Looking out into the black of the night, Elise gazed upward to marvel at its beauty. Suddenly, the folds of Elise's gown cupped and clung to her body as if to embrace her in love. She stood, giving herself up to it.

The vision was real to Elise. She saw his tall, lean body, his arms resting on the railing of a ship. Strong hands with long slender fingers cupped his chin as he scanned the vastness of the churning waters. He was deep in thought, caring not that his unruly dark hair blew over his face. So vivid was this image to Elise that she saw the opened neck of his shirt baring his chest with the gold medallion resting on the bed of curly black hair. His mouth was set tight, and his black eyes danced aimlessly over the dark horizon. As if in answer to her plea, she could almost feel the sweet, assuring warmth of his lips caressing her, softly whispering, "I'm coming love—just as fast as the winds will carry me. . . ."

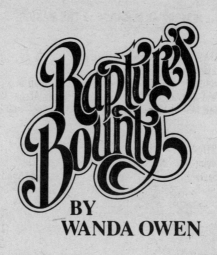

Rapture's Bounty

BY
WANDA OWEN

ZEBRA BOOKS
KENSINGTON PUBLISHING CORP.

ZEBRA BOOKS

are published by

KENSINGTON PUBLISHING CORP.
475 Park Avenue South
New York, N.Y. 10016

Printed in the United States of America

As I promised, this one is for you, Leslie Gelbman. Thanks for your faith in me!

Prologue

Strong, stiff winds filled the sails of the two-masted, trim-lined schooner, the *Elise*. The ship's captain, Lance Edwards, welcomed the sight of the billowing canvas because it meant they were finally on their way again toward their destination, New Orleans. The ghostly calm of the last two days had disturbed his patience and nerves, as well as his crew. Now, with the schooner plowing through the waters, he stood by the rail looking out over the horizon enjoying the wild assault of the wind whipping his shirt and blowing his black hair over his face.

That usual devil-may-care, reckless attitude had not been his when they departed the coast of England. He realized it was the precious cargo aboard. There was a young son, along with the beautiful wife he adored. The sooner they reached New Orleans, the happier he'd be. He bloody well must be getting old, he chided himself, for becoming so damned serious. Watch it, Edwards, he cautioned himself privately, or he'd never be able to hold on to that vixen wife of his!

He had not sensed her approach as he stood by the rail until her two dainty arms encircled his waist and her sweet jasmine fragrance wafted to his nose. Then he turned to see her smiling face looking up at him.

Her jet black hair fanned out, enhancing the loveliness of her oval face. Her emerald green eyes sparkled bright and alive as they always did when she was excited. Her soft lips creased in a smile invited him to kiss them and he bent to do just that.

"*Ma petite*, we are on our way again. Are you as glad as I am?" His arm went around her tiny waist, pulling her up closer to him. Her small figure had not changed since the birth of their son, and he was proud of her for not retaining the excess weight so many women seemed to after having children.

"You know I am," Elise Edwards told her husband. "I can't wait to show off our son and see our new home. Zack's letter made it sound so wonderful—the perfect place to raise Andy. Except for that short time spent together at your townhouse in London, it will be our first home."

"Then it's about time, isn't it love, that we found our little 'nest' after being married over five years now, eh?" His black eyes adored her as he spoke.

"Oh, yes, *mon cheri!*"

They stood in silence, each having their own private thoughts. There was a serenity abiding within them without any words being spoken.

Her nearness warmed him to the core of his being for never would he have believed himself to be so consumed by love for one little slip of a woman. So it had been and so it remained.

Never would he forget that night in the winter of 1805 on the coast of Le Harve. Her father, Andre Cartier, an old friend, had owned and operated the Seafarer's Inn down by the wharf. At Andre's request he'd smuggled Elise and her older sister out of France and taken them to London to reside with their aunt.

When she'd bounced into the old inn's kitchen that night and his eyes had beheld her ravishing beauty at age sixteen he'd lost his heart, even though he dared not admit it to himself. When circumstances placed them alone one evening aboard his ship, the *Seahawk*, during the crossing of the English Channel, his sanity deserted him as they'd finished dining and she prepared to return to the cabin shared with her sister. All evening he'd restrained his wild desires to take her in his arms and kiss those rosebud lips. Never before had he denied himself any woman he wanted and usually any woman he met was eager and willing to jump in his bed.

The hand of fate seemed to thrust Elise too close to him that night as she started out the door, and in the next moment she was in his arms. Like a wild fire out of control, flames of passion swept over him with a fury he'd never known before.

By the time he deposited the deflowered young French maid with her aunt, she had stolen his reckless heart. Nothing would ease the ache and longing for her until he made her his wife.

A cruel fate was to test them shortly after they were married. Standing there now with Elise by his side he still shuddered at how swiftly she'd been abducted by his old enemy Joaquin Ruiz and carried away from England on his ship. Endless months of searching and lonely nights of heartache finally were rewarded when he found her alive in New Orleans. But new pain and torment tore at his soul when he found her ready to marry the man who had rescued her from Joaquin. That man was Clint Barron, an American sea captain who lived in New Orleans and who they would be seeing soon, along with their other friends, once they made port in New Orleans.

Elise's wispy voice interrupted his musings at that point, and he let the past be forgotten. "Sorry, love, what did you say?"

"I said the wind has rather chilled me and something hot would taste good. Would you join me, *Capitaine?*"

A devious smile broke on his tanned face. "Do I ever refuse you any request, *ma petite?*"

"Well—almost never!" She giggled and turned sharply to go below to their cabin.

He smiled, trailing her. Always, even when she was sixty he'd wager, she'd retain that girlish innocence, even though she'd endured more than most women without losing that indomitable spirit. Even the many months when she was held captive by Joaquin Ruiz, the cruel Spanish buccaneer, and kept in Havana had not broken her. How could he fault Clint Barron for falling helplessly in love with her when he found her on that secluded Havana street. That was the past.

They entered the lavishly furnished cabin he'd provided for them to travel in from England back to the New World where both wished to live and make their home. Across the hall was the cabin occupied by their son and his nurse.

He realized her idea was a good one. He suggested she remove her wool shawl while he sought some coffee from Cook, along with a bottle of good brandy. Elise gave him a nod of her tousled head, surveying the horrible damage to her hair in the mirror over the small gilded dressing table. "Oh, Lance, perhaps some croissants, too!"

"Lord, woman, are you pregnant again? For such a tiny miss you eat a lot." He laughed lightly, closing the cabin door behind him. He saw not the sly smile on her face as he departed.

She stood, tediously trying to work the comb through the mass of tangles. "*Mon Dieu*, what a mess!" She worked with the brush and comb until she was tempted to take the scissors to a

11

couple of stubborn clumps.

When Lance finally returned with their refreshments on a tray, she sat exhausted with her glossy black hair in two plaits hanging down over her breasts.

"What do we have here, an Indian maiden?" Her husband teased her as he placed the tray on the squared oak table with four chairs placed around it situated in the center of the cabin.

"Madame." He urged her to join him.

"Hmmm, to this Indian maiden it smells so good. To be served by such a handsome buck as you really makes for a delightful repast." She wiggled into the cushioned velvet seat he held out for her. She still marveled at the grandeur of their cabin and all the special furnishings he'd installed for their comfort.

Lance laced his coffee with a generous dose of the brandy and listened as his wife chattered away about their new home; Montclair. "We were very lucky that Zack acquired the fine old estate for us, and such a bargain, too."

"Zack Hart has been a true friend to me since the first time we met. I'm damned glad I kept the partnership in the fleet lines when we sailed back to England two years ago. Old Zack seems to be prospering, according to his last letter." Like any father, Lance had started dreaming about his son Andy following in his shoes, and it was comforting to know that Zack would keep the business running smoothly.

"It will be a wonderful life, Lance. I am so excited. I have a million plans going through

12

my mind on what I'll do in our house. We'll be seeing Clint and Susan again, and there's those wonderful Le Cleres. They were the dearest people. Annette has to be one of the most beautiful ladies I've ever seen."

Lance agreed, adding, "For an older woman, *chérie.*"

"Older or not, she is beautiful, and so gracious and kind. I'll never forget how nice she was to me when those catty women stuck their claws into me so," Elise snapped, remembering the snobby way some of the ladies had acted toward her when she resided at Shady Oaks as Clint Barron's guest. Clint had insisted she stay with him after he'd rescued her in Havana and nursed her back to health. It had not taken the countryside or the city long to explode with the gossip about "Clint Barron's mistress," and while the gentlemen envied him, the ladies and wives resented the adoring raves about the beautiful French miss residing under Clint's roof. With the exception of Zack Hart's daughter Susan and Annette Le Clere no warm acceptance came forth from the other women Elise met.

Lance appreciated Elise's feelings but he dared not voice his true feelings; that she would forever have that stigma to live with. Instead, he sought to tease her. "All the gents seemed to make up for their women as I remember it though. Can't figure out why?" He broke into a deep, throaty laugh.

She said nothing for a moment, allowing him

to have his fun. Cocking her head to the side with a look of mischief playing there, she purred softly, "Can't you now?" Moving out of her chair, she came around the table and eased herself down on his lap. His firm, muscled thigh radiated its heat to her and she wiggled her hips sensuously.

Before his very eyes he saw that trait in Elise that was so rare, and yet so exciting to him. From sweet childlike innocence she'd turned into a sultry temptress, playing him as he adored her to do. The look on her face provocative and bold, and her eyes were telling him she desired his touch and caress. As a man who had known many women from different walks of life, he could have sworn she was not aware of the changes. It was as natural as her breathing, no game or act. Just that beautiful free spirit of hers giving in to the urge for her own desires, and dear God, he prayed she'd never change.

Already swollen with desire, his mouth sought hers anxiously. Her lips, half-parted and moist, accepted his, as her fingers trailed through his curling sideburns.

Feeling the hardened manhood prodding her thighs, she trembled with the sensations it aroused, along with the searing caress of his hands on her breasts, teasing and taunting the pulsing orbs.

"Oh, *mon cheri*," she moaned with delight, urging his head to her breast. Fumbling impatiently to remove the barrier of her gown,

Lance's hands moved hastily.

"Love! Love! I want you so," he gasped huskily. Pushing the bodice of her gown down to her waist, he laid her back in his arms, cradling her there as his lips took the sweet nectar she offered so freely.

His hands swept under her legs, lifting her up in his arms, and in two giant strides he placed her down on the bed. Flinging aside his shirt, he sat down on the bed to hastily remove the black leather boots, then practically leapt out of his tight-fitting brown pants. Boyishly, he smiled, admitting, "Woman, when you get me like this I go crazy."

She laughed, wiggling so the gown would be more easily removed, "You're not the only one. Come on, I can't wait!" She moved over on the bed.

When he joined her on the satin coverlet and she pressed close to his broad chest sprinkled with the same black curls of hair as on his head, he sought to quench her thirst for him. Burrowing himself between her thighs, he waited no longer to pleasure them both. His thrust was all power and conquering. He was her master, but she delighted in his quest and conquering.

At the peak of their frenzy of passion, he suddenly reversed the role. She, like him, enjoyed the change of position. His head reared slightly, his mouth taking the jutting tips of her breasts, each in turn.

"Dear God, it feels good, *cheri!*" Higher and

15

higher she felt herself soaring, and he responded to her rapturous ecstasy, unable to deny himself any longer.

Serene, deep sleep fell upon them as they lay stilled and contented afterward. Only the harsh rap on the door two hours later roused the resting couple on the massive bed in the captain's cabin.

"Captain Edwards!" The voice of his first mate called impatiently. Tom McTavish did not like the turn of the weather and the look of the sky. While he'd agreed some eight hours ago that they should take the northern route instead of the southern he had some doubts now.

Lance recognized the voice and replied, "Just a minute, Tom." He reached for his pants and slipped into them. The boots were on and he struggled to button his shirt as he opened the door to Tom.

"Sorry, Captain, to disturb your . . . your afternoon," Tom said, a slight smile on his youthful face. It was not too hard to figure how his captain had been spending his time off. Damned if he blamed him. Since signing on as first mate in London to journey on the *Elise* back to America, he'd secretly admired the pretty, petite wife of the captain. Her presence aboard had been a bright spot during the weeks since they'd left the shores of England. It certainly proved to be false about a woman's presence on a ship being bad luck. At least, up to now!

Being a practical fellow, he'd not blame anything bad on that tiny lass. With that angel's face and sweet, friendly smile, it would not be possible. A good little mother she was, too.

Lance shrugged aside Tom's disturbing him as they walked up on deck. Tom explained his concern over the weather the last three and a half hours, since the captain had been in his quarters below.

"Damn! What a hell of a change," Lance exclaimed, finding it hard to believe the calming of the galelike winds he and Elise had been whipped by before they'd gone below. The air was thick and oppressive and the schooner seemed to be moving at a snail's pace now.

"Let's take a look at the charts, Tom," Lance suggested, knowing even before he checked them that they had been a few days away from entering the Gulf of Mexico even with the strong winds behind them. He prayed that fate wasn't sending a hurricane their way from down in the Caribbean. Cuba and Haiti lay ahead, and the Carolinas were to the west. But they would make none of those ports before this approaching storm was upon them.

Tom gave vent to his thoughts. "No way, Captain. We'd just have to ride it out as best we could. Thing is, Captain, ain't the season for hurricanes."

"There's always the exception, Tom. Like you, I always labored under the impression they started in August or September, but an old

17

seaman with me on my ship the *Seahawk* swore to me one hit a ship he sailed on in May. Like the ladies, the weather's unpredictable."

With orders given to Tom to alert the crew, Lance went to the cabin below where he was sure young Andy would be awake from his afternoon nap. He still swelled with overwhelming pride when he looked upon the tiny piece of humanity created by him and Elise. It still was nothing short of a miracle to him.

Elise swore Andy was the image of Lance, and he'd not deny the fact pleased him exceedingly. Like so many things about his wife, he found it amazing that she managed so cleverly to give birth to Andy on his own birthday.

When he opened the door of the cabin occupied by Andy and his nurse Maggie, his son leaped up from the floor where he and Maggie were sitting on a pelted rug looking at one of the many books they'd purchased for the ocean voyage.

"Good afternoon, Monsieur. I was just showing your son the many different animals of the world. I think you must have you a horseman here." She laughed. "His favorites seem to be the pinto pony and the zebra."

"So you like the horses, Andy?" Lance laughed, lifting the boy up in his arms and tousling his black curls, which Elise found difficult to cut away.

Andy gave his father an enthusiastic nod, giving a hint of trying to say "horsey." Like his

18

mother, he was a warm, outgoing little fellow and gave Lance an eager kiss on the cheek. "Come, Andy, you show Daddy all the animals while Maggie goes and gets your supper, eh?"

"Show Daddy!" Andy chuckled excitedly as Lance sat him down on the floor and the boy got the book, flipping back the pages to the front. Lance sat down on the floor beside him and the two turned page after page. Andy pointed to the cat, dog, and bear on the pages, trying his best to remember what Maggie had titled them. Lance found it interesting to watch Andy's mind work tediously when he could not come up with the name of the animal, and equally he would be pleased with himself when he did remember.

Elise entered with Maggie. Feeling all warm inside at the sight of father and son together, she mused what a pair they made at that moment. Lance had to have looked much the same as a tad. She was so grateful their firstborn had been a son.

Maggie chirped, "Are you hungry, lad? Maggie has some good hot biscuits that you like. Shall we eat now?" Unless his father urged it, Maggie knew she would not stand a chance of getting the boy to settle for eating. But the captain would insist, for he did not wish a spoiled brat, even though he loved the child very much.

Elise gave him a kiss. "Go eat for Maggie, Andy, and we will see you before bedtime darling." She smiled at Lance urging himself up off the floor. He gave out a grunt, which young Andy found funny.

After they left their son Lance excused himself quite abruptly, mentioning nothing to her about the usual stroll around the deck before they dined. What was the matter with him? Especially after making love as they had only a few hours earlier. His mood was usually so very tender. True, he had not been sharp or snapping with her, but just very preoccupied and troubled. She wondered why.

Without further ado, she bolted out of the cabin, determined to find out for herself just what was going on. As she mounted the last step before stepping onto the deck, she braced herself for the galelike winds she expected to whip around her, only to find the gentle calm. *Mon Dieu*, it was so still and calm!

The air was warm, she noted, taking the ecru shawl away from her shoulders. The pale blue-sprigged muslin gown she wore was comfortable enough. As she walked on out on the deck there was no sign of Lance or Tom. Two young seamen walked past her giving a friendly nod of their heads and smiling, but intent about going about their appointed duties earnestly. She walked on, more aware of the muggy air, and for a moment she was reminded of an unbearable summer day in New Orleans when she'd been at Shady Oaks, Clint Barron's plantation.

Looking out over the horizon, she finally saw the dark, ominous clouds in the distance.

Perhaps a storm was coming up and that was Lance's concern. She hastened her steps to find him, knowing that he was most likely in the chart room. She directed her footsteps that way.

She bounced into the room, surprising both Lance and Tom who were bent over the long wooden table. Elbows pressed and faces cradled in their hands, eyes studying the maps lain out, they both turned in her direction. "Am I allowed to know what's going on, gentlemen?" Ambling up to the side of her husband, she smiled so fetchingly Lance could not be irked at her unannounced entry. Tom stood up straight as he always did in her presence, for he felt that way around Elise Edwards. She reminded him of some beautiful princess or queen to be treated royally. If any woman could make a man feel like a king she would be the one. He could not help envying Captain Edwards his good fortune. The young Scot hoped to be as lucky someday.

Lance had hoped to spare Elise any concern until it was absolutely necessary, but he knew he could not lie to her now. He gently pulled her over closer, kissed her lightly on the cheek and casually remarked, "A little turbulence coming our way, *ma petite*. The next hour will tell the tale, we think. We could be on the fringes or right in the middle of it."

She knew him so well that she saw right through his attempt to be casual, but she allowed him to think otherwise. "I see. Then

I'd best leave the two of you alone and tend to my own affairs. See you for dinner in a little while, *mon cheri?*" She swished around to leave.

"In a while, Elise," Lance mumbled in an off-handed manner, for his eyes and mind were back on the charts.

Elise went directly to her son's room and told Maggie of her suspicions. She directed her to empty the huge wicker chest purchased specifically to house and hold Andy's multitude of toys for the voyage. "Pad it with covers and secure it with the ropes to the posts of your bunks. If the weather should get nasty you would be doing good to hold yourself in the bunk. Andy will take it as a fun game, we'll hope."

"Yes ma'am. Perhaps, I should remove the glass pieces in the room and place them in my sewing basket? Better than them falling from the chest or shelf, I'd say."

"Very good idea, Maggie. In fact, I'll do the same," she declared, rushing out the door to go to her cabin.

Lance entered his quarters a half hour later having no inkling of the scurrying around the two women had been doing. Elise sat, looking relaxed and lovely. Their table was spread with the dinner the galley cook had brought, and candlelight dappled her face as she sat in one of the velvet cushioned chairs already sipping a glass of wine. She'd felt the need of it for she could not deny she was somewhat frightened.

"Well, madame, you are a feast to my eyes, I

must say," he said, closing the door behind him. His eyes went to the glass in her dainty hand. "What's this? You have a glass of wine. Where may I ask is mine?"

She immediately came out of the chair and hastily poured a glass of wine for him and took it to him. "My pardon, m'Lord. The truth of the matter is I didn't know when you would be joining me." Shrugging her shoulders and tilting her head nonchalantly, she purred, "A lady has to keep herself from being bored, you know."

"Lord, woman! You are a demanding wench. A man could kill himself trying to please you." He laughed, swatting her firm bottom playfully.

"Speaking of pleasing, does the dinner not smell good. I'm famished! Shall we enjoy it before it gets cold?"

"I'm for that. And you, *ma petite* must have a tapeworm the way you're eating. Let me just change out of this shirt and we shall gorge ourselves, eh?" He, too, found himself hungry, and better to eat now while there was time to enjoy it.

Devour it they did. In part it was hunger, and in part it was tenseness and nerves.

It did not surprise Elise that Lance once again took his leave from the cabin to check with his first mate. Both had played at being lighthearted during the dinner hour. He could not have reached the deck before Elise heard raindrops pelting against the porthole glass.

She searched the darkness outside to see if she could see anything. No thunder was erupting in the skies but in the distance she could see the streaks of flashing lightning dancing deviously across the black sky. It seemed far away and she prayed it stayed there.

A soft rap on the door and Maggie's voice alerted her and she went to answer the call. "The lad sleeps soundly, ma'am. I thought I might fetch myself a glass of milk, if that would be all right? Good for the nerves. Is it all right?"

"Of course, Maggie. I'll listen for him," Elise assured her.

"I won't be long, ma'am." The young English woman hurried down the passageway. Elise watched her go, feeling how lucky they'd been to come upon Maggie. She was a conscientious, hard worker, and she and Andy had hit it off at once. During the weeks she'd traveled with them, Elise trusted her completely with Andy.

True to her word, Maggie returned, all excited and, Elise could tell by her face, light in spirit.

"Ah, ma'am, the worst may be going around us old Sam says. I asked him why he said that and he said he felt it right here," Maggie exclaimed, gesturing to her chest.

"Mon Dieu, I hope old Sam is right!"

"He said there was this certain feeling always hit him in the chest when a bad storm was going to it. So far, all we are having is a little rain coming down."

"Well, suppose we just leave Andy's door open and you sit with me and enjoy your milk in my cabin," Elsie suggested. It might just be a long, dreary night before Lance joined her in the quarters.

The two women settled themselves at the table and engaged in casual conversation as Maggie drank her milk. Her mistress was a rare one, not one haughty bone in her body. She thought to herself she had to be the luckiest of nannies.

"Ma'am, I've just got to say it for it's on my mind," Maggie stammered, feeling a slight embarrassment now that she'd spoken.

"What is it, Maggie? Are you regretting your decision to leave your country and go to this strange new place with us?" A frown creased Elise's forehead. It was almost asking too much to find one so perfect to tend to Andy.

"Oh, mercy be! That's the last thing on my mind. No, no, I was just going to tell you how grateful I am to be in your employ and how fortunate I feel to have such nice people to be serving. I've never seen or known such dear, loving people as you and Captain Edwards. I surely haven't, ma'am."

Elise heaved a deep sigh of relief and broke into a giggle, "Oh, dear, you had me worried, Maggie. I'm so pleased you feel that way for you've become a part of our family in the short time you've been with us."

Her mistress's praise meant more to Maggie

than a pouch filled with gold. Without realizing it, she drifted into an easy, flowing conversation bringing Elise up to date on her life before this job, and how she'd happened to be living with her aunt in London instead of Sussex with her parents.

"I shamed them, ma'am. Gave my heart to a rascal . . . the only beau I'd ever had. Found myself with a wee one and had it not been for my kindhearted aunt I'd been out on the streets, I reckon. I miscarried less than two months after I got to Aunt Carrie's and I guess you could say it was a blessing."

Maggie erupted into shaking sobs, suddenly realizing all she'd told Madame Edwards. Her freckled face, damp with the flood of tears jerked up to look at Elise. "Oh mercy, now you'll not think me fit to care for Andy. Oh, Lord!"

Elise rushed over to her and hugged the trembling girl. Compassion flooded her as she soothed her. "Shhh, stop that kind of silly talk this minute, Maggie. So you're not perfect! Well, neither am I. One would have to be sealed up in a room not to make a few wrong moves. Now wouldn't that be a dull, boring existence." Elise laughed lightly, patting the girl on the head.

"Oh, thank you, ma'am. Said it before and I'll say it again, you have to be the kindest lady I've ever known," Maggie stammered, wiping her eyes and nose, both red by now.

"Maggie, my dear, I could tell you some facts

26

that would surely curl your toes, but I shan't for then you might not want to work for me," Elise teased. The girl laughed, declaring that would never be.

Their gay, jovial mood was shortlived as the cabin gave a sudden, sharp surge. An exploding crackle and bright light lit up the cabin and deafening thunder caused their eyes to widen with fear and concern.

"Oh, dear Lord!"

"*Mon Dieu*, it's hitting! We'd best see about Andy, Maggie." Elise wasted no time rushing across to the other cabin, but her son slept soundly.

A young seaman by the name of Josh gave her a message from the captain and then turned to hurry back topside. "Just a minute Josh, is it going to be a bad one?" Elise prodded him.

"Not as bad as it could have been, ma'am. Captain says the worst of it is passing far south of us and on to the east. Don't mean though we ain't goin' to get a little bouncing around. That's why he told me to tell you to secure yourself in the cabin so you won't slam against something. Best get back now, ma'am."

"Yes, yes. Thank you, Josh," Elise called as the lanky youth was already running back down the passageway. She was forced to grab at the facing of the doorway to keep from being thrust forward.

"You all right, ma'am?" Maggie worked her way to Elise's side and the two of them sought the bunk by the side of the wicker basket cradling the still sleeping Andy.

They sat huddled together on the bunk with hands securing the basket to prevent its movement. Their closeness was a comforting feeling to one another. The ship pitched and bucked like a wild mustang being broken, and its lumber moaned and groaned like a wounded animal. Elise and Maggie could hear the torrent of rain beating against the deck above and the sides of the schooner. Shuffling feet rushing to and fro could be heard from time to time during a lull in the rumbling thunder.

Elise almost wished to be up there instead of where she was, not knowing how Lance was, so she constantly repeated a prayer for his safety. The minutes dragged like hours for her. Then suddenly there was a slackening of the beating rain, and the thunder, still rumbling, was less intense and seemed farther away. With this change, Elise's heart began to pound slower, and she let out a sigh to relieve the tightness engulfing her chest. Perhaps the worst was soon to be over. Still, she and Maggie sat on the bunk holding tight to one another and the basket.

Several minutes passed before they heard footsteps on the passageway. When the tall, towering figure of her husband invaded the doorway, Elise leaped into his arms, ever so grateful that no harm had come to him and completely uncaring that she pressed herself against his drenched clothing.

Hair fell over his face while rivulets of water

28

ran down his cheeks. Elise looked up to see a flow of red mingling with the moisture. "You've been hurt, Lance!" She jerked away from his arms to survey him more closely.

"Only a scratch, *ma petite*. But I am in need of some dry clothing. Everything's okay down here, I'd say."

"Just scared to death, but yes, we're fine," Elise assured him. "Come, *mon Capitaine*, we'll see about getting you dry." She urged him across the passageway, bidding Maggie good-bye for the time being.

With dry clothing on and three fast slugs of warming brandy inside him, Lance lay back on the bed, exhausted and weary. They'd been lucky, he told her, to have not had the full assault of the freakish storm. With only a very brief comment about how the decks were a rampaging river for a while, he shut his eyes and fell into a deep sleep. Elise lay down beside him and she, too, went to sleep, in need of the rest more than she had realized.

In the days to follow they encountered fair weather and smooth sailing. Overjoyed, Lance informed Elise that it was the warm gulf waters they were now plowing through. Even the crew seemed jubilant as the Louisiana coastline came closer.

On their last night aboard the schooner before docking there was a gala celebration of feasting and drinking. With the cares and worries of his ship's safe passage over and their destination almost reached, Lance's mood was the most jovial of all. His relaxed, devil-may-care air took over again, and he realized that he had been more concerned than he'd dare admit to himself. Damnit, it was impossible to be the daring, reckless privateer he'd been when he'd first met Elise. Time and love had changed all that. Precious cargo, he carried now. His life would have no meaning or purpose without that beloved wife and adored son. Oh, yes, it changed a man's thinking!

The hour was late when he and Elise finally sought the solitude of their cabin. Elise had praised his idea about allowing the crew to celebrate within reason as far as drinking was concerned. While he would not have allowed overindulgence, a couple of drinks caused no problem, he felt. Elise agreed, feeling the crew appreciated the gesture.

As they undressed, Elise admitted she was so excited that sleep would be impossible for her. "I will arrive with red-streaked eyes and they'll be all puffy. I'll look awful!"

Her fragrance intoxicated him far more than the wine he'd drunk. He pulled her over to the bed where he sat to remove his boots. Mischief played in his black eyes and he murmured softly in her ear, "Got an idea about something we could do that never fails to induce sleep, love!"

"And what might that be, *mon cheri?*" She smiled impishly, knowing full well what he was hinting at. By now, she had changed into a sheer gown of blue green, lavishly trimmed in lace, and daringly low cut at the neckline.

"This, *ma petite!*" Taking her by the shoulders he lifted her over to cover the length of his firm body. His smiling face looked up at her. "Damn waste putting on that gown." His hands slipped the sheer bodice away to reveal her rounded breasts. His lips sought each in turn, caressing the orbs slow and unhurried.

Elise's moan of pleasure told him she adored his touch there, but he still delighted in hearing her voice it as she was now doing without a care. "Oh, Lance, I love for you to do that."

Her hands worked feverishly, tousling his thick mane of hair. Once again, their lips met and without breaking their hold, he turned her on her back to cover her with his powerful body. He adored to look upon her face when it was so flushed with passion, and for a second he did just that with black eyes blazing with desire.

She arched eagerly to him, seeking and wanting. He gave out a husky laugh. "Hmmmm, you always feel so good! You know how much I like to love you, Elise."

"Oh, yes, 'cause I feel the same way," she purred, burning with the heat of his touch and caress. "Oh, Lance!" His firm body slid between her opening thighs. Burying himself deep within her, he gave out a moan of his own, swelling with elation that he was capable of pleasing her so.

Elise gave way to wild abandon as his movement increased, and together they soared to the lofty heights of a world where only the

31

two of them existed. "Ah, yes, love . . . love me! Love me!" Elise felt the warm heat of his being flooding her.

When the savage ecstasy calmed and they floated back down from the towering heights, they stayed entwined in one another's arms, enjoying the lingering warmth.

Finally, it was Elise who broke the night's quietness. "Oh, *mon Dieu,* Lance. Do you think we'll still be able to . . . you know, do this when we're fifty?"

A roar of laughter erupted. "I bloody well am going to try my best to stay healthy, little vixen, so I can take care of your needs." He patted her bottom. "Now go to sleep!"

"Yes, *mon Capitaine.*"

He felt her body relax, and he, too, closed his eyes. Somehow, he could not rid himself completely of apprehension and concern. He knew he probably wouldn't until they docked in New Orleans. They were so close to land nothing would go wrong, he tried to assure himself.

At least Elise slept, and he was glad. His head rested on the palms of his hands and he stared at the ceiling, listening to the constant lapping of the water on the hull of his ship. Willing himself to think about their future together and what a fine life they'd have making the old Montclair plantation a showplace, he began to relax. He was glad he'd had Zack acquire the place for them, even though he realized they'd have been welcome guests at Zack's, or Clint

32

Barron's fine place, Shady Oaks. Lance had to give credit where credit was due, for Clint had, indeed, proved himself one hell of a gent when he helped get the two of them back together. How could he really fault the man for falling in love with Elise? Especially when Elise, as well as Clint, thought he was dead. Hell, forget it, he urged himself. That was over two years ago and nothing mattered now that he and Elise were together. Nothing would separate them ever again!

He felt his eyes becoming heavy finally and gave in to the feeling. But that feeling was interrupted abruptly by the sound of heavy footsteps rushing across the deck, along with loud shouts and the explosion of gunfire. "What the bloody hell!" Leaping out of the bed and hastily struggling to get into his pants, he knew something bad was going on, and his worst fears were a reality.

"Lance?" Elise was still in a sleepy stupor.

"Get something on fast! Hurry!" He urgently commanded her, taking a fleeting glance at her luscious, inviting nakedness. He felt sick, like a booted foot had kicked him in the groin, just knowing what a feast to the eyes she'd make to the invading enemy overrunning his ship. He felt a terrifying helplessness to protect her from the vermin who would be busting through the door any second.

His hand was almost ready to grasp his pistol when the door opened and a huge giant of a man stood before them. His lusting black eyes focused in on Elise, who was just pulling on her silk wrapper. One breast was yet to be covered, and she felt she could retch reading his evil thoughts so easily. Her stomach churned from the fetid, animal odor wafting over to her. Lance's firm, muscled body was tensed and he looked ready to spring on the three men now in the cabin like a panther, and she prayed he would do nothing foolish.

"What is the meaning of this. I demand to know!" Lance knew all too well what it meant. The fear he felt for Elise's safety dominated his thoughts.

The burly, black-bearded pirate ignored him completely. "What do we have here? Ah, men, did you ever see such a rare jewel? Sebastian is lucky tonight, eh?" His hands rested low on his wide girth and his legs were spread wide in baggy, dirty britches. His two comrades laughed, nodding their heads.

Black rage consumed Lance. "The lady is my wife, you bastard!" Again, the cabin resounded with loud laughter.

Sebastian sauntered over to the side of the bed where Elise sat. Never had his eyes beheld such ravishing beauty. Her eyes were like jewels, the most magnificent emeralds. The skin looked like pale gold satin, thick black glossy hair streamed down over her dainty shoulders, and her lips were so sensuously sweet that nectar must lie there. God, he could hardly wait to taste her once they returned to his ship.

His hairy hand lifted her defiant chin up, but she jerked away haughtily. Ah, there was fire in this one, Sebastian saw. Automatically, Lance leaped at the man like a raging bull. A sharp blow exploded and Lance fell across the bed.

"You animals!" Elise screamed, flinging herself over her husband's limp body. She was so concerned about Lance that she had no awareness she was bare to the waist until Sebastian's hairy arms pressed against her flesh as he lifted her up like a sack of grain. Fighting him like a tiger, she struggled against his granite-hard body until a stinging blow stopped her. With her remaining ounce of strength, she once again struck him with legs and arms. The next blow was so harsh that blackness engulfed her.

She knew very little about what went on the next thirty minutes. There was a foggy vision of a blood-spattered deck with bodies everywhere and mammoth flames leaping up through the darkness of the night. There was the vague memory of being carried like a sack of grain over a man's shoulder. She was mercifully spared the crude, vulgar conversation of the trio when she was thrust into the cabin of Sebastian's ship. But she would have been relieved to know they took their leave after locking the door. However, Sebastian was relating with gusto his intentions for the beautiful lady, and his two companions grinned and nodded their heads, visually picturing Sebastian's evening in his hut back on Barataria. It wasn't difficult to figure out his impatience to return to their fortress.

Mingled with the fragrance of jasmine, the billowing smoke choked Lance. He felt his last reserve of strength waning as he struggled across the passageway to the cabin occupied by his son and the nanny. He knew instinctively that the jasmine aroma was all that remained in the cabin of her; his darling wife.

As he stumbled through the door, the bloody, battered body of poor Maggie told the story of her last moments alive. The whimpering sound coming from under the bunk was the blessed evidence that his son lived. He urged the frightened tot to come to him quickly.

With his son in his arm, he made his way up the steps realizing there was no where to go but in the waters below, humbly putting their lives in the hand of God. Flames danced everywhere like crazed demons, and the smell of death hung like a shroud around him as he jumped from the burning ship.

As he plunged into the blackness below, violent explosions ruptured the schooner. The timbers splintered and broke apart and flames and smoke billowed skyward.

Amid the floating debris, Lance Edwards floundered and struggled in desperation, but still he held tightly the son he was determined to save.

He had failed to save Elise so he must not fail Andy.

Part I
Love's Stolen Bounty

Chapter 1

Barataria, forty miles south of New Orleans
Spring of 1811

A violent, raging fury swept over the handsome, swarthy face of the Frenchman as he
paced back and forth at the foot of the massive
bed. Each time his eyes darted down upon the
still, petite figure of the woman he clinched his
fists and gritted his teeth in anger and agony.
To think that one of his men had done the
dastardly deed causing the bruises on that
lovely face made Jean Laffite want to retch.

Many months ago, he'd met the enchanting
Elise Edwards, and being a connoisseur of the
most beautiful women in the city of New
Orleans he considered her the prize. She was
breathtaking! This was not how he'd envisioned her being in his bed, but he had, in deed,
dreamed about the delight she would be lying
where she now rested.

Under his breath, he vowed the bastard Sebastian would die for defying his direct orders to not prey on any American ships. He cussed and damned the devil, knowing now that he should have listened to his brother's suggestion that they not welcome him to their midst.

In all the months Lola had been with Jean she'd never seen him so angry, and she trembled as she went about cleaning the dried blood from the woman's face and hands. Her heart went out to the poor thing remembering how Jean had rescued her from a Spanish slaver. To some, he might be a "river rat," but to her he was her savior, her patron. Always, he'd been kind and gentle and so it had been when he finally took her to his bed after she'd been with him for several weeks. When he awakened the wild ecstasy within her, Lola was amazed by the surprising delights a man's touch could stir. Since that time she'd eagerly enjoyed the moments spent with Jean, although she knew she was not the only woman in the Frenchman's life.

She tried to ease his concern over the woman. "Monsieur, she is breathing just fine now. I think it will merely be a matter of rest and gaining back her strength." Her dark eyes looked up at his tense face. She'd never seen this Jean Laffite.

She brushed back the straying wisps of jet black hair from the lady's face to allow him to see how much better she looked with all the

40

blood cleaned away. The woman's long, fringed lashes lay against her cheek, her eyes closed in sleep. The even heaving of her breasts under the blue satin coverlet denoted she had calmed since being brought to the room after her rescue by young Julio Vega. What a reward he would receive from Jean for his brave stand against Sebastian, Lola mused!

Jean's hand reached down to gently touch the woman's forehead, and he seemed satisfied with Lola's observations. "Stay with her awhile, Lola. I have to attend to something immediately and then I'll return. I'll have Mama John brew up some of her nourishing broth for Madame Edwards so when she rouses she can have it." He turned sharply on his heels to leave the room, and Lola knew what he was about and where he was going without him saying more.

So that was the woman's name, Madame Edwards. A married lady or a widow?

It was dark when Jean returned, and he ordered Mama John from the room in a sharp, curt tone unfamiliar to the huge black woman who had served him as housekeeper and cook for many years. For once she gave him no argument, for she had only to look at "her Jean," as she called him, to know he was in no lighthearted mood. Knowing him as well as she did, Mama John knew this small miss held a special meaning to her master. Yet, she'd never seen her here before, nor at his house in the

41

city where she'd accompanied him from time to time when he'd spent time there.

She shook her kerchief-covered head as she sauntered slowly down the hall, pondering who their guest was and what she was to Jean. "Sho' 'nuf, that one will be de one to break his heart. Purty thing tho'," she mumbled to herself on the way back to her kitchen.

Moments later as she busied herself with her pots and pans she fumed and fussed still. Since the time she'd come to Jean Laffite, she'd assumed the role of mother hen, and he'd allowed her the rare privilege of bossing him as no other person would dare to do, along with running his house. None of the other servants questioned an order from Mama John.

Jean took no notice of the huge woman glaring down on him as she left. He sunk down deep in the chair and looked upon the woman. The deed was done and he heaved a deep breath, feeling some satisfaction of revenge for the sake of Elise Edwards. He was torn by the two conflicting emotions sweeping over him. He wanted nothing so much as for her to get well and alert to the world around her, but then he dreaded to face those accusing eyes.

He could vividly envision the last time he'd seen her, so enchanting and devastatingly exciting. Her jet black hair was piled high atop her head and away from that beautiful oval face, and her eyes were sparkling like two exquisite emeralds. Holding her tall, good looking husband's arm as he led her out the door, she had given a soft, lilting laugh looking up at Lance Edwards. Such love burned in her eyes, and Jean envied Lance at that moment as he'd never envied any man. To have this woman's heart would be like owning the world.

Although Elise Edwards did not know it, Laffite sat throughout the dark night hours by her bedside, sleeping fitfully in the chair. Only as the sky began to glow with the light of dawn did he seek out the guest room across the hallway.

Lola figured as much as she brought a tray of light breakfast to Elise. The door was ajar to the guest room and she saw Jean's prone figure, still clothed. She was certain that he had sought the comfort of the bed from sheer exhaustion.

Elise's eyes opened and Lola hastily answered her questioning look. She wanted her to remain calm and not upset or rouse Jean with an outburst or scream of fear. "Madame? Are you feeling strong enough for a little food?" Lola smiled kindly down at her and kept her voice soft.

"Uhh, who are you, and where am I?" Elise wanted to know. It was a great relief just to be looking upon the kind face of the young girl instead of the hairy monster her eyes had last beheld. Then the blackness had devoured her and that was all she'd remembered. How long ago had that been?

"My name's Lola, madame and I've been tending to you since late yesterday. I am so happy to see how improved you look!" Lola

43

smiled and placed the tray on the nearby table so she could prop the woman up with an additional pillow.

Elise accepted the girl's help, for she found she was very weak when she tried to make the effort on her own. Weakly, she murmured, "Thank you, Lola. I appreciate your kindness to me. I am also indebted to your master." She wondered where she was, but it mattered not, for wherever it might be she was being cared for and was free of the horrible animal aboard that slimy ship. How it had all come about she would find out in time.

"Monsieur will be delighted to see you looking so well. However, let's get this nourishment down and you will feel much better," Lola urged her. She could have envied the woman if she had not felt such pity for her. She hadn't liked the evil, foul-mouthed Sebastian from the first minute she'd seen him here, but Sebastian was no more, she was certain. Jean would have seen to that last night.

Elise obeyed the young girl, feeling as helpless as a baby in her weakness. However, she felt that she would not be able to swallow even a mouthful of the soup. Surprisingly, she did, and allowed Lola to spoon-feed her almost the whole bowl. Lola exclaimed her pleasure at the amount she consumed.

"Mama John will be pleased!"

"Mama John?" Elise prodded.

"Mama John is our cook here, and she

44

considers herself the boss." Lola laughed lightheartedly.

Elise managed a wan smile and sunk back deep in the soft pillow. "Tell her for me that it was delicious, Lola."

"Well, I will let you rest for a while now. Perhaps, by this afternoon I might comb and brush your hair, madame?"

Elise gave her a nod.

Lola wished not to tax the poor woman too much all at one time, and the untangling and unmatting of her thick black hair would be a tedious task. She'd noticed the broken nails of her hands: no doubt she'd fought furiously at the brute Sebastian. Lola's appraising eyes had not missed the magnificent emerald and diamond ring and gold bracelets she still wore. Just one of the gold bangles would have made Lola feel like a queen. The woman wore five.

Ah, there was no doubt about her being a lady of quality and existing in a world far removed from Lola's. She could not help wishing to be petted and pampered in a similar fashion.

These were the thoughts sweeping through her head as Jean entered the door. He questioned her with his dark eyes before he spoke up. She quickly assured him Elise was fine. "Why you would not believe how much soup I got her to eat, Monsieur Jean!"

"*Magnifique*, Lola! I am pleased. Perhaps I could get you to run down and have Mama John

45

fix me some coffee, eh? And Lola, bring it here!''

Lola left to do his bidding and Jean moved closer to the bed. His dark eyes glowed warm with adoration and a depth of emotion he'd never felt for anyone before.

Elise Edwards was not asleep, but even with her eyes closed she could feel the warmth of the man's eyes boring into her. Slowly, she opened her eyes but closed them dejectedly when she saw the black-haired man was not her beloved Lance. For one fleeting moment she thought her dream had come true, that Lance had indeed rescued her from the ship that had been bearing her away.

Oh, that same horrible dream had occurred again, as it had haunted her in the past when she and Lance were separated. Once again he'd been on one ship and she stood by the railing of another. In the maze of fog and mist, she'd call out to him and just about the time the two ships would be parallel Lance's ship would be engulfed by a massive, giant wave. Now through the narrow openings of her eyelids, she saw that the handsome face and black hair were not Lance's. She sought to close her eyes against the disappointing, stark reality. However, she felt no fear of this man, whomever he might be, and perhaps that was because something about him reminded her of Lance.

She knew he was still devouring her. She could feel it even though her own eyes remained closed. Something urged her to see this stranger standing over her and slowly, she forced herself to open her eyes.

"Ah, madame, I'm so glad to see you looking so much better," he said, sinking down in the chair by the side of the bed. Relief registered on his face instantly.

Instinct told Elise this finely attired man was certainly no pirate, and he would not harm her. Weakly, she murmured, "I thank you, monsieur, for all you've done for me."

"It has been my pleasure, Madame Edwards."

"I fear you have me at a disadvantage for I do not know your name, monsieur."

"Ah, forgive me, madame. I am Jean Laffite and we are not the strangers you might think. A long time ago we met at the Le Clere's soiree. So you see, we have mutual friends. Perhaps you won't recall the occasion I speak of." He would never forget the beautiful vision of her in the stunning gown of rich green velvet and her magnificent emerald jewels. She looked like a queen!

"I believe I do remember the night." It was a gala affair that Elise had remembered, for she'd been impressed by the lovely Annette Le Clere that night and afterward they'd become very good friends, before she and Lance had departed to return to England.

The man's black eyes danced over her. Such warmth seemed to be reflected there. "I shall be forever grateful to you, Monsieur Laffite for the truth is, you've surely saved my life."

47

Laffite quickly admitted that he could not take credit for that and informed her of the name of the young pirate who had saved her. "The important thing now is for us to get you well. My home and my servants are yours, Madame Edwards. All you have to do is let your wishes be known." Jean had not heard Lola enter the room with a carafe of coffee. She saw him holding the lady's dainty hand in an almost loving caress and something close to worship in his dark eyes.

How gracious and kind he was, Elise thought. Try as she might she could not remember meeting him at Annette Le Clere's party, but she did remember the night. Even in her weakened state, she was impressed now by his swarthy handsomeness and elegant attire.

Jean took her thoughtful mood to be the result of weariness and decided he should linger no longer. Giving her a smile, he urged her to rest; he would return to check in on her later.

Elise gave him a weak smile, watching him leave the room.

Jean found he did not want to leave Barataria at this time for he still felt concern over Elise. He went to seek out his two most trusted men, Dominique You and Beluche, and inform them they were to go to New Orleans in his place. He reminded himself to include a message to be delivered to his current lady love, Elena Sanchez. Knowing the effect of his message and long absence, Jean smiled, thinking about the

48

furious, pouting Elena he'd encounter when he went to New Orleans. A fine trinket would soothe her ruffled feathers though.

Elise did welcome the hours she could sleep for her hours awake were a hellish torment. Thoughts of those horrible flames destroying the *Elise,* and the bloody decks made her want to start screaming. Poor Maggie, along with Lance and Andy, had to have been engulfed in that blazing inferno.

Brief moments of tranquility came upon her when she could force herself to recall their last evening together, standing by the railing of the ship, looking out over the rushing gulf water. Lance had exclaimed his pride of his newly adopted country for he considered himself an American now, not English.

With his strong arm around her waist, he'd spoken of his plans for their future together in the exciting New World, and how happy he was to be arriving after being delayed longer than they'd anticipated. As they sailed away from New Orleans, they could not have known it would be two years before their return to the country they'd become so fond of. By the time they'd landed in London, Elise knew she was pregnant and Lance was adament about his decision that they would remain there until Andy was born and old enough to travel without any danger to his well-being.

Their delay and prolonged stay delighted Elise's sister and Colette. So it was that they settled into Lance's townhouse, where they'd first lived after their marriage, to await the birth of their child while Lance disposed of all his holdings in England.

It was a wonderful time for them. It seemed as though they went back in time to those glorious days of bliss. Elise could not help remembering from time to time how those days were so swiftly swept away by the tragedy that changed both of their lives and eventually took them to the New World.

Even at this late date, she could remember her abduction by the Spaniard Joaquin Ruiz when she and Lance had gone to the small coastal town for a spring holiday. For many months she'd been aboard his ship, leaving England far behind. Then in Havana, she'd managed to escape only to find herself the victim of a couple of drunken, evil seamen. Had it not been for her rescue by an American sea captain, Clint Barron, she never would have lived through the ordeal their lustful intentions implied.

Clint became her protector and took her with him to his home in New Orleans. Feeling Lance was dead, and knowing Clint loved her, Elise finally agreed to marry him after many months in New Orleans. She had no way of knowing that Joaquin had lied to her about Lance's death, or that he'd searched for her all those months, often going on the slimmest clues left behind in ports where the *El Diablo*, Ruiz's ship, had docked. When Lance finally arrived in the cresent city and fate placed them face to face, it was a bitter, cruel reckoning, for each was in the company of another. Each of them suffered pain and hurt that seemed to be insurmountable. Loving one another as fiercely as they had, the thought of someone else invading that private domain proved to be a maelstrom of ravaged pride.

It took the self-sacrificing Clint Barron to bring the two stubborn, proud lovers together. He knew Elise could never love him as she did Lance Edwards, and he gallantly stepped aside. Never had a decision been harder for Captain Barron to make, but he knew he must, for all their sakes.

After Lance and Elise had left the city, Clint did get married to a vivacious girl he'd known all his life. Susan, the red-haired daughter of Zack Hart, became the mistress of Shady Oaks, Barron's plantation.

Lance Edwards retained his partnership with Zack Hart during his two years absence and Hart-Edwards Fleet Lines prospered and grew during that period. The two men kept in constant contact with their plans and ideas for the future when Edwards would return to the city.

Elise kept in contact with Susan and could not have been happier to learn that she'd become Clint's bride. That Susan had been infatuated with Lance and that they had briefly been lovers when he first arrived in New Orleans Elise willed herself to forget. They had

51

all been victims of the most unusual circumstances.

For months, the gossiping ladies gathered at their teas or sewing circles, speculating and pondering. The puzzling, mysterious liaison of Clint Barron, Susan Hart, Elise, and Lance Edwards became rather shopworn before the busybodies moved on to a new subject.

Behind fluttering fans, the name Elise Edwards had been whispered by both the men and the women since the minute of her arrival on Clint's ship. For one as beautiful and sensuous as Elise, the men spoke with envy and wistful yearning to be in Barron's shoes. The women's remarks vented their jealousy with smirking, catty retorts.

That last night together and a million memories paraded through Elise's mind that night and the nights to follow. She knew that Jean Laffite hovered by the bed to observe her and the girl, Lola came with food. But Elise had no determination or fighting spirit to get herself strong enough to leave the bed. It was not like the time when she was the captive of Joaquin Ruiz. Always, she plotted her escape from him.

Elise was not aware of her curt, snapping remarks to Lola as the days passed by, nor of just how trying she was to the young girl. Lola had to bite her tongue from her increasing desire to tell Elise Edwards what she thought.

Jean could not understand why she did not improve after all the constant care of his household.

Then came the day that Elise did realize what a shrew she'd been with Lola and she swore she would not do it again. After all, they'd all been so kind and considerate of her for weeks now. But that very afternoon when Lola patiently brushed and combed Elise's long hair, she lashed out at the girl again. This was just too many times, as far as Lola was concerned and she hurried down the hall muttering, "The bitch! The haughty bitch!" She vowed she would speak to Jean that same night.

Lola lifted her thick, heavy mane of hair off her neck as she swayed down the hall. It was such a balmy, sticky day and the hair away from her neck gave a cooling effect. As she ambled toward her room the idea of a cool bath appealed to her. For tonight, she planned to give special attention to her appearance. She was tired of Jean never coming to her room. It wasn't hard to figure out why. It was over that woman that Jean acted like a lovesick school boy.

She plotted how tonight would be different, and she would have him in her bed, one way or another.

That evening Lola perfumed herself and changed into a clean thin cotton blouse cut low in the front. The pretty new floral skirt flowed gracefully to her ankles. She wore the soft leather sandals old Angelo had given to her and for a final touch she tucked a red hibiscus in her hair to the side of her head. She knew she looked beautiful; her mirror told her so. The white batiste blouse molded to her firm, jutting breasts and as she turned sideways to take a final look at herself in the mirror she was pleased.

Jean greeted her pleasantly enough and took the tray of wine she brought to him. But when she playfully wrapped her arms around his waist and told him how lonely she'd been his tone chilled her to the core of her being. "Christ, not tonight, Lola! My mind is not on folly tonight!" He rudely shooed her out of his room. The pain stabbing her chest made her gasp and as soon as she was outside the door tears spilled down her cheeks.

Damn the woman and damn Jean Laffite, she spit under her breath. She would show them both, especially the arrogant Frenchman. The next time Alfredo Vega gave her the eye she would encourage him. *Madre de Dios*, he certainly had given her reason to think he was interested in her. Perhaps she'd just test him out while Jean was away. Mama John had told her Mister Jean was leaving early in the morning for the city.

Elise was unaware of all the activity centering on her, or of the strict order given to Mama John, Sulky, and Bess about the constant care to be given the woman occupying his bedroom.

As each passing day darkened the circles under Elise's eyes and she refused the good food brought her, Jean became more perplexed. Agitated that the stubborn woman would not obey his demand and bend to his will, he insisted that the servants take shifts of spoon-feeding her, even if they managed only one or two spoonfuls. Damn her, he cussed under his breath! He would not allow it. He knew with restored strength that face would become beautiful again, and the spirited, vital woman he'd looked upon at the party would be again. Such waste would be unforgivable and he was determined to not let it happen.

Mama John listened as he told her of his plans to consult with a doctor friend of his. The black woman shook her head in despair and declared, "Tha' little thing is goin' to just slip away from us if'n she don't eat. That's fo' sho'."

"No, Mama John! I *won't* let that happen!" he angrily spit at her before turning swiftly on his heels to leave the room. She started to hum and move around her kitchen, her own spirits lifted. That adament look on his face erased any doubts Mama John was harboring: she knew him too well. He would win! He always did.

So later it was carefully that she instructed the servant girls and Lola what they should do. It would be her fault, if anything went wrong.

Resolutely, the old woman tended to Elise in Jean's absence and the results brought a broad smile to her face three days later. Feeling quite smug, Mama John bubbled with delight and impatiently anticipated Jean's return from New Orleans.

Chapter 2

The swampy bayou never seemed to sleep, even during the darkness of the night. The night-birds gave out a high-pitched vibrato that was almost deafening, and it was this sound that roused the bruised and battered man lying on the boggy ground. Clutched in his bleeding arms was his curly-black-haired son. He listened for a moment to his son's breathing, mingled with deep sobs. He patted the boy in hopes of soothing his anguish, although he knew that his own would never be eased.

His body lay atop a huge piece of rough lumber, which represented what was left of his magnificent ship, the *Elise*. Dear God, how could he endure life without his beautiful Elise. The Elise of his thoughts was his wife, not his schooner. He could always get himself another fine schooner but never was there a woman like his Elise.

That God should have taken them both was

his desire. But the warmth of his little son's body burning against him reminded him that Andy needed him!

Poor little lad, he was all he had left of her now. Andy represented the all-consuming love they'd shared together. Since the minute he'd set his eyes upon the breathtaking loveliness of the French girl he'd claimed as his bride, no other woman had entered his life. She had been his everything, the power that made his world revolve. He, the elusive, reckless Captain Edwards had been tamed by the little green-eyed vixen.

He pulled Andy closer to him, holding the small body protectively against the cold night air. It would be foolhardy to move one inch without the light of day to guide him. Besides, he was devastated with weakness, and rest would allow him to gain some strength, he reasoned.

With the remnants of his coat he covered his son as best as he could and planted a kiss on the boy's fevered brow before sinking into a deep sleep.

Peter Beigerone's gruff demand for his young, impetuous daughter to wait for him did not stop her from scampering on ahead of him through the teacherous swamp. The impish Gigi hurried on, giving out a gust of lilting, lighthearted laughter for she knew how easily she could wrap her papa around her little finger. Spoiled and pampered by four older

57

brothers, she was used to getting her own way and Papa was more indulgent than the boys. His daughter was the "apple of his eye," and Peter admitted it. That Gigi would be their last child made her even more cherished. His wife Lisette could have no more the doctor had told them.

He watched his precious child dart through the wooded area like a spirited nymph and saw her stop short. "Papa, hurry! Hurry!" In huge striding steps the lanky Peter rushed to see what Gigi had come upon to excite her so. His heart pounded rapidly, expecting to see a deadly snake coiled at her feet, but her discovery proved to be of a man and small boy. Both looked more dead than alive, and as Peter bent down to check them he felt that he'd arrived too late to help the pair. However, the lad had a strong pulse beat, rapid because of the fever in his body. The man was another matter.

Gigi stood, shocked and disbelieving when her papa cradled the boy in his arms and urged her to come along. "But we can't leave this poor man, Papa!" She stood firm refusing to leave.

"You dare to question your papa, Gigi? I can not take the man and the boy. We'll go for help and return for the man. Can you carry the man, eh? Now, hurry! You are causing us to waste precious time!"

With a bowed head, ashamed of her thoughts, she stumbled along the path following her father to their canoe. She should have known

58

her papa would not just leave that poor man there.

The sun was almost directly overhead when they arrived at their small cottage situated on the bank of one of the many creeks that seemed to wind and finally flow into the muddy Mississippi River. Peter thrust the boy into Lisette's arms with a brief explanation of how he'd found him before rushing off to find two of his older sons, Paul and Etienne.

When they returned the sun was beginning to sink in the western sky and a billowing circlet of smoke rose from the chimney of the cottage signaling Lisette was preparing the evening meal. Lisette's two husky sons began to anticipate their mama's good cooking and their fine, muscled bodies bore witness to the fact that they ate well of their simple fare. While Paul was twelve and Etienne was fourteen, the two could have passed for twins.

Young Henri held the door for his brothers to carry the injured man into the cottage, but Andre was too busy helping himself to a fine chunk of fish in the chowder to be concerned about anything but his own needs. While his mama's attention was not on him, he rewarded himself a second time.

"Stop that, Andre! Take your dirty hands out of the rest of our supper," Gigi bossily shouted. Even though he was older, she was not in awe of him for he was the runt of the family and as short as Gigi. She prided herself that she could whip him in a scuffle anytime.

"Shut up, brat!" Andre smirked, sticking out his tongue.

Lisette chose to ignore them for she was tired and exasperated. The last thing in the world she needed was two unexpected guests to care for and feed. But her warm heart had gone soft at the sight of the curly haired lad as she'd doctored him and settled him into Gigi's bed a few hours ago. Now she knew the handsome man had to be the boy's father.

"Peter, you tend to the supper while I clean the man's face and arms," she urged. "I'll join you later after I'm through. The child is sleeping and that's the best thing for both of them. The rest is going to lie in God's hands anyway."

"Can I get something for you first?" Peter helped her remove the man's coat and shirt. He let his hands trail over the soft, fine cut of the man's pants. How nice it felt and Peter knew it had to be expensive. He also knew he'd never own such a garment, but perhaps his sons would know a different world and enjoy luxuries he'd never known in his lifetime. On occasion, the man allowed himself the pleasure of leisurely daydreams before drifting back to reality. How different their lives could have been if he'd been a wealthy man; he could have decked his beautiful Lisette in silk gowns and jewels. Instead she'd done nothing but hard work since they'd been married. It had made both of them age, and left its mark.

"Peter!" Lisette nudged him to help her pull

the clothing off the man. Peter mumbled an apology for his dawdling and went about the task. "Go on, Peter," she urged him, pulling her falling tresses away from her face and informing him that she could take over now to get the man comfortable and cleaned up.

As Peter left to wash up and see about their supper, Lisette busily cleaned the man's face and arms. As her hands swiped the warm cloth across his broad chest garnished with black curly hair Lisette was stirred by the handsomeness of her patient. Such a fine face, and the longest black lashes lay limp against his tanned face. Oh, he was one fine man, she thought! About Peter's age, or perhaps a little younger. His hands lay atop the sheet and she noted no calluses, no harsh redness or little cuts from laboring. No, this man was a gentleman, for sure.

Having no knowledge of any man other than Peter, Lisette had a curiosity what it would be like to feel another man's hands caressing her body and kissing her. She allowed her imagination to run wild there in the dimly lit room of her cottage.

Feeling guilty, she lifted the sheet to steal a look at the man's nakedness. Strong muscled thighs and legs rested slightly parted, exhibiting his bold maleness with a shield of black, curling ringlets. There seemed to be no injuries below his waistline, Lisette decided as she rolled him over gently. Then turning him slowly back on his back, she tucked the cover up under his armpits. It justified her lingering ogling of his body, but she knew that it was more than just checking his body for injuries. Curiosity urged her to do it.

For the longest time, Lisette had felt cheated by life. It was not to say she did not love her children and Peter. But life had given her no excitement or riches. All she'd known was working from daylight to dark and having babies. She felt tired and worn, as if she would soon grow old and die, she told herself. There'd been little time for laughter, and of late Peter had rarely come to her bed. Not since Gigi'd been born. While she appreciated that he wished not to endanger her life with having another baby, she ached with the hunger of a passionate woman. She'd always been that, and now that pleasure had been denied her. She had become nervous and snappy at the children and Peter, completely drowning in desperate self-pity.

She moved aimlessly through the days, not caring whether her hair was combed or her dress neat and clean. There was no incentive for Lisette to make herself attractive anymore. Yet, there were still hints of the pretty young girl she had been when she'd first married Peter. Her thick glossy hair shined no more from her constant brushing, and the sweet fragrance of verbena water dabbed behind her ears was forgotten. Leisurely baths she allotted to herself as a special private time to relax and enjoy herself when the small children took their naps were not indulged in anymore.

It was little wonder that her family was shocked beyond belief when they entered the cottage a few evenings later and saw their mother in her clean, neat muslin dress and her dark hair nicely combed into a neat coil.

Paul whistled and Etienne gasped, "Mama, you're beautiful!" She looked almost girlish with the curly wisps of hair tickling her ears. Mother or not, his fourteen year old eyes could appreciate her trim figure and fine bosom.

"Why, thank you, Etienne," Lisette said, obviously pleased by her son's remark. Peter's eyes blazed with desire for the first time in months and it delighted her.

"Is it a holiday or something, Lis? Have I been so busy I've forgotten it?" Peter inquired, noting the good smell of her herbed chicken and dumplings steaming in the iron pot on the stove. He saw all the special, little touches she'd added around the cottage, like a crock filled with green foliage and a glass filled with purple wildflowers. It was obvious she'd spent hours during the day baking two pies and pan bread for their supper that night.

Gigi, Henri, Andre, and the young lad they'd rescued sat in the other room playing some child's game, but in a quiet, mannerly fashion. All Peter could tell himself was that a small miracle had happened in the last ten hours.

"No, Peter, I just felt full of energy and . . . well, perhaps, it was the day. It was such a beautiful day. I . . . I just got going and couldn't stop." She gave a soft giggle and Peter was reminded of the Lisette he knew so long ago. In fact, he was so warmed by the sight of her and his cottage that even as tired as he was from working a long day, he'd liked to have stole her away from the eyes of their children, rushed into their bedroom and made wild love to her. So strong was the desire that he took the hat off his head to place in front of him to hide the bulge of his pants. He felt the swelling and hardening of himself and was embarrassed.

"It's . . . it's really nice, Lis and so are you," he stammered, rushing on out of the room to clean up for the nice meal awaiting him. He wondered if his weathered, tanned face was showing a flush. As her older sons followed their father and the younger children continued to play their game, Lisette smiled smuggly to herself. Only she knew the secret inspiration for all her special efforts and toilette. Only an hour ago she'd carried a refreshing cup of tea and a bowl of broth to the ill man and even his eyes had warmed to the sight of her. It was a great enough reward for her. They'd even chatted for a moment and he'd been able to relate to her how he and his young son, Andy, had come to be on the bank of the river and the misfortune befalling them. She envied with all her being the wife he anguished for! His dark eyes filled with pain as he spoke of "his Elise."

He'd touched her hand lightly, his eyes warmed with gratitude as he thanked her. "I owe you and your family my life, Madame

Beigerone. As soon as I can get on my feet I plan to do something about all the trouble I've put you to." Even the way he called her "Madame Beigerone" made her feel like an elegant lady, and the dark, lazy look of his eyes made her tingle, not to say anything about the touch of his hand. They're strong hands, and powerful, she wagered, when he's himself.

"Oh, Monsieur Edwards, you owe us nothing!" She assured him, feeling flushed and embarrassed. Her hand shook from the unsure, timid feeling overwhelming her in his presence. Lisette had never met a man like Lance Edwards before. She gave way to her nervousness by prattling on and on about what a pleasure it had been. "Why that dear little boy of yours has been so good and he's such a handsome child. Why he looks just like you!" Lord, she realized she sounded like a silly school girl, and she knew her face must be a rosy red from the heat rushing to her head. Actually, she was experiencing a giddiness.

"Thank you, madame. I truly thank you from the bottom of my heart. However, in Andy I can see only my wife. But he does have my coloring." He gave her a weak smile.

Lisette saw that he was desiring to close his eyes again to sleep and she excused herself, urging him to rest.

Damn, he was weary and it disgusted him thoroughly. All this wasted time when he could be on his way. As soon as he arrived in New Orleans, he plotted out how he'd seek out the help of Zack Hart and Clint Barron.

When he slept, it was a restless sleep and filled with nightmares of despicable acts of violence inflicted against Elise. He'd heard tales of men such as the cutthroats who'd captured his wife. Worse than rutting animals in the fields, they were!

For Elise's sake, it would probably be a blessing if death had come fast and swift. God forbid, he could not wish that, but neither would he want her to suffer. When he was thinking rationally, he had to admit that there was little hope that she'd survive this long. Brave, she certainly was, and a wildcat of a fighter, but her tiny body could not withstand the brutish, harsh treatment she'd receive by that giant of a man.

He'd killed before for her and he'd search until he found this pirate bastard. The name was branded in his soul—Sebastian!

Should she truly be dead, Lance knew her presence would forever be with him. Like the colorful blossoming of spring, the torrid heat of summer, the golden harvest of autumn, or the exhilaration of a cool winter's day, Elise was eternally a part of him as long as he breathed.

Was it too much to expect that a rapture such as theirs could have been but a brief span of time on this earth? he solemnly mused.

Chapter 3

The balmy breeze and warm sun washed over the sandy dunes and its effect was like a tonic to Elise as she playfully ran her toes through the almost white grains of sand. She sat by the side of the short, pudgy pirate Jean introduced as Dominique You. Each day he escorted her along the beach for a stroll and she'd come to look forward to it.

The chubby Dominique You swelled with pride that he was the man chosen as Elise's protector when Jean was busy with other duties. In very explicit terms, Laffite had described what punishment would befall any man approaching her, but knowing how easily any man could take leave of his senses where a ravishing, breathtaking beauty like Elise was concerned, Jean appointed You.

All the lovesick looks on You and Laffite's faces sickened and disgusted the little Spanish miss, Lola. She gave out a hiss and kicked at the sand as she stood leaning against the massive palm this particular afternoon. This had been the regular afternoon schedule since Jean's return from the city. What a couple of fools they both were, she mused silently.

You's hands gestured busily as he sat telling Elise about his exciting times in Haiti when he fought against Toussaint l'Ouverture and Elise's eyes widened as he came to the part of the bloody battle. Dominique hastily changed the subject to a more lighthearted topic noticing her lovely face frown. The barrel-chested You looked like a court jester entertaining his queen. Lola shrugged her shoulders and laughed at the thought. What did it matter now, she had Alfredo. While she had to be honest that in Alfredo's huge arms she did not find the wild passion of Jean's lovemaking, she was amazed at the gentleness of the bearlike Alfredo. He was a tender lover, considering her feelings above his own, and he tried to pleasure her as well as himself. She found she liked the Spaniard very much.

Lola lingered to watch Dominique help Elise up from the beach and he supported her arm like she was a fragile doll leading her back to the house. It was such a funny sight to Lola she put her hand over her mouth to suppress a giggle. The squatty, little pirate was so out of his element and awkward playing the gallant.

After he'd seen her to the door and made his way down the path where Lola swayed toward him, he greeted her with a big smile plastered on his face. Lola sighed under her breath. What a lovesick fool he looked like. Aloud, she hailed a friendly greeting. "Hello, Dominique. Beautiful afternoon, isn't it?"

"Sure is. How you been, Lola?" He truly wanted to know, and Lola could not help warming to Dominique. He was far too outgoing and friendly for anyone not to like. Yet, she'd heard tales about his fierceness as a fighter when the need arose. There was no doubt about the high esteem Laffite had for the man.

"Been just fine. I see you took Madame Edwards for her outting today," Lola remarked.

"Yeah, I did. Such a delicate little thing and such a grand lady. Yes sir, there's a real lady of quality, Lola." He kicked at the dirt and swung his arms absorbed in his thoughts like a romantic young lad in love for the first time. Lola could swear his dark face glowed with a blush.

"Yes, I know, Dominique . . . a real lady, indeed!" She spit out the words: she'd heard the same thing from Mama John and the young black girl, Prissy. Christ, she was sick to death with all the praises about Elise Edwards. For the life of her, she could not figure out Jean Laffite. Lola knew that it was not the lady's wishes that she still remain on Barataria. No, it was Jean who kept insisting she was not up to making the trip into the city. Being quite honest, Lola had observed with her own eyes that Madame Edwards did not encourage this constant devotion Jean bestowed upon her. The arrogant Laffite she'd known was not the man she saw now.

Like a thief in the night, Jean had arrived at his house in the city, and upon his arrival he instructed the servants he was retiring. His plans called for an early morning call on the Le Cleres.

Jean had many friends in the city but highest on his list was Francois and Annette Le Clere. They, along with most of the French Creole population, were loyal to Laffite and kept him informed about his sworn enemy, Governor Claiborne. Francois enjoyed a lukewarm friendship with the governor, but his wife and the governor's wife were very good friends. Jean adored Madame Claiborne and admired her greatly. On occasion, she'd enjoyed the bounty from his warehouses, like Annette Le Clere.

While Jean cared not what most people thought of him, he cared very much about the impression Francois might form about these latest rumors floating around the city about his attacking the Edwards ship. As for most of the wealthy planters, the ones who damned him to the governor were the same hypocrites greedily bartering for his rich goods in the warehouses on Grand Terre.

So it was not unusual with his many connections in the city that Jean found himself at the same grand functions of the social elite of the French Creole citizens.

There was no finer plantation around New Orleans than Bellefair and there was no planter more gracious than Francois Le Clere. So when Jean arrived to a rather cool, aloof manner that morning, he was admittedly hurt. But what Jean could not know was the depth of feeling Francois and Annette bore for Elise and Lance Edwards. They were crushed by the news of the dastardly deed.

Jean could not finish the cup of coffee served to him by Henri, the Le Clere's house servant of many years. "Francois, we've been friends far too long for you to doubt me. I will come right to the point before I take my leave. You, of all people, should have more faith in me than to think what I know you are sitting there thinking!" With that declaration, Jean rose from the chair, preparing to hasty departure.

"Jean, I—"

"I had no knowledge of the act and the man has been punished—executed. I could not undo what was already done, *mon ami,* but I have devoted myself to the lady, Madame Elise Edwards and she is now well."

"Oh, Jean . . . forgive a foolish old man. Come sit down and we shall talk some more," Francois insisted, feeling terrible that in his mind he condemned him without giving Jean a chance or hearing his side of the happening. Brutally unfair, he'd been.

They talked for over an hour and Francois

71

insisted that Jean must bring Elise to them, for nothing would please his wife Annette more. He assured Jean that nothing had reached the city of Captain Edwards's survival, but he directed Jean to call upon Zack Hart or Clint Barron for they would surely know.

"Can't say I look forward to calling on Zack Hart, and I've never met this Barron." Jean smiled. He and the American fleetline owner had never hit it off too well. Once again, he rose from the chair to take his leave, assuring Francois that he would bring Elise to Bellefair very soon.

The two men moved down the long hall toward the front door. In a more lighthearted mood, Jean remarked, "Tell your beautiful wife I'll allow her the first choice of some of my new bolts of silk and brocades."

Francois laughed. "Ah, you spoil her, you know?"

"Ah, but a beautiful lady like Annette deserves spoiling," Laffite teased, knowing his older friend pampered his adored Annette.

Francois patted his shoulders assuring Jean that Annette would be sorry she'd missed him. Before departing, Jean could not resist the devious urge to inquire, "How is old Claiborne?"

Francois chuckled. *"Mon ami,* I fear you give him a daily attack of indigestion!"

Pleased at that prospect, Jean admitted that he hoped so and left Francois to go to Harwood to speak to Zack Hart. However, upon arriving at Harwood Hart's majordomo informed him that Mister Hart would not be returning home until early evening. So Jean proceeded on to the Barron plantation to seek out its owner.

While Jean had known the parents of Barron before their fatal accident when their carriage had overturned due to runaway bays, he had never met Clint. The elder Barron had been a fine man and an excellent horseman. The accident had been just one of those freakish incidents where the team of horses had been frightened, sending them into a frenzy that the elder Barron could not bring them out of even with all his expertise.

On his ride up the country road toward Shady Oaks he pondered if the fine old plantation had retained the grandeur of the time Clint Barron's parents had been the mistress and master there. It was a fine showplace then with its magnificent grounds and the impressive home.

As the roan galloped up the long, winding drive bordered by boxwood shrubs, he had to admit it obviously was well cared for by the younger Barron.

He leaped down from his horse, handing the reins to a young black boy, and strode up to the impressive entranceway to receive admittance into the house. He was glad to hear Barron was home and the manservant led him down the highly polished cypress floor of the long hallway to the morning room.

There, sitting in a chair with his foot propped

up on a footstool sat Clint Barron. Before Clint turned to greet him with a broad, friendly smile, Jean thought he looked like some Viking warrior. Clint was a powerfully built man with a heavy mane of blond hair framing a strong, rugged face.

So this was the man who had married Zack Hart's vivacious red-haired daughter Susan, Jean thought to himself. Since Jean had ears and eyes all over the city of New Orleans even though he spent a lot of his time on Barataria, he still knew everything that went on in the city of New Orleans. He'd heard the gossip about Susan Hart Barron, but he'd never met the young lady.

In that moment he lingered in the archway waiting for the servant to take his leave, Jean surveyed the lavishly furnished room, admiring Barron's taste in the dark wood furnishings and fine works of art decorating the walls, along with a fine exhibit of firearms. The windows gave a perfect view of the magnificent gardens just outside, with its many colored blossoming flowers and shrubs. Two portraits of Clint's parents hung over the massive mantel of the fireplace.

The two men exchanged smiles and Clint apologized for not standing up to greet him due to his injured foot.

Clint urged him to have a seat and ordered refreshments brought to the two of them. "It is a pleasure to finally meet you after all this time.

I've heard about you for so long now." The tales about the Frenchman sold the man short, Clint considered, taking in the striking figure across from him. Not only was his fine attire impressive but his dark good looks were enough to turn any woman's head. He'd heard the gossip about the man's winning ways with the women of New Orleans. Susan would be cussing herself for not being home this time, he thought privately.

"I fear, sir, I could not possibly live up to a lot of the gossip circulated around the countryside about me. However, I am honored to finally meet you and I find it curious that we've not met before. Anyway, now we have." Laffite liked the man and despite his overpowering body and rugged appearance there was a gentle air about Clint Barron.

Laffite told him the shocking story, watching Barron's face flinch with varied emotions. Clint sat stunned afterward and mumbled, "Dear God! Poor Elise!" His thoughts traveled back to months and months ago. Holy Christ, he cussed himself so many times for allowing her to slip away from him so easily. So many times he'd wished he'd fought harder for her.

"You say Elise is recovering and staying with you on Barataria?" Clint quizzed, trying to sort everything out in his muddled head.

"Yes, monsieur. She is getting the very best of care. I've just this minute left the Le Clere's to inform them about her condition."

75

Clint cussed his injured foot and his incapacity, for otherwise he would have requested of Laffite that he be allowed to accompany the Frenchman back to his fortress to bring Elise home. Oh, yes, he remembered long ago the night when he'd gathered her petite body in his two arms and carried her to his ship and nursed her back to health. God, it galled him that he could not rush to her side now. The memory burned brightly in his mind of the time Shady Oaks was her home after they returned from Havana where he'd found her crumpled body on a deserted street after two drunk seamen had attacked her.

Months ago, he'd realized he'd never stop loving her. His marriage to Susan Hart had been a big mistake and they'd both paid bitterly. God, how they'd paid!

Jean felt awkward at the man's long period of quiet thoughtfulness, but Barron broke the long silence. In a serious, somber manner, he remarked, "Monsieur Laffite, let nothing happen to her. I will be happy to care for her as soon as you can bring her to the city. She means ev— very much to me. I've known her a long time."

Susan had not made her presence known. Walking down the hall she had heard her husband talking to another man and stood in the arch before announcing herself. It was at that moment she'd heard Clint's declaration to the gentleman sitting across from him. She stopped short, moving no farther through the archway. Who was this strange, handsome man?

"Madame Edwards is a lucky woman to have so many good, devoted friends," Laffite replied.

"Elise Edwards is a most unusual, outstanding woman, Monsieur Laffite," Clint informed him.

Susan now knew who Clint was talking about earlier, and replaying his words she was convinced more than ever that he'd never stopped loving Elise. But what was all this about—this discussion with Monsieur Laffite about the Edwardses? What connection did Laffite have with Elise, she wondered? She sauntered into the room.

"Gentlemen." Susan was impressed by the good looks of her husband's guest. While she heard about the famous Jean Laffite, she never met him, and now as she was about to she could clearly see why the women were so taken with his charms. To her, there was the reminder of Lance Edwards in his tall, dark countenance. As his dark eyes turned in her direction and his mouth curved on one side in a smile she felt a flutter in her stomach remembering Lance.

Clint made the introduction and noted the bright flashing in Susan's eyes. Christ, there was not one ounce of discretion in his redheaded wife, he observed.

Jean greeted her in that gracious, warm

manner of his, but cautiously warned himself that this was a woman who could be dangerous. "Madame Barron, it is a pleasure to meet you. I just wish our first meeting could have been one of happier circumstances." Susan returned his greeting graciously.

She took a seat and turned to Clint with a questioning glance. She listened as he related Laffite's news to her, and gasped unable to hold back the tears, for the impact of Lance Edwards being dead was bitter to accept. From the minute she'd heard about their returning to the city, she'd been filled with the wild anticipation of seeing him again. He was a man no woman could forget easily.

During that time when the four of them had been involved she could understand so easily why Elise postponed answering Clint's proposal of marriage. Of course, she had not known Lance Edwards at that time and she'd thought Elise was crazy not to grab a man like Clint Barron who wanted to place the world at her feet. Then Lance came to the city and she met him not as Elise's husband, but as a stranger coming from England to their city. She was completely enamored with him and diligently tried to lure him. One brief night in his arms was all they had, but it was enough for Susan to know that most men paled in comparison. Yes, even her husband had been a big disappointment on their wedding night and she knew that the path she'd traveled since marrying Clint was a futile search to recapture that same glorious rapture she found once in Lance Edwards's arms down by the river bank. No, she could not believe that marvelous, vital man was dead, and she could not stay in the room one minute longer with her tears flowing. So she mumbled a feeble apology and staggered from the room to seek solitude.

Instead of her bedroom, she rushed to the stables and ordered her mare saddled. Moments later as she struck the quirt to the mare's rump she was struck with a terrifying thought. If Lance was dead, Elise would be a widow—free to remarry. What could that do to her life? Would Clint leave her to go to Elise? He'd never got the woman out of his system, she'd accepted that shortly after their marriage had taken place.

Elise. . . . Elise. . . . Elise! With each beat of the mare's hooves on the dusty, dirt road, it beat like a drum in her aching, throbbing head. Why wasn't Elise dead instead of Lance?

Jean took his leave to return to the city. The trail of dust swirling over in the distance caught his eyes and he recognized the wild, flying red hair of the rider as Susan Barron. What a savage little minx she was, he wagered watching her gallop like demons were chasing after her! Perhaps, they were, he mused.

Something about the young lady warned him to stay well away from her. Dear God, he'd squirmed in their parlor as she ogled him with unabashed boldness in the presence of her husband. He pondered just what kind of man Clint Barron was to allow such behavior out of his wife. Shrugging his shoulders, he had to admit that one mistress at a time was the best way. A wife was another matter. For Elise, he would make the exception!

Chapter 4

Jean Laffite rode away from Shady Oaks with
some very puzzling questions gnawing at him.
The handsome couple were two complex
personalities. He'd be the last man in the world
to not admit that the red-haired Susan Barron
was not a good looking woman with a fine
figure. That pert little face of hers was almost
childlike. But there was something about her
that spelled danger and watching her ride out of
the grounds like that pointed out a wildness
he'd seen before.

His first impression of the blond giant Clint
Barron was that he liked the man immensely.
Mon Dieu, how his revelation about the
Edwardses had affected the man! Laffite felt it
had more to do with Elise Edwards than her
husband.

Somehow, he knew that Elise had played a
very important role in the couple's lives. He
pondered the strangeness all the way back to

the city. There were no two ways about it, a kind of chill fell in that parlor when Susan had joined the two of them. There was another point that Jean could not forget. Clint's firm insistence that Elise be brought to Shady Oaks instead of the Le Clere's plantation.

Jean did not relish the role facing him upon his return to Barataria for he had hoped to have encouraging news to tell Elise. He dreaded looking upon her beautiful face when he must tell her that there was no word of Lance or the young son in the city. Had he known what was transpiring that very moment back at his fortress, he would have been irate. Elise, with the help of Lola, finished her toilette. Her green eyes blazed at that moment from the discussion she'd just had with the devious Lola. The girl, in an innocent manner, had let it slip to Elise that the man who'd attacked her husband's ship and taken her captive was Laffite's lieutenant. The naughty little Lola derived a certain amount of pleasure watching the woman's face distort in shock.

Still playing the innocent, Lola hastily added that her patron had put Sebastian to death for his terrible deed. "Oh, madame, he is a marvelous man. He felt terrible about the thing this Sebastian did." Elise paid no attention to the praise Lola bestowed on the man. It mattered not to Elise; it was one of his cutthroats who had destroyed her son and husband.

The next day she fell into a quiet, thoughtful

mood that puzzled Mama John. The young lady had been improving and when she even refused the goodhearted You's suggestion to go for a walk on the beach Mama John became concerned.

"Let me check you head, missy!" Her black hand came to rest on Elise's forehead. "Nope, you cool's a cu'comber. You tell Mama John what trouble'n you?"

Elise smiled up at the black woman. She certainly felt no malice toward her; she had been kindness itself. "You don't worry about me, Mama John. I'm all right. I'm just a little low today."

Mama John gave her a knowing nod of her kerchiefed head. Poor little thing certainly had a right to feel low. After all it had been only a few weeks and a woman didn't get over losing her man and her boy in a short time. However, she had been so perky lately and that pretty face of hers had glowed so with restored vitality that Mama John was discouraged by this despaired manner.

Mama John turned to leave the room. "Maybe t'morrow be better, honey." Elise replied that perhaps it would.

Dominique You was crushed by her refusals to take their daily walks along the sandy beach. But Elise could not tolerate his company now, and she had enjoyed the chummy, good-natured pirate before talking to Lola.

So she exercised within the confines of her room, walking what seemed like miles during the long, boring days. Determined to gain her strength, she attended to her own toilet and other needs for she wanted only to leave Barataria as soon as possible. As soon as Laffite returned, she was determined to demand he allow her to leave. She wanted no more of his charity for it could not make up for her loss.

Mama John was more than pleased when she returned her plate of food with every morsel gone. No one, Lola included, realized the thoughts and plotting going on behind the mask Elise wore those next few days.

The Elise Edwards presenting herself at his dinner table the night Jean returned from New Orleans pleased him as well as stirred him with desire. She was breathtakingly beautiful, with a glow in her cheeks. The added pounds enhanced her small, petite figure. He had not taken note of just how short she was until they stood side by side. The top of her head came to his shoulders.

Her eyes seemed unusually bright as they looked over at him and she inquired, "A pleasant trip, monsieur?"

"A safe one, shall we say." His dark eyes swept over her, warm with adoration. "I don't have to ask how you are, Madame Edwards. You look marvelous and I think it calls for a drink to celebrate your good health."

"Yes, I think that's a wonderful idea." It was very difficult to be pleasant to the man, even though he was most charming. She would gain nothing with this man by being overbearing. So this night she would be an actress.

Laffite decided not to mar the evening just yet by telling her what he learned in the city. He was also puzzled to find her so gay tonight since Lola had informed him that she'd refused to accompany You on walks and stayed mostly in her room.

Elise played her role magnificently, and Jean could not remember when he'd enjoyed a candlelight dinner more. He sat letting his eyes devour her beautiful image. One minute her eyes were the bright green of emeralds and the next moment they seemed to change to the hue of a topaz. The pale shade of her gold satin gown seemed to blend in with her tanned flesh. He found it easy to imagine her naked sitting before him. It seemed the gown was surely molded to those firm, rounded breasts, with its neckline cut just low enough to tease him. With her dark hair piled high atop her head, she looked so fashionable. No queen could have appeared more regal than Elise Edwards, he thought to himself.

Overcome with wild desire for her, he tried to sound more casual than he was feeling by commenting about the exquisite diamond and emerald ring and the gold bangle bracelets she wore. Elise remarked that her husband had given them to her.

"He had magnificent taste in many things, I must say."

"He was a magnificent man, monsieur!" Elise hastily remarked. Jean assured her he had

85

no doubt about that. He went on to tell her of his visit with her friends, the Le Cleres and the Barrons. Elise was more than grateful when he spoke of the Le Clere's suggestion that she stay with them for she could not cope now with residing at Montclair. He finally admitted that he could not find any evidence or news about her husband; he was presumed dead.

Her lovely face was like stone, no hint of emotion played there as he spoke. When he finished speaking, she remarked in such a cool, chilling tone it rather unnerved Jean. "I wish to leave as soon as possible, Monsieur Laffite. I've put you to enough trouble already—too long."

"Madame, you—"

"Monsieur, I must insist that you take me to New Orleans as soon as it can be arranged," she interrupted him.

"You have been ill, Madame Edwards. We shouldn't chance it yet."

"I am fine, Monsieur. I assure you I'm no delicate little flower. I can make the trip to New Orleans, I tell you," Elise declared in a sharp, assured tone that dared Laffite to contradict her.

Little she might be, but she was a firebrand, Laffite realized suddenly. It was the first time she'd exhibited this trait. When she was herself and not ailing, Jean mused privately, she must be a very independent individual with a will of iron.

"I assure you, Madame Edwards, I have not

the slightest doubt of your courage, but merely concern that you would overtax yourself," he said, amusement playing on his face.

"I appreciate that, but after all, I will have to be the judge of my feelings," Elise retorted.

Her mercurial personality this evening taxed his patience, but it also challenged him to unravel its cause. She was no ordinary woman in any sense of the word. Her gay mood had changed too swiftly to a stubborn defiance.

Seeking to put her back to the former gay, casual atmosphere, he said, "Please, shall we just call one another Jean and Elise. I feel after the time we've been in each other's company we should not be so stiff. We aren't exactly strangers. Here, another glass of wine to celebrate your good health, Elise." Jean put all the charm he could in his manner and speech. He had a right to feel very self-assured about that charm that never failed where ladies were concerned.

Elise was not immuned to the electricity he created for she had a man whose strong personality was similar. Even after they were married, Elise never forgot what an impact Lance made on the ladies. Smugly, she'd watched the reactions of women when Lance's lazy long-lashed eyes turned in their direction. She knew the secret yearnings going on within them.

Let him think he is having his way, Elise silently thought. She wanted to have her way about leaving this place and him. For all his charming ways and expensive clothes, he was just a thieving pirate who lived off the stolen property of others. After what Lola had revealed to her, she could not stand to take another day of his charity.

"Yes, monsieur, I will drink to that, but I assure you my health is fine." Jean devoured her carefully. She was mysterious tonight and he would have given anything to know what was going on behind that beautiful mask.

"Please, call me Jean." He sipped from his glass, letting his black eyes lock onto hers. "You are most beautiful by candlelight, Elise."

The cad, she fumed vehemently! He would not win her over with his fine words for she hated what he represented.

"You are kind, Monsieur Laffite." She forced herself to smile but Jean could almost feel the chill in it.

To bolster her courage to do battle with him, she drained her glass of wine. It took her a brief moment to realize that she was beginning to feel the effects of the wine consumed during the evening. She'd not drunk that much for some time.

"I'm feeling very tired, Monsieur Laffite. If you will excuse me, I think I shall retire," she announced, rising up from her chair before he could assist her. She swayed and found Jean's arms encircling her. Pressed against his broad chest, she lingered to steady herself.

Jean lifted her face upward and slowly bent his head down, letting his lips consume her warm, inviting mouth. A volcano of desire erupted within him, the likes he'd never experienced before from a mere kiss. Elise's response was as natural as breathing, and for a moment she forgot that it was Jean Laffite kissing her. The haze lifted and she hastily pushed away from him with all the strength she could muster.

"Jean . . . stop! You've no—" His mouth attacked her again, demanding she return his kisses. Her legs felt like jelly and she trembled, fearing she would surely faint.

For a woman like Elise, whose body was so tuned to making love, the impact of Jean's quest was taking its toll. She knew it and it stirred a maelstrom of conflicting emotions. Yes, she could easily let him have his way and the fleeting thought raced through her that she could enjoy that pleasure very much. At the same time, it sickened and disgusted her! At the same moment, she could have cussed Lance Edwards for opening the door of such raptures the body can enjoy.

"Dear God, my darling! You are perfection!" Jean gasped in a heavy, labored voice. Obviously shaken by the effect she'd had on him, he knew he must have her. What had delighted him was her own brief response, but now she was fighting him. Damned if he'd let her!

Without any hesitation, he swept her up in his arms and made his way up the stairs. Elise felt her head whirling at the swiftness of it all. "I've adored you from afar for so long, you beautiful angel." His words came to her. The magnetism of him was, indeed, overwhelming.

She heard the door opening and knew he was now in the bedroom she was quartered in. Feeling herself gently placed on the massive bed and looking up at the face of the man bending over her, she reacted. Jean was completely unprepared for what happened next.

"Get out! This minute—I want you to leave me!" Elise sat upright in the bed, arranging her gown down over her legs and knees. Jean removed himself from the bed as swiftly as if she had slapped him across the face. "What . . . what did you say?"

"I think you heard me, Monsieur Laffite! I asked you to leave." Elise swept the falling hair from her face and jumped up from the bed. Yanking up the neckline of her gown, she realized just how far his caresses had gone; one breast was exposed.

He trembled with confusion and his face burned with rage. The throbbing ache in his groin made him gasp and cuss. He moved slowly, heaving with a heavy intake of air, trying to regain his wits about him. He was damned near close to throttling her.

Drawing on all his willpower, he gave her a smirking smile and informed her, "Madame, the woman hasn't been born whom I'd beg to go to bed with me!" Bowing gallantly, he turned and laughed. "Pardon my *faux pas,* but I could have sworn you wanted me to continue. In fact,

Madame Edwards—I think you did!"

He stood, raising a skeptical brow and still smiling. He managed to slip out of the door just before a satin slipper smashed against the frame and a flood of French cuss words echoed inside the room.

It was true what he said and the thought sickened Elise. Disgust flooded her being. She wanted him to make love to her and she ached from the emptiness engulfing her now. Was she as wanton as Lance had often teased her about being? But his teasing had been filled with love and she knew how it pleased him that she desired him so eagerly. More than ever, she felt the need to be away from this man, Laffite!

Lola was puzzled by the black mood Jean displayed the next morning, but Mama John wore a sly smile on her face and assured the curious Lola, "Oh, it's nuthin', child. It's nuthin'—just an ornery mood of Mister Jean's."

When Lola left her kitchen, Mama John let out a restrained laugh she'd held back. That special candlelight dinner, fine wine and Mister Jean at his most charming best had not won him the prize last night. Probably for the first time in his life Jean Laffite was refused!

Chapter 5

It had been a week since Jean had attempted to make love to Elise. His new aloofness left her perplexed and disturbed her almost as much as his earlier attempts to possess her. It was as if he was playing some devious game with her. On occasion she'd notice his dark eyes devouring her and a smirking smile on his sensuous mouth. It made her stay at Barataria miserable.

Each time she'd suggested that he get her into the city to her friends, he'd shrugged her wishes aside, saying he couldn't make the trip yet. This inflamed her and he knew it. She'd bounce out of the room, cussing him under her breath. Damn him, he was enjoying this power over her and she hated him for that!

Perhaps his beguiling charms worked on other women, but she vowed they wouldn't work on her. Yet, at times they did, and she hated herself for allowing it. At night, she'd pace her room like a caged animal.

This particular night, she could stand it no longer. Walking out on the terrace outside her bedroom in her sheer blue wrapper, she told herself it mattered not what the hands of the clock said. One day was the same as another, as well as the nights. So she walked down the steps, halting to remove her slippers, to walk on the white sandy beach.

She stood for a moment absorbing the gentle, balmy breeze teasing and caressing her face. Then she inhaled the smell of the island's flowering blossoms wafting to her. It was a beautiful paradise here, she had to admit. Jean had himself a little kingdom here. Looking out on the moonlit bay, she was quickly reminded of her husband viewing the towering masts of the ships moored there. The lazy, lapping of the tide seemed to whisper his name. . . . Lance. . . . Lance. . . . Lance.

She had no idea that she was being observed from the shadows by a figure leaning against a giant palm tree. Actually, Jean had been preparing to go to bed, but he'd seen the gossamer shadow pass his window and he dared not investigate what she was about. Yet, he felt certain most of the inhabitants were asleep.

He was so absorbed for those first few minutes observing the beauty of her curved body with the gentle breeze making the gown cling close that the realization startled him. Dear God, he'd never given that possibility any thought since she'd been here on Barataria over a month now. But she had been married, and the possibility did exist!

He watched her sink down on the sandy beach and even in the darkness he could make out that her head was cupped in her hands. She was crying and it pained Jean to know she was so sad. So small and tiny, she looked like a lost child and he felt more than just a man's wild desire for her. There was the urgency to cradle her in his arms and give her comfort. Damnit, she needed him and if that was all he could be to her at this time, then so be it!

Elise did not hear his approach until he sank down beside her and enclosed her in his strong arm. Then she started to protest but Jean would not allow it. "No, Elise, you need me and I want nothing from you, *ma petite*." His warm lips rested on the side of her cheek and he gently smoothed the hair from her damp face. She clung to him and he whispered softly in her ear, "I'll always be near if you need me, little Elise. Remember that, will you Elise?"

"You're a good man, Jean Laffite," she sobbed, kissing his cheek. "I adore you!" It was not the words he yearned to hear but it was a beginning. He was not a man to give up without a fight.

"And I adore you, my little Elise." He soothed her as he would a small, lost child, and it pleasured him to do so. It was the assurance she needed at that time and place.

"Oh, Jean . . . can you believe me when I say that I truly wish it could be more. You deserve more than I can give. I'm . . . I'm carrying

Lance's child and I never had the chance to tell him." Again, she shook with sobs and he allowed her to cry it all out. He was content to be her comforter.

"I know, little one, or at least I suspected it," he told her. These strange stirrings of compassion for someone were new to him. Now his hot-blooded desires to be her lover were superseded by this need to comfort her.

"I've never felt so lost and alone in all my life," she confessed. "I truly don't know how I can ever repay your kindness."

"Elise . . . Elise, listen to me. You are not alone. Dear God, I'd give anything if the child you carried was mine. I—" he stopped short what he was tempted to say. Instead, he decided to make an alternate suggestion in a most casual, lighthearted way. "Perhaps, you might repay me by being my guest for a few days before going to the Le Cleres. Not my mistress, Elise . . . only my guest. I have a house in New Orleans, staffed and ready anytime I wish to spend time there." Damnit, he didn't want to part with her!

"Oh, Jean! Yes, I will," she exclaimed, smiling through her tears. All hate harbored against this man was swept away there on the sandy beach. They sat there laughing and swaying in one another's arms. Neither seemed aware of the sun rising on the eastern horizon.

The strange camaraderie born that night on the beach between Jean and Elise would have been hard for most people to understand. It had that effect on Mama John and Lola. That her "Mister Jean" seemed happy was all that mattered to the mammoth black woman, but Lola was confused and perplexed. Jean came to her no more, but late at night when she slipped down the hall to listen at Elise's door she heard nothing. The soft, sweet moans of pleasure were not coming from within the room as she expected. So she'd returned to her own bed, more confused than ever.

Knowing Lola and Mama John as well as he did, Jean could read the turmoil going on in their minds. He found it rather amusing and decided that it was good enough for the two of them. His life was his own to live any way he saw fit. He and Elise shared this amusement from time to time when they realized they were being thoughtfully observed.

Yet, Jean was smart enough to know that his platonic existence with Elise could not go on too long; his blood was too hot and his desire far too strong. His nerves were stretched too far and he exploded violently a few days before they were to leave for the city.

Elise had walked in on his conversation with a gentleman from New Orleans. She shuddered violently when she heard them speaking about slaves and Jean's providing the planter with several.

Later, she questioned him about it. "*Mon Dieu*, they are human beings . . . not . . . not cattle! I find it hard to believe a man who's been so kind to me could do such a thing!"

The green fire blazing in her eyes excited him even though her words angered him, and the mixture of the two strong emotions brought forth a different Jean Laffite. Elise did not know the stranger exploding fiercely at her.

"You dare to look down your nose at me, eh? Well, Madame Edwards, I sell to your friends, the refined planters. Never have I gone to Africa. My only sin is preying on the ships that have been guilty of the crime. I'm no 'blackbirder' and I will not be called one . . . even by you! I take all the cargo on any Spanish ship, and if it has slaves then, yes, I take them!" Black was the color of his eyes and his pained, furrowed face was flushed. He left the room with his fists clinched and slammed the carved oak door so hard that Elise was sure it had cracked.

She leaned back in the chair and gave a deep, long sigh. The look on his face when he left lingered there in her memory and for the first time since she'd been at Barataria she thought of him as he was reputed to be—a menacing, fierce pirate.

The thought of sitting at the end of the long table and dining with him that evening left her apprehensive and edgy. She asked just to be served a tray.

However, Elise changed her mind by dinner time. If nothing more, she joined him for the change of scene. It was a quiet, thoughtful Laffite she witnessed during their meal. In fact, she would have almost preferred the violent, screaming one to this cool aloofness.

There were few words exchanged between the two of them until they finished Mama John's delicious desert and Jean requested an after-dinner liquor for them.

"We will be leaving for New Orleans in the morning, Elise," he abruptly announced. The short notice surprised her and he sensed it at once. She gave him a slight nod of her head, saying nothing. "I just happened to receive a message this evening that makes it necessary I go at once. I had not planned it quite this soon." There was almost an apology in his tone, Elise concluded.

"I see. Well, in that case I'd best say good night, Jean. I'll be ready." She hastily downed the drink and took her leave with no knowledge of the sadness in Jean's eyes.

It was not a spectacular house Jean brought her to when they arrived in New Orleans. It was a Creole-styled house, generously trimmed with wrought iron at the windows and small balconies on the second floor. The grounds were walled in and the entry gate was wrought iron. But it was lovely, Elise thought, and it was inviting and homey. While the outside might not have been impressive, once inside the front door the lavishness made her gasp. She greatly admired Jean's impeccable taste.

Jean's almost formal air with her left her bewildered and ill at ease though. His house-keeper smiled warmly at her, seeming to sense her uneasiness.

Having been Jean Laffite's housekeeper for the last three years, Dorrie concluded this strikingly, beautiful woman had to be his latest conquest. Lord, the man paraded a bevy of beauties through these portals, but this one had to be the loveliest of any she'd seen. She could understand why the ladies fell victim to his overwhelming charms. This charm endeared him to his servants; he was always kind and generous unless his orders were not obeyed. Then he could be a very hard taskmaster. A devil, he could be then!

"Dorrie, I'll be at home to no one! Is that understood?" Jean informed her, leaving no doubt in Dorrie's mind how he wished her to handle any callers.

"Yes, monsieur. Anything else you wish before I get mademoiselle settled?" Her eyes darted over to the petite lady standing there acting rather perplexed and lost. Dorrie felt compassion for the tiny miss.

Jean told her that was all, dismissing her to take his refuge in the study. He did take a brief moment to inform Elise he would see her at dinner as Dorrie guided Elise from the room. The sharp ears of Dorrie had picked up immediately that he had referred to her as madame. Now what was this, Dorrie pondered? Was this a married lady Mister Jean was bringing to his house? Perhaps she was a widow?

Upstairs Dorrie moved around Elise to open

the door of one of the rooms. "Here we are, ma'am." Elise went through the door into a bright, spacious bedroom. Her eyes went directly to a massive bed with a velvet-covered headboard of gold with a matching coverlet. Dozens of various shaped pillows of silk and satin lay in a cluster. Accent colors of blue and green were used in the matching chairs and dressing table stool. The tufted chairs were placed on either side of a small fireplace. The Carrara marble mantel held exquisite cut-crystal candleholders and crystal vases filled with white roses and greens. It was even brighter and inviting when Dorrie opened up the drapes allowing the sunshine to flow in.

"How pretty!" Elise exclaimed, slowly letting her eyes move around the room.

"Yes ma'am—Master Jean lak purty things around him," Dorrie told her. She went behind the paneled screen to check to see that the chambermaid had placed towels, scented soaps and oils as she always did when Jean brought a guest to the house.

"Will madame wish anything before I prepare the warm bath?"

Elise turned to Dorrie, taking note of the pleasant manner of the quadroon. "No, thank you. I think that and some rest is all I desire."

A low back pain struck sharply and Elise sought the comfort of the bed, almost wishing she could forget about the bath and just take a nap. She let the lemon colored slippers slip from her feet and removed the kid gloves from her hands. Taking two jeweled combs from the sides of her head, she swished her hair in a roll, securing it up on the top of her head with the combs.

A soft rap sounded on the door as Elise was undoing the many miniature buttons down the front of the bodice of her dress and she invited whomever it was to enter, assuming it was Dorrie.

"Hello. It's me—I'm Jessamine," the pert voice said. Elise noted the fiesty, smiling young girl standing before her as she wiggled out of the lemon colored sarcenet dress.

"Come in, Jessamine." Elise returned her smile, impressed by the delicate beauty of the mulatto child who had to be about twelve.

The child inquired boldly, "You Missy Elise?"

"Yes, I am, Jessamine."

"Dorrie sent me to help you with your bath." The girl announced, picking up Elise's gown. "She seein' to dinner."

"Well, you're as sweet and pretty as the flower I bet you were named for, Jessamine. That just happens to be my favorite fragrance," Elise informed the girl.

"How'd ya' kno tha'? Why my mama named me tha'. She say I was a purty one jus' lak the yellow ones growin' down by the river."

Elise gave a light laugh. "My, I guess I must be smart, mustn't I?"

"Sho' are, Missy Elise, and you are purty, too. So was my mama." With an authoritative air, she added, "She lak me and Aunt Dorrie, but my papa—well, he was white." There was a prideful boast registered there, Elise noticed.

"I see," Elise remarked. She admired the young mulatto girl's utter frankness even though it rather stunned her for a moment. She had no way of knowing that it was young Jessamine's instant liking of her that had ignited the honesty.

As Elise luxuriated in the warm, relaxing bath, the stabbing pain in her back faded and she listened to the talkative Jessamine chatter away. A sudden thought swept over her looking upon the face of Jessamine. A child like Jessamine, who was almost white, could have been created by Clint Barron and his octoroon mistress-housekeeper. She wondered what had happened to the tawny-skinned Delphine since Clint had married Susan? She had grave doubts that the sensuous Delphine had been allowed to stay at Shady Oaks. No, Susan would never allow that, she felt certain.

What a rare beauty Delphine had been, with that satiny, deep golden skin, and her sensuously swaying hips! She was a hot-blooded temptress who could cause any man, white or black, to burn with desire for her. Oh, what hate had burned in those black eyes of hers when Elise had arrived at Shady Oaks with Clint. She remembered even now how Delphine had vented her dislike for her presence there. Only near the end of her sojourn at the plantation did the two of them reach an understanding, one to the other. Both, being women of passion and boldness, had to respect the other.

Thinking of Delphine, her thoughts went to the other people she would soon be seeing. Oh, if only it could have been as she'd anticipated, with Lance by her side. Her hands rubbed her slightly rounded belly where a part of him was nestled.

Coming back to the present out of her jumbled maze of thought, she lathered herself generously with the scented soap and realized that Jessamine was still chattering away, but she knew not what she'd been talking about.

Finally, Elise rose from the tub and allowed the young girl to dry her off. The bed looked inviting and she was weary with thoughts of the future. It seemed a heavy burden to bear without Lance. Dismissing Jessamine, she sought the comfort of the bed.

Jean indulged himself with his favorite brandy late into the night and searched for some kind of answer to the strange dilemma he found himself in. He could almost despise Elise Edwards for the quandary he struggled in.

Even so, Jean knew he'd be Elise's protector as long as she needed him, if he could not be her lover. She was a fever in his blood, and never more than now, sitting alone in his study, did he realize that. Only a short distance away waited the eager arms of his current mistress, Elena, and normally he would have been anxious to go to her upon arriving in the city.

Her curvaceous body moved and delighted the throbbing in his groin with the wildest, savage stirrings. He'd enjoyed that pleasure many, many times, so why, he asked himself, was he sitting here in solitude tonight?

Down by the milling, busy wharf that same afternoon, Lance Edwards arrived by boat. With his young son, Andy, he'd traveled down the bayou with the eldest son of the Beigerones, Etienne. The shy, lanky youth had politely refused the offer of drink and food before boarding his boat to row back up the bayou. He felt nervous about the strange sights, noises and crowds of humanity.

However, Lance insisted that he accompany him and Andy to the bank. "I must repay your family, Etienne, for you saved my life as well as my son's." Lance led him to the livery to hire a gig, and Etienne trailed close to his side like a scared pup. An hour later, he delivered him back to the levee and his pirogue.

Etienne stepped into the pirogue with the heavy pouch of gold given to him by Lance. He was so overwhelmed by the vast amount given him that his breath was coming fast and furious. In his fourteen years he'd never seen so much money, and he stammered his thanks and gratitude over and over again. His parents would be in shock when he showed them the generous gift from Monsieur Edwards.

"Safe journey, Etienne, and I hope we shall

meet again," Lance called out as Etienne paddled away. Waving with one hand, he took Andy's small hand with the other.

As Lance lifted his son up on the seat and climbed in beside him, he felt so strange and alone. As the one-horse carriage rolled along, it seemed to him that the bright, challenging future he'd dreamed about here in the New World had been swiftly swept away without Elise by his side. To pick up the remnants of his life now seemed like an insurmountable mountain. Yet, he had never been a man to know defeat or be conquered. He knew that to survive meant he would have to climb that mountain one step at a time.

By the time he'd bought himself and Andy some presentable clothing and reined the gig in the direction of Zack Hart's plantation, Harwood, he was smiling. One step at a time. A minuscule spark of spirit burned within him.

Hart's majordomo, Jonas, greeted him with a broad smile on his ebony face. "Sho' good to see you, Captain Edwards! Yes, sir and this be ya' fine son?"

"Yes, Jonas, this is my son, Andy. Zack home?" Lance inquired, following Jonas's lead into the hallway he remembered from his previous days as a guest at Harwood.

"No, sir. He won't be home til late, but me and Sadie git you all settled in jus' fine!"

The two had been trusted house servants of Zack Hart's for years. Jonas's wife Sadie had taken charge of Zack's daughter after his wife's death. Sadie took charge of young Andy while Jonas welcomed Lance with Zack's best whiskey and imported cheroots.

By the time Zack arrived, Andy was tucked in bed for the night and Lance had been served a fine meal. Now he relaxed in Zack's study helping himself to some cognac, waiting up to greet his old friend.

It had been a long day and weariness washed over him. The warm cognac dulled his senses somewhat as he rested in the overstuffed leather chair. He did not hear Zack coming through the door until he spoke.

"God Almighty, is that really you?" Zack strode over, embracing his younger friend in a bear hug. "Damn, Lance, I'm glad to see you!" Zack exclaimed exuberantly.

"Good to see you, Zack!" Lance's spirits soared just being with his friend again, and with Zack's genuine delight of the sight of him. Never in his hectic life had he needed a friend more than now. Zack Hart sensed that at first sight.

The evening lingered into the late night hours with the two old friends drinking and talking. By the time Lance finally went to his room his sagging morale was lifted.

Zack Hart's logic painted no encouraging pictures for him, but he had to admit he was probably right about Elise, and said he should not dwell in a fool's paradise expecting the impossible. As Zack pointed out, one tiny woman was no match for animals such as the cutthroat pirates who had carried her away. "It's just the damned truth, Lance! Face it!"

It was true that Lance of all people knew she was a spirited, brave woman with lots of guts, but the vermin who had her would have no mercy, and she could not stand the violent battering her small body would have to take. No, Zack made good sense when he said with a sad, anguished look on his face that they should just pray it was a brief torment for Elise.

"Son," Zack pointed out, "you were blessed with a fine son and if I knew that little green-eyed vixen of yours like I think I did, you better do a good job by him or she'll come back to haunt you." Zack's words brought a smile to Lance's furrowed face.

"You know Zack, you're bloody well right. That I'll certainly do, for he's all I have left of Elise."

Fate surely sat on Lance's shoulder that evening, laughing at him and playing a cruel trick. Had Zack Hart been home when Laffite paid his visit to Harwood he would have known that Elise was safe and sound, and very much alive. That very night Lance, in turn, would have known the startling truth. Zack Hart did not know, thanks to his daughter Susan.

As it happened, Zack's majordomo only informed him that a gentleman called, not leaving any name, and the paths of Clint Barron or the Le Cleres had not crossed with his the last few days. Zack had not seen any of them for over a week.

Normally, Clint would have ridden over to Harwood a couple of times during that first week Lance resided there, but a freakish accident resulting in a sprained ankle confined him to the house, so it was Susan who rushed to Harwood upon learning about Lance's arrival.

Zack saw her obvious disappointment upon arriving to find Lance not there. But young Andy was and she clutched the young tot in her arms, wishing for all her life that he was hers and Lance's.

"Oh, Papa, he's beautiful, isn't he?" Her hands played on the boy's curly, black hair falling over his forehead. He was the image of Lance, with the same long black lashes framing pitch black eyes, and a sturdy little body. He seemed to warm to her immediately when she gave herself to him, and Susan realized he was probably missing the motherly love she knew Elise had given to him. When Susan prodded him to say her name, he managed to mumble something close to "Susu" and it was close enough to please her.

"Well, Andy, something tells me you and Susu may be very good friends. Okay?" The little boy gave her an agreeable nod of his head and she kissed him on the cheek, allowing Sadie to take him upstairs for his afternoon nap.

Zack knew, before she spoke, what she was about to ask. It saddened Zack that his beloved daughter, apple of his eye, had been disillusioned by her marriage to Clint. His hopes had

108

been so high for the two. Wherein the fault lied, he did not know. In truth, he liked and respected his son-in-law too much to fault him alone for the failure.

"What's Lance up to, Papa?" Susan raised herself up from the floor where she'd been playing with Andy and took a seat in the chair opposite her father. Zack informed her he was seeing to the loading of cargo aboard the *Southern Star* for shipment to Cuba.

"He insisted. I was of the opinion that he should take it easy for a while after his ordeal. Not the same man, Susan, don't expect to see the Lance Edwards you knew."

"What are you saying, Papa?" Susan's face was etched in concern.

"Oh, it isn't something one puts a finger on. It's . . . well, it's his manner. I guess that's it. You'll have to judge for yourself, daughter. Told me he wanted to jump right into the swing of things. In fact, he wants to take the *Southern Star* to Havana himself."

"Are you going to let him?"

"Hell, he's part owner, remember? I couldn't very well stop him, could I?"

"When will he sail?"

"Due to leave day after tomorrow," Zack told her.

"I see," Susan mumbled, deep in her own private thoughts. "Well, Papa, tell him I'm sorry I missed him and we'll try to see him later. I guess I should be getting back home, what with Clint all laid up and all."

A conniving devil took possession of Susan Hart Barron and she committed a despicable deed. She left Harwood without telling Zack about Laffite's visit to them and the revelation that Elise was alive and well. On her ride on the roan gelding toward her own home she was seized with an attack of fierce misgivings. She should have told Zack so he could have informed Lance at once. She found it hard to look herself in the mirror that evening. It was cruel and heartless. "You're a miserable bitch, Susan Barron," she sneered at the image she saw in the gold gilded mirror. But then why should she make it so easy for everyone else when she was so utterly miserable herself. No, damn it, she wanted company!

She wanted company—Elise's company. Why should she reap the glorious harvest of love from a man like Lance Edwards. Sweet Jesus, he could keep more than one woman spellbound and content, if she was any judge of men. Lord only knew she'd tasted enough samples the last two years. Each time, she'd come away unfulfilled and unsated. Always, she'd found them lacking that certain something that had been hers that night down by the riverbank when Lance had taken her with a savage urgency. Oh, she could never erase the memory of that masterful maleness of him in his quest to possess her. The fire of his touch seared her until her whole body blazed with flames.

She damned Clint Barron for not having the

110

same capacity to fill her with that rapturous pleasure she'd known that one night with Lance Edwards.

Clint Barron sat in his study with a glass of brandy for company. He swished the dark amber liquid slowly, watching the motion. He was so deep in thought that all other sounds of the late night were blotted out. A person should never settle for second best in life. Sweet Jesus, if only he had it to do over again! He felt damned well cheated. Better he'd let Elise go and resume the relationship he'd thoroughly enjoyed with Delphine. But no, after those wonderful months with Elise he'd come to realize that he wanted a wife, a real home, and children. All the things he could not have with Delphine. So when he was dangerously vulnerable, he'd succumbed to the frivolous charms of the red headed Susan. She'd been as letdown as he upon learning that Lance was married to Elise. Perhaps, it was only natural for the two of them to drown their sorrows in the warm embrace of one another.

For a while, it had worked until the first glow of passion was spent. He'd known after the first six months just how shallow and meaningless their feelings were.

—God forgive him. He cared not that she took a lover from time to time! He also knew the sheer hell she went through to cover her tracks, and he found a certain amount of devious pleasure from that torment. He just didn't give a damn!

111

Let her have as many lovers as she could handle!

Every day since Laffite had informed him that Elise was in his care Clint could not deny the trembling anticipation he felt about seeing the beautiful Elise once again. Elise. . . . Elise. . . . Elise! How often, like a gentle summer breeze, he'd whispered her name as he'd stroll to that secluded spot in the woods where they'd made love on the thick carpet of grass one night so long ago, or sometimes, when he rode over the path down by the bank of the river on his huge black stallion the odor of wild jasmine had reminded him of her.

There were also those times when he found himself damning her for lingering in his memory. Like a poison in his blood, she rested there always. Yet it was not Clint's nature to hate, and Elise had always been completely honest with him from the very first. Christ, that in itself was more than he'd had out of most women! He'd always admired that trait in Elise.

If he could have known the perfidious act his wife had done that very afternoon, he would have beaten her within an inch of her life. However, Clint summed up her nervousness that evening at dinner as a qualm of conscience about her newest lover.

He recognized this little role she played. How foolhardy she was to think he was so stupid! That was what galled him to the core of his being.

112

Chapter 6

With Jean by her side in his fancy carriage pulled by the prancing, high-stepping bays, Elise took in the sights of the city. It was a golden autumn day and it was having its effect on Elise. She was remembering the first time she'd seen the sights of New Orleans here in this New World in the company of a certain Clint Barron. It was as if the city greeted her with open, welcoming arms with all its familiar French influences flourishing all around her. She loved New Orleans.

Now it was 1811 and evidence of a few years' growth and additional buildings were obvious. Elise was more than impressed with the newness. The fun-filled days and nights she shared with Jean passed swiftly for they did not live by the hands of the clock, only their whimsy. It came to her on their last night together just how much Jean Laffite had embedded himself in her life. The idea of being no longer under his protective wing left her a little frightened. While she considered the Le Cleres good friends, she would still be alone . . . a third spoke in the wheel.

That last night on the city Jean had comforted himself with the knowledge that he would enjoy the pleasures at Madame Fifi's the following night. It had been sheer anguish to be such a gentleman lately, and his manhood demanded fulfillment. It had been a tormenting agony to escort Elise to all the fine establishments, wining and dining her and attending the theater. The perfection of the evenings was marred by kissing her lightly at her bedroom door when he burned with such passion to take her to bed. Damn her, he could swear she was fighting the urge herself! Did she really think her husband lived? Was it that ghost that prevented her from coming to him?

It was not a matter of conceit, but truth, that he was a charmer of women. While many women openly admired his tall, dark handsomeness, he knew the "secret" of his winning ways was his true appreciation of a beautiful woman. He savored their time together, enjoying himself while he gave completely of himself for the lady's pleasure. It was a delight to his ears to hear his lady softly moan in her wild passion for his lovemaking. He would have given all he owned to hear the sweetness of Elise's moans under him just once. Even the thought of it made him burn. For the first time in his life, a woman denied him.

The morning he was to escort her to the Le Cleres had arrived and he had already had breakfast when he heard her descending the stairway. Even though he'd consumed a large amount of brandy, his sleep had been restless. Both Dorrie and Jessamine were surprised to see him downstairs.

"Miss Elise up yet, Mister Jean?" Jessamine asked, as she sat the cup of coffee in front of him. Jean answered her, preoccupied with his private thoughts. His manner prompted Jessamine to question if they'd had a lovers' quarrel the night before and she voiced her opinion to her aunt.

"They aren't lovers, Jessamine," Dorrie corrected the impertinent young girl. "And what would you know about love, girl?"

"I know!" Jessamine gave a shrug of her small shoulders and turned toward her aunt. Her big doelike brown eyes gleamed brightly with mischief. "I sho' do!" Jessamine heard Elise's soft voice greeting Jean in the dining room. Then she heard Mister Jean greet her. "Ah, *ma petite* Elise." He found it difficult to sound casual and not exhibit the sadness engulfing him about parting with her.

She returned the smile he gave her and seated herself in the chair he'd pulled out for her. She, too, had a lump in her throat about leaving Jean, and for that reason she wanted only coffee, politely refusing any food.

"I think I ate too much last night, Jean. Never have I ate such fabulous *filet de sole*

115

dieppoise and the *tarte aux fraise* were like nectar from heaven! Ah, such wonderful strawberries," she sighed.

Jean laughed, remembering her biting into the strawberry tart the night before. It was truly amazing; she kept such a trim figure and he found it a miracle that she was less than five months away from giving birth to a baby. Had he not seen her that night on the beach in the sheer gown, he'd still not have known about it.

"Good, *chérie!* I'm glad they were the best strawberries you've ever eaten, for you see you ate them with me," he teased her flippantly. Elise saw beneath the surface of all this lighthearted gaiety.

Reaching over to cover his hand with hers, she sighed, "Oh, Jean, it . . . it has been good, hasn't it? You've been so good and understanding and I will never forget it. I confess to trying desperately to hate you for what your man did to me and my family. I can't!" Tears started streaming down her cheek and she wiped them away hastily, hating herself for being a whimpering ninny.

"No, Elise! Cry it all out, *ma petite,*" he tried to sooth her and moved over by her side. "Oh, my darling! If only I could . . . if only you'd let—" He stopped himself, letting his lips touch her forehead and taking her clinched little fists in his hands to his lips. His dark eyes looked into green ones, so woeful and pained.

When he spoke it was in a serious tone and cracked with the strong emotion he felt, leaving no doubt in Elise's mind of his sincerity. "Remember, Elise, anytime you need me or want me to come to you all you have to do is send word to this house. The message will get to me. Then there is one other place here in the city, you may get word to me. There is a smithy shop in another part of the city and I will write down the location for you. You understand what I'm saying, don't you, my sweet? *I mean anytime!*"

Elise flung herself into his arms and clung to him. He held her for the longest time with neither of them speaking a word. He never wanted to let her go, but if she was going through with her plans to stay with the Le Cleres for a while then there was no need to prolong the agony.

"Are you sure you want to leave me, Elise? Sure you couldn't go on as we have? I'd marry you . . . I've told you that, and the baby would be ours. No one need know the difference. I would be proud as a peacock."

"No, Jean, not at this time. Not that I'm not humbled and honored, but I've a lot of thinking to do and this is what I'm going to do. Please, my darling Jean, please try to understand?" The look on her face tore at Jean's heartstrings.

He gave her a nod and rose from the chair pulling her up with him. "Shall we be on our way to the Le Clere's plantation then?" He could offer her no more, he reasoned.

"Yes," she answered, wondering if she was a fool to give up what Jean had so generously offered for her uncertain future.

Neither spoke much on the short ride to the outskirts of the city, and Jean did not linger long at the plantation after they arrived. However, as he prepared to take his leave he told Elise he would return to the city in about a month's time. After a farewell kiss he was gone, and Elise strolled back into the parlor.

The house seemed like an awful void when Jean returned from the Le Clere plantation, and he was certain his friends sensed the friendly intimacy between him and Elise. The only solution he could think of to cure what ailed him was a rollicking night at Madame Fifi's, where he'd drown himself in liquor and spend the night with Fifi's choice ladies. So without further ado, he dressed in his finest evening attire and left the lonely house drenched with memories of Elise.

Clint Barron sought solace from the torment in his soul with a bottle of whiskey. The soothing effects of the drinks relaxed him and his thoughts, like Laffite's, were on Elise Edwards.

A few miles away, another man also dwelled upon the same woman and searched his being for the right answer. He'd folded away the maps and charts he'd studied earlier that evening after he'd accompanied Sadie tucking his young son in his bed. The child adored Sadie and had adapted to his new life in Zack's home. How easy it seemed to be for children! Damned, he envied Andy. It was going to be a long, hard struggle for himself.

It was for this reason he'd decided to make the run to Cuba on the *Southern Star*. The sea had been his first love before Elise entered his life. Perhaps the sea would be his salvation. When he returned, hopefully with his head cleared, he could take his son to their new home, Montclair. Then he would try to start a new life for himself, he projected in his thoughts about the future.

Between the attentions of Jonas, Sadie, and Zack, young Andy would be well cared for, and the biggest favor he could do himself and Andy was get his life together.

Having no idea the woman his soul cried out for lie sleeping only a few miles away, he, too, found sleep, satisfied with the plans he'd made for himself.

So it was that neither could know what a bitterly cruel trick fate was dealing them.

Elise's sleep was not peaceful. Already, she was lonely for Jean, and there was no need to deny it. Being dishonest with herself was not one of her faults. Lance had always chided her for that brutal honesty of hers, but he also always admired it, she remembered. Good or bad, it was the way she was.

Madame Annette Le Clere had tried so graciously to make her feel at home upon her arrival, and it was good to be reunited with the petite French lady she'd first met when she had been Clint Barron's houseguest a few years ago.

Annette Le Clere knew the story about Elise's past, and it had drawn her to the beautiful girl for her own life had not always been easy. The truth would shock their friends.

When their friend Jean Laffite arrived with Elise that day, Annette Le Clere was sure of two things: Jean was in love with Elise, and Elise was enceinte.

For one fleeting moment, she pondered if it was by Jean or Lance. Counting the time Elise had spent at Barataria with the charming Laffite, she immediately felt guilty about her wicked thoughts. Being almost fifty, she was safe from his winning ways, but Elise could hardly be immuned to that dashing pirate, she mused.

She allowed Elise a few days after her arrival to rest and adjust to her surroundings before an outing. This quiet, reserved young woman was not the spirited, lively miss she'd remembered, and Annette decided a ride around the beautiful countryside was the tonic she needed.

Elise seemed eager when she suggested it, and Annette ordered the carriage readied at once. It was nice and refreshing traveling down the country lanes, chattering away.

Their conversation continued in a light, casual manner until finally, Jean's name came up. Annette confessed, "Francois and I adore the man. These . . . these smug Americans who frown at Jean are the first to seek him out for his fine merchandise. This makes me so mad!" Her lovely face displayed her contempt.

Elise remembered when she was there on Barataria the gentlemen visiting his warehouse on Grand Terre.

"Well, one should never sell Jean short. He is clever and not easily fooled. When he is your friend he will do anything for you. This, Francois and I know. I tell you this, *chérie,* Jean adores you," she told Elise and gave her a wink. His adoration for Elise was undisguised.

"I know, Annette." A pang of sadness swept over her thinking back to a few days ago of the time she'd spent with the handsome Frenchman. There had been happy times.

They had gone a few miles to the south over the back roads. Over in the distance Elise saw a familiar sight. She had not realized until now that they were that close to Shady Oaks until she viewed the stately home of Clint Barron. In that same instant, she saw a rider with bright red hair coming toward them. It could be no one but Susan atop the horse.

Elise was jubilant as Susan reined her horse to the side of the carriage. Susan was dressed in fine-tailored blue twill riding attire, and she was as excited as Elise as she dismounted. "Elise! Oh, good Lord, it's good to see you!" Crazy as it might seem after all she'd done, she was glad to see her.

"Oh, Susan! Susan!" The two fell into one another's arms in a warm embrace. Annette looked on in silence, having her own personal thoughts about the young woman who had just joined them. She pondered what Elise would think when she found out what Susan had become this last year.

The local gossip had reached Madame Le Clere's ears about Susan's outrageous behavior this last year. She knew for a fact that Clint Barron's manner had changed and he was not the same young man he'd been when Elise stayed at Shady Oaks.

While Annette did not believe everything she heard from the busy tongue-waggers, she knew something was wrong with the Barron marriage. Since most of the time she and Francois stayed at Bellefair and rarely resided at the house in the city, Annette was not as involved with women's social gatherings as she'd once been. Actually, she enjoyed the life in the country much better.

She realized that Susan was slightly intimidated by her presence. It was understandable, for she had known Susan and Clint all their lives.

Elise hugged Susan in a warm embrace. "It is so good to see you again. And . . . and how is Clint?"

"Fine, Elise! The rascal is laid up with a sprained ankle but he's ornery as ever," Susan exclaimed, so unnerved that she trembled as her blue eyes darted hastily from Elise to Annette. "Forgive me, Madame Le Clere, I was just so glad to see Elise. I didn't mean to ignore you."

Annette's cool, poised face seemed to put a

hex on her. She gave Susan a smile, assuring her it was perfectly understandable. The older woman's demeanor was shaking Susan to the core, and she had to pull on a reserve of strength to carry forth a conversation with Elise in a lighthearted, gay manner. Madame Le Clere frightened her.

What were Susan's true feelings toward Elise? Annette wondered secretly as she sat observing the two in animated conversation. Was Susan really glad to have Elise back in New Orleans? After all, had Lance Edwards not arrived when he did, it would have been Clint Barron Elise would have married.

Annette wondered if Elise took notice of Susan's highstrung manner before she bid them farewell. The dinner invitation issued by Susan for the following evening was accepted by Madame Le Clere. The evening at Shady Oaks could be most entertaining, she thought to herself.

As Susan Barron left the two and rode back toward her home, she realized abruptly what a mess she'd created for herself. One lie would beget another, and somehow it would take Clint's help. Of course, he would be innocent and unaware of it. Dear Lord, what is happening to me, she wondered!

Guilt swept over her like a mighty tidal wave as she realized how cruel she'd been. It was within her power to give Elise back the world she'd thought was lost to her forever. How wicked and evil she'd become!

Shrugging her shoulders, she willed these tormenting thoughts aside. She'd go crazy if she didn't. Instead, she turned her energy to how she'd lay a new foundation for another web of lies. Clint must never find out what she'd done!

Oh, how she needed Zack to fight her battles for her now as he had all her life. On her own Susan realized just how ill-prepared she was to meet life. Under her breath, she muttered, "Papa, you did me no favors giving me my way about everything." For every hurt and pain he'd saved her, she seemed to be paying tenfold now. What a protected, cloistered life she'd led, she realized more and more all the time.

Chapter 7

All that syrupy sweetness dripping from her rosebud lips could mean only one thing, Clint Barron told himself as he struggled, with the aid of his cane, into his study. Either she was feeling guilty as hell over a new lover or she sought the purchase of some fine piece of jewelry she had seen when shopping in the city.

Lying the cane beside his chair after he'd situated himself, he sipped on a brandy and prepared himself for her entrance. He was not disappointed as she came in. The swishing of the rich, wine-colored taffeta skirt alerted him of her presence, and gazing up at her he had to admit that the pale pink top she wore was flattering to her gardenia white skin. Her flaming curls were piled atop her head and a pink velvet flower comb was placed at the back of her head to hold the curls in place.

There was a sensuous quality about his wife he could not deny, and he decided to try warming to her. Inviting her to join him in a drink, he apologized about his not being able to play the gentleman to help her into the chair.

"Don't be silly darling! And I will join you. It . . . it was a nice dinner, wasn't it? The quail were deliciously tender and no one makes rice like Callie, I have to admit." She gave herself a generous helping of cognac before seating herself opposite her husband. For a few minutes, she chatted casually for Clint's mood seemed light and relaxed and she wished it so when the subject of Elise came up.

Clint agreed with her about the meal and sat enjoying his cheroot. Feeling very content, he inquired about her afternoon. "Did you enjoy your ride? I'll be damned glad when I can do the same thing. I'm tired of being a hothouse plant!"

"Yes, it was a wonderful afternoon, Clint," she said softly. Should she mention Elise now? Might as well, she reasoned. "As a matter of fact, I came upon Madame Le Clere and Elise. She's arrived, Clint." Her eyes watched for his reaction.

Guardedly, he tried to remain calm, but his hands gripped the arm of the chair. She was here, only a few miles away. "How . . . how is she? Is she doing all right under the circumstances? God, to have thought that her husband and son were dead then the trauma of finding out they were alive. What a hell of a shock, both ways!"

He was not prepared for Susan's sobs. "Now,

126

what in the hell is the matter with you. What have you got to cry about?" Irritation was reflected on his face.

"You'll hate me, I just know you will, but I couldn't . . . didn't say anything, Clint!" Susan dramatically wailed.

Rage made him tremble and he shouted, "God, woman! Do you know what you're saying? You didn't inform her that Lance and Andy are alive?"

She convulsed in another flood of tears. "Clint, listen to me! I assumed at first that she knew, and we were both so excited about seeing each other. Then Elise said something—I can't remember what it was—that made me know neither she nor the Le Cleres knew about Lance's arrival in the city. I . . . I didn't know what to do then, Clint."

Damn, he wanted to believe her but something gnawed at him. He stared at her as if to try to convince himself that she told the truth. Susan looked up at him through the river of tears, wondering if she had played her role convincingly. Something told her that if he should ever find out the truth her giant of a husband might wring her pretty neck with those powerful hands of his. She shuddered, remembering that Zack could give her away anytime. How stupid and foolhardy she'd been by not telling her father Elise was alive while Lance was still in the city.

"I invited them to dinner Clint, and we'll . . . we'll tell Elise everything. All right? She'll be so very happy and I think it will be better coming from you, dear," she urged. Praying he would see the logic of her statement, she waited for what seemed an eternity for his reply.

"It will have to be that way now, Susan, but if it wasn't for my inability to get around I assure you I'd ride to the Le Clere's plantation this minute." Shaking his heavy mane of blond hair, he muttered with disgust, "Damned if I can understand why you'd not tell her."

Susan said nothing more. Leave well enough alone, she decided. If she tipped the scales or tripped herself up with a slip of the tongue. . . .

Later, alone in her bedroom, she knew where she must go the first thing in the morning before her father left for his offices in the city. Zack wouldn't like it and already she could hear him cussing like some river rat or salty seaman, but that she could endure. All the same, he would protect her and cover up her horrible lie. With her fears slightly calmed, she drifted off to sleep.

Sleep escaped Elise that night and she pondered why. Was it seeing Susan again and so many memories rushing through her mind? Possibly so. Yet, more disturbing to her were Annette's reactions as she talked about Susan and Clint. They weren't direct comments as much as innuendos Annette seemed to be making. Elise knew her friend well enough to know she was trying to prepare her for her meeting with Clint. She could only come to the conclusion that the Barron marriage was not serene.

"Aren't Clint and Susan happy, Annette?" Elise was always direct so she could not resist pressing her friend for the truth.

"I'll let you be the judge of that tomorrow night, *chérie,* when you see him, eh? You know the man much better than I. But I am hedging with you, so let me just say that I feel Clint is most unhappy about something."

Elise had finally bid her dear friend good night and retired to her room with the Barrons very much in her thoughts.

Elise found herself anticipating the evening during the next day. She and Annette broke into a gale of laughter over how much more comfort was realized with the easement of one seam of Elise's gorgeous green silk gown. Elise broke out with a deep sigh of relief as she slipped it back on.

Annette told her she still was no bigger in the waistline than most women. "But then you always had such a wasp-like waist, *chérie.*" She had to bite her tongue for almost blurting out that Lance's huge hands could span it easily.

Annette's maid styled Elise's hair on top of her head and placed jeweled combs at the back. Splashing a dab of jasmine water at her throat and behind her ears, Elise went to join Annette and Francois downstairs.

Coming face to face with her dear friend and former lover, Elise found herself in a very emotional state. Always, Clint would be very dear to her, and she saw that same warmth in his brilliant blue eyes as he strode up to her. He greeted her with a warm embrace. During that first hour, Elise could have sworn Annette was wrong about the Barrons.

Clint took Elise's arm and smiled that broad smile of his she remembered so well. "Come with me, Elise. There's someone just dying to see you."

Elise smiled. "Callie?"

"That's right!" He led her away from his other guests and through the door down the long hallway. A familiar voice called out to Elise and she moved hastily toward the black woman she'd loved so much and considered her friend.

"Oh, Callie . . . my dear, dear Callie!" Hugging the huge girth of the woman with her two arms, tears creeped down Callie's cheek as she whispered Elise's name over and over again. The beautiful lady hugging her brightened up the kitchen, and Callie could not help comparing the different aura abiding in the house these last few years. Like yesterday, she recalled, standing there now, the night she'd readied Elise's valise for poor Mister Clint to take her back to her husband. Course she'd not known that night she would not be seeing her again for a long, long time.

"If yo' ain't a sight for ole Callie's eyes, sugar. Lordy, ain't she purty as a speckled pup, Mister Clint?" She looked up to see his eyes sparkling as they'd not for a long time. Pity for the young man washed over Callie, for she knew the depth of his love for Elise. Now she knew it was still burning there hopelessly.

When he spoke, Elise knew that Annette had probably been right. His words were flattering, but disturbing to her. It was just not the thing a happily married man declared in front of his servant.

"Prettiest thing that ever graced Shady Oaks. Good to have her back, isn't it Callie? Hasn't been the same since she left." His blue eyes were bright with adoration.

"Oh, you two . . . why you'll spoil me!" Elise teased, trying to have a lighthearted, casual air about her that she hardly felt at the moment.

Relishing these moments with Elise and Callie, Clint was carried back in time and seemed to forget that he had a wife. Jovial and gay, he declared, "Can't think of anyone I'd enjoy spoiling more!"

Elise and old Callie exchanged smiles, both slightly embarrassed in the knowledge of what was going on in Clint's mind. She patted Callie's shoulder and suggested that they should be joining the others. Callie smiled, giving her an understanding look. Mister Clint was bubbling with happiness!

The dinner was delicious, and Elise finally began to relax as the atmosphere around the dining table was gay. The presence of the others was reassuring: Elise felt the heat of Clint's

131

eyes constantly on her. She was not the only one aware of it. Why did he have to be so obvious?

Clint must think that she's blind, Susan furiously mused. The only time he wasn't ogling Elise was when Francois engaged him in conversation. Annette noticed it, too. Never more certain that the handsome Captain Barron was still in love with Elise, she engaged Susan in conversation for she'd seen her mounting vexation. It was taking every ounce of Susan's willpower to keep her mouth shut. Tonight she knew she must be the sweet, docile wife. It galled her!

The evening began to drag at a snail's pace for Susan, and it seemed the opportunity would never come for Clint to get Elise alone. Clint seemed to have forgotten about the task of enlightening Elise about her husband and son being alive.

"Darling, why don't you get Elise a glass of that wine and I will return with Annette and Francois in just a minute. I want their advice about my new painting and which wall I should hang it on, all right?" Susan impatiently urged both the Le Cleres from the room before Clint could even answer her.

Susan revealed her reason for her strange behavior as soon as they were in the hallway. At the same moment, Clint poured Elise a glass of wine, inviting her to have a seat.

Elise sat on the settee, sipping the wine Clint

had served her. It was as if he read her thoughts as he remarked, "Seems like old times, doesn't it, Elise?" She smiled and nodded. "God, was it only two years ago? Seems like a lifetime to me!"

"Please, Clint!" Why was he doing this to her? Didn't he realize the futility of dwelling on the past.

Moving with the aid of his cane, Clint went over to her side, realizing she was upset by his remarks. "Sorry, little darlin', I didn't mean to hurt you. You know me, Elise, the clumsy oaf!" He gave an uneasy, forced laugh and looked like a young boy who'd been scolded.

Elise sighed, "Oh, Clint! My dear, dear Clint! Never have you hurt me. I'm afraid it's the other way around. And you . . . you are not an oaf! But we can't go back, Clint, we're both married." In the same instance, she realized she was now a widow but could not bring herself to accept the horrible fact. The cruel truth brought forth tears she could not hold back.

Falling into Clint's waiting arms, she moaned, "Oh, Clint, I can't bear the thought of him being dead. I love him so much." Wiping the tears away, she asked him to forgive her display of weakness. But once again, tears flowed down her cheek.

Clint cradled her in his huge arms, savoring the precious moment of having her close: it might never come again. "Hush, Elise. Listen to me, honey! You have no reason for tears."

Elise reared, jerking away from him. "I . . . wha—"

"Lance is alive and so is Andy," he said. When she calmed after the first minutes of excitement, he quietly and calmly told her about Susan seeing her son at Zack's. It seemed once again the wonderful Clint Barron had given her back the one man she loved more than anything in the world. She was overcome with joy to know that her darling son was safe only miles away. It took the edge off of the fact that her husband had left the city thinking she was gone from him forever. Ah, but he would return and she would be waiting! Just to know that he lived was all she asked.

Suddenly, it was all too much for her and she fainted. Clint rushed for a cool cloth, not calling to the others. He wanted this time alone with her and he vowed to himself as he held her that he'd win and woo her if he could. The devil could take the hindmost; he cared not what anyone thought. As he well knew, one day or night could make a difference in a person's life. Nothing was forever!

Elise did not hear his whispered words. "Oh, little darlin', I love you so damn much it hurts."

The great joy of hearing Clint's revelation had overshadowed his comment about Susan seeing Andy. Therefore, it was a detail she had not questioned then or later.

One person did question Susan's surreptitious actions after the initial shock eased. Annette privately cursed the red-haired wench for the unforgivable deed. But she remained silent, saying nothing to even Francois about her suspicions. When they'd met Susan the day before she'd known and had not mentioned a word to Elise. For the present, she decided to keep her secret, but her eyes and ears would be alerted as far as Susan Hart Barron was concerned. Every opportunity that presented itself, she would delight in letting Susan know she was aware of her treachery.

Chapter 8

Like most men when they looked upon Elise Edwards, Zack Hart was affected. He could understand a younger man like his son-in-law being fired with desire. Clint made no effort to explain or excuse the time he spent at the Edwards's estate now that Elise had taken up residence there with her young son to await Lance's return from Cuba.

On occasion, Elise found herself entertaining Clint, Zack, and Jean Laffite all in the same afternoon. It was nice to have their company for her confinement was drawing near and the days were long. However, this time she had not grown so huge as she had with Andy because her appetite was lacking. Her loneliness for Lance was a part of it.

She treasured the friendship and concern of the three men during her trying time. Both Zack and Clint conferred with the competent overseer, Dake Coulter. Elise, in turn, daily spent time going over the reports and records to acquaint herself with the running of the huge plantation. The social events that gathered the ladies together, such as teas and sewing circles, were boring and dull to Elise and she much preferred afternoons at home in the company of her young son. However, she did enjoy Susan's visits and the company of Annette Le Clere.

Elise had no inkling of the mask Susan wore during those weeks and months she called at Montclair. That she adored Andy was obvious to Elise, and outwardly Susan was the same warm, friendly young woman Elise had been drawn to. Inwardly, Susan was an erupting volcano.

Her resentment and hate for Clint heightened daily, and her own father filled her with sheer disgust with his devotion to Elise Edwards. Sweet Jesus, all the men seemed bewitched by the woman, even with her enlarged in pregnancy. She could not say one harsh word about the woman without either of the men jumping to her defense. Clint had made this quite clear.

Even her own father had sharply told her off the day before when she made a devious remark about the curiosity of Jean Laffite supplying Elise with her new lady's maid.

Zack's thick brow arched and his bushy white head turned in the direction of his daughter. "So?"

"So, Daddy, that Jessamine is some white

137

man's brat. Good Lord! That's what!" Susan vented a disgusted air.

Zack threw back his head and laughed. "Good Lord, Susan, that is nothing new or unusual. Where you been, girl? You're a married woman yourself now and I dare say that I could count on one hand the planters I know who haven't taken a negro servant to bed." He turned his back to Susan in impatience.

"Daddy . . . I . . . I can't believe you can be so—"

"Susan! Stop this! I'm being truthful and you're no young innocent anymore. Two years ago I would not have spoken so bluntly." Zack's eyes bored into hers and she stomped out of the room, leaving Harwood immediately without another word to her father. Zack watched her go, more disturbed about his daughter and the state of her marriage to Clint Barron than he cared to admit. Lance Edwards's absence was not helping the explosive situation.

His esteem and respect for his son-in-law was obvious long before he married Susan, so he found it hard to fault the man. Yet, Clint's attentions toward Elise did trouble Zack.

Now, this latest development with Lance perplexed him, and there was nothing he could do about it. The rascal had no damn business making the extra run into Venezuela to deliver firearms for rebels fighting for their independence. He would not only be delayed returning to New Orleans, but it was a very dangerous undertaking. Zack cussed the fact that a rough storm had delayed his dispatch sent by the *Southern Star*'s sister ship, but Lance had already departed from Cuba when it finally arrived. Zack did not want to think what the repercussions would be.

Edwards's wife was such a rare beauty that even her swelling pregnancy did not dull the constant attentions of Laffite or of his own son-in-law. No, her type of woman was too damned tempting to be left alone without a husband, Zack told himself. But Edwards had no knowledge of this, so he could hardly fault him for that. Neither could he fault Laffite or Barron for he, himself, was affected by the sensuousness of Elise.

Lance's dispatch to Zack was enthusiastic about the rich cargo he'd be returning to New Orleans with for sale in France and Spain, since their ships had been driven from the seas by the British Navy. The reckless rascal was enjoying his escapade.

Zack applauded his cleverness. American shippers daring to defy the danger could make a vast profit. War with the British came closer every day and President Madison had called for an early Congress. England's new minister, Francis J. Jackson, was insolent and uncooperative. He had arrogantly insulted Madison and his wife Dolley. Negotiations with Jackson had become impossible. The talks between England and America had deteriorated since

Erskine had been replaced by Jackson.

Erskine had been married to an American lady and he was more willing to listen and sympathize with the arguments presented to him. As long as he was the minister there was a ray of hope.

Heavy thoughts dominated Zack's being as his buggy carried him down the dirt road toward Montclair. He'd always admired the glorious setting of the old estate, and it seemed fitting that its mistress was now Elise Edwards. With its beautiful grounds and gardens, it was so picturesque. Zack had to pat himself on the back for obtaining the services of Dake Coulter for Elise's overseer. The man was dependable and a hard worker.

He dreaded telling the pretty lady her husband would not be returning as soon as he'd first calculated. He'd figured the sister ship had made contact and by all odds Lance would have been sailing back toward New Orleans by now. He could remember as if it were yesterday when his own little Irish wife was expecting Susan. She wanted him near her when the time came for the delivery of the baby.

With trepidation, he entered the house and asked to see Elise. One hour later, he left Montclair with the task behind him, knowing that she fought bravely to keep the tears from flowing down her sad little face. Seeking to make it easier on her, Zack made a hasty departure and Elise was grateful.

She rushed up the stairs and flung herself

across the bed. Burying herself in the mountain of silk pillows, she allowed herself to cry and cry until she was drained.

Then she continued to lie quietly, looking up at the ceiling. Someone listening might have thought she was crazy, for she spoke to the shadows in the room as though she was speaking to Lance. Could he hear her crying out to him as he had in the past? Theirs was an unusual closeness, and she did not consider the possibility that the many miles of ocean would be a barrier.

There was comfort for Elise in the thoughts and weary exhaustion washed over her and she slept. In sleep she was to dream once again, the same old dream that haunted her sleep while being Joaquin Ruiz's captive and those first months spent with Clint Barron.

The *Southern Star* was anchored in the secluded cove, where it had been for many weeks now. This small area was one of the few places not blockaded by Spanish ships along the coastline of Venezuela. Inside the captain's cabin of the *Southern Star* there was the air of tenseness, and Francisco Miranda knew it well; he'd been a soldier of fortune for too many years not to recognize the signs.

A year ago he'd returned to Venezuela to direct an army to win the country's independence. Upon his arrival he'd been elected president of the junta. Simon Bolivar had returned with him after their meeting in

London and Bolivar was installed as governor of Puerta Cabello.

Miranda, Bolivar, and Lance Edwards had developed a mutual admiration since Captain Edwards had delivered the arms so badly needed for their cause. The American sea captain from New Orleans rated high with Miranda and Bolivar for his cleverness to maneuver through the tight blockade of the Spanish fleet. It was an almost impossible feat, requiring guts and courage coupled with expert skill.

Now he was preparing to use those same tactics to leave their shores for his return to his home. Their thoughts were heavy with concern for his safety.

During the week's stay the three had sat in the evenings drinking and talking long into the night. Simon shared Lance's grief about his wife; he had lost his beautiful wife to yellow fever. They had only shared eight wonderful months together.

"You were at least blessed with a son, Captain Edwards," Bolivar lamented one of the nights when they were well into their cup.

Since that night Lance's thoughts had been on his son and the urge to get started home prodded him. His time to leave was now hastily approaching. The three were having their farewell toast. The quiet, thoughtful manner Lance exhibited was not from fear or dread for what he faced the next few hours before reaching safe waters. This thing consuming him was almost eerie and unexplainable.

For the last hour there in his cabin, Elise's presence had floated before him and he could have sworn he smelled the sweet fragrance of jasmine wafting through the porthole. At first he'd shook himself back to reality. Chiding himself for being a fool, he'd reasoned that it was only the tropical breeze blowing the scent of the many blooming plants flourishing along the coastline.

It was crazy and he was intelligent enough to admit it. Yet, as he sat trying to make conversation with the two men, their voices were not what he heard. It was Elise's wispy voice murmuring in his ear. If he let his imagination go wild he could almost feel the touch of her honey-sweet lips caressing his cheek in that special way of hers. So warm and moist they were!

Was it not true that he'd experienced this awesome, shaking experience when they'd been apart, he argued silently with himself. Was it not true that he'd later been reunited with her? Wonder of wonders, could it be possible that she *was* still alive?

An hour later, he had bid a final farewell to his comrades of the last week and they'd taken a boat back to the shoreline. Lance had given the orders to prepare to leave the secluded cove his schooner had been moored at since his arrival. His coffers were rich with the gold paid for his services to Bolivar. Now, if fate deemed it, he would run the blockade with a prayer on his lips and hope in his heart he'd find Elise.

As he stood there on the schooner, the moon that had been shining down so bright and full was blotted out by clouds. His hands pressed tightly on the railing as he looked up at the black horizon. He gave out a deep laugh as he spoke to the wind and a few stars shining up there. Then the moving clouds blotted out their brilliant light as well. His crew would have thought him slightly daft had they heard him urging the wind to take his message to his beloved Elise; he was homeward bound. "I love you, Elise, my love," his voice moaned like the timbers of his ship, beginning to move and sway in the waters of the hidden cove.

A gusting wind invaded Elise's room and she roused from her sleep to find the doors leading out to the balcony ajar. Getting out of her bed, she went to close them. There was a warmth to the gulf breeze touching her skin clothed in the sheer nightgown, and she stood for a moment to enjoy it, inhaling deeply. Looking out into the black of the night, she gazed upward to marvel at its beauty. Those same stars were shining down on Lance at that very moment. "Oh, my darling . . . my darling! Hurry home, *mon cheri*, I miss you so."

Suddenly, the folds of her gown cupped and clung to her body as if to embrace her in love. She stood, giving herself up to it.

The vision was real to Elise. She saw his tall, lean body bent over, his arms resting on the

144

railing of a ship. Strong hands with long slender fingers cupped his chin as he scanned the vastness of the churning waters around his ship. He was deep in thought, caring not that his unruly dark hair blew over his face. So vivid was this image to her that she saw the opened neck of his shirt baring his chest with the gold medallion resting on the bed of curly black hair. His mouth was set tight, and his black eyes danced aimlessly over the dark horizon. As if in answer to her plea, she could almost feel the sweet, assuring warmth of his lips caressing her, softly whispering, "I'm coming, love. Just as fast as the winds will carry me."

She believed what her heart told her for it had been so in the past. It surpassed time or space. She knew soon she would look upon the face of her beloved.

Chapter 9

The *Southern Star* moved from the cove under the cover of the dark night like some giant hand in the sky had intended to aid them. The crew greeted the cloud cover as a blessing as the schooner veered north and west to leave the shores of Venezuela.

Lance Edwards was joined by the ship's first mate, Jack Parsons, one of Zack Hart's most able-bodied seamen. He'd spent ten years with Zack and after all the many weeks Lance had spent with him, he could see why Zack Hart praised him as a damned good sailor.

"Give or take ten miles and we'll be in safe waters, Captain. Can't say I'm not ready for the sight of New Orleans myself. Never saw so many strange bugs and critters as I have back there. Made me sure appreciate my little place back home, I can tell you."

"Jack, on that I'd have to agree with you. Cheroot?"

"Thank you, Captain. Believe I will." Jack accepted Lance's offer, as the two of them stood shoulder to shoulder with their eyes riveted in the direction of the enemy.

All they had to do was get in the open waters and Lance felt he could outdistance any approaching ship. The hold of his ship was carrying little cargo, for he had had to forego a huge cargo when he left Cuba in order to carry the shipment of arms to Miranda and Bolivar. It had been more than worth it to get the handsome reward he carried home in gold from Bolivar.

During those long nights in the company of Bolivar and Miranda, Simon had told him of the financial support he'd received in Europe when he traveled through France and Spain seeking allies to his cause.

Ah, yes, Lance could see old Zack's mouth fly open when he slapped down the heavy pouches of gold. The anticipated cargo from Havana would be forgotten.

The two men puffed contentedly on the cheroots and both shared the mutual thoughts that their departure was going to be uneventful and without incident. Lance relished the idea wholeheartedly, and if this trend continued, he decided he might just find the comfort of his cabin to indulge in a generous amount of his favorite whiskey. To pass the rest of the night with dreams of Elise and the prospect of seeing young Andy again filled him with pleasant delight.

Jack Parsons was having similar thoughts about what he'd do once they docked at the wharf in the city. He was ready for a retreat of being "ground crawlin' drunk," as he dubbed it, and then seeking his sweet, juicy little Denise; a little spitfire he'd taken a fancy to since the first night he'd walked into the Red Dolphin Tavern. Just to think about her made his huge, stocky body swell with yearning. Just the right size for his sinewy arms to hold and curve to his massive body. Pint-size, she made him feel like so much the man and master.

With hair as gold as cornsilks and eyes blue as field flowers she looked as delicate as a Dresden doll, but he knew she was certainly not fragile. As big and ugly as he knew himself to be, she seemed to adore him.

As smooth as silk the trim-lined schooner made its way through the calm waters, its sails sucking the wind around its canvas. Suddenly, the moon came out from the shroud of clouds and Jack Parsons strained to see if he saw what he thought he saw in the distance.

"Captain, did you catch sight of a ship over to the east?"

Before Lance could reply, Jack's bass voice interrupted any answer his captain might have given him. "Christ Almighty, I think there's three, and damned if I don't think they're plowing right toward us!"

"Then we'll just have to outrun them, my friend," Lance declared and shrugged. To surrender would be a sentence of death by the

Spaniards, he knew for sure. The *Southern Star* was not armed to compete with the Spanish ships blockading the coastline.

A lookout called out the sighting in the next minute as Lance was already giving orders to his men to take advantage of all the available wind.

He still had not spotted the approaching vessels as Jack and the lookout had, for the clouds had shifted back over the moon. "Christ! Can't see a damn thing, Jack. Can you spot them now?"

Jack peered into the distance, saying nothing for the longest time. "There, Captain Edwards. Over there! I'd have sworn there was three, but now there's only two coming this way. Wonder what happened to the third one?" Jack scratched his head, pondering if his eyes had played a trick on him or if the third ship had departed from the convoy. Why had it left the other two if they were in pursuit of them?

"There *are* only two, Jack. I see them now. But if I'm any judge of speed they're coasting along at a slow snail's pace. I wonder—"

"Captain! Does it look to you what it looks like to me, sir?" Jack Parsons could not believe that the ship was cruising toward the shoreline instead of following the other two toward them. Why?

"We're of the same mind, I'm thinking Jack," Lance said. Had they been luckier than he'd hope? Perhaps they had not been spotted at all by the Spaniards.

A few more miles out of the bay and they'd come into swifter currents and that would play in their favor, he reasoned. Could they possibly be that lucky?

A volley of explosions cut through the gentle tropic night and Jack and Lance exchanged looks. Both knew in that moment what was taking place back at the cove. Bolivar and Miranda were providing a deceptive diversion.

"Those cagey bastards!" Jack Parsons roared with hearty, delighted laughter. "I hand it to 'em, Captain."

"So do I, but one is still heading in our direction, Jack. I got a feeling he's going to keep coming."

The exchange of gunfire over to the east of the coast could still be heard by the two men. Lance knew lives were most likely being sacrificed for he and his ship's safe departure. He would forever feel a debt of gratitude to Simon Bolivar and General Miranda. If for no other reason than that he had to outmaneuver the oncoming Spanish ship. Selfishly, he had his personal reasons for wanting to resist an altercation. New Orleans beckoned to him with an urging summons still compelling and strong. "I'm trying to get to you, Elise," he moaned under his breath.

Jack Parsons left Lance standing at the point observing the approaching enemy to attend to his duties. Lance could still see the flashing lights of yellow, gold, and red over in the distance. They looked like lightning playing over the coastline in the black of night.

He desperately wished the *Southern Star* was armed for sea warfare in that moment, but damned if it was. He knew for all his daring and cleverness as a seaman it would be useless if the Spanish got within firing range.

Suddenly, with a thunderous burst detonating to the starboard of the *Southern Star*, a massive surge of water sprayed. Seamen scurried over the deck and Jack Parsons rushed up to Lance shouting, "The goddamn fools! They're too far away—missed us a mile almost!"

Taking off his cap and scratching his tousled head, Jack said, "They're crazy, sir. They're too far away. Can't figure it out as to why they'd waste the shot."

"Nor can I, Jack. Maybe for show—a final effort." His spirits were lifted for now he felt certain they could outrun the patrol ship without too much effort, and an upsurge of breeze heightened his spirits. God smiled on them. The two men exchanged smiles, saying nothing. They were homeward bound and each minute now put the blockade farther in the distance. The futility of the Spanish ship's single volley had seemed to have convinced them to pursue the *Southern Star* no longer.

Overjoyed and jubilant, Lance slapped his first mate on the shoulders and suggested, "Join me in the cabin for a drink, eh?"

A broad grin beamed on Tom's boyish face, "*Yes, sir!* I feel the need." He swung around to match his stride to that of the captain's, and his only hesitation was to inform Mike Bowen to take charge while he was with the captain in his quarters.

Lance's mood was relaxed and lighthearted, as it had been when he and his former first mate Jud Morgan had made port back in London during the years he was a privateer. He recalled the two of them disembarking from the schooner and making for a tavern on Fleet Street. It was a good feeling, getting roaring drunk and bedding some wench to pleasure them. He had to admit he missed the witty Irishman he'd shared many a good time with— as well as some narrow escapes from danger.

When he'd finally reunited with Elise in New Orleans and the decision had been made to return to London where he would dispose of all his holdings so they might pursue a life in the New World, Lance had told Jud Morgan farewell. Their parting had taken place in London after Jud had accompanied them back there.

There had been a certain void when he bid his friend good-bye, and even Elise felt it as they watched him board the boat on the Thames. Jud was going home to Ireland, his first trip back in several years.

He could hear that Irishman jesting as he waved to them. "Ah, we'll meet again, my friend! Tis for sure, we will!" With a wink of his devious blue eye, he'd cocked his head of curly brown hair and added, "Elise, my darling, knock hell out of him for me if he doesn't behave."

Lance knew that even Jud Morgan had felt something akin to love for his ravishing, beautiful wife. A smile lit up on his tanned face.

Jack's voice broke up Lance's private musings. "Must be pleasant thoughts you're having, sir." Lance jerked himself alert and busied himself generously filling two glasses with whiskey.

"That they were, Jack. Here, enjoy yourself. Take a seat. I think we can rest assured the crew can manage without the two of us for a while." He motioned to one of the wooden chairs at a small table centered in the cabin. Lance sunk his large frame into the chair behind his desk and propped his booted foot atop the fine mahogany.

Both took greedy gulps of the whiskey, followed by another, until the glasses were emptied. Lance wasted no time in pouring them to the brim again. The two fell into an easy banter.

"Got someone waiting for you back in New Orleans, Jack?" Captain Edwards asked him, for his thoughts were intense about his own woman. The thought of her stirred an ache in his groin; the nights and days had been long and lonely since the fateful night the fierce Sebastian had invaded the cabin of the *Elise*. He'd not taken any woman to his bed during that time. Once, while in port in Havana he had been tempted, and once again in the camp of

Miranda a beauty of a peasant girl had eagerly offered herself. That night he had come even closer, having hoisted her skirt, when a ruckus outside the campsite had broken the mood. Afterward his ardor had cooled and he sought not to rekindle it.

"Yeah," Jack admitted. "I got the cutest, sexiest little kitten you've ever laid eyes on. She purrs so sweet! You know what I mean, Captain?" The whiskey had a delightfully relaxing affect on him.

Jack painted a colorful picture of his doll with the golden hair and sky blue eyes. "She is one little hellcat though when her temper is roused. Damn, I got the scars to prove it!"

Lance laughed, relating to his description of Denise. He was reminded of his green-eyed vixen. "Got a few of those scars myself, Jack."

"That right, sir? Well, I got a theory about the ladies. I like 'em to have a little of the spitfire, hellcat in 'em. Always give you a better tumble in the hay, I always say."

"I won't argue with you there, Jack." Lance saw his first mate was feeling the effect of the fast shots of liquor and he wasn't too far behind him. Perhaps he should go topside and allow Jack to catch a couple of hours sleep in his bunk. Both of them couldn't be drunk.

He was just about to voice his decision to Jack when his first mate hit him with the same question he'd earlier asked.

"You got a woman waiting for you, Captain Edwards? I never heard you mention one."

154

'Yes, Jack, I have!" He felt so certain that it was true, that Elise was there in New Orleans waiting for him. She could not be dead. He knew that now.

"Tell me about her," Jack invited, sprawled lazily in the chair.

In a voice unusually soft with love, he answered his first mate. "She's got hair as black as a raven's wing and eyes as green as emeralds. Skin so soft it looks like satin—pale gold satin. So tiny I can span her waist with my two hands." Lance had no idea of the love coming from his lips as he spoke or the look on his face as he praised the woman he loved. Caught up in his own revelation, he envisioned her there, standing by the side of the desk. "And soft lips that taste like honey."

"Dear God, she must be something! Don't need to be told you're in love with the lady." Jack had barely got the word out before he tumbled out of the wooden chair, falling to the floor with a thud. Past caring, Jack lay there, still and content.

Lance gave a chuckle and made no effort to bother him. Striding out the cabin door, he spoke, but Jack was past hearing him. "I guess there's no doubt of that at all, Jack my friend. I shall forever love her."

He walked down the passageway with wild anticipation pounding in his broad chest. He vowed to give out a howl of joy that would deafen his crew when the coastline of Louisiana was sighted.

The day the *Southern Star* left the Gulf's waters and entered the mouth of the river winding toward New Orleans, Lance gave out a mighty roar and some of his crew joined him. The milling wharf, the pungent smells of the vendor's wares, the men working, and the boatmen coming in off the river were beheld in wonder by the crew of the *Southern Star*.

Chapter 10

In the sharp spasms of pain Elise tossed and turned on the bed, unaware that Annette Le Clere had left the room and the doctor had arrived. She joined her husband and Zack Hart in the parlor where they were indulging themselves with the Edwards's best brandy and were in deep conversation about how nerve-wracking an event like this was. To this remark Annette responded with no sympathy for either of them, but for the woman upstairs.

Bending down to kiss her husband, she teased playfully, "Oh, poor Francois . . . you are working so hard, *mon cheri*." Both men had to see the comedy of it all and laughed for the first time during the night.

The three of them drifted into conversation to pass the time away, and none of them heard the carriage's approach to the front entrance or the servant greeting the stranger at the door. It was only the ring of a deep, familiar voice echoing through the long hallway that made them turn their heads to the archway of the parlor. All of them jumped up in unison and rushed toward the tall, towering figure of the man standing there.

"Annette? Zack . . . Francois!" Lance's voice trailed off along with his gaze around the parlor. Everyone but the one beautiful face he yearned to see was present.

"*Mon ami* . . . thank God you are here!" Francois grabbed him around the shoulders. Zack chimed in with his delight at the sight of his partner's return to the city.

But it was Annette's words that made him rush from the room and lunge up the steps in huge strides to get to his wife, knowing now that she had, indeed, been calling to him to come to her. To know she truly lived is all he'd ever ask of the gods. He realized just as he reached the door of the bedroom to make his entry that the little vixen had known she was carrying their second child before they left London. How like his Elise!

Even though he was impatient just to set his eyes upon her, he slowly and quietly opened the door. Still, his overpowering image made Jessamine gasp and brought forth an indignant inquiry from the doctor attending Elise.

In a cool, imperious tone, Lance enlightened him at once. "I, sir, am Captain Lance Edwards—the lady's husband!" By the time he'd spoken the words, he was by Elise's side bending down to kiss her smiling face, her eyes wide with wonder and delight. He let his cheek rest for a moment on her tear-dampened face, daring the doctor to say anything.

"It's all right, my love. I'm here now and I love you, Elise," he whispered softly to her. With the easement of pain and a brief moment before the next one, she sighed.

"Love you Lance *cheri*."

As the next pain struck its brutal blow, Lance's strong hand was there to squeeze. His great strength radiated through her and comforted her so.

Had the doctor been a perceptive man, or had he noticed the new calm settling over his patient, he would never have spoken his next words. "Sir, I must ask you to leave or I will never get this babe into the world."

The old wizened face of the doctor looked over at Lance, unaware of the fury gathering there, for Lance's eyes remained upon Elise. But he'd heard the old doctor and had to restrain the overwhelming impulse to punch his smug face. How dare he tell me to leave my wife, he muttered under his breath. No one had that right!

Lance turned to the doctor at the foot of the bed. His eyes bored into the doctor's glaring ones. He held Elise's small hand tight and secure, but he made no motion to leave his wife's side. Through clinched teeth, he spit at the doctor, "Sir, you tend to the birthing of the baby and I'll tend to my wife."

As the stunned doctor started to protest,

Lance stopped him. *"I am staying, sir!"* There was nothing to do but allow the determined man his way, Doctor Harper decided. The fury in his black eyes convinced Harper the man could be dangerous if crossed, and after all it was his wife.

It was obvious that his powerful presence pleased the beautiful Madame Edwards. Upon examination it would appear the young Edwards heir was now eager to greet the man and ready to emerge.

"Bear down with all your might, madame, with your next hard pain," the doctor urged Elise. She did as he requested, grasping her husband's hand so hard that it pained him.

To have fathered a son had pleased Lance so that he'd swelled with pride, and he'd sworn nothing could have been more gratifying. But now, he felt he'd witnessed a miracle with the birth of his daughter. This time he'd shared the agony, as well as the excitement of her entrance into the world. He could think of nothing to compare with this experience. He would forever cherish it.

Elise had managed one weak smile before drifting off in an exhausted sleep. He kissed her tenderly and told her, "Yes, *ma petite*, you've worked hard enough. Now rest, my precious love." His hand lovingly traced her forehead and her long eyelashes fluttered lazily before closing.

Jessamine washed the baby and after wrapping the small being in a warm, soft blanket, she presented the baby to its father for inspection. Lance took the babe with ease and Jessamine was surprised at his assured manner. There was no awkwardness, Jessamine noticed as she watched the tall handsome man standing close to her. My, he was a handsome devil and she could see why Missy missed him so.

"Sure de' purtiest baby I ever seen, Cap'tan Edwards," Jessamine said, smiling up at Lance with her dark eyes.

"Of course she is!" He turned to her with his own dark eyes beaming with pride and excitement. "Now, tell me what is your name, eh?"

"Jessamine, sir. I'm Missy's maid, sir!" The sloe-eyed girl announced as though she was boasting. She obviously adored her mistress and that endeared her to Lance instantly; he also admired the girl's proud manner.

"Well, Jessamine, I think we will be very good friends, and since you are so capable I'm going to leave my two loves in your safe keeping and see a young man who should be told he has a new baby sister." He gave her a wink of his eye and handed the babe to her waiting arms.

Already Jessamine was captivated by the new master of Montclair. As she watched him exit the room, she gave out a deep sigh, voicing her thoughts aloud. "Hmmm, he's somethin'!"

An hour later, Lance had not only informed his young son about his new sister, but with the boy in his arms he'd joined his friends downstairs for drinks and cheroots in the parlor. He'd been so elated over the event he'd even passed the teakwood chest holding the cheroots to Annette Le Clere. She'd laughed and graciously refused while all the gentlemen exploded into laughter.

A little later they'd taken their leave from Montclair, declaring it was time the Edwardses, including Lance, needed some rest.

After they departed and young Andy was taken back to his room, Lance realized he was weary from all the excitement and the romp with his young son.

When next he looked in on his wife, after waking from a four hour nap, he was amazed to see her propped up against the pillows, certainly looking as though she'd not given birth some eight hours ago.

He stood just inside the door absorbing her smiling face and her long black hair fanning out on the pillows. Gowned in a pale pink that enhanced her light olive complexion, she looked lovely.

She held out her arms to him and he went to them eagerly, sitting down beside her on the bed. "Oh, my precious darling, can you possibly know what it means to me to hold you once again in my arms," his voice cracked with emotion.

Tears dampened her face for she, too, was filled with the deepest emotions as he held her tenderly. Never did she want to be without those strong, protective arms again. It seemed to her that he'd always been her protector.

All she could utter over and over was, *"Mon*

cheri! Mon cheri!"

"Yes, sweet! Oh, love! Never will I ask more of life, never!" He continued just to hold her reveling in the sweet contentment her nearness brought.

Later, he insisted on having his dinner tray brought to the room; he wished not to leave her for one minute. Jessamine did so, feeling even more impressed by his obvious devotion to his wife.

It became his habit for the next two days to dine with Elise in her bedroom. The rest of the days were spent getting acquainted with young Andy once again. Elise had never known such happiness, and her body thrived and healed rapidly. She was convinced it was from such bliss. Impatience gnawed at her to get out of bed, but Lance firmly demanded she stay there for a few more days.

"Oh, Lance." She pouted impatiently, irritated.

"Not yet, *ma petite!* I don't want you falling and smashing that beautiful face. Now that's final! Another day or two and we'll see." She knew he would not be swayed, and she could not deny that he was probably right, remembering Andy's birth and her confinement in London.

She decided to abide by his wishes, but only for two more days and then, she promised herself, she would do what she wished.

The newly arrived master was very much in evidence around Montclair. Lance made his presence known during the first week of his arrival, and his young son trailed behind him like a shadow. Nothing could have pleased Captain Edwards more.

Young Andy enjoyed riding in front of his father on the huge horse over the acres of land. Lance decided that the lad would have his own mount as soon as he was old enough.

Elise's recovery was amazing, and she turned a deaf ear to Jessamine's plea that she was getting out of bed too soon. When she stubbornly insisted on going downstairs to dine with her husband after a week of having trays in her bedroom, Lance agreed only if she would let him carry her down the stairs. Elise smiled her sweetest smile and eagerly hugged his neck.

Lance was more than pleased when Elise told him the name she'd chosen for their daughter, Lanissa. "For you, *mon cheri*. Lanissa for her handsome father, Lance Edwards." She smiled lovingly up at him and his broad chest swelled, ready to burst with a bounty of emotions. Her sentiment and cleverness amazed him once again.

That first month home was bittersweet for Lance. Having been apart from Elise for so many months now that he was home it was sheer hell not to be able to crush her in his arms, making love to her as he ached to do. So to spend himself in order to fall asleep, exhausted and weary, he worked around the plantation from sunup to sunset. He'd take long walks down by the river, occasionally taking a dip in the river to cool his flushed body.

Elise could not help feeling sorry for her poor darling, and she dared not let him see the smiles of amusement on her face, knowing well his virile, amorous nature.

As the days passed and her own body healed, she, too, became impatient for the feel of his strong arms and powerful body. She needed no doctor to tell her she was finally ready to welcome her husband back to her bed.

When Annette Le Clere invited Elise and Lance to accompany the Le Cleres into the city for carnival time, Elise eagerly accepted. The baby was now six weeks old and Lance had insisted on a wet nurse for her so Elise could sleep through the night. A few days away from Montclair would be nice, she thought. A wonderful retreat with her husband!

That evening after Annette's afternoon visit, Elise told Lance about Madame Le Clere's invitation as they were having a candlelight dinner. Lance readily agreed. His heart beat wildly as he leaped out of his chair to go over to Elise. He knew what she was telling him in her own special way. Elise giggled in spite of herself; he reminded her of young Andy about to devour his favorite chocolate cake.

He edged his chair up close to her. "Ah, Elise, it will be fun. You should have some new gowns for the occasion, and I'm ready for some social life." His dark eyes were so alive and bright.

"Yes, *mon cheri*. You've been working entirely too hard," she said, smiling. Lance saw the provocative look in her eyes and realized she was aware that all his toil and sweat was a release for his tensions. The little minx! He'd been a fool to think he could fool her; they were far too close for that.

"Damn right! Now I want to play and it's you, *petite amie*, I want to play with," he teased, arching his brows in a suggestive, inviting way. She felt a tingling, warm heat creeping over her as his eyes danced over her face, down her throat and to the lowcut neckline of her gown.

She had purposely chosen one of her most attractive gowns, and the soft clinging material exhibited the fullness of her breasts and clinched the small waist. The rich gold color was always flattering to her. Lance always complimented her on the off-the-shoulder style, declaring her satiny skin was inviting to the touch.

His hand played on her bare shoulders. "Hmmmmm, you smell delicious!" His voice was husky with passion, disregarding his caution to get control of himself.

"And you, darling smell very manly. All man!" She gave a sigh that spoke for itself, of her desire to be loved. Her body pressed lovingly against him, feeling as though it was melting and blending with his.

"Oh, God, Elise. . . ." was all he could manage to say, for he was ready to explode with her responding heat flaming over him. "Should we? Can we?" Nervous anxiety washed over him.

"*Je t'aime*, Lance." Her arms encircled his neck and it was all the urging he needed. His hands slipped under her thighs, lifting her up into his arms. Leaving their glasses of wine unfinished on the table, they departed the dining room for their private haven upstairs. Enthralled with one another and murmuring their little messages of love, they did not know they were being observed with wonder and curiosity by Jessamine, who stood giggling about the scene she was observing. It sure seemed to Jessamine like the two were having fun, and she was curious to know what it would feel like to be held by a man and kissed like that. Missy sure did like it! Bet she would, too. Already, there was a strange new awareness of her blossoming body.

She took herself to her bed with her imagination running wild about Missy and her husband.

Moonlight played across Elise's face as she lie waiting for Lance to hastily remove the remaining barrier of clothes restraining him. She could not suppress a soft, teasing laugh at his impatience.

"I'll make you pay for that, you little vixen," Lance promised her, knowing why she found him so amusing. Laughing with her, he snuggled into the bed beside her.

Pulling her over to cover him, he could not

167

control the deep intake of breath as her firm breasts pushed against his chest. Their thighs entangled and lips sought the sweetness of feel and touch. Their two bodies met in unison, with a familiarity they knew so well.

"God, Elise, you feel so good!" He was calling on all the power he possessed to allow the paradise of passion to last. His darling Elise was so eager, writhing with her own wild urgency, and her sweet lips sought his mouth and throat with soft, pleased moans.

"Yes, love. Love me! Love me!" He was beyond caring now as he laid her back on the bed and she arched toward him as if she was afraid he was leaving her.

It was impossible to be as gentle as he'd willed himself to be with his little wife's wild eagerness destroying all his good intentions. With her so willingly giving of herself, he did not hesitate to take of the sweet nectar she offered.

Elise gave out soft, pleased moans of the pleasure she was feeling as Lance's hands cupped her firm, rounded hips, urging her even closer against him. Again and again Elise gave up to the dams of ecstasy breaking loose within her. Lance was unrelenting in his quest to carry her to those wonderous heights with him, and she went willingly.

"Hmmmm, I love you," she moaned after they'd soared to the heavens and beyond. He sunk down by her side, giving light kisses to her cheek and ear. "My darling, my beautiful darling! It was so damn good to love you again," his deep, husky voice declared. It was the last word spoken by either of them as they drifted off for some much-needed sleep.

It was Elise who woke up first, but she remained encircled in her husband's arms. She smiled, remembering a time when she'd tried to slip away from that muscled, restraining arm the morning after he'd deflowered her in his cabin aboard the *Seahawk*. Lying by his side now, that was the last thing she would want to do, and gazing on his handsome face, she saw so much that resembled their young son Andy.

Someday he would be stealing some beautiful maiden's heart just like his father had done with her's. But how wonderful it had all worked out, she mused, snuggling closer to her husband. Lance had vowed that it was written in the stars that they should meet and be lovers. For all his rugged exterior, he was truly the romantic, this husband of hers!

Lance slowly opened his lazy eyes to see this look of adoring love written on his wife's face and he moved up to plant a kiss on her lips. "Good morning, sweetheart," he whispered softly. His hand caught a long, straying wisp of her hair resting across her breast. They shared a moment of silence, just gazing at one another with the hint of a knowing smile on their lips.

"Good morning, *mon Capitaine*," she purred.

He knew without being told what she was

thinking about. He smiled broadly, quizzing her. "You've never been sorry, have you, *ma petite amie?*"

"Never!" Looking so temptingly sensuous with the sheer gown molded to her body, she bent over him to invite another kiss. The kiss whetted the appetite of both and so it was late in the morning before Lance and Elise emerged from their bedroom. As they indulged in a mammoth brunch, he told her of his plan that they should go into the city for the afternoon.

"I think it is the time to purchase you some new gowns, love, and this is what we will do." He did not add that he wanted to buy a special gift in honor of the birth of their new daughter.

Elise was delighted with his idea and gobbled down her food so she could get dressed.

Their visit to Madame Vivienne's exclusive salon was welcomed enthusiastically by Vivienne Delavigne. A most generous spender he was, and only one other man in the city of New Orleans was as strikingly handsome as Lance Edwards. That man was Monsieur Jean Laffite. *Mon Dieu,* both men had a devastating effect on her. Interestingly enough, they did resemble one another. She'd have to conclude in the sizing of them that Edwards was more powerfully built and an inch or two taller than the dark, handsome Frenchman.

She was to learn in a brief time that Monsieur Edwards had an eye for fashion, for he picked her most beautiful creation, a blue

170

green watered silk with matching cape of velvet, trimmed with rich sable fur.

When Elise tried on the gown for Madame Vivienne to take up the rather large waistline, the seamstress was awestruck, noting how the young woman's eyes seemed to turn the shade of the gown.

Elise modeled the gown for Lance's approval and he, too, saw what the seamstress meant about the gown and Elise's eyes. Caring not that they were not alone, he reached over and kissed Elise. "Ravishing, love! Now, I'll leave you with Madame Vivienne to pick out two or three more gowns while we're here. I must run on an errand, but I'll return before you are through."

He had some special shopping to do so he made a hasty exit, leaving a smiling Elise and a gaping Madame Vivienne, who would have enjoyed the experience of being Elise Edwards just one day.

Elise chose a deep red gown trimmed with black lace and jet beads with a matching pelisse. Vivienne pointed out the perfect hair adornment, an aigrette of black plumes and red colored stones.

She chose the material and pattern for a gown of satin with an ecru overlay of lace imported from France. By the time Lance returned Madame Vivienne had figured in her head the handsome fee coming to her. She assured Elise that the gown would be ready before the end of the week.

A deep voice interrupted the two women's chattering. "Have you finished, *ma petite?*" Lance stood, feeling proud and smug about his special purchase, resting concealed in his pocket. How perfect the ring and bracelet would be with the blue green gown. Before he left he could not pass up earrings for her dainty ears, too.

Elise assured her husband she had made all her purchases and was ready to leave. Madame Vivienne had one of her helpers carry the packaged goods to the awaiting carriage in front of her shop and personally escorted the couple to the door to bid them farewell and assure them the great pleasure it had been to serve them. Elise and Lance were in high spirits and a gay mood as they started to board their carriage. Someone observing the two would have thought they were experiencing those first moments of romance.

Two ladies down the street were about to board their carriage. A gentle breeze blew the bright-colored plumage of one of the ladies' bonnets across her eyes and she impatiently pushed it back to get a view of the striking couple.

"Dear God, it's him . . . them!" the woman gasped!

"Who . . . what, Susan?" Linda Gentry questioned her companion whom she'd just shared a delightful luncheon with in the little tearoom.

"Lance Edwards and . . . and Elise!" Forgetting Linda's ever-wagging tongue, she muttered, "Sweet Lord, he has to be the best-looking man anywhere."

"I don't think Clint would appreciate that, Susan dear." Linda smirked smuggly. Susan Barron was a horrible flirt!

"Pooh, who cares? I assure you, Linda I don't! So don't go tattling that tomorrow at the sewing circle. While we're on that subject, I regret I just can't make it tomorrow, dear." Susan had other plans, but as far as Clint was concerned it was where she was spending the afternoon. Her "sewing circle" was the secluded cottage used by J. William Burke's eldest son, a rake and well-known womanizer.

Susan accepted Linda's invitation to visit awhile before returning to Shady Oaks since she would not be coming to the gathering the next day. The next hour at the Gentry's home was spent gossiping. Linda let Susan know the thoughts of some of her genteel friends, and their catty remarks about the name Elise had picked for her daughter.

"Think about it, Susan. Lanissa could be for memories of Laffite, instead of her husband Lance. After all she *was* with him for many weeks, wasn't she?"

Susan said nothing in defense of Elise and guilt plagued her later. It was vicious and unfounded, and yet, she'd done nothing to halt Linda's poison tongue. Linda's instant dislike of Elise was due to Jeff Gentry's open admiration of her beauty. His open, but lavish compliments had ignited overwhelming envy in his rather plain, colorless wife, whom he married for wealth and status.

The craziness of it all. As far as Susan Barron was concerned she liked Elise much better than the dull, boring Linda Gentry. The thorn in her side was that Elise had everything Susan yearned for.

Susan had found in Lance the Prince Charming of her dreams, and the futility of the last two years had been, in part, the constant comparing of Clint to Lance. Dear God, Clint came up short in Susan's eyes! Disillusioned and disappointed, she began an endless search jumping into one man's bed and then another. She'd always left them and felt unfulfilled. To dull the ache and blot out the emptiness of her life at Shady Oaks, she indulged herself more and more with liquor. For the first time in her twenty years, Daddy couldn't make things right. Nor could she turn to Zack Hart with this problem, for he would take Clint's side, she knew.

So Susan entered into a lifestyle of allowing herself to do as she pleased and saying, "The devil take the hindmost."

Shady Oaks came in view and depression settled in. Shrugging her shoulders she pacified herself with thoughts of her latest paramour, Charles Burke. Now that she'd finally met the fascinating Jean Laffite her interest was aroused. The rumors she'd heard about his spellbinding charms were obvious to her now, since their brief encounter.

Dear Lord, it made her tremble just thinking about being with him at Barataria as many weeks as Elise had been! That minute a devious idea hatched in Susan's warped mind.

Chapter 11

For many weeks now Jean's news about Elise
came through the Le Cleres. Since her husband's arrival in the city, he'd made no trip to
Montclair to see her. He knew about Lanissa's
arrival into the world and gave Annette a silver
feeding spoon and cup to present to Elise for
the baby. "Never mind telling her I sent it,"
he'd instructed Madame Le Clere, confident
that Annette understood.

Often he thought of her and yearned
desperately to see her, but logic told him it was
not wise. Besides, more serious thoughts had
occupied his time. He was still furious from
Governor Claiborne's latest act against him and
his men. It did not faze him that he'd been
arrested along with his brother Pierre, and
tossed in jail. His capable lawyer had them out
in a short time. But he did resent being caught
by the damned patrol as they'd made their way
through the bayou with a load of merchandise

going to the city.

His last trip into the city was made out of curiosity. When he saw with his own eyes Claiborne's proclamation offering 500 dollars to anyone who captured him he doubled over with laughter. A devious idea came to him and he declared his own proclamation; a bid of 15,000 dollars for anyone who would bring Claiborne to Barataria.

Now Claiborne was pushed into a corner, and his pride had to be salvaged so he turned to the courts. A warrant was issued against him and his men. When Pierre was arrested the second time, Jean was past the laughing stage about the governor's foolishness. It was becoming a damned nuisance. Jean had more important business to conduct. However, once again he outsmarted Claiborne's militia by cleverly disguising his men in uniforms and rescuing Pierre from jail. Upon their return to Barataria, Jean and his men celebrated the night away.

It was then and there Jean decided he would attend the elegant carnival party given by the wealthy J. William Burke. It was a costume affair and he might just stand next to old Claiborne before the evening was over.

His invitation had been issued personally by J. William's much younger wife Andrea when they'd happened on one another a few weeks ago. He had grave doubts that Burke would have approved if he'd known. The aging banker did not approve of him, Jean knew. Andrea Burke was another matter, and Jean just

177

happened to be privy to some well-guarded secrets in regards to the lady's past. He knew it was the wealth and position Andrea found attractive about being the banker's wife. Even with her fancy clothes and expensive jewels, the woman was coarse, and her acceptance by the elite society of the city was out of respect for her husband. She was about the age of J. William's oldest son, Charles. With Charles's reputation, Laffite would bet he'd been in that honey-pot a few times. Sweet innocence, Andrea Burke was not!

For days Andrea had anticipated the soiree. Finally the gala evening was approaching. With her lady's maid, who had become her confidente since marrying Burke, she giggled and twittered like a schoolgirl about three of the handsome gentlemen who would be attending. That devilish rogue, Laffite, and the big blond giant Clint Barron were both intriguing, but her curiosity was whetted about the man she'd heard about but she was yet to meet. She'd heard his name tossed around by Flo Maynard, Susan Barron, and even her fiesty, mulatto maid Celine. From all the tributes paid, he had to be nothing less than a Greek God. Susan Barron called him a handsome devil with black, dreamy bedroom eyes, and Flo's remarks had been influenced by his magnificent, muscled body. However, it was the earthy Celine's remarks that had painted the most interesting picture for Andrea.

"Lord, how he moves that body of his—like a big, black cat. Makes you tingle all over." Celine giggled, rolling her dark eyes suggestively. Andrea knew exactly what she meant for the two had shared girl talk many times about men. There were times that she'd have been terribly bored had it not been for Celine in the big house she now called home.

"He's somethin'. . . . Know how to make a woman squeal in bed, I'll bet. Hmmmm, mercy. Eyes make you feel naked. You get my meaning, Mistress?" Celine swayed her young body as she turned back to face Andrea.

"I know what you mean, Celine. You make me more anxious than ever for the night to get here," Andrea told her, running her slender fingers through her long, blond hair. Sitting quietly while Celine started to style her hair, she was certain she'd picked the perfect costume for the evening. Her firm, full breasts would be emphasized in the Cleopatra costume and should attract the eyes of one of the three interesting gentlemen. Then she exploded into a gale of laughter thinking about the fat J. William in his toga. Dear Lord, he was revolting! Often she'd asked herself if the wealth was worth the effort. In bed, he was worse than a grunting pig, and she'd learned a little trick to rid herself of his fat, heavy body. What he took for instant excitement on her part was merely an act, knowing he would give a release sooner and she could be rid of him. The dumb idiot had no idea how repulsive he actually was to her.

As it would happen there were two other Cleos at the party, but the other two ladies had chosen more concealing costumes than Andrea's. There were kings, jesters, and queens. Indian maidens and fierce Vikings paraded through the large ballroom. A gentleman wearing buckskins talked with a beautiful Spanish *señorita*. The room seemed to revolve in bright colors and Andrea's head swam as she looked out over the mob of guests milling around. The gay atmosphere sparked wild excitement in her.

There was a tiny Chinese empress in a magnificent slit gown being embraced by a pirate. Many wore wigs to conceal their identity. She was certain though that the impressive man disguised as a swarthy gypsy was the charming Laffite and the black-haired gypsy girl with the bright red flower in her hair and gold hoop earrings was his lady of the evening. But where were the Edwardses she wondered?

Seeing the massive figure dressed in a toga coming in her direction, she rushed through the archway out of his sight. She welcomed the sight of one of the servants coming toward her with a tray of glasses filled with champagne. She grabbed one for herself. Taking a large gulp, she sank back against the wall and let out a deep sigh.

"Ah, my beautiful Cleo, you are outstanding tonight!" A deep male voice whispered in her ear and she turned to see a ferocious-looking pirate smiling down on her. "At last we meet tonight." How tall he was, she noticed looking up at him.

"Monsieur pirate, you scared me!" The man's powerful presence made her tingle. Was this what Celine was talking about? Was this that dashing Lance Edwards?

The spot they stood in was rather secluded. He bent down, teasing her ear with his lips as lightly as with a feather. "Forgive me, *ma petite*, I didn't mean to scare you. In fact, I'm so taken with you I might just take you captive on my ship and sail away with you, eh? Would you like to sail away with me, beautiful Cleo?" His husky laugh taunted her.

Andrea felt she could hardly catch her breath and her breasts swelled with excitement from the touch of his warm hand snaking around the sheer jeweled midriff top. Trying to sound flippant and casual, she replied, "And where would we go, pirate, and what would we do?" Her body betrayed her by swaying wickedly against him. This was the old Andrea, the real Andrea—the Andrea who had been caged too long.

"Wherever and whatever the lady wishes," he told her, his hot breath tickling her neck. Andrea was so engrossed in this flirtatious game that she did not see the angry Roman marching hastily toward her. Neither did she see the distraction causing the pirate to turn from her to ogle the swishing floral skirt of the gypsy girl going through the terrace doors.

Her long black hair swung in the same swaying motion as the gypsy's skirt, short enough to reveal her ankles, and her feet were shod in golden sandals. The pirate was intoxicated by the soft, bared shoulders of the peasant-style blouse. He smiled, knowing at once who it was. What a perfect little gypsy she made, wild and wonderful!

He was unaware of the two loud voices next to him. Already he'd forgotten Cleo and Andrea chided her husband for screaming at her. "Shut up, Bill! Do you want all our guests to hear you?" Oh, God, he'd ruined the night again, she cussed under her breath. Dejectedly, she allowed him to pull her away, but she turned back to see the pirate strolling away in the opposite direction. Taking some degree of satisfaction in the thought that he was as disappointed as she was, she went along with her husband. The night was not over yet!

Separated from Lance in the vast, milling crowd, Elise felt the need of a breath of fresh air. Noticing the cool-looking darkness of the terrace, she decided to take advantage of it for a while. Feeling free from prying eyes, she pulled the ruffling of the blouse out to allow the cool breeze to reach her bosom. It felt divine! Again, she urged the drawstring opening of the blouse to expand to cool herself. Then she tied the ribbons back and lifted the heavy, thick hair off her neck for the same effect.

Jean stood silently watching her unsophisticated, spontaneous actions. She could not realize how beguiling he found her out there in the darkness. Such naturalness, without a care in the world, it would seem. A fairy queen or a wood nymph—he could not decide which.

Remembering suddenly that he'd had the forethought to hastily take two glasses of cool champagne before following her, he finally spoke. "A refreshing drink, little gypsy?"

She turned, knowing who the voice belonged to, and a radiant smile flashed on her face. "Jean! Oh, Jean!" She rushed up to greet him and he bent, still holding the champagne, to peck her forehead with a friendly kiss.

It had been a long time since he'd last seen her, and her obvious delight to see him pleased him very much. He throbbed with ignited passion to enfold her in his arms. She was more beautiful than he'd remembered.

"How are you, little one? Obviously, very happy or else you wouldn't look so bewitching."

"Oh, I am happy, Jean. And you?" Elise followed his lead toward the bench and they sat, sipping the champagne. Elise told him about her new daughter. Time passed with neither of them aware that an angry gypsy man had covered the ballroom many times looking for his missing wife.

Jean was enjoying her delightful company, caring little about the festivities going on inside. The fact that Jean held her hand seemed only natural and right as they continued to talk. Finally, he inquired, "And where is your husband, *ma petite?*"

"Here!" A powerful figure in a bright red silk shirt and black pants stood in the doorway looking down on the two. Had he not been masked, his face would have spoken of the fury blazing there.

Jean Laffite felt that blazing fury as sure as if he'd wore no mask when he extended his hand, introducing himself. "It's a great pleasure to meet you, Captain Edwards. Your wife has been telling me about your new daughter."

For Elise's sake he hoped to soothe the Englishman's ire, for he sensed the immediate danger of the situation.

"As she's told me of you, Monsieur Laffite, and I take this opportunity to thank you for saving her life. I . . . I can't deny that I would have preferred to kill the bastard myself." Lance's words were laced with the venom of hate, and Elise could feel the tenseness of his muscled arm placed possessively around her back.

Here was a man who gave no quarter, Laffite sensed in the strong, arrogant tone of his voice, and no one took what was his. He immediately admired and respected that trait in Elise's husband. He shared the same traits.

"I respect your feelings, Captain, and understand them. Since he was under my command it was my job to see him made an example. I tolerate no disobedience," he

184

parried back at the tall man, whose black eyes pierced him from the openings in his mask. Both knew neither allowed insubordination.

Elise was puzzled by the two men on either side of her. Her soft laughter interrupted the tenseness as she flippantly remarked, "You two! Shall we drop the morbid subject. I'm fine and you my darling husband, and you, my friend, will please change the subject . . . *oui?*"

Jean laughed. *"Oui!* Besides I must seek out a lovely lady I'd ask for this dance. I ask you two to excuse me now. Nice to meet you, Captain, and good to see you again, Elise." Jean turned to leave the two with a very definite opinion of Lance Edwards imprinted in his mind.

As he entered the ballroom, he vowed to get one dance with Elise later. Now was not the time though. As he mingled into the crowd, he looked back at the two. "Yes, one dance I'll have, Edwards, before the evening is over."

He watched Captain Edwards lead Elise toward the dance floor and enfold his powerful arms around her. She was dwarfed by the tremendous size of the man. He smiled, detecting a slight mellowing of the man's fury now that he held Elise possessively in his arms and they danced.

Mon Dieu, he could not blame him for that! He, too, would have felt the same rage at finding her alone in the dark if he were her husband. If he dared to be honest, he saw with his own eyes that he was the man who could handle and harness the wild little gypsy in his arms.

For the first time he realized how many different women were wrapped up in the petite lady. He recalled the exquisitely gowned, jewel bedecked, sophisticated beauty he'd escorted to the finest places in New Orleans when he'd first returned with her from Barataria. Then tonight she was the earthy gypsy girl. A woman of many moods and mysteries!

Lance had said nothing to Elise as they began to dance, and some innate feeling told her to say nothing. He held her so tight she could barely breathe, but the closeness of his body affected her. With the look of love on her face she gazed up at him, and his face suddenly softened, she saw.

His black mood eased as he looked down at her. He knew she had no inkling of the hellish torment racing through his being. Joaquin Ruiz's face haunted his thoughts and Clint Barron's time in Elise's life pricked at him still. Yet, he knew the little minx loved him, and that was his salvation. It always erased these devilish thoughts.

With the innocence of a child, she snuggled close and prodded, *"Mon cheri,* are you all right?"

He whirled her as the music came to an end. "Fine, love. Just fine!" He lied, willing himself not to let anything mar the festive evening. Something about Laffite troubled him.

The next hour passed with each of them

changing partners with each new dance. He'd just danced with the exotic looking, elegantly gowned Chinese empress, Annette Le Clere, and left her with Francois. Now he was ready to search for his wife among the crowd.

The music started up again as Lance scrutinized carefully the gathering crowd of dancers, unable to spot the tiny gypsy miss anywhere. A shapely lady in a sheer gown and flaming red hair pounced upon him, insisting, "My dance, monsieur." He took her in his arms, knowing at once it was Susan Barron. From her slurred speech, he also knew she was drinking far too much. Instantly he wished the dance over with.

"Lance, I swear I was beginning to think you weren't going to ask me to dance all night," Susan said, snuggling close, pressing her body against his.

He looked down, his face etched with a frown. What the bloody hell was she trying to pull right there on the dance floor for all their friends to witness? Was she so drunk she was not aware of her actions?

"I see Clint over there. Oh, yes, that's him with Elise," Lance remarked, purposely moving toward them.

"Who cares! I certainly don't!"

Christ, the music seemed to never come to an end. Lance had lost sight of Elise and Clint the next time he whirled the stumbling Susan around. She felt like dead weight in his arms. This was what must have been troubling his old friend Zack lately. It was at this minute he began to notice the prying eyes of couples around them giving questioning looks at Susan. She giggled for no particular reason. Lance's eyes turned from her in disgust.

"You don't like me very much anymore, do you, Lance?"

"Of course I like you, Susan. That's a foolish thing to say." Christ, he didn't want a sobbing drunk on his hands.

"There was one night you *really* liked me, real good, Lance," she laughed. "Boy, that was a night!"

"Susan, shut up! Oh, I see Clint again." He gave her a firm, harsh jerk on the arm to catch up with Clint and Elise.

With his strong, supporting arm removed from Susan's back he saw her begin to sway. Christ—she was drunk! He stretched out his hand to her and urged, "Come on, Susan!" His eyes darted over the room in search of her husband or perhaps Zack. Only moments ago he had seen Zack in his buckskins engrossed in conversation with his lawyer friend Robertson. Now they'd disappeared from sight. The evening was fast becoming a nightmare for Lance, and he wanted only to rid himself of the burden tugging on his arm.

"Gotta' get some air, Lance! Please!" Susan pleaded, almost childlike.

"Damn! All right, Susan. Just shut up and quit talking so bloody loud." He made no effort to be courteous or charming with the young lady hanging on his arm. She was truly proving to be a pain in the ass.

By the time he had led her into the hallway any gentleness was gone. He jerked her roughly on. With a surge of strength that surprised him, she separated herself from him and bolted. Lance gave out a disgusted sigh, tired of appeasing her.

A taunting voice beckoned to him from the doorway of one of the rooms off the hallway. "Bet you can't find me!"

"For Christ's sake, Susan. Quit playing child's games!" He sauntered into the room where the sound had come from, totally unprepared for the attack of arms, body, and mouth.

"What—what the hell is the matter with you?" Lance untangled himself, flinging her away from him. She was crazy as well as drunk. He was embarrassed for Clint, Zack, and himself!

She giggled and swayed seductively forward. "Don't want to play with Susan, eh? Oh, I could show you some fun games, Lancie." Her act of the temptress did not impress him.

"I'm going to pretend this hasn't happened, Susan, and tomorrow you're going to wish it hadn't."

"Oh? Got to be true to Elise, eh? Silly! You're entitled to some extra fun just like her."

"You bitch!" Sanity returned to stop his clenched fist, but the temptation to sock her was overwhelming him.

189

"That, I am! But I'm not the only one and that, my dear Lance is why you're the *fool!*" She threw her head back and gave a wild laugh. Trying to stand up straight, she pointed her finger at him and declared, "Hear me well, for I tell you a fact—there is not a woman in New Orleans who wouldn't jump in Jean Laffite's bed eagerly, and if you think your precious Elise stayed with him for weeks without doing it then you are a fool!"

He turned from the disgusting sight. A lowly waterfront whore could have been more appealing than Susan Barron. Grinding his teeth, he hissed, "You are a foul mouthed slut, and I hope you rot in hell!"

Striding from the room, he didn't hear her reply. Susan crumpled in a heap on the carpeted floor, mumbling, "Oh, I probably will." The remorse and shame gushed through her and resentment exploded. Lance had not been tempted by her. His insults would linger forever. Her only salvation was to find Charles Burke fast, before she went raving mad.

Lance sought the privacy of the terrace to cool his temper before joining the crowd in the ballroom. He could not forget Susan's tormenting words. He could tell himself he did not believe the drunk woman all he wanted to, but he still could not erase them from his mind. He cursed her for that!

He returned to the ballroom to see Elise dancing with Jean. It took all the willpower he could muster to keep from going over and jerking her out of his arms. When Jean brought her to her husband, his aloof manner was obvious to Laffite and Elise.

"Remember you can have your pick, Elise," Jean reminded her before taking his leave. Lance inquired what he meant and Elise explained that he spoke of bolts of silk material.

"I will supply your silks, madame!" He barked, jerking her along to go join the Le Cleres.

She could not do battle with him there on the ballroom floor, but her eyes flashed as they turned away from him, and she held her head high in defiance.

"He was merely being nice, Lance. Annette was given the same privilege, if you must know," she muttered, allowing him no doubt of her anger with him at that point.

"I don't give a damn about Annette! *We'll* not buy his plundered goods Elise, and that's final!"

He needed to say nothing more for Elise to know her husband did not hold Jean Laffite in very high regard. While the man walking by her side held her love, as well as her heart, she could not deny that Jean held a small part of her, too. She felt Lance was being absolutely unfair toward the man who had saved her life and been nothing but kind to her for many weeks. He could act civil, at least!

Suddenly, his childish behavior inflamed her so she yanked her arm away from his viselike hold to hasten her steps, leaving him a few paces behind her. Caring not about the prying eyes around them, Lance took two steps to catch up with her. "Damn you, Elise! Don't you ever do that again!" This time his arm snaked around her tiny waist, with his long fingers burrowing into her flesh so that she dared not move faster than he led her.

Annette saw the volcano brewing in the handsome Englishman's eyes as well as the cool, green fire in Elise's eyes and she had a notion it had to do with Jean Laffite. The first day Elise had arrived at Bellefair, Madame Le Clere had seen the love in their friend Laffite's face.

The ride to their home in the city was subdued. The two ladies excused themselves to retire, leaving the two gentlemen downstairs to have a nightcap.

Elise only pretended to be asleep when she heard Lance enter the room. She'd fumed the whole time he'd been downstairs with Francois. His stupid actions had ruined a glorious evening and she found it hard to excuse it.

Lance's temper had cooled by the time he'd wearily climbed the steps to their room, and he was feeling rather foolish. Slipping quietly through the door, he saw the tiny figure of his wife lying on her side on the bed. Moonlight played across the room, lighting up certain areas, and Lance saw her clothing tossed on the floor and chair. He could not suppress a smile imagining his little spitfire in action earlier. It made his passions rise as he slipped out of his clothes and crawled in the bed beside her.

He made no motion to reach over and plant so much as a kiss on her cheek, and yet she could feel the divine heat of him next to her. She ached for him, wanted him most desperately. But she'd be damned if she'd roll over to make the first gesture of making up. No, he must!

The soft curves of her body taunted him as he lie looking at her back. This was the little gypsy who'd looked so sensuous and tantalizing all night long. Now they were alone and he could have her if only. . . .

This was not his Elise, who yielded so totally and eagerly, for she would have come immediately into his arms. The pain of this realization hit him square in the gut and turned like a knife in his belly. What neither of them could know was the frustration drowning the other one.

Each shifted their bodies at the same moment—only a slight turn. It was enough that flesh touched flesh. Instinctively, Lance's arms went around her, pulling her savagely against him and holding her there.

"You vixen, you drive me crazy!" He declared huskily, searching for her mouth and fiercely invading it with his tongue. He'd take her by force if he must, for his blood boiled wanting her so. The long kiss left Elise breathless.

193

She remained silent, giving him no hint about her feelings. A stubbornness within her took over and she was determined not to respond anxiously and wildly as she normally did. Let him subdue and conquer!

It was having a maddening effect on Lance, she realized, watching him rise up slightly to look down upon her face. In those onyx black eyes she saw the message that he would have her.

His pulse pounded wildly as he wondered if she was so mad she'd try to deny him. God forbid if she did. His blood boiled at that moment; he was obsessed by one maddening desire.

He pulled her soft body to fit the curve of his, wishing to hear her soft moans of pleasure. Even though a searing liquid heat flowed within her, she said nothing. Nor did she resist him.

His surging thrust conquered her and her body arched upward. His heated breath played against her throat as he gasped, "I want you damnit, whether you want me or not! I'll bloody well have you, my darling."

She yielded sweetly to him, and he sighed. "Ah, yes, love. Come to me, give to me what only you can."

His overwhelming maleness invaded and conquered her. Her own breathless voice echoed, *"Mon cheri! Mon cheri!* Hmmmmm, you feel so good!" Elise cried out his name in response as his mouth and hands caressed her

194

body, stirring sensation after sensation. Together now, they climbed to the peak of passion's rapture. There was no hint of the chilling winter's night just outside their bedroom window for the torrid heat of summer consumed them, flaming and burning out of control.

Part II
Love's Bittersweet Betrayals

Chapter 12

Clint Barron had hunted for his stray wife in every corner of the Burke's palacial home. He was tempted to leave her wherever she might be. He should take out for Shady Oaks without her. What a tidbit of gossip that would make. He was weary of the stupid deception and fallacy of their so-called marriage. Life was too short to live this way!

Susan's perfidy bore no cleverness. God knows, she was not the sly little fox she thought herself to be, Clint mused with disgust. That was obvious to him a few minutes after he'd returned from searching the garden area to join Zack Hart. Zack could pity him looking upon the troubled face! He, too, knew what was going on.

When his wife came rushing around the corner with the good-looking Charles Burke trailing a few steps behind her it didn't take too much intelligence to know what Susan had been doing. Even her curls were askew, and her gown was creased with wrinkles. Clint noted the sly smile on Andrea Burke's face, but then she had put in a busy evening flirting with every man in sight.

He made hasty farewells and was none too gentle leading his red-haired wife out to their waiting carriage. Zack observed, saying nothing. He could not fault Clint for his anger.

The Barrons traveled to Shady Oaks in a chilling silence. Upon entering the house he marched up the steps to his bedroom as Susan staggered down the hallway to the liquor chest. Clint cared not if she drank herself into oblivion. He sought the solitude of his bed, and there he relived the precious moments of holding Elise in his arms as they danced. That was the high point of the whole evening for him. But a man could not live his life on a few rare moments. It suddenly galled him that the other men must be talking behind his back, and his male ego reared against the repulsive situation he'd been bogged down in too long. He would not dwell in the gutter too much longer with Susan, he vowed, lying there in the darkness of his room.

Old Callie tugged at the worn, gray robe draped around her heavy body and ambled back down the hall to her quarters. She shared Mister Clint's opinion that the young mistress could drink herself to death if that was her wish. Poor Mister Clint! One look at his face told of his misery. Lord Almighty, it was so different when he and Missy Elise had come home from a party all bubbling and laughing. Mister Clint would be looking down so lovingly on her pretty, smiling face. Lordy, where would all this lead to, Callie pondered sadly as she slipped back between the sheets of her bed.

Susan poured a generous glassful from the bottle containing the amber liquid and gulped it down hastily, hoping to blot out the haunting look of disgust on Lance's face. She filled the glass again. Oh, she wanted to reach that state of soft, floating clouds of forgetfulness. She had to erase the image of Charles and his sickening remarks, muttered as he'd taken her on the filthy cot in the stable at the back of the Burke's mansion. His lascivious acts brought forth no thrilling memories now, only disgust with herself. God, she wanted to retch!

She flung the glass to the floor with all the fury boiling within her. Damnit, why was she still sober and able to think . . . remember every sordid detail? She wanted so to erase his scurrilous touch from her breasts and body. She felt soiled and dirty, as though she needed desperately to soak for hours to remove the vile rot of Charles Burke once and for all.

Why had it not seemed that way the night by the river bank when she had laid on the ground at Harwood with Lance? Why was it that she did not feel debased or degraded that Lance had taken her there in the open, as though they were animals mating in the fields? Instead, it had seemed right and wonderful, and she felt

201

no shame or remorse. She felt all woman, happy and fulfilled. There was no hint of feeling the slut!

Her being cried out his name over and over, and her body shook with deep, hurting sobs.

Rising up from the chair was a tedious effort, but she had to have another drink, and then another if it was necessary. Staggering over to the corner where the glass had landed, she picked it up with a trembling hand.

"Gonna' forget! Gotta' forget! Go crazy if I don't!" Her smudged face wrinkled with anguish. Hair fell over her eyes blocking the flow of the liquor. The glass overflowed but Susan cared not that the liquor flowed on the fine teakwood table. She greedily gulped the contents, making no effort to move from the carpeted floor. By now her body was numbed in a drunken stupor.

Jean Laffite's evening had been very pleasant. He had escorted the beauteous Antonia Delgardo home and ended up spending the night and part of the next day with her.

Jean returned to Barataria, worn and weary from his interlude with the insatiable Antonia Delgardo. The usually alert and clever Laffite had no inkling that he had been pumped for information about the city and certain people during that sensual episode. Nor would he suspect any connection between her and the arrival some two weeks later of a British ship at Barataria.

However, as soon as Jean had left Antonia's residence she had hastily flung on her sable-trimmed velvet cloak and gone to the hotel where her contact was staying. She hated the little weasel of a man she knew as Granville Harris. Even though he sent a chill down her spine it was a part of the job. As a British spy she had a lot to put up with. By the same token, the very expensive cloak she had over her shoulders was the compensation. She received a generous fee for each mission she accepted.

Laffite would serve their purpose perfectly, she'd concluded. He had all the qualifications, and after she'd passed these facts on to Granville her part of the mission would be over. She would leave New Orleans and proceed to Natchez. The sooner the better!

An hour later she boarded the carriage again. Her reticule was heavy with her reward. Granville had seemed pleased with her information about Jean's habits and his vast circle of friends. She'd obtained information about his fortress and the number of men under his command. Her impression of his loyalty was that Jean Laffite bowed to no mortal man. Barataria was his kingdom. Yes, he was perfect for what the British had in mind, and she knew riches whetted his appetite.

As Antonia made her plans, so did Granville Harris.

Cannon fire alerted Jean and he jumped out of his bed to dress hastily. As he rushed out of

203

his quarters, he saw that his men were preparing to blast a ship out of their waters and he yelled orders for them to halt. They obeyed, holding their fire as a white flag unfurled aboard the ship.

Two men in a long boat rowed to the shore as Jean stood observing them from the shoreline. Who were these strangers daring to land on his island? With ten of his men falling in step with him, he approached the boat carrying the two strangers. Wading in the shallow water after the boat had been tugged up on the sandy beach, one of the men declared, "We seek Jean Laffite."

In his snowy white ruffled shirt, Jean's tall, impressive figure stood out among his men's in their attire of dark-colored tunics and baggy trousers. "I am Jean Laffite, monsieur, and who might you be?"

"Captain Robert Winters, sir—commanding officer of the *Royal George,* anchored there, and this is my friend, Granville Harris," came the reply. Granville stepped forward to greet Laffite, and Jean suggested the two follow him to his quarters for whatever it was they wished to talk to him about. Harris never would have imagined it to be so easy to actually penetrate the great fortress of the pirate. The rumors he'd heard about the fierce pirate had been highly exaggerated, he decided. Laffite appeared to be more aristocrat than cutthroat pirate to him.

He was even more impressed as they drank and dined in the grandeur of his quarters. They were not the surroundings one would expect a pirate to reside in. Laffite lived like an English nobleman, and his attire was impeccable, as well as expensive, Granville observed.

Finally the time came to get to the point of their visit, and keeping in mind what Antonia had learned about this man before and after the party at the Burkes Harris knew Laffite would be easy prey.

Without further ado, Harris told Jean that the British were prepared to reward him handsomely if he would join forces with them when they invaded the city of New Orleans.

Granville's snakelike eyes beamed wickedly as he spoke. "It will be soon, Monsieur Laffite, and you could take great pleasure in the revenge you'd enjoy on your old friend Claiborne. You see, we are aware of your long-running feud with the stupid American governor. In fact, it might amaze you to know how many friends we have in the city who resent the Americans dominating their city."

Jean detested the little weasel sitting across from him almost on sight, and his hand grasped his wine glass so tightly that he suddenly realized he could have shattered it. But he was determined to play a convincing role. "What, Monsieur Harris, what are the British prepared to do for me, eh?"

Almost conceited about his expertise in dealing with Laffite, Granville Harris quickly responded that he would have rank, along with a sizable sum of money.

"I see. When would I receive these tokens?"

"If you agree, monsieur, half the sum tonight and the other half along with the rank when victory is ours. And remember, it will be very soon."

"The hour is late and I must sleep on it. I suggest we retire, and I shall give you my answer tomorrow." Jean stood, declaring the meeting over, and waved to his servant to usher the guests to their appointed rooms.

He remained at the long table, slowly sipping the glass of wine. A devious smile creased his mouth. The two fools could not know his deep-rooted hatred for the English, who'd been the enemy of France. It left a sour taste in his mouth to think about beautiful New Orleans, with its French culture and atmosphere, being overrun with the conquering English. No amount of money or no rank could sway him to fall in league with the British. However, the pirate in him urged him to outfox the two foolish Britons, and that he would do.

When the *Royal George* sailed away from Barataria Granville Harris was elated that his mission was successful. Jean had the pouch of gold. His conscience did not bother him, though he had lied to little weasel Laffite and taken his blood money. That evening he prepared to make his way through the bayous and go into the city of New Orleans. It was imperative that he seek out Francois Le Clere, whose opinion Governor Claiborne respected. He, of all people, knew how ill-prepared Governor

Claiborne's militia was. New Orleans could be overrun by the British troops in a matter of hours.

Heavy fog shrouded the bayous and Jean's trip was long and tiring. A chilly mist fell during the night to add to the discomfort of the journey. Jean was glad to reach the city and settle in the comfort of his house. He sipped on his favorite brandy and while Dorrie warmed up dinner, he would indulge in a few hours' rest before going out to Bellefair to talk to Francois.

He slept for two straight hours before summoning the carriage to go see Francois. As was the Le Clere's habit, they were enjoying a late brunch. The majordomo ushered Laffite in. He glimpsed the very animated conversation they indulged in, having no idea he was the one being discussed. Annette had been confessing to Francois her concern about a misunderstanding the night of the party. She'd observed Lance's displeasure about Jean where Elise was concerned, and she had also noticed Susan's horrible display. "The girl is a tramp, Francois. Pure and simple. I will not see Elise hurt! This, I tell you!"

Francois was soothing her as Jean appeared. "Elise is a lot like you, *chérie*. Don't worry about her. After all she's been rather confined with a new baby. I'll bet you right here and now that you have nothing to concern yourself about, my darling Annette."

"I hope not, Francois, but I just don't think

Elise realizes what a little bitch Susan has become over the last year."

Jean heard Annette's last statement and it almost seemed out of character for the very refined Madame Le Clere. He could not resist remarking, "Francois, I'll back your bet." He enjoyed teasing the delightful Annette.

The Le Cleres both looked up, broke into laughter, and greeted their friend. Annette gave him a warm kiss and hug and ordered an extra cup and plate brought to the table. "You must try Henri's newest concoction. It is delicious, Jean!"

Jean had to agree with Annette after enjoying a second helping. Sensing the serious air about Jean, Annette excused herself, leaving the two men in private. Annette concluded that the Burke's party had had an unpleasant effect on the guests.

Jean's revelation stunned Francois, for it left no doubt that the war was very real. Up to the time the news had been of attacks made many miles away, up to the north and east. Francois could envision the British fleet landing along the long coastline of Louisiana, or coming down the Mississippi River, and the city of New Orleans being overrun in a matter of hours.

He told Jean the news he received from an old army friend back in Washington. "The true enlistment figure is so far from the truth, Henry says. The thirty-five thousand on paper is more like ten thousand. As you know our state militia is depleted."

"I should know." Jean laughed. "Claiborne sends them to Grand Terre and we have them running with their tails between their legs in short order. That, or they just give up and join us for some drinks while laughing at Claiborne."

"You know I'll relay your news to the governor, and intercede for you as well. He can't be foolhardy or allow his pride to stand in the way of what's best for New Orleans." Francois was thoughtful for a moment. Remnants of his youthful handsomeness still lingered on his fine chiseled face. "The news that the British took command of Lake Erie and our forces retreated to Detroit suddenly has more impact now. What was so far away now seems so close, eh?"

"Closer than I like, *mon ami!*" Jean declared in a serious tone. As quickly he changed back to his devil-may-care personality and informed Francois that he must take his leave. "Speaking of the governor, he's been such a bother to me lately my business suffers. That red-headed madam is going to let that wild Irish temper of her's flare, and she'll have my scalp if I don't get her order of whiskey and brandy to La Maison. A real hellcat, that one!"

Another woman occupied his thoughts, and he intended to pay a call on Antonia Delgardo after his brief stop at Fifi's. But Fifi must be taken care of first, and in his pocket he carried a gift that would delight his old friend. The moment he'd spied it in some recent booty he'd thought of Fifi and her voluptuous figure. The garish collar, gold encrusted with rubies and diamonds, would overwhelm most women, but not the blasé Fifi.

He left Bellefair and reined the roan mare in the direction of La Maison. The old mansion would be quiet this time of the day; all of Fifi's girls would be resting. He'd always credited Fifi La Tour for her good treatment of and honesty with the luscious lovelies she carefully picked for her establishment. Who was Fifi really? he wondered. After all this time, Fifi La Tour remained an enigma.

These were the thoughts running through his mind as the black giant Titus greeted him at the door. Jean had barely stepped into the hallway before he saw something was amiss there. It was too early in the day for all the activity.

These nocturnal lovelies were never up this early. Something was wrong!

Chapter 13

An array of curvaceous beauties scampered to and fro down the long hallway, skirting around the overturned walnut table. Fifi's fine silver urn lay on the floor also.

Jean recognized Rita, a Spanish lovely, chattering away excitedly with the tall, willowy Swedish girl called Marta. The two of them were joined by a golden-skinned mulatto, Tawny. Her sensuous body was revealed under the diaphanous crimson robe. She seemed to be in disagreement with Rita over some matter. Jean ambled up to the archway where they stood.

The greeting room, which was a large, lavishly furnished parlor, was a shambles. It had been dubbed "greeting room" by Fifi because this was where her clientele were greeted and given fine wine or champagne before picking their lady for the evening. Its furnishings were rich and vivid: red velvets and brocades, silver urns and candleholders, huge gilt mirrors with swan-necked cartouche, and imported crystal chandeliers.

"I tell you, Rita it had to have been after midnight. I saw her," Tawny corrected the Spanish girl. "But she left her baby. Did you know that?"

"*Madre de Dios!* I wouldn't have believed that. Duke must have done a real selling job on her to get her to leave her little *chiquita* behind. She worshipped that little girl," Rita remarked.

Whatever had taken place at Madame Fifi's had all the girls atwitter. He greeted them, breaking up the serious conversation.

"Ah, Monsieur Laffite! Is it not a mess?" Tawny swayed up to him, swinging an arm around his shoulder in a familiar manner. Like all the girls, she adored Jean.

"I'd say so, but what is all of this about?"

"The woman Delphine. She left last night with the gambler Duke Donavan. Madame Fifi is fit to be tied. It was after that that all hell broke out here. This man . . . the American planter, came here and proceeded to get roaring drunk. He was madder than hell about Fifi allowing Duke to be with Delphine," Rita told him, disregarding Marta's nudging her to shut up.

"As usual, your mouth's going too fast, Rita," Marta's husky voice cautioned.

"Oh, pooh! Everyone knows that Delphine was here as Barron's private property. It's no great mystery, Marta. Sure, she was only a maid when Mister Clint Barron was not spending the night. Just like everyone knows Dominique is his little daughter. *Dios,* he couldn't have Delphine out at Shady Oaks when he married the snobby little Hart girl, so our good-hearted Fifi took her in for him." Rita gave out a soft laugh and added, "Course, Fifi is rewarded for her heart of gold."

"Do you suppose I could see Fifi, Tawny?" Jean inquired, for the whole affair did not interest him at this time. Yet, it would explain the strangeness about the couple he'd met many months ago when he sought Clint Barron in Elise's behalf.

"Take your chances if you will, Monsieur Laffite. She's upstairs with Barron. Finally got him quieted down after he went on a rampage when he found out about his woman leaving with another man."

Fifi welcomed Jean's company and they retreated to her rooms. The magnificent collar brought a smile to her weary face, caked with makeup of the night before. She brightened up with the delight of a child and flung her arms around Jean. "Damn, you're a good, dear man, Jean Laffite, and I'd call anyone a liar who said otherwise!"

Jean gave her a deep laugh. "And I'd say the same, so we are in agreement, *chérie.*"

"Course you know the both of us are thought to be rascals in certain circles? But what do we care, eh?" She gave him a sharp nudge in the ribs.

213

She rang for her man Titus to bring a fine bottle of brandy and the two of them settled into serious talk. Fifi told him all about the ruckus that took place the night before. Jean listened, for she seemed to have the need of a friend to talk to.

"I just couldn't help it, Jean. I felt sorry for her. She was so damned lonely, and Duke was struck blind the minute he laid his eyes on her. I saw it happening and I did nothing to stop it."

"In affairs of the heart, Fifi, you and I know there is only so much anyone can do," Jean pacified her.

Fifi agreed, drawing deeply on the brandy. "I'd grown very fond of her, and that precious baby of hers has become our plaything. My God Jean, it is a beautiful child! I'll swear, if I had not known I'd never have suspected she or the baby had colored blood. Delphine could have passed for a white woman. I don't know whether she ever told Duke or not."

Fifi left nothing out about her arrangement with Clint Barron to take Delphine. "She had Dominique right here, and during the first two years he came constantly. But this last year he rarely showed up. Damn him, he has no one to blame but himself. Delphine was a hot-blooded woman and Duke's attention was flattering. I got to admit I'm shocked that she'd leave the baby."

"And I am correct in assuming this child is Barron's? Perhaps this woman hopes that he will take the child?" Jean pointed out to Fifi.

"No Jean that was not her hope at all. I might as well tell the whole truth. There was a note from Delphine and that's what puts me in the middle of this mess. I could care less what Clint Barron thinks of me. It's not my fault that Delphine ran away." She fumbled in the pocket of her silk robe and pulled out a slip of paper.

Jean took the note with its neat writing. He remarked about it to Fifi and she explained that Delphine had been taught to read and write by Clint during the years she'd served as his mistress and housekeeper at Shady Oaks. The note said simply:

Please forgive me Madame Fifi, but this I must do. I must take this chance Duke is offering me for he does love me. We are going to Natchez to seek a new life for ourselves, and I beg you not to tell Clint. I trust you'll take care of Dommi for me until I come for her in the Spring. Please!
Love,
Delphine

Jean handed the note back to Fifi. He saw the dilemma poor Fifi floundered in. When she sought his advice, he dared not tell her. Knowing Fifi as he did, he had a feeling she'd do as Delphine asked. He could only laugh a few minutes later when she declared, "I won't tell him. He offered her nothing but a few stolen moments when it suited him. At least Duke, rascal that he might be, has asked her to share his life. Now, that little girl is another matter. I can't hold her if Clint Barron decides to take her from me."

Before Jean left Fifi he saw the beautiful child fathered by Clint Barron. Why any man would hesitate to claim such a pretty little girl Jean couldn't understand. Gazing upon the child he realized what a great pleasure he'd denied himself in life.

Looking on the child's oval face he saw promised loveliness. She bore the mixture of her blond father and mulatto mother. Her olive complected skin was Delphine's, but her curling hair was neither blond nor black, as her mother's. It was a warm chestnut color, and those eyes like topaz were flecked with gold and brown.

Susan Barron resented the quizzical, puzzled looks old Callie kept giving her during the morning hours as they met in the house. Finally her temper flared when Callie informed her Mister Clint would not be home in time for lunch. Susan snapped at the old woman, "Nor will I!"

She flounced out of the room and up the stairway to change clothes. A ride on her mare might act as a tonic and release. It mattered not to her that Clint had most likely spent the night in Madame Fifi's, but to embarrass her by staying away all day without a word riled her. Always before he'd had the decency to return to Shady Oaks in the early morning hours, and

216

it had caused no gossip among the servants. He'd gone too far this time.

She rode out of Shady Oaks aimlessly and let the mare have her way. Suddenly she reined up with the realization that she was at the long, winding drive leading up to Montclair. Why had she come here?

"Well, perhaps I should just drop in on my good friends, the Edwardses. I just might find my wayward husband." She giggled, as a nasty thought took hold of her. How startled Clint would be if he should be visiting Elise in Lance's absence and she made an appearance.

Ushered into the sunny morning room and finding Elise there with her children left Susan stammering with embarrassment. It was certainly no clandestine affair but a scene quite the opposite. Susan was filled with envy looking upon Elise's serene face. She had so much love surrounding her, it seemed to Susan. Looking down at the baby Lanissa lying contentedly in her cradle and young Andy playing on the floor at Elise's feet Susan mused silently that this was how it should be.

Elise sensed Susan's apprehensions and she assured her she needed no invitation or excuse to stop by Montclair. "We're friends, for heaven's sake!"

Susan took a seat on the bright floral settee and began to relax. Of all the women she knew, she felt she'd had more in common with Elise. From the moment they'd met the two had been able to talk together freely. Yet, there was this gnawing thing, this poison within her she could not control.

After a while they fell into lighthearted conversation and Susan was ever so grateful she had found Elise alone. She had no desire to face Lance Edwards after the other night.

However, he did appear later, and the sight of him set her heart pounding wildly. Dear God he took her breath away, standing there in the door in tight-fitting fawn colored pants with his shirt sleeves rolled to the elbows. His hair was slightly rumpled and he ran his fingers through it to remove it from his face. His black eyes stabbed at Susan with questioning fury. He gave her a curt greeting and left with a brief comment to Elise.

He could not believe his eyes as he stomped out to the stables. Dear God, she was a brazen hussy! How could she sit there with Elise, being so friendly after what she'd said to him only a few nights ago? He felt a pang of sorrow for Clint Barron.

He vowed he'd kill the bitch if she was there for some more of her devilment. Her venom was still lingering within him, and he cussed himself for allowing it to remain there in the deep abyss of his thoughts.

He strode to the stable, kicking at the earth like some raging bull. If he was Barron, he would beat the hell out of her for the display she made of herself in front of his friends.

Back in the morning room Elise noticed the sudden change in Susan's manner. It was not like her to not show Andy attention, for she'd always acted like she adored the boy. Nor was Elise prepared when Susan jumped up from the settee and announced she had to be going.

"But you just got here Susan, and I wanted to gossip about the party with you. I didn't have more than five minutes' conversation with you the whole evening, and that was when we first arrived," Elise said, rising up from her seat.

"I know, but we'll do it the next time," Susan replied, almost rushing for the door.

Elise was left perplexed but gave it no more thought as the children demanded her attention.

Susan mounted up, but she reined the gelding toward the stable and her appearance there was too much for Lance. "I have nothing to say to you, Susan. Get the hell out of my sight—now!" He turned his back on her and walked away. He knew then and there something had to be done about the woman.

Susan gave out a wild kind of laugh watching Lance turn from her to walk into one of the stalls. She swore and cussed him under her breath and vowed he'd rue the day he'd turned his arrogant back on her. She'd make him pay dearly!

Lance was not the only one having tormented thoughts the rest of that day. Elise happened to be looking out of the window as Susan exited the stable and the shock of seeing her husband following her was more than she could swallow. Lance had made a hasty exit from the house after Susan's departure. They both had acted odd in the presence of the other.

Never had she had any reason to question Lance's faithfulness—until now. Should she come right out and ask him at dinner? Her head whirled and she felt queasy. If he admitted to an affair with Susan what would she do? *Mon Dieu*, how could he after all their love had endured?

The afternoon was a maze to her. First, she'd gone to her room and cried, then she'd washed her face with cold water, changed her gown, and sat by the window just to think. Once they'd been reunited, she'd never quizzed him about the many, many months they'd been apart when she was Joaquin's booty. Perhaps he had sought solace in the arms of women. Could she fault him for that? Had he faulted her for being the Spanish buccaneer's woman—mistress—during that horrible interlude of their life. Then there was Clint, who'd rescued her in Cuba and brought her to Shady Oaks. Yes, she'd been Clint's mistress, too. She covered her face again and gave way to tears. She did not know whether she could stand it if his love belonged to Susan.

An hour later she rose from the chair. The vixen he accused her of being took over and once again she changed her gown. Then she styled her hair and dabbed some jasmine water behind her ears and along the soft crease of her breasts before going downstairs. She'd be damned if she'd be a weeping, meek little wife.

The firebrand in her would not tolerate it.

Lance's handsomeness overwhelmed her as they dined by candlelight that night. Her breasts swelled with love and sadness at the thought of any other woman lying in his arms. His unusual quietness only pointed out to her that what she'd witnessed was significant.

He looked up to see her eyes gazing at him. What lay behind those beautiful green eyes? he mused. Never had she looked more beautiful or desirable to him. Soft, satiny skin exposed and invited the touch of a man. That was only a part of the vision. The honey-sweet lips parted slightly as if she wanted to say something. Her hair; what a crown of beauty it was tonight with the sparkling brilliance of her jeweled combs. Those eyes fringed with thick black lashes seemed to be saying something. But what? Although Elise could not know it, Susan Barron was the last thing on his mind.

Their talk was casual; of routine things. Elise concluded if his encounter with Susan was innocent then he would have explained how it happened.

Lance decided as he studied her ravishing beauty that perhaps it was asking too much for him to expect that a woman like Elise could have resided on Barataria with Jean Laffite without sharing his bed. Laffite had a magnetic charm, he'd agree. She'd lived all those weeks thinking he and Andy were dead.

Loving a woman like Elise could be heaven and hell, he dejectedly surmised.

Jean Laffite swam and struggled in a sea of dejection as well as puzzlement when he arrived at Antonia's home to find her and her servants gone. The strange servant who answered his knock knew nothing of the lady's strange departure. He returned to his mount and rode off in the night.

Laffite headed toward the smithy shop to join his brother Pierre and Dominique You. He could not have known that he had passed the carriage carrying Antonia and her older sister Lucia like ships that pass in the night. They had now completed their secret rendezvous with Granville Harris, and he'd escorted them to the hired carriage to be taken out of the city.

Granville was glad to be rid of the despicable pair. Never had he liked the two Latin women, not anymore than he cared for many of his cohorts in the game of spying. For the most part it was a dirty business, and its players were a lot of misfits in society.

Being an English spy seemed most unlikely for a lad who had been born on American soil, in Charleston, South Carolina. Most likely, it would never have been had he not seen his young sister Elvira raped by American soldiers, not the British soldiers from whom his family was fleeing during the war. It was at that point Granville vowed vengeance for his sister.

Many families were fleeing just ahead of the invading British that night so long ago. It was just outside the city that a troop of soldiers stopped them, relieving their wagons of their goods and food supplies. Two of the soldiers decided to satisfy their lusty appetite with his fifteen-year-old sister. The trauma had an overwhelming effect on the seventeen-year-old Granville. Another young hellion and his family had fled the city that night, and since that night Granville had not laid eyes on his youthful friend until a few days ago.

He recognized Zack Hart immediately when he almost bumped into him in the Grand Hotel lobby. But Zack never blinked an eye as they exchanged brief, darting glances. However, Granville didn't need to look in a mirror to know that life had not been kind to him and he looked much older than his actual age.

Chapter 14

Cloudy, overcast skies and daily downpours had lingered over the delta countryside, making the journey up the Mississippi River anything but pleasant for Duke Donavan and Delphine. By the time they finally arrived in Natchez Delphine was ill, running a fever and chilling.

Duke secured quarters for them and got Delphine in bed as soon as possible. Feeling awkward and helpless, he insisted she finish all the hot broth and tea he'd ordered. When he saw that she was going off to sleep, he told her to rest while he sought out the man who'd promised him a job. His pockets were not filled with enough funds to keep them long without a flow of money coming in.

Delphine merely nodded as he left the room. For the first time in his vagabond life, Duke felt an honest concern for someone other than himself. His love for the beautiful octoroon was genuine. For a drifting rascal such as he it was a new, slightly disturbing advent.

All the way up the river Delphine had been just as perplexed about her new status in life. It seemed she'd been Clint Barron's woman forever, but she could never be his wife. At least Duke Donavan wanted her, and she had no doubt that the good-looking gambler really cared for her. For months Clint had not even sought the senuous pleasures of her body.

Her life before going to live on the grand plantation was a blur. But when the sixteen-year-old servant was taken to the bed of the handsome, blond master of the house her life began. Each time he returned to Shady Oaks from a voyage at sea he sought her out. By her eighteenth birthday, Delphine was exalted to his housekeeper and mistress. She was filled with pride and lorded it over the other servants.

She yearned for no more the rest of her life. However, Captain Barron returned from the Caribbean one day with a beautiful woman whom he supposedly rescued from a shipwreck off the coast of Cuba. For many months the woman remained his guest. She became his mistress and Delphine knew she'd never have that kind of doting love from Clint Barron. Elise Edwards had bewitched her man, and life was never the same at Shady Oaks.

Only when the dashing Lance Edwards came to New Orleans in search of his wife did Clint Barron relinquish his claim on Elise. Delphine had hoped desperately that he would turn to her, but instead it was Susan Hart he turned to.

Shortly after Susan's marriage to Clint, Delphine found herself employed at Madame Fifi's fabulous house of pleasure. She also found out that she was expecting Clint's child. For almost two years it had been a happy arrangement; Clint visited her regularly and Fifi was kind and good to her. Clint's baby daughter Dominique filled her heart and her hours. She was still Clint's woman, so she was content.

At first, Clint's perplexing absences from Fifi's puzzled her. Then through the grapevine of gossip she heard about Elise's return to the city. She'd blamed her for Clint's staying away from Fifi's.

Then one day Clint called on her and played lovingly with his little daughter. He spoke freely and openly of Elise and told Delphine about the Edwardses' new baby.

Somehow Delphine knew that Clint was staying away from her for reasons other than Elise Edwards. Remembering the beautiful green-eyed woman and the great passion she felt for her hsuband, Delphine could not fault her. No, she knew deep in her heart what kept Clint from her and would always keep them apart, that drop of negro blood in her veins. With "the black Irishman," as Duke jokingly called himself, it had not mattered. This had urged her to make the decision she made, but she had hardly been away from Fifi's thirty minutes when she was tempted to go back. A part of her remained there, and a foreboding prodded her that she might never see her baby again.

As they'd traveled farther away from the city up the muddy river, reaching the bend in the river and the high bluffs announcing their arrival in Natchez, Delphine had grown more depressed and frightened. Even Duke's strong, loving arms did not offer the safe, secure feeling she needed so desperately.

The country road was a wet, spongy mire due to the constant rain. The sudden breaking out of the sun had inspired Elise to get out of the house. Lance's constant bragging about his new thoroughbred Satan had whetted Elise's curiosity. Once she walked over to the stable and saw the handsome white beast she fell in love with the spirited animal.

With the mischief of an impetuous child flashing in her green eyes, she rushed back into the house and changed into her riding clothes. Returning to the stable she ordered the stable boy, Baptiste, to saddle the horse for her.

"Madame, Monsieur Edwards will have my hind for this," he declared with concern etching his face.

"And I will have your hind if you don't, Baptiste! So hurry!" Softening her sharp tongue, she added, "Do not worry, Baptiste, I will clear you of any blame should my husband voice any objections."

The young Creole could not have refused her

anyway. Like most of the servants at Montclair, young Baptiste was infatuated by his mistress. Awestruck by her beauty, he found himself embarrassed in her presence, and by the strange, exciting effect she had on his fifteen-year-old being. When she smiled so sweetly, as she was doing just then, he felt like he was slowly, but surely melting into the ground.

"Satan is ready, Madame Edwards. Please take care," he could not resist cautioning her. The fine animal was already prancing, proud and full of fire and fury. Elise allowed Baptiste to help her mount, and she reined the horse around.

Baptiste said a silent prayer as he watched her ride away. Finally, her dark green attire blended into the countryside and he could see her or the huge white horse no more, so he went about his chores.

Elise was in the best of spirits, feeling like her own petite body was fused to the animal's, and she was feeling very smug that she was handling the high-spirited animal magnificently.

She had gone over a mile down the road bordering the north edge of their land. The waters of the river were higher than she'd imagined from all the recent rains, and in some of the lower spots the river spilled over the banks. She was unprepared for the covey of quail that rushed out of the underbrush, and their surprised flight frightened Satan as well.

He reared up and Elise felt herself going

backward. Too late she tried to tighten her grasp on the reins. The soft mud sprayed over her as she slammed to the ground and her hat flew into a small pool of standing water. She was furious when she tried to pull herself up only to slide back down in the bog again.

"Sweet Jesus!" She flung her hands up in despair and just sat there a moment to regain her composure. Her lovely outfit was a mess and she needed no mirror to know her face and hair were smeared with mud. She could not even wipe her face, for her hands were covered with mud as well.

The fine white animal stood quietly by and Elise looked up at him. He seemed to be smirking at her there in the mud puddle. "Don't look down your arrogant nose at me, Satan! You weren't spared either. You aren't so lily white now yourself," she fumed. Placing her hands in front of her, she raised forward hoping for a better balance.

Had it not been such a comical sight, Lance would have been furious with his wife. He'd been riding through the field approaching the road to take the shortcut back home when his stunned eyes caught sight of the white thoroughbred galloping down the road with his wife atop him. He'd reined his mare with the intention of intercepting her.

He was some 200 yards directly behind her when he saw the horse rear up and Elise tumble into the mud hole. At first he gasped with fear that she would be hurt, but then he saw that she was more mad than hurt and he roared with laughter.

Riding the horse slowly toward her, he said not a word to alert her to his presence and merely observed her. Served the little vixen right, he mused, smiling devilishly. Instead of rushing to her side as a gallant, thoughtful husband should, he allowed her to struggle, slipping and sliding in the quagmire. Elise had no idea that he sat atop his mount, watching her with a broad, amused smile on his face.

She stood up finally, shaking one soaked foot and then the other like a tabby cat. Lance could not suppress his laughter any longer.

"Well damnit, help me!" Elise was mortified. Of all the people to come upon her why did it have to be Lance.

"Madame, how fetching you look!" he teased her, leaping down from the horse. Then and there the idea emerged, as Elise looked upon his teasing face. His devious black eyes surveyed her and it made her even madder. Besides the wet clothes pressed against her, chilling her to the bones.

She looked up at her amused husband dressed in his warm brown jacket and matching pants, so neat and spotless. Mischief ignited within her and she determined he should suffer along with her for laughing so at her misfortune. She urged sweetly in her most helpless voice, "Just stretch your hand out to me, *mon cheri*, and then you won't have to get in that awful mud hole, dear. I think I can make it then."

Having no inkling what she was plotting, Lance reached out his hand to her and gasped with surprise and utter shock when she gave a sharp tug, causing him to slide and tumble down by her side.

"Why you little—"

Elise convulsed into laughter until she felt his two strong arms encircling her legs, causing her to slide back down just as she'd managed to rise up. Shrieking and cursing in French, she found herself back in the mud again. Lance laughed so hard tears ran down his cheeks. Finally, Elise joined him, declaring that she prayed no one else was witnessing their insanity.

"Got a marvelous idea, love. Let's go home, share a warm bath, crawl in bed with a warm brandy and—"

Elise interrupted, "Monsieur, you are dreadful, but let's go!" Together, they helped one another up. On the ride to the house one or the other would explode with a laugh thinking about their silliness.

"What will the servants think of us, Lance?" Elise asked him. He gave her a sly wink of the eye, answering, "Who cares, *ma petite!* It will give them something to talk about for a day or two."

"Especially Jessamine." Elise laughed.

It was true what Elise had said about Jessamine. She began forming a romantic plot even as she sauntered slowly down the hall, hearing the soft laugh of her mistress echoing from the room. She'd been dismissed after serving them two snifters of brandy.

Elise's skin glowed from the warm bath scented with bath oil, and the sight of her golden skin intoxicated Lance far more than the brandy. She gave him a lazy smile, enjoying the appraising way his black eyes danced around over her body. He needed to say nothing out loud.

Placing his glass on the table and snuffing out his cheroot, he walked over to the bed. His slightly damp hair formed ringlets of small black curls on his long sideburns, and the same curly ringlets on his broad, tanned chest. She thought to herself he had reason to flaunt his maleness so conceitedly, for he was a most magnificent man. That he was her man filled her with a certain female smugness, she'd not deny.

Like a magnet and a pin they came together, both eager for the feel and touch of the other's body. That was always a glorious moment. Slowly and easily, he adjusted her to him. "Ah, you fit me so perfectly, *chérie!*" His breath was a sweet warmth, like a soft plume teasing and fluttering across her neck.

The satin coverlet enclosed them like a cocoon, blotting out the afternoon sun. Lance leisurely made love to her, waiting until she could stand it no longer and demand that he fill her. He loved to watch her impassioned face as he gave that first magnificent thrust, and feel the responding arch of her body eagerly meeting his with a penetrating liquid warmth.

Elise's hand urged him on. "Lance? I—"

"Yes, darling!" He answered, his breath coming in heavy heaves, burying himself deep to fulfill her plea. Elise moaned a pleased sigh feeling his heated flesh within her, undulating sensuously. As the tides moved in and out, so did their bodies, faster and faster until they were swallowed up in one gigantic tidal wave, tossing and turning, swirling and rotating them in a whirlpool of sensations. With the ebbing tide, both sank exhausted and sated ready for sleep. A serene sweet sleep!

At Shady Oaks, a serene sleep had evaded Susan Barron for nights now. During the days Susan was haunted by the all-knowing black eyes of old Callie. Dear God, the black woman drove her crazy! She made Susan feel as though she was the intruder instead of the mistress, and from the minute Susan had arrived at Shady Oaks she sensed old Callie felt it was Elise instead of Susan who should be mistress. There were times when she wondered if the old woman put her voodoo hexes on her. She knew the old woman watched her like a hawk. Perhaps Clint had instructed her to do so, Susan mused. To be rid of her would, no doubt, please him.

Clint had maintained his distant, aloof manner since the night of the party, and she'd hardly seen him. His nights were spent away from the house and he offered no explanation as to where he was. It was an embarrassment, but then she'd lost the last ounce of pride a long time ago. She knew the gossip going around the servant quarters, but that didn't matter. She couldn't care less.

Since the night of the party Clint had sought solitude, hoping to come up with some solution to his problems, which could not go unchecked. It was obvious to him that his wife became more unstable each day and drank more. He was troubled about what to do for his young daughter. One thing was for sure; he could not bring her to Shady Oaks. It was for the child's safety, he considered. That Susan knew she was his daughter by Delphine mattered not to him. If only she was older he could have sent her to his friends in London.

If only he'd had good sense he would have taken Delphine away for many months and returned with her as his bride from Europe. No one would have been the wiser, for Delphine could have easily passed for Spanish, French or Italian. What a fool he'd been. It was too late for that now. But he would seek the counsel of someone he respected.

The next day Susan watched from her bedroom window as her husband rode out of Shady Oaks, as was his habit lately. She had no idea where he was off to for they continued to live under the same roof like strangers.

The last remnants of winter remained over the countryside, but hints of spring seemed to be emerging, it seemed to Clint as he galloped down the dirt road. When Shady Oaks was out of sight he suddenly reined up on the mare to enjoy the serene beauty of the golden day. A lightheartedness abided within him that he'd not felt for a long time, and he knew it had to be the simple fact that he was seeing and talking with his dear Elise.

The creatures of nature seemed to be alive and active. He chuckled watching a couple of squirrels chasing one another up and down a tree, and a fat robin sitting on the branch of one of the young saplings near the road. It dawned on him that it was the first time he'd laughed in a long time. God Almighty, a man should be able to laugh more often! He was a healthy man in his prime, and he had a fair amount of wealth. He had a lot of living to do. Hell, was it thirty-five years old he was on his last birthday?

It was this surge of vigor and zest to enjoy life he felt as he arrived at Elise's. Zack had told him that Lance had left for Mobile. He'd not deny for a minute that the prospects of his absence from Montclair pleased him. Now he could visit with Elise alone.

He tied his mare to the hitching post and jauntily walked up the boxwood bordered path leading up to the front entrance. However, he never mounted the first step. His eyes were pulled to the south of the house in the direction of the stable.

Her black hair was flowing, loose and free.

235

Her tiny figure was molded in perfection in her simple muslin gown, and a light shawl was covering her shoulders. But to Clint Barron she looked like a princess. Her face brightened radiantly when her eyes met his, and she threw up her hand to wave. He watched with utter delight as she walked hastily toward him. What tantalizing grace she moved with. Clint Barron knew for a fact that Elise didn't, nor probably had in her life, realized the overwhelming effect she cast on men as they encountered her. Even he could not pinpoint it, and God knows, he'd tried. But it was more than the beautiful face and figure.

"Clint! So good to see you. Is this not a perfect day," she declared, smiling so charmingly up at him that he ached to take her in his arms.

"Yes, perfect. I don't have to ask how you are, Elise. I'll swear you just get prettier all the time," he said.

"Oh, Clint, you're sweet!" In a flippant gesture, she curtsied. "I thank you for your nice compliment." They both laughed, with Clint taking hold of her arm as they casually walked toward the house. Neither could know that a pair of angry blue eyes were watching and reading false meanings into the scene they were observing.

After she could no longer see them and they'd gone into the house, Susan rode away. So the sonofabitch was making hay while the sun was shining and Lance was gone, she

236

muttered under her breath.

Clint sat in the morning room appraising Elise's well managed home and envying Lance Edwards his happy home, fine young son, and baby daughter. All that and Elise, too! How could one man be so darn lucky?

For a while they talked in an easy, casual manner, but Elise sensed that something was bothering Clint, and she said as much. Clint broke into a boyish, sheepish grin. "Your knowledge of me is a little disquieting Elise, and you are right. I do have something I'd like to talk about."

For the next hour, Clint bared his soul to Elise, leaving nothing out. Elise knew now what Annette had hinted about many times regarding Susan and Clint's marriage. Somehow she felt she was to blame for a part of Clint's unhappiness, for he had given so completely and she'd taken of his kindness and generosity.

"I had wondered so many times what had happened to Delphine. Oh, Clint, your . . . your daughter must be a beautiful child. I'd love to see her!"

A wan smile emerged on Clint's face. How like Elise to throw convention to the wind. She was unconcerned what people would say or think. "She is, Elise, absolutely beautiful. Perhaps, you can sometime."

Elise firmly urged that the child remain at Fifi's for the time being, after what he'd told her about Susan. "There has to be something, some way to work this out, Clint. Let me think on this. It has all caught me by surprise, as I'm sure you can understand," Elise told him. She knew at that moment she was going to seek the wise counsel of Annette Le Clere, for she could trust her older friend. She knew, too, that the Le Cleres felt a deep respect for Clint as a person.

Compassion and tenderness flooded her as she walked him to the door, and she was proud he was able to talk to her. After all, he had certainly helped her when she'd needed help most desperately, and that she could never forget.

Clint could not resist pulling her into his arms for one brief moment and planting a kiss on her forehead. "Oh God, Elise, why did things have to change? Why could they not have gone on?" His voice cracked with anguish.

Elise pulled away from his huge arms. "Please, Clint! Don't do this to us, please!"

Repentant, he hung his head. "I'm sorry, I shouldn't have said that. Better go, I guess."

"I'm glad you came to talk to me, Clint. After all, that's what it's all about with friends," Elise comforted him. In a way his visit had comforted her, for she had been vexed by Lance's announcement that he was making the run to Mobile. She let him know it before he left by inquiring why one of his captains could not as easily make the run. But his manner had been

238

evasive, and she had given way to various imaginings sleeping alone since he'd been gone.

Once again the gnawing thoughts returned about seeing Susan come from their stable. Elise was a woman possessive of the man she loved, and she could never share any part of him with another woman. With a man as virile and alive as Lance, she could not help pondering the possibility that he might yearn to return to his carefree days as a privateer and adventurer.

As quickly as possible Lance tended to his business in Mobile and set sail for Louisiana. His only stop once he'd disembarked in port, except for a brief conversation with Zack Hart, was Madame Vivienne's. His wife's wrath would hopefully be soothed by his special purchase. It pained him to have to keep her in the dark about his hasty mission but it was necessary.

As he approached Montclair, he saw Clint Barron's huge stallion galloping away; there was no mistaking Clint's lion's mane of golden blond hair. What the devil was he doing there? Lance wondered. If it wasn't Laffite sniffing around, it was Barron. He'd never fooled himself about Clint, even though he'd helped him and Elise come together by bringing Elise to him aboard the *Elise*. It was true that Clint had helped bridge the gap keeping them apart after Lance had found out Elise intended to marry Clint. But even now, when Clint was around Elise Lance saw the adoration in his eyes.

When he walked through the front door of his home and saw his wife's lovely face and his young son trailing behind her full flowing skirt any misgivings about Barron's visit were swept away.

Dropping the bundle he carried, he gathered her in his arms for a long, lingering kiss. Sweeping up Andy in one muscled arm, his other arm snaked around Elise's waist and the three of them went up the steps. After a few minutes playing with Andy, he took his son to the nurse and left Elise standing by their bedroom door.

Once his protesting son was deposited in the nursery he told Elise, "Be back in a minute. I got to get something. Wait right here, love!" He hurried down the stairs.

Elise ambled through the door of their bedroom. He was home and all loneliness was gone now, and all doubts. She realized how he breathed life into her with his dominative personality. Perhaps, she thought to herself as she waited for his return, that was why Clint could have never filled Lance's shoes, or taken his place in her heart.

He stood in the doorway. "I have something for you!" She turned and started to giggle. Mischief sparked in her eyes as she observed him standing there. "I see you have, *mon capitaine!*" She spoke not of the package but the tremendous mound exhibited in his tight-fitting deep blue pants.

It took a moment for her remark to register and then he, too, broke into laughter. Grabbing her, he muttered, "Ah, I'll make you pay for that. It's wicked you are, Elise Edwards!"

"And you made me so, Lance Edwards!"

Chapter 15

Elise played the coquette for Lance, kicking up her leg to display the new half-boots he'd surprised her with. Watching her scrutinize her reflection in the cheval glass, he was glad he'd detoured to Madame Vivienne's to pick up the new riding ensemble he'd ordered for her. She'd ruined her other one that day Satan tumbled her into the mire.

"Madame says it's the latest fashion from Paris, and I must say, love, you are the perfect model. Every woman in New Orleans will want those fancy boots," he declared.

The bright green of the outfit was no brighter than her eyes. The jacket and sleeves were trimmed with black braid. The black half-boots were laced and fringed in the same bright green. He'd even bought matching kid gloves to complete the outfit.

"I love it, Lance!" She rushed to him and sat on his lap, smothering him with kisses. Her long hair swept over his head and shoulders and he moved her ever so slightly in his arms so that she was reclining in his arms. With one hand he smoothed the thick mane away from her face.

"I'm glad, kitten," he whispered softly in her ear. His lips moved to capture her lips with fire and fury, and he found himself impatient to rid her of her new outfit.

"Lance?"

"Hmmmmm?"

"Let me up," she urged anxiously. Reluctantly, he released her. "My outfit, my darling," she reminded him standing up to remove the jacket. She stood in the small circle of space between his wide-spread legs and he watched admiring the teasing art she employed. Impatience took over and he raised to relieve himself of his shirt and pants.

It was only later that the two of them realized that Elise, in her haste to enjoy their love-making, had not removed the fringed half-boots. Both of them shook with laughter.

"Monsieur, you have to be the most wicked man to make your wife so wanton. 'Tis sinful!" She teased him with the intoxicating light-heartedness that washed over her.

Lance grabbed her, rolling her atop him. "Saint or sinner I may be, but you, my love, have to be a witch! You cast a spell on me with your beguiling ways." Giving her a swat on her bottom, he added, "Get up, you wanton! It's time I saw my son and little daughter. After all, I don't want them forgetting their father."

They both dressed hastily and made their way down the hall, arm in arm. Only then did he question why she had not mentioned the fact that Clint Barron had just left their home.

It had been almost a year since Elise had received any word from her beloved Tante Colette in London. Her letter had been months in finally arriving, and Elise read and reread it. It seemed London was a beehive of social activity and Colette wrote of the lively period they were enjoying. It stated how a certain Mrs. Fitzherbert was setting the fashion mode for London and played the hostess for the Prince Regent's famous parties. Viscount Wellington was made a Marquess, winning victory after victory for England against the French, and Prime Minister Spencer Perceval had been assassinated in the House of Commons.

Colette vowed that someday she and Jean Louis would journey to New Orleans to see them. Elise still had to remind herself once again that the former French nobleman who had married Tante Colette was her real father. To her, the Le Harve innkeeper Andre Cartiers was her father, for he had cared for her until his death. But she had liked Jean Louise de'Aumalie and had instantly warmed to him that first moment they'd met in London.

It was good to hear the latest news from her sister Olivia and her husband James Ashley. James had been thrilled to witness the launching of the first steamboat on the Clyde River as they just happened to have been vacationing at the Ashley's lodge in Scotland.

That part of Colette's letter interested Lance, for he was a firm believer in the advent of the steamboat and the advantage it would have in the future of shipping. The subject of shipping reminded him he must tear himself away from his wife and return to his offices in the city to see to business. So he bid her good-bye, reminding her it could be late when he returned home that evening.

Elise informed him that she thought she might pay a visit to Annette Le Clere that afternoon.

Fifi La Tour had not experienced such an overwhelming helplessness since God knows when. She'd sought the solace of her room and a bottle, pulling the rich, velvet drape to blot out the dreary, overcast day outside that seemed to reflect her mood.

Duke Donvan's unexpected visit with the news of Delphine's death had affected her more than she cared to admit. She'd become fond of the young woman during the many months she'd stayed at La Maison. Now she was pressed to make a decision on little Dominique. She couldn't raise a kid in a whorehouse, no matter how fancy or prosperous her establishment was. It was still a whorehouse, Fifi frankly admitted to herself.

Fifi decided she must seek out the wise counsel of her old friend. As it had been over the many years this bond of friendship existed cloistered in secrecy. Never did their paths cross socially. Yet, fate deemed that their paths cross when the two were mere girls, so young and disillusioned with the cruel world around them. What a lifetime ago that seemed now to Fifi!

Even then the two had come from totally different backgrounds and it was the older, Fifi, who had taken charge of the sheltered young miss who had been used to a life of servants tending to her every need. But that terrible night she'd been tossed from a moving carriage on a foggy London night with a chilling mist of rain moving in over the English Channel, Fifi had taken one look at her and dubbed her "Chickie." Throughout the years it was this name Fifi called her. For if ever she'd seen a drowned chicken, it was the beautiful girl who was now the poised, charming mistress of Bellefair.

It seemed they'd both shared the same fate that night on the desolate streets of London, and so they found refuge together. When the dashing young Frenchman took them under his wing and stowed them aboard the ship he was to travel aboard to the New World, they were both delighted and eager to accept his offer, having no other solution to their dilemma.

By the time the ship docked in Boston, it was obvious to Fifi that the good-looking Frenchman was in love with her friend. They left Boston after a few days to journey to New

Orleans. What a strange trio they made!

Seeking a new life, all decided to give themselves a new identity and name. So it was that her friends became Monsieur and Madame Francois Le Clere. She became Fifi La Tour and Fiona Kelly faded into the sunset one evening as they traveled down the muddy Mississippi River toward New Orleans.

Francois's gambling expertise won the fine plantation of Bellefair and the boarding house the three had first stayed in upon their arrival in the city. It was Francois who gave Fiona the house and furnishings now known as La Maison.

Dame Fortune had been generous to all three and often they laughed about the magnificent charade they'd pulled off. Whom of their friends would believe the fantastic tale if it was told? The aristocratic, wealthy Le Cleres and Fifi La Tour were dear friends dating back over twenty years.

Without further ado, Fifi sent the usual message to Bellefair when she wished or needed a meeting.

Madame Fifi's girls were always curious when the veiled, exquisitely gowned lady arrived at the establishment and was ushered directly to Fifi's suite upstairs. The sweet fragrance always trailed behind in the hallway. Wildflowers was what one of the girls had dubbed it.

As the two women closeted themselves there for an hour or two, Titus was the only one allowed to enter. The few times one of the girls had had the audacity to question who the woman was a sharp tongue-lashing was forthcoming from the hefty madam.

The visit this time was like the others, with Titus taking in a bottle of Fifi's favorite sherry and making a hasty exit.

Inside the room the two women warmly embraced one another and then sat down with their glasses of sherry. Fifi told her of her dilemma and Annette listened intensely. When Fifi finished, Annette patted her hand assuredly.

"I have the perfect solution, Fifi. Bessie just lost a baby. She and Sam would be delighted, and the child would be a delight for me and Francois. That is the one thing Francois and I weren't blessed with. I'd love having a darling, little daughter. You know how I always yearned for one."

"I know, Chickie. That brings me to another subject, and you know what I'm talking about."

Annette smiled sheepishly, "No, Fifi, not yet! I can't bring myself to tell him. Somehow, the right time has not come."

Fifi raised a skeptical brow, shook her head, and sighed. "Well, if he's half the man he must be he'll be happy to know that you are his mother. You've spoke so often of him and his wife and what good friends you are. You see, he already likes you, *chérie*. Besides, our days fly by so fast. I, for one, realize that more and more."

"They do, don't they, Fifi?" Annette remarked thoughtfully. While she knew herself
to be fortunate to have retained her smooth
skin and a presentable, trim figure, she had to
admit she took more time to sit and rest,
reading or sewing. It had come to her attention
that Francois, her darling Francois, seemed to
have aged so the last few weeks. Perhaps the
young girl would be good for him, brightening
his days. Yet, he vowed he felt wonderful when
she quizzed him about his health. Annette had
never questioned Francois's word.

"We have no right to put off anything,
Chickie—not at our age." Fifi laughed, slapping Annette's knee. Annette broke into a
laugh herself. As always, a visit with her dear
friend lifted her spirits, but it was time for her
to be starting home so she could reach there
before darkness fell over the countryside. She
pulled the dark veil down and said farewell to
Fifi with the madam's admonishing words
ringing in her ears as she made her way to her
carriage. "Tell your son the truth!"

All the way home Fifi's words wafted to her
ears. Did she dare and chance the look of hate
emerging there? At least she enjoyed a friendship with him and Elise. She knew he admired
and respected her. Was this not better than
chancing him despising her?

Chapter 16

A vociferous, celebrating crowd lined the sandy shores of Barataria. Lighted torches dotted the beaches and a cluster of the pirates sat drinking. Some couples were in the act of making love, shameless or uncaring that they were being observed.

This was the scene greeting Jean Laffite and his brother Pierre when they returned from New Orleans. In order to make their way to Jean's house, they had to step over the bodies, empty bottles, and foodstuffs scattered about.

While Jean had participated in similar celebrations himself many times, tonight it repulsed him. He did not seek out or congratulate the couple for whom the fete had been staged. In fact he'd been so preoccupied that he'd forgotten that Vega asked his permission to take Lola for his wife.

He wasted no time once inside his quarters but went straight to his bedroom to undress for bed. A fleeting thought about Vega's young son crossed his mind seeing his neatly laundered shirts placed on the bed. How had he taken the union of Lola with his father? Jean pondered. The shirts tediously washed by old Nadja were always picked up by Julio and brought to the house, so he had been there today.

In the next room by the massive stone fireplace a blanket-covered body lie sleeping soundly on a pallet near the hearth. It was at Jean's house young Julio had sought refuge from the feasting.

Tonight he was tired but tomorrow he must check with his lieutenants and see what had been going on in his island home, his little dynasty here on Barataria. For to the residents there he was the patron and their ruler. They looked to him for guidance and protection.

His men serving him had joined for many and varied reasons. There were misfits of society, drifters, and sons of wealthy families from New Orleans among his cohorts. The women had been taken as bounty from the ships they preyed on, while others had come along due to a fondness for one of his men, desiring to be their lovers and mistresses. All looked upon Jean as the leader.

They had their own code of laws and justice in this colony of people from all walks of life and nationalities.

The next morning he took his usual jaunt around the compound. Encountering his friend Vega, Jean gave his congratulations and a fat pouch of gold coins. Only as he took his leave from the obviously happy bridegroom did he realize that his "little shadow," Julio, was not trailing around with him as was his habit. Where was the youth? he wondered.

An hour later, after he'd surveyed the rich bounty of Black Jack's recent raid, the thought gnawed at him again as to where young Julio might be. He sauntered aimlessly along the path, throwing his hand up to wave at the island women at the doorways of the huts. It was a hodgepodge of humanities abiding there, he mused thoughtfully. Nevertheless, it was his kingdom!

His hands examined the magnificent etched silver dagger Black Jack had just given to him from the bounty. It was an excellent piece of workmanship, and Jean realized with appreciation the skill exhibited there.

At that moment, Jean's dark eyes glanced over to old Nadja's humped figure sitting near her doorway, and it was Julio's black curly head he recognized popping up behind her. He smiled, walking over to speak to the boy. Old toothless Nadja was surely filling his head with her nonsense about the future. Declaring herself a Romany, she swore she could tell anyone who'd listen what the future held for them. Jean put little stock in the old gypsy's forecasts.

"Julio!"

"Ssssh! Don't disturb Nadja!" The old woman chided him, pointing her bony finger in his direction.

Like an obedient servant, Jean complied with the old woman's command. No harm in pampering the old woman, so he stood silently to hear what she was telling the boy. With the same bony finger she'd shook at Jean, she now drew the letter L in the sand. "Your greatest joy and your greatest sorrow will come from this." Julio looked at the letter drawn in the sand.

"To the east and the south, my son, there lies your destiny." Her words made no sense to him at all. Never could he imagine leaving Barataria and his idol, Jean Laffite.

At the old lady's insistence, Jean sat in Julio's spot. She looked him sternly in the eye, declaring, "You will not get what you desire, for it was written otherwise long ago. Forget it, Mister Jean. To pursue would be to perish." The wizened-faced old hag frowned and gave a sudden jerk.

"What's the matter, old lady?" Jean prodded.

"Danger, but not to you. A black-haired lady."

Did she speak of Antonia? Could it have something to do with her sudden exit from New Orleans?

"What kind of danger, Nadja? Can you tell me that?"

"The worst—her life!"

While he was not a superstitious man, the old woman's revelation troubled him as he and Julio walked along the beach. "I think we would have both been lighter of heart had we not talked to Nadja." Jean laughed, hoping to bring a smile to Julio's face. But the boy only nodded.

Laffite flashed the dagger in front of the boy. "What do you think of this, Julio? Is it not something?"

The boy examined it almost cautiously and finally he turned his dark eyes up at Jean. "Oh, Mister Jean, it is a fine piece!"

"Then it is yours. I'm . . . I'm truly sorry I've been so remiss in rewarding you properly for your brave act against the evil Sebastian. It was a daring thing you did in saving my friend Madame Edwards, and I was far too long in not letting you know of my appreciation," Jean beamed pridefully at the youth and patted him on the shoulders.

"Oh, thank you, Mister Jean!" Julio trembled with pride and the special tribute Jean Laffite had just paid him. In a cracking voice he asked to take his leave, for he could not wait to display his fine gift to all he came upon and tell them it was the great Laffite who had presented the dagger to him.

Jean waved for the boy to be on his way and sauntered alone along the beach. The mention of her name and the soft slapping surf teasing his boot brought the vivid image of her to mind. A petrifying thought grabbed at him like a giant claw squeezing his chest. Could there be a grain of truth in old Nadja's words? The woman's face he envisioned was not Antonia's, but Elise's.

Was he, the great Laffite, never to be rid of the fever in his blood for the married woman he could never have? Was that what Nadja meant when she told him he'd not have what he desired most? Perhaps the old hag was right!

His pirate's heart told him that should the opportunity ever present itself, he'd take her without a qualm of conscience.

Not far away from the site where Jean had sought the solitude of the beach, young Julio had flung himself down on the sand, smiling happily and breathing hard. He'd scurried all over the place to boast of his reward from Jean Laffite. His dark face was flushed with excitement and the broad smile seemed cemented to his face.

He lie with his head cradled in his hand gazing up at the skies of azure blue. Lazy daydreams paraded through his youthful head. He envisioned strange places he'd go to and the wildest of adventures he'd undertake. He'd take rich bounty and conquer beautiful women like Mister Jean had.

With these random thoughts dominating his being, he'd forgotten all about the disturbing fact that his father had taken as his bride the spitfire Lola. Let him have her, Julio told himself! He'd certainly never consider her his mother, for she was far too young. Besides, he became nervous and flustered by her nearness. His young body experienced wild, strange sensations, and his heart pumped so fast he felt he couldn't breathe. Besides, her eyes smiled at him when they moved down and over his trim body, and he felt naked standing before her.

Julio had no knowledge of the promising handsomeness an experienced woman could see so readily. His firm, rounded buttocks and muscled thighs were obvious, and his small waist tapered upward to his broad shoulders and chest. His flashing white teeth looked even whiter framed against his olive skin. With his jet black, wavy hair and dark eyes, almost black, he could have passed for Jean's son. While his nature was a serious one, there was a devilish gleam in his dark eyes that gave him the air of a rogue.

But young Julio had yet to discover these traits about himself, and it would be a few years before he did. He could not know this day how his dark handsomeness would melt a young girl's heart whose life at that moment was so remote and foreign to him. Had someone told him all these things, he would have laughed at the absurdity. Old Nadja knew, but she dared not tell him more. It would happen, it was written in the stars.

This same day, far away from Barataria on the veranda of the plantation house at Bellefair, children's laughter rang out. A small boy in his striped duck pantaloons and dark blue jacket scurried across the carpeted grass to capture the bright red ball he and the little girl had been playing with.

A smaller little girl clapped her dimpled

hands with delight, watching the two older children play. The two women watched the three with unguarded pride for all were beautiful children.

"It's like we've found the fountain of youth, Elise. Why, Francois has surely lost his heart to the precious little girl already!" Annette told her friend.

"Your face tells the whole story, Annette. I've never seen you look more radiant," Elise declared. "And I know how happy Clint must be to know his little daughter is safe and secure with you and Francois." Elise had been tempted to take on the child, but even the hint of it did not set well with Lance. She measured the cost to go against his wishes and decided to drop the subject. As everything had turned out, she was glad she'd not been her usually headstrong self.

Lance's impression of the situation was that no one should have to assume Clint's responsibility. He left no doubt that he considered Clint's failure to do so a weakness. His brief curt retort to Elise had been, "The child is his. If he were man enough to get her, he bloody well ought to see to her care!" Upon that snapping remark, he'd walked out of the room.

Annette interrupted Elise's musing with the comment that Clint came over about twice a week. "I could swear, Elise— I know that once I saw that red hair of Susan's skulking back there under that grove of trees. I'd swear she'd followed him and spied on him the other day.

Francois thinks I've just imagined it. A vivid imagination, he jokes."

Regardless of Lance's feelings, Elise felt sorry for Clint and hoped that he and Susan would have a happy marriage. There seemed to be little hope for that now.

Once again Annette's soft accented voice broke into her thoughtful musings. "The girl is unstable, Elise. I know you and Susan have always been friends, but please bear that fact in mind, my dear." Annette felt she must warn her little friend for there was no doubt in her mind that Susan Barron's resentment and envy of Elise was deeply implanted and she could be capable of any evil trick.

Lance had only to look upon her face when he picked her up at Bellefair to know she was troubled. They rode toward Montclair, saying little. When they did finally break the silence, their conversation was to end with both snapping at one another.

Elise had casually remarked about the little girl's presence bringing new life to the elder couple. Lance surmised frankly, "I admire both of the Le Cleres very much as you well know, but I still say it will not work out. Sorry if I offend you love, but I still question the guts of our friend Barron."

His whole manner riled Elise. Why was he so harsh and critical of Clint? First it was Jean and now Clint.

She turned slowly on the seat and searched his stern, firm-set features. "That is your privilege, Lance."

It was not her words, but the tone of them that angered him. He practically spit out the words, "Yes, it is!"

It wasn't his remark but the blazing fury in his black eyes that made Elise turn away from him to look out over the land. What was bringing on all this hostility in him? Did this mood he was in have anything to do with the longer hours he'd been spending at his office?

Many things had bothered Lance the last few weeks that he'd not discussed, and he'd tried to not give in to the long weary hours of having to carry the burden of his duties plus Zack's. Lance blamed Zack Hart's troubled mind on Susan's wildness. It was nothing to observe her and Charles Burke jaunting around the city in his opened carriage, as if to announce her brazen behavior for any or all to see.

As if it wasn't enough to have rumors flying all over the city, she had arrived at the Hart-Edwards Lines one afternoon. As one of their captains was leaving Lance's office, Susan had rushed in, making remarks that would have left the impression of a clandestine meeting between her and Lance. He had been tempted to wring her pretty neck, but he had too much respect for Zack.

The captain had already made a hasty exit by the time Lance told her off in a stern, insulting way that should have embarrassed her. However, Susan only threw her head back and laughed, "Oh, Lance, you're really becoming an old fuddyduddy! A real bore!"

Lance smirked. "Then madam, why don't you remove yourself from my boring presence. In truth, I find you the same; dull and boring!"

"Oh, I'll make you sorry for that, Lance Edwards! You wait and see!" She swished her ruffled skirt and marched out of the office. His laughter rang in her ears infuriating her more. How dare he insult her like she was a trollop!

Hell, Clint Barron seemed unable to handle anything in his life. Poor bastard, Lance thought to himself, shaking his head in disgust! He had forgotten somewhere along the way how to be a man.

Lance decided he must gamble on the long friendship with Zack Hart. He wanted the old rough and ready Zack Hart back and this depressed lethargic Zack had to go.

He sought him out in the warehouse to suggest a couple of drinks and some man-talk about the latest news the packet ship had brought back about the developments in Florida.

Zack accepted and the two went to a nearby tavern. Lance informed him about General Jackson being given the command by the Department of the South in Mobile. He had succeeded in driving the British out of Pensacola.

Zack openly admired the general and had for many years. For the first time in ages, he broke out in loud laughter. "Well, I'll be a sonofabitch!"

After Zack's mood was relaxed and casual talk about their mutual interest in the fleet line was discussed, Lance spoke of Susan in unrestrained honesty, telling Zack everything.

Zack's face displayed a contrast of emotions. One minute Lance could have sworn he was coming at him with fists clinched tight, the nerves in his jaw twitching in anger. The next moment he saw a mist gathering in his pale blue eyes.

Lance steeled himself in the chair for whatever came his way. Damnit, he liked Zack Hart! There were times he warmed to the man as he would have liked to have warmed to Sir Malcolm, his true father. There were other times when he looked upon the rugged Zack Hart as an older brother, for he had never felt any brotherly kinship toward his younger half-brother with his effeminate ways.

Finally, Zack's demeanor seemed to come to terms with the anger. He looked across at Lance. Slowly he reached out his hand. There was a slight cracking of his voice as he spoke. "Thank you, my friend! I needed the truth pointed out to me about Susan. And . . . and I know what it cost you to have the guts to spell it out to me."

Lance's broad chest felt like a heavy load had been lifted, and he heaved a deep sigh. A broad smile came to his face slowly. He clasped Zack's hand in a firm handshake.

"In fact, I think the next time I see Clint Barron I'll give him my permission to turn

Susan over his lap and beat the hell out of her with my blessing!" The two exploded in raucous laughter, caring not that the other patrons of the tavern were staring in their direction.

"A woman's gotta' be tamed, Zack. I, of all people know that!" Lance joked.

"Yeah, but it can be a hell of a lot of fun, as I remember with that pert little Irish lass of mine. Susan's mom was a little spitfire, real hellcat!"

"I agree with you. I've enjoyed every minute of it . . . well, almost every minute," Lance confined, winking his eye.

By the time they parted company late in the afternoon Zack Hart was in high spirits. Lance rode toward Montclair elated with the transformation he'd witnessed there in the tavern. He could not help being pleased that he'd helped bring it all about.

His spirits soared even higher the next day learning that down in Venezuela Simon Bolivar had won his fight for independence and was declared the virtual dictator. Again, he felt a small degree of satisfaction that he'd shared a small portion in the historical event. He wished Bolivar well and pondered if General Miranda was there sharing the rewards of victory.

Without the much needed firearms and ammunition that were so vital to their endeavor the end of the struggle could not have been accomplished. At least, Lance reasoned, it would have taken much longer, and taken more lives. Yes, he felt a certain gratification and pride that his efforts had helped the cause. The cargo he'd carried into Venezuela from Cuba surely aided Bolivar and Miranda's fight for independence.

Chapter 17

Since the day of old Nadja's predictions Jean had been obsessed by thoughts of Elise Edwards. It was madness, and he knew it! Why could he not shrug aside his feeling for her as easily as he had for Antonia Delgardo. With the firey Latin lady it had been as easy as with all other women in his life.

The overwhelming urge to see her came over him during the late night hours as well as during the daytime. Was it possible the old toothless gypsy's words bore a grain of truth? Should he warn Elise?

He never battled such a war of conflicting emotions. He tried stripping away all his masculine pride by asking himself honestly if it was her indomiable will not to be conquered by him that urged him on.

For one brief moment, he knew she'd responded to him with a fired passion of her own. He'd made love to far too many women before and since not to recognize it that night so long ago when she was on Barataria. Then, in the next moment, she'd turned on him like a little wildcat. Damnit, he knew it then and he knew it now: She was fighting! Any other woman who had allowed him to go that far he would have taken by force, but he could not have done that to Elise.

He knew that he needed to do no more debating about the subject; he must go to Elise. Nothing, not even the formidable Lance Edwards would stop him!

The old Montclair mansion was a picture of grandeur and splendor, so fitting for its beautiful mistress. The old majordomo greeted Jean and bid him enter. He was just attempting to tell Jean that the mistress was out when a young girl coming down the hall shrieked out his name.

"Mister Jean!" Jessamine rushed hastily toward him.

Jean greeted her, appraising the many changes in the young mulatto servant he'd allowed Elise to have as her lady's maid. Her deep-olive complected face beamed at him, obviously glad to see him, and the soft print of her shift molded to her girlish figure; slim and trim except for the budding breasts.

"My, my, Jessamine . . . you are getting so grown up, and I can see you are very happy here with your mistress," Jean told her.

"Yes, sir. Sho' am happy here."

"I'm glad, Jessamine. You suppose I might

265

see your mistress?"

"Sho' could, but she not here."

"Oh?" Jean was crestfallen at the thought of the trip from the city being for naught.

"Come, Mister Jean. I'll get yo' somethin' cool to drink 'for yo' start back to the city." Jessamine urged him into the parlor, her hand at his arm and a more serious look on her face. "'Sides I sorta' hav a bad feelin' about the mistress."

"What are you talking about, Jessamine? Where is Elise?"

"Tol' me she were goin' to the Le Cleres. That's funny, too. 'Cause they had a dinner to go to over thar tonight. But Missy Elise say she don had a urgent message from Missy Annette to come quick. Jus' don' lak it tho', Mister Jean!"

A deep male voice interrupted any answer Jean might have given to the young girl. "Don't like what, Jessamine?"

In the doorway Lance Edwards stood looking down at the two. His dark eyes blazed, looking at Jean Laffite sitting so casually in his parlor. One arched brow raised, questioning the reason for his visit.

To her master Jessamine repeated the story she'd just finished relating to Laffite. As she hastily mumbled it out she instinctively sensed the tenseness wafting through the room. Lance sauntered to the liquor chest to pour himself a generous drink of whiskey.

"Thank you, Jessamine. You may go." Lance

curtly dismissed the girl. He turned to Jean and said, "You will have to excuse me, Monsieur Laffite. I must go!"

Jean excused his coolness, for it was obvious Lance Edwards was concerned. "Pardon, Monsieur . . . may I offer my services? I mean—"

"That won't be necessary," Lance cut him off. He cursed himself as he bolted through the front door and down the steps, for only this morning he'd meant to caution Elise not to ride alone. He, along with some of the other land owners, had planned to investigate the strange fires at night down on the river banks and goings-on around the countryside like chickens missing and goods missing from their houses and barns.

Lance was too preoccupied with these troubled thoughts as he galloped off on his huge stallion to take note that Jean was following.

There was a dense wooded area between Montclair and Bellefair. The towering oaks and massive cypress trees blotted out the rays of the setting sun. This was a secluded, desolate strip of road with its enclosure of trees. Lance was beginning to calm the hard pounding of his heart as he saw the end of the woods ahead. He kept telling himself he would find Elise sitting calmly, having refreshments with Annette, and would feel very foolish. But that did not seem very likely when they had been due to dine with the Le Cleres two hours later. No, logic told him different.

It was only in another second that his eyes told him differently. He had only to view the white mountain lying up on the dirt road to know it was Satan, Elise's mount. Once again he felt a tightness in his chest as though he could hardly breath as he reined his horse to a halt. Leaping off, he hurried to the fallen horse and there she was.

"Oh, God!" Never would he have thought he would welcome hearing her moan, but he did. She was alive! He gently stirred her, afraid of where or how she was injured. Again, she gave out a moan of anguish, but by now he cradled her in his arms, kissing her dirt-smeared, bleeding face, and at the same time soothing away her fears.

"L . . . Lance?"

"Shhh, love. Yes, my precious it is Lance and you're . . . you're safe," his stammering voice assured her. By now he sat flat on the dirt road with her in his lap and his attention had been distracted to the dead beast, his magnificent white thoroughbred. The horse had been shot, not Elise. She had suffered whatever injuries she had due to falling off the animal. What or who could have possibly engineered this atrosity?

"*Mon Dieu!*" Jean gasped, obviously shocked.

Dazed, Lance turned and saw Laffite standing there as numbed as he was. "Elise lives?"

"She lives, monsieur. Mainly shocked, and some cuts and bruises, I pray," Lance informed

268

him. Elise stirred slightly and her eyes opened slowly. Blurred faces with two black heads seemed to merge together, but she was too tired to try to sort it out so she laid against the chest of the man holding her and gave way to the tiredness engulfing her.

Laffite supported Lance as he rose off the ground with the limp body of his wife. Laffite's super senses detected a noise over by the underbrush and he listened.

Lance sat securely on his horse with Elise in his arm, reining with the other hand. There was an eerie quiet except for Edwards's voice assuring and comforting his wife. Now Jean started to mount up, only to hesitate and listen. Something disturbed the otherwise quiet and Jean's alert senses caught it. It was a sharp, crisp sound of a breaking branch, or a footstep on the underbrush, it seemed to him.

Lance was far too concerned about Elise and paid little attention to Laffite's comment that he was going to snoop around the area for a while. He rode off, leaving Jean behind. Disregarding his fine attire, Laffite moved slowly and tediously, plowing into the thick underbrush where he'd thought the noise came from. Amazingly, only some twenty feet back, there was a small clearing. Jean carefully scoured the ground for hoofprints or any clue that might give some information as to who had done the dastardly deed.

At the point of giving up and riding back to Montclair his gaze fell upon a bright blue object, which when pulled from the branch proved to be a piece of fabric.

Blue! Unusual color! Jean's mind whirled with the wildest ideas. Being a man of impeccable taste in clothing and expensive materials, he knew the swatch was just that. He questioned who the wearer might be.

Pocketing the small piece he prepared to mount up, knowing before he returned to New Orleans he had to satisfy himself about Elise's condition even though he'd seen enough of life to know she was not seriously injured. A guardian angel had been sitting on her pretty shoulder this day, but what about the next time. If they were being observed, as he was certain now that they were, then the culprit knew the attempt had failed.

Shrugging his shoulders he concluded he should not sweep aside old Nadja's words too lightly any more. The black-haired woman she spoke of had to be Elise. He tarried at Montclair long enough to hear Jessamine's report that Elise was going to be all right and then he started back toward the city.

Lance knew nothing about Laffite's return to his home because Jessamine considered it wiser not to mention it. The master did not share the warm, friendly attitude toward Laffite that her mistress did, Jessamine realized.

Much later, after the doctor had examined Elise and departed, Lance forced himself to eat a light dinner and retired to his study to have a brandy, hoping to sort out his thoughts and the insanity of the day. The serious impact hit with a fierce blow: how close he'd come once again to losing his beloved Elise. How much he loved her made him tremble with a new fear for the future! But who would wish her dead? Who hated her so intensely as to plan such a horrible act? There was no doubt that it had been premeditated, the forged note sent to Elise showed that. Then the bastard had waited for his unsuspecting wife to ride down the road. He ended up with no suspects as he went over the names and acquaintances knowing of Elise's habits and daily routines. Weary from so much thought he laid his head down on the desk and the brandy lulled him to sleep.

Other people pondered the same happening. Jean had dinner with Fifi La Tour and after the two of them finished the fine beefsteak along with a bottle of wine, Jean told her about the events. Fifi almost choked on the wine in shocking disbelief.

"I need a woman's opinion, Fifi," Jean said, pulling out the piece of material.

"Well, I don't know how great my opinion is, but for you honey I'd try." Fifi laughed. In the next moment, she realized that Jean was more than a little concerned by the incident.

"Fifi, take a look at this. Would you say this came from a woman's garment?" He lay the swatch of cloth on the table.

"Most likely . . . it would." She frowned, questioning what Jean was getting at. "What . . . what's this all about, Jean?"

271

Jean explained where he'd found it, and like Lance he had figured out that the incident with Elise had been planned, but bungled by a poor marksman or a trembling hand. A woman, he deduced.

"God Almighty, Jean! What woman?"

"Can't say, Fifi . . . not for sure. Like the man or not, I feel compelled to present this evidence to Edwards."

Fifi smiled that all-knowing smile of hers, playing casually with the lace ruffling at the neck of her gown. "You still aren't over her, are you honey?" Her blue eyes demanded a straight answer from him, and he readily admitted the truth to his old friend.

"She's like no other woman I've ever known, Fifi."

She reached across the table and patted his hand. "Yes, and you've yet to get her in your bed and that, dear Jean, makes the wanting even more desperate, eh?"

"Fifi, why do you have to be so damn clever?"

"Because, my pet, I know men, all kinds. There is nothing stronger than the urge a man gets for a certain woman. Hell, Laffite, kingdoms have been lost and fortunes squandered. If anyone knows, I do. I see it nightly."

"Is that why you never married, Fifi?" Jean asked, always curious about her past.

"No, sweetheart. I only loved, really loved, one man, and he loved another. I never met another who could match him. It's just as simple as that, Jean." Fifi was dead serious as she spoke. Her one and only love was Francois Le Clere, and that was one secret she could not share with her dear friend, Chickie. Annette Le Clere never had an inkling of the feelings harbored there.

Jean reached over to plant an affectionate kiss on her cheek. "Whoever the gentleman was, he lost one damn good woman. That's all I have to say."

"Ah, but he got a damn good one, Jean—the best!"

Jean pondered her words and wondered how any woman could be so generous toward someone who had taken the man she loved. Shaking his head in wonder and amazement, he declared, "You're some woman, Fifi La Tour!"

Fifi threw back her head, gave him a sound slap on the shoulder and laughing, she retorted, "I am, aren't I!"

Chapter 18

The shocking, contemptible act against her little friend Elise shook Annette Le Clere to the core of her being. That something like that could occur within the boundaries of two fine plantations like Bellefair and Montclair during the daylight hours was frightening and alarming. Nothing Francois could say to her calmed or soothed her.

This was her mood the morning Lance Edwards rode over from Montclair, and it was Elise he came to discuss, knowing the close friendship of the two.

"I need your help, Madame Le Clere," he said, concern reflected in his dark eyes.

"Annette," she corrected him, smiling sweetly.

"Annette. You know how crazy she was about that horse and that I can replace it, although I know she'll not respond to the new one for a while. It won't be like Satan. I guess

I'm driving her crazy with this overprotective attitude, but until I can find something out about what happened that day, I've kept her so housebound she's ready to scream. You know Elise. She's a free spirit and I don't think she's taking this whole thing seriously."

That he'd come to her made her swell with pride, and she agreed with him completely but she knew Elise, too. "I am in complete accord with you, my dear," she replied. How close she'd come to saying "my son." How easy and natural it seemed, and Fifi was right; she must chance telling him soon.

"Has any progress been made in turning up anything?"

Lance shook his head dejectedly. "I've covered every foot of ground myself. It's like the gunman vanished into thin air. One thing is for certain though, and that is that whoever did this came by the river, by boat, or their horse was left back quite a way. No prints were visible on the grounds by the time I went back."

"It is for sure the act was premeditated though. There is no shadow of a doubt about that," Annette remarked, feeling almost sick to her stomach to think someone would wish to kill the darling Elise—so sweet and beautiful. That she had come so close to death was a startling fact.

"Oh, yes, there's no doubt of that, and when I find out who—well, you know without my saying it, don't you? I shall take the greatest pleasure in killing them," he vowed, black fire

275

blazing in his determined eyes.

"I have no doubt, my son," Annette said almost in a whisper. The two were so involved with their thoughts about Elise that neither put any significance on the fact that Annette had given way to the subconscious urge to call him her son.

They parted company that day with Annette suggesting that she get Elise involved with planning the party she was to give for Francois's fiftieth birthday. Lance thought it a great idea. It would brighten Elise's depressed state over the loss of Satan.

Helping Annette with the invitations and shopping for new gowns and a birthday gift for Francois brought about wonders and renewed radiance in Elise. Lance felt grateful to Annette Le Clere.

Camaraderie and gaiety flowed generously the day before the party was to be held. Lance arrived at Bellefair to find Elise and Annette putting the final touches of the decorations in place. What a magnificent pair they were! A generation divided them, but they enjoyed one another's company so much. It dawned on him the two shared the same type of striking beauty. Both were of French descent with their green eyes and petite statures. While Annette Le Clere's hair was now streaked with gray, Lance could envision hers being as jet black as Elise's glossy mane.

As he stood there in the archway observing the two women giving out a moment of soft, amused laughter about something, he felt a strange closeness engulfing him for the older woman; a feeling akin to love. It was a puzzle he could not piece together, and it caught him up and held him. He had no knowledge of how long he lingered there deep in thought before making his presence known.

Returning to the present, he jauntily entered the room to greet them. Elise rushed to his side and raised to plant a warm kiss on his cheek. *"Mon cheri,* doesn't it all look wonderful!" She gave a sweeping motion with her hand for him to take in the colorful, festive room that Annette had decorated.

"It's perfection . . . like the two of you." He smiled lovingly down on her radiant face. Annette warmed just looking upon the two of them with a natural mother's pride swelling in her breast.

With a flippant air Elise whirled around to face Annette. "You can see why this rake stole my heart so completely. He's such a smooth-tongued rascal, is he not?"

Annette gave that soft laugh of hers and replied, "And so handsome, *chérie.* Ah, yes, it is easy to see how he stole your heart."

"I vow the two of you will give me a swollen head," Lance jested.

It was with this same lighthearted air that the Edwardses bid Annette farewell to travel home to Montclair, and it was good to see Elise so alive and excited again. He listened to her chattering all the way home, enjoying every minute of it. She had not mentioned the loss of Satan in the last few days, and she had no idea that soon there would be the delivery of a new horse to Montclair. This thoroughbred would be a jet-black animal.

The night of the party sparkled with crisp autumn chill and as Lance placed the blue velvet cape around Elise's shoulders he could not resist stealing a kiss. The bareness of her neck was attractive; Elise needed no adornment. In fact, her only jewelry was the pearl earrings encircled with diamonds that was perfect with the pale blue silk gown with Valenciennes lace on the bodice. The sleeves were blue net, matching the sheer blue overlaying white satin. Lance knew she would outshine every woman there as he admired the woman he was proud to say was his wife.

Later when they arrived and he surveyed the guests he was certain of it. The way Francois was adoring his lady Lance was also certain he was feeling the same masculine pride.

In the secret abyss of his thoughts no one could know what this night meant to the distinguished-looking Francois. It was a magnificent climax of his glorious life with his precious Annette. He desired that she would remember it so. He would forever see her as she was in her favorite pastels of green and pink, pink rosebud of velvet in her upswept hair, and pale green satin slippers on her dainty feet.

The governor and his wife arrived and she, like Elise, was dressed in pale blue and white.

On her dark head she wore a fashionable blue satin turban adorned with white plumes.

Susan Barron made an attractive picture in her yellow gauze with its raised dots of velvet. Annette greeted her with a warmth and graciousness she did not feel. Yet she detested feeling this way for it was not her nature. From Clint and Susan she moved on to speak to other guests.

The flamboyant Andrea Burke was gorgeous in her rich wine-colored dress and abundant display of rubies. Annette noted that she'd remained only briefly at J. William's side before engaging Jack Maynard in conversation, which Flo was quick to notice and she rushed over to Jack's side.

Francois enjoyed the many toasts and good wishes his friends were bestowing upon him before dinner was announced. Elise knew all the special dishes old Henri was preparing for the special night and anticipated tasting them.

The crayfish soup brought forth sighs of delight and approval from the governor. But it was the governor's wife who admitted she'd love to abduct their cook when she took a bit of the thin-sliced veal in a rich brandied sauce. "What is this, Annette? I've never tasted anything so delightful!"

"Henri calls it *Escalopes de veau a la royale*. But beyond that I don't know how he fixes the cream sauce. I'd hoped you would enjoy it as much as Francois and I always do."

All the guests agreed that they certainly did,

for each new course seemed to surpass the last one. Annette was more than pleased and gave Elise a wink as she looked down in her direction.

The elaborate dinner left the guests ready to move around so the ladies moved to the parlor or upstairs to repair their toilet while the gentlemen enjoyed their brandy and cheroots before rejoining their ladies for the dance to begin.

With the ladies absent, the men's conversation turned to the unpleasant subject of the war and Jackson's anticipated arrival in New Orleans. Jack Maynard prodded the governor, "How much can we expect, governor? How many men?"

"By the time they leave Florida—4,000 strong, I'm informed, Maynard."

Lance listened intensely. But what if the British arrived before Jackson. Claiborne's militia was ill-prepared.

Francois found it a most opportune time to intercede for his friend Jean Laffite and did not hesitate to do so. "I for one would welcome the help of Jean Laffite, sir. He has warehouses filled with arms and hundreds of men we could find ourselves sorely in need of."

Lance grimaced, finding it unpleasant to ally himself up with the Baratarian, and the governor obviously did not agree with his friend Francois. But he did not get a chance to answer for Clint Barron interrupted whatever Claiborne would have said. "The damn British would be running over New Orleans in a few hours' time with the pitiful militia we've got right now."

Lance broke into a slow grin, for it was at that moment he noticed Clint was into his cup. His words were frightening and true. The governor's face looked like a thundercloud, and Francois was regretting that the whole subject had come up, but he did agree with the younger man.

Hearing the music begin was the godsend he needed. With great relief he announced, "Gentlemen, I suggest we join our ladies or we might just be having a battle here at Bellefair tonight." All the men chuckled except the governor who hung back to walk beside Lance Edwards.

Claiborne sensed somehow that Monsieur Edwards, like himself, was not taken in by the so-called Laffite charm as was their mutual friend, Le Clere. His attention had been repeatedly whetted by the impressive path cut by the Englishman since coming to New Orleans and becoming Zack's partner.

"What about you, Monsieur Edwards? What are your thoughts about the possibility of invasion by the British?"

"My priority would be the fortification around Lake Bourne and sixty miles northeast, sir. Saint Louis Bay. We cannot deny that we are ill-prepared compared to the seasoned British fleet, can we, governor?" Lance tactfully pointed out in a low, deep voice that somehow didn't rub Claiborne the same way

Barron had.

"Uhhh, well, yes. What you say is true."

"I have some knowledge on the subject, having been a privateer a few years ago, and any help I might offer you, sir—you have only to ask."

"I greatly appreciate that, Monsieur Edwards." The governor was affected by the strong, self-assured manner of the man he'd heard so much about from Francois Le Clere, and he saw tonight for himself why. Not only was he a good-looking gentleman, he was intelligent. Just as they approached the cluster of ladies, Claiborne suggested, "Yes, I would like to consult with you at length, Monsieur Edwards. Your advice could be very valuable."

On that note they shook hands and Lance spotted the smiling Elise coming to meet him.

The music played and the dancers whirled around the floor. To the observer just outside the terrace doors in the dark garden it was a scene of merriment he chose not to interrupt. It was Francois's special night, and he'd not chance causing it to be anything less. He strolled down the flagstone path to sit down on one of the benches on the inside of the arbor entwined with the climbing night-blooming jasmine. Always the fragrance of its blooms reminded him of Elise. Only a moment ago he'd caught a fleeting glance of her as her husband had turned her over to Francois for the next dance. He envied his old friend, wishing it was he who was holding her at this minute close to his chest.

There, alone in the night's quietness he swore for his ears alone—if only once, he must have her. For just one wild, wonderful interlude he must possess her. Yet, he was wise enough to realize the act could be the dance of death. Lance Edwards would allow no man to live who tried to take what belonged to him. He could not fault him for that. He, too, shared the feeling.

The night's chill was too harsh to linger long and he wanted only a brief moment to wish his old friend congratulations and present a gift he'd purchased especially with Francois in mind.

He made an entrance through the kitchen door, and was greeted warmly by old Henri. One of the servants guided him down the back hall to Francois's small study, and then rushed away to inform Francois of his visitor. Jean was more than delighted at the unexpected sight of Elise hanging on Francois's arm. He had not expected to be so lucky tonight.

"Francois! *Ma petite*—you are breathtaking tonight!" Warm exchanges of hugs and kisses were made between the trio before Francois was to inquire, "But why this, Jean? You should be in there with our other guests and dear friends."

"No, *mon ami*. I would not cause havoc in your parlor. I wanted only to give you this and toast you with one drink." Jean knew at this time a face to face meeting with the governor was not wise.

Francois took the case and upon opening it gasped with admiration as he saw the black opal stickpin nested on the velvet lining of the case. "It is magnificent, Jean and I shall truly treasure it!"

"I'm glad you like it, Francois."

"Now, we must share a toast. But, Jean you must promise me to never stay away from our home ever again. I won't stand for that. Now, I must go find Annette or she will have both of our heads." With the instructions that the two of them remain there in the study, Francois rushed from the room to get his wife.

Elise and Jean exchanged lighthearted laughter. "He is enjoying this night so much and Annette has worked so hard to make it special for him," Elise remarked, sitting back down to await the two of them. Jean could not have been more pleased to have this private time with Elise.

"They are both very special people I adore very much, as I also adore you, Elise," he said, his eyes devouring her beautiful face flushed with radiance tonight.

Elise could not help being affected by the intensity of his eyes, so hungry and impassioned. It made her suddenly realize that for her and Jean to be alone like this was not wise, especially knowing Lance's thoughts about him. While she realized her husband did not approve of Jean, Elise could not pretend Jean did not exist or that what they'd briefly shared had not happened. It had, and she did feel a warmth in her heart for the man sitting beside her. Oh, it was not the love she felt for Lance, nor could it ever be, however, there was feeling there she could not deny.

Francois was finding it difficult to spy his tiny wife among the mass of milling guests. When at last he caught sight of her pink and green gown, he hoped she would remain talking to the couple until he could elbow his way to her.

Lance, like Francois, had been scanning the huge room for the last half hour. Andrea Burke had cleverly had him cornered and the woman was too careless with her hands, giving generous pats on his leg and thigh. While his masculine ego was flattered, he found himself bored with her little game. God forbid, he mused to himself, he must be getting old. There was a time when he'd have swept a female like her up the steps, found a guest bedroom, and bedded her without a qualm.

Andrea's sultry voice murmured softly but he was so preoccupied letting his eyes dance over the room he did not hear her. He saw the governor talking to Maynard and Clint was by Susan's side. The last sight he had of Elise was when she was dancing with Francois over an hour ago. She wasn't with him. Now Francois was standing with Annette talking to the Maynards. Where the devil was the little vixen?

"Monsieur? I do not think you heard what I

said." Andrea nudged him. With an abruptness that puzzled and infuriated her at the same time she lost his attention completely. It was a terrible blow to her vanity, for at last she'd cornered the handsome devil and had him all to herself. Thinking to herself that Elise Edwards could not have too high a degree of intelligence to leave a man such as him loose this long, she'd used the time to the fullest. Now this!

His gracious excuse to leave her brought on a deep, dejected sigh.

Elise was not on the terrace, he saw quickly enough, and it was for certain she was not in the ballroom. Lance ambled aimlessly down the hall toward the winding stairway. Could she be upstairs attending to her toilet?

He leaned against the balustrade and drew on the cheroot becoming more impatient and flustered. When he heard the ring of her light laughter coming from the room he knew to be Francois's study, he bolted in the direction like a man possessed. Less than twenty feet away, Francois and Annette were approaching. "Oh, *Mon Dieu*, Francois!"

The perceptive Annette shuddered at the prospects of what would happen when Lance found Elise alone with Jean.

As Annette and Francois came up to the doorway, Lance made his presence known, and his displeasure. Elise's face was pale from his outburst as she summoned him. "Lance? Wha—"

Annette left Francois, urging him to console

Elise. She would talk to Lance. With a strength that halted him Lance gave way to the pressure of her hold on him and turned sharply on his heels. "Madame Le Clere, I beg—"

Annette stopped him before he could continue. "And I beg you, my son—do not act the fool." She trembled with her own fury, paying no heed to the fury in his face. Her outburst took him by such surprise that he could not react. So he stood for a moment as if frozen in his boots. How dare she speak to him so? What right did this woman have to tell him how to act or what to say?

Each glared at the other, unflinching, with eyes locked onto one another. For one swift second he'd had the urge to deal her the blow he'd yearned to punish Elise with.

An uncanny feeling engulfed him. The French called *déja vù*. He'd before experienced it. He batted his eyes, demanding himself to take control. No woman had ever stood up to him like this, with the exception of Elise. He suddenly felt like a small lad being reprimanded.

"I think, perhaps, the temper needs some cooling, eh?" She looked up at the handsome face of her son, suddenly shocked at the motherly liberties she'd taken so naturally.

"I will be on the terrace, Madame Le Clere," Lance told her. "You might inform my wife, if she's interested."

Stubbornly, Annette shook her head. "No, monsieur, you will tell her. After all, you are

287

too wise to make it easy for a man like Jean Laffite, eh?''

How clearly she seemed to see right through him! He looked upon her knowing face and saw an amused look in her eyes. Damn the woman! Yet, he found his anger diminishing, and a slight hint of a smile emerged on his own face as he bent to plant a kiss on her cheek. ''Madame, I think I adore you!'' She watched him go and her heart felt like it could explode with the joy she was feeling at that moment.

Lance was ready to explode for other reasons. While the matronly Madame Le Clere had calmed the immediate fury seething in him, the spark remained. He resented everything Jean Laffite represented, and his role in Elise's life, even though it was a brief period.

All the reasoning he'd tried to apply—that she felt grateful to the Baratarian for saving her life—did not calm the monster jealousy. She was his! His alone for no other man to share! Yet, he knew no man would ever master her completely—not Elise!

Remembering Annette Le Clere's words, he turned swiftly on his heels to return to the festivities inside. No, he'd not make it bloody well easy for Laffite. Madame Le Clere was a wise, clever woman!

Guests were beginning to take their leave as he strode through the hallway. Annette and Francois stood together saying their farewells. Elise was not in sight. He heard the voice of Andrea just around the corner of a small alcove. Just as he started to turn away, for he wished no encounter with that one tonight, he stopped short, hearing his name mentioned.

"Monsieur Edwards is a most charming man. He kept me delightfully entertained earlier while you were . . . uuh, elsewhere, madame."

"You are very gracious, Madame Burke, and I appreciate your compliments about my husband. I'm sure he was as entertained by your company," Elise remarked. While Andrea Burke might not have been aware of it, Lance did not have to see Elise's face to know what she was thinking.

Andrea purred, "Why aren't you just the sweetest thing, Elise Edwards."

In a confidential tone, as though she wanted no other ears to hear her words to Elise, Andrea confided to Lance's wife, "I think you and I should become better acquainted, dear. I just bet you are like me—you get bored with these fancy fluffs, eh?"

A smile broke on Lance's face, wondering what Elise's next comment would be. He didn't have to wait long.

"Oh, I'm sure we'll become better acquainted, Andrea, as time goes by. Between two babies and a very demanding husband I find I have so little time." Her soft voice was syrupy sweet. "Now, I must ask you to excuse me." Elise whirled around to leave Andrea Burke, pondering if she'd succeeded or not in her efforts to establish a friendly relationship with the wife of the devilishly handsome man she'd love to lure to her bed.

Lance lunged out to catch Elise's arm as she dashed by the alcove. The little minx! A demanding husband, indeed! What a little vixen she was!

"Madame, were you looking for me?" He held her arm tighter than he realized for he still felt the fury of the episode with Jean Laffite.

How presumptuous of him, after he'd stalked out of Francois's study earlier in a pique without even allowing her the courtesy to hear her out! His strong arm and hand held her fast to his side and she glared up at him with green fire in her eyes, biting her lower lip in anger.

Every fiber of her petite body rebelled against that superior look on his face, and she hissed, "Not really!"

"Oh, forgive me, madame! Well, I was looking for you. It is time we leave," he snapped, pulling her along with no gentleness. "Ah, there is Annette now. Come, we must tell her good night."

Elise smoldered as they came up to their hostess, and the smile given to the dear lady was forced. Bending over to kiss Annette's cheek, Elise told her it was a lovely evening. "I'll come over in a few days for a visit, Annette dear."

"I'll look forward to seeing you, *chérie,*" Annette replied, patting her hand. The perceptive Madame Le Clere sensed all was far from settled between the two.

"Good night, Annette." Lance turned to

Francois and the two men exchanged a few words. Turning his attention back to Elise, he suggested, "Shall we go, Elise?"

The ride home did not improve either of their tempers. Her husband puzzled Elise, and she found it hard to forgive him for spoiling Annette's party with his outrageous jealousy. Why couldn't he understand her feeling for the man who had saved her life? What did he expect of her? Whatever it was, it was too much! She would not turn her back on Jean and not be civil.

It was apparent to her that he had not been exactly twiddling his thumbs, from the way Andrea Burke was bubbling over about him. How obvious the woman was!

The longer they rode in silence, the more irritated Lance became. This "quiet" Elise he did not know. God, why did she not rant or rave? He felt like he was sitting next to a volcano ready to erupt. Even in the dark, he could see the fire in her eyes. Crazy as it might be, he was washed by the overwhelming desire to crush her defiant little body to him.

When they arrived at Montclair she still had not uttered one word to him. She marched into the house and up the steps to the bedroom. He followed, only to be more inflamed with desire watching the sensuous swaying of her hips. Damn, he would have her tonight!

Carelessly flinging her cape aside, she sat down on the stool to remove her slippers. Lance prepared to undress while she did the same. He stood with his chest bare when he noticed her observing him in the mirror. What was the little she-cat thinking?

Elise felt disgust with herself, sitting there now removing the ornaments from her hair and proceeding to attack her hair with the silver brush. She told herself there had to be a wicked wantonness in her. She felt desire stirring within her as she looked up in the mirror to see him standing there. His magnificent body bared to the waist stirred her, and he knew it.

His black hair fell carelessly over his forehead as he bent to remove his boots, and she ogled the firm roundness of his buttocks. While his chest was broad, his waist was trim in comparison. Was it any wonder Andrea Burke or any other woman would not want that superior body making love to them?

By now she had changed into a diaphanous lavender nightgown, which Lance thought was daringly attractive on her. He was reminded of the exotic tropical blossoms he'd seen during his stay in Venezuela. He was bloody well on fire, watching her crawl in bed, and he knew only one way to put it out.

He joined her on the bed, aware that she sought to lie as far away from him as the bed allowed. Her supercilious manner would not cool his quest though.

Strong hands flung her around so fast she gasped in shock and surprise. "Lance! I . . . I have a headache. It is late." Determined to not succumb to his always intoxicating male charm, she stiffened herself against his hot body.

"It is late, indeed! But I wish you to lose no sleep, *ma petite*, because of a headache. Let's see if I can cure it, eh?" His mouth first took her lips and then moved slowly over her face and temples. "Feel good, love?" Her body could not deny his anymore than he could hers once they touched, and he felt the stiff restrain sweep away as his lips found hers. By the time his lips had trailed down her throat to the tip of one jutting breast, Elise knew she was under his spell.

"Hmmmm, it feels a little better, I guess," she moaned softly.

"Ah, we'll have to keep up the treatment then," he suggested, smiling down on her impishly. His eyes were heavy lidded, as if he was lazy and sleepy. Elise called them dreamy-looking eyes, and they spoke of the consuming passion mounting within him.

She arched, undulating her body to the curve of his body, wanting to join him. "Oh, yes, my darling. . . . I . . . I need treatment at once!"

He laughed, thrusting himself between her thighs and giving her the pulsing manhood that was his. She moaned with pleasure, enclosing herself around him.

"Oh, God, Elise!" His chest heaved with his heavy intake of breath, wanting more and more of her honey-sweet pleasure. He felt himself drowning in the warm liquid heat of her.

Elise felt herself being swept up in the swift currents of ecstasy as she clung to Lance. Together, they let it bear them away and beyond.

Chapter 19

Francois paid a visit to the doctor, and he left the office knowing that he had little time left. His only hope was that he could continue to conceal the truth from Annette as long as possible. More than ever he realized how important it was that she tell her son the truth, for soon she would be needing the comfort and support of her son.

As he started for home, he was urged to stop at La Maison and speak to Fifi. She was so strong, always had been like the Rock of Gibraltar. He felt the need of her strength.

Fifi was not prepared for Francois's revelation, nor was she as strong as he imagined. The realization that Francois was dying hit her with a devastating blow. After he left she went to her room and cried a river of tears. Afterward she remained in her room the rest of the day to drink herself into a drunken stupor. He never suspected how much she always loved him, she realized. His thoughts were totally concerned with the blow it was going to be for his beloved Annette. Dear God, it hurt so bad! If it was any other woman but Annette she'd have tried, for just one wonderful moment, to get him to her bed. She'd have bet any amount of money Francois had never taken another woman but Annette.

Francois traveled home lighter of heart after seeing Fifi, and there was a new found hope within him; a new faith abounded there. It was wonderful to be alive and he would enjoy whatever time he had left. Why, he mused to himself, one minute could be a lifetime!

In this state of mind he arrived home and greeted Annette with such an amorous kiss that it left her breathless. His face—dear God, he looked to her as he had so many years ago. There was mischief there, for his eyes were bright; so alive. Annette floated in a cloud of complete contentment, without a care in the world to disturb her the rest of that day and evening. It could be said that Francois Le Clere had succeeded in giving his wife the sweet peace he desired for her.

When Elise rode over on the new horse Lance had acquired for her to replace Satan, she mentioned how marvelous Francois looked. Annette contributed it to the delightful presence of the adorable Dominique. "She's been like the fountain of youth."

As she rode out of Bellefair that day, Francois's arm encircled his wife's small waist as the two of them watched the pair fly down the road. The new stallion's coat was as glossy black as Elise's raven black hair, and Francois admired the perfectly matched grace and beauty of the pair.

He did question if Lance realized Elise was out riding alone, for he knew his concern after her close brush with death. When he voiced this to Annette she shrugged her shoulders, remarking, "He knows, *cheri*, that there is no making a prisoner out of Elise."

After Elise was out of sight and they were strolling back to the house, Francois gently but firmly urged her, "You must delay no longer, Annette, this thing you should have settled long, long ago."

She said nothing, but her thoughts covered a vast period of time as they made their way down the long hallway and settled in the bright, sunny morning room. She relived that shocking moment when first her eyes came to rest on the gold medallion worn constantly around Lance Edwards's neck.

It was at the gala affair of Clint Barron's party; the one that was given to announce his engagement to Elise. The party became a strained affair, and the announcement was never made. Annette just happened to be witness to the aftermath of Elise and Lance's first encounter.

Only moments earlier she'd first seen the handsome newcomer arriving with Susan Hart, elegantly attired in a bottle green coat and creme-colored pants. He wore a silk waistcoat of the same creme color, making his good-looking face look even tanner. Annette had no idea this was her son she looked upon. She'd pegged him as the son of a wealthy Carolina shipping family, remembering that Hart had originally migrated to New Orleans from the Carolinas years ago.

Everything happened so fast after he and Susan had arrived at Shady Oaks. Susan stood talking with Clint and the stranger Lance Edwards had moved as in a trance to the couple engaged in conversation a few feet away. That couple was Zack and Elise. It had been the soft, familiar voice of Elise that had pulled Lance like a magnet toward her. Their eyes met in the same moment she'd remarked about her coming marriage to Clint Barron. Annette stood, awestruck as she observed the black eyes of the stranger. First, the pang of anguish reflected there, and quickly the change to fury and rage as he turned, almost staggering for the nearest door.

Something she could never explain to herself compelled her to follow him. There on the Barron's veranda he tore off his fine coat and opened the neck of his white ruffled shirt as if he was suddenly choking for breath. Then she saw the gold medallion nestled in the cluster of black hair on his tanned chest. She gasped, having trouble getting her own breath. Before she could get her wits about her, he hurried down the steps and across the carpeted grass toward the stable. She knew without a shadow of a doubt she'd just gazed upon the face of her son. They'd yet to have been introduced, but his name would be Landon or Lance, named by his Uncle Albert. What a pity Lord Malcolm could not have been the wonderful, kind-hearted man his brother Albert had been!

Never could she imagine Albert tossing his young wife out of a carriage on a deserted London street on a dismal, raining night when he was caught up in a frenzy of rage. Malcolm had done so to her many years ago. His angry voice raged that she'd never see her young five-year-old son again, and he'd be told she was dead. So it had been.

It was ludicrous even now. She thought back over the many, many years since all this had taken place to remember that Malcolm's accusations that she had been untrue to him were false.

So far away were Annette's thoughts that she took no notice that Francois had slipped out of the room to go to the solitude of the study and sink into his waiting leather chair. Like a giant tidal wave, total exhaustion had engulfed him.

Young Baptiste sighed with great relief when he saw his mistress returning atop the huge black stallion. The animal's size made her seem all the more fragile and delicate. Yet he knew his mistress was anything but fragile or helpless. Nevertheless, he was glad to see her returning, since this afternoon was the first time she'd taken the fine black horse out. He was not the powerfully built animal that Satan had been, but just as fiesty and high-spirited.

Baptiste knew the master had intended that he would be on hand when she rode the new horse the first time, but the impetuous mistress decided to ride today. He admired her independent spirit, even though she'd defied the master's direct, firm orders. Baptiste knew it was useless to try to persuade her to obey them.

Like his master, he found it hard to refuse her requests and he would have protected her by laying down his life, if necessary. The young Creole was enamored of his mistress, worshipped and adored her in his heart and soul.

He returned her wave as she galloped toward the stable and the place he stood awaiting her. A beautiful flush showed on her face from the vigorous ride she'd just had and she looked marvelous, Baptiste thought.

"Ah, Baptiste, he's wonderful—a magnificent animal, and I've thought of the perfect name for him. You know what I shall call him?" Her face beamed with excitement, and the beauty of her bright green eyes was something to behold.

"No, Missy Elise . . . what is he to be called?"

"Midnight, Baptiste! Isn't that perfect! He is as black as midnight."

"Oh, yes—it is the perfect name for him."

Leaping down from the horse, she handed

him the reins and patted the silky black mane lovingly. Young Baptiste admired this trait in her. As it had been with Satan, she showed such loving care for the animals. No wonder the master was such a happy man, he privately mused. His young romantic heart could easily imagine how it must be between them. She was a woman of warmth, and her feelings flowed forth naturally and unreined at times; Baptiste had witnessed them. The young lad was unaware of their recent tiff.

She was unpredictable, never with the same smile pasted on her pretty face, or the constant stern, harsh look of the lording mistress of a fine plantation like Montclair. She was more like the constantly changing wind, Baptiste thought. Baptiste could understand how the indomitable Madame Edwards could hold the attention of a man like his master.

The youth smiled as he thought about Monsieur Edwards's surprise when he learned that she had already acquainted herself with the new horse. Lance Edwards had returned home daily to find her awaiting his arrival, freshly gowned and hair styled. But each day that week she'd taken the horse out for a jaunt over the countryside, and by now she and Midnight were good friends.

Baptiste could not miss the mischief in her green eyes, knowing she could not wait to have her husband see her expertise come that Sunday when they would ride together over the plantation. She'd show him!

*   *   *

This particular afternoon was like the past few days; he handed the reins up to her and she and the huge black animal trotted down the drive. The threat of rain was in the air. But it was not a threatening type of storm approaching, rather, it held the promise of a brief passing shower. Elise cared not if she got caught in a few drops of rain. She'd been riding only a short while when she was forced to seek the shelter of a chinaberry tree.

She laughed softly observing two squirrels scampering for the cover of the trees. The serenity around her was suddenly interrupted when she was distracted by a buggy rumbling down the narrow lane that cut through the sugarcane field. Who would be coming down that lane with such haste?

As the buggy passed her by the lone driver took no notice of her, but she saw the familiar face of the man. A man she thoroughly detested from the first minute they met. Why would Charles Burke be down in the sugarcane fields on Barron property? she wondered. It seemed the most unlikely place he would be.

She sat there pondering it for several minutes before continuing her ride, now that the rain had ceased. Charles's appearance puzzled her very much.

A noise came from the nearby thicket and Elise listened. A moan of anguish came to her ears and she reined Midnight toward the sound. The thought of some poor animal injured prodded her to dismount and investigate.

She stood cautiously, pulled back the branches and listened. Her eyes could not see anything but more underbrush. Bending down on her knees, she searched the ground slowly. The moan came again and this time Elise began to tremble; the cry was human.

"Where are you? Tell me!" Elise urged frantically.

"He . . . elp me . . . please!" The lady's voice cried out and Elise frantically pulled at the branches. She recognized the voice as Susan's.

"Susan! It's Elise! I see you now," she called out, catching a glimpse of blue among the greenery. Crawling on the ground through a thinner section of the thicket she made her way to the bruised, bleeding Susan Barron.

Of all people to come upon her! Susan wished it was anyone but Elise Edwards. However, she hurt so bad that that thought passed as swiftly as it had come.

"Dear God, Susan! What happened to you?" She shrugged aside Susan's effort to answer, for her mouth was covered with her own blood and a swelling was already beginning under one of the eyes. "Can you help me just a little, dear. We'll get you out of here."

Susan nodded weakly and placed one of her arms over Elise's shoulder. "That's it. Just scoot along with me, all right?"

Both of them were heaving by the time Elise had guided her to the clearing. "Now, if we can just manage to get you up on Midnight we've got it made, Susan dear."

Elise could not know the mental anguish or the physical pain engulfing the red-haired woman. She stammered out a "thank you" to the same woman she'd tried to kill only a few weeks ago. Dear God, it was almost too much to bear.

Elise's breathing had finally returned to normal. Compassion swept over her looking at Susan's battered face. "I know it's not my affair Susan, but I must ask. Did Charles do this to you?"

Susan's bowed head nodded. Elise gently pulled the tumbling hair from Susan's face and pinned it in a coil. She wiped some of the oozing blood away from Susan's lip. "We've got to get you home, Susan. You need tending to."

"Wait, Elise—before we try to go I must talk to you."

"Later, Susan, after I get you to Shady Oaks. Then we'll talk."

Atop the huge black horse with the injured Susan in front of her, Elise guided the animal toward Shady Oaks. Susan's prayers were answered, for upon their arrival home it was only Callie and old Jess who met them at the door.

As Callie got her mistress situated in her bed and ointments and salve applied to the cuts and bruises, Elise went down to the kitchen to fetch some coffee for the two of them. She, like Susan, felt extreme relief that they had not encountered Clint upon arriving at Shady Oaks. Other thoughts consumed her there in the familiar kitchen.

Callie left the two young women, but her curiosity was whetted to a fine, sharp edge. Just what had taken place this day that would send the mistress home in such awful shape? Shaking her head, she knew it was something bad—something Mister Clint would suffer pain over. Poor Mister Clint! That red-haired miss was nothing but trouble.

When Elise left Shady Oaks an hour later it was with a heavy heart. Yet she knew for the good of all concerned she must bear the burden alone. She hated to think about what Lance would do if he knew what Susan had just revealed to her. But how—dear God, how would she ever manage it with those piercing black eyes looking right through her?

Elise had experienced a maelstrom of feelings during Susan's startling confession. Shock, disbelief, and dismay desolved into pity and compassion, for Susan did not spare herself. The pain of the truth hurt so!

She'd promised the humbled Susan to forgive her and keep her terrible secret. However, she wished that she could have been spared the cleansing of Susan's soul. Hearing that it was Susan who had tried to shoot her was a traumatic shock. Never had she had any inkling of the envy or resentment her friend now confessed to. It overwhelmed Elise, but the other parts of Susan's revelation were equally shocking.

The day had been exhausting, and upon her arrival back at Montclair Elise had Jessamine prepare a warm bath for her. She chose a cool, blue gown with matching blue slippers to greet her husband in when he arrived home. He could not know what she'd learned this day. She feared his reaction.

Even now she was pinching herself, wondering if she'd dreamed this nightmare.

Lance was not fooled later as they sat dining. Her mood was quiet and guarded and he knew her all too well. What was she hiding from him?

Elise was never any good at pretending, and her attempts at deception were miserably obvious. He sunk into a quiet mood, going through the motions of eating but discreetly observing her. Her cool, icy attitude bothered him.

Once he caught her looking at him lovingly. Had he been able to read her thoughts he would have known she was considering herself the most blessed woman in the world to have him as her husband. Yes, she could understand easily why Susan envied her. Kindled with these gratifying thoughts her eyes were those of a woman in love.

Lance pushed back in his chair, impatient for her to enlighten him about whatever mystery she was involved in. "What it is, my *petite renarde?*" He forced himself to ask her.

Her spirits could not resist being lifted when

306

she looked down the length of the table at his teasing dark eyes and naughty smile taunting her. "A fox, am I?"

"A more sly lady I've never known. I'm starved for a kiss, so come here." He placed the napkin by the side of his plate by the time she'd walked down to him, and he urged her down on his lap. "You, *mon chérie*, never starved for a kiss in your life, I'd wager!"

His need for her was made known as she sunk down on his lap. He needed to say nothing, but their eyes met in understanding. With the flick of his finger, the neckline of her gown lowered and he nuzzled her neck, letting his lips move over the jutting tip of her breast.

"Ah, Lance!" She sighed with a lazy moan of pleasure. Anything troubling her thoughts was hastily swept away. He felt her supple body press urgently against him and impatience to have her flooded him so that he lifted her up in his arms, striding out of the dining room down the short distance to his study. His lips never left her mouth except for the short second he turned, making sure his booted foot had slammed the door shut to the study.

He withdrew from her passion-heated body only long enough to remove his clothes before going back to her waiting arms. His voice, husky with desire, confessed, "God, I wasn't about to waste time climbing those bloody stairs, love." Elise cared not where she lie, for all she wanted was his handsome body filling her with his love.

"Then don't waste time, *mon cheri*," she coaxed.

"Lazy wench—I must undress you, too?"

"*Oui*—it is more exciting when you do it."

He yanked anxiously at her garments, not caring that the seams could not withstand his impatient hands. The only thought dominating him was to burrow himself between her thighs. Like a leaf being tossed by turbulent wind, they moved until the savage storm churning within them passed into a serene calm.

Only then did each become aware of the confined space they lay in. Lance laughed. "Lord, this might make an old man out of me."

"Then I will just have to find someone to take care of my needs, *mon cheri*," she said. His hand applied a sharp slap to her rounded rump. Cradling her pert chin in his hand, he told her firmly, "Hear me well, my sweet; be it the bed, the floor, or on God's good earth, I'll be the man taking care of all your needs. Now gather yourself up and we'll go up to bed, you wicked vixen!"

But she knew that already. Saying not a word, she did as he ordered, smiling all the while.

Chapter 20

Clint Barron could not have told anyone the minute it happened. His heart had softened toward the woman who had been his wife for over two years. He found he was even enjoying the dinner hour together, and he had taken notice that she took only one glass of wine.

The days following the incident, which had been explained as her being thrown from her mount, had satisfied Clint. The next few days Susan had stayed mainly in her room, doing a lot of soul searching and making some commitments about her future. She started by being kinder to old Callie, and the black woman was amazed herself as to how she responded to her red-haired mistress.

Susan took it minute by minute, doing battle with the urge to rush to the liquor chest. Clint did notice this in the evenings when he helped himself to his favorite brandy. Each day she became stronger and realized what a drugged haze she'd been in and how so many things had become distorted. It was startling!

After several days she pridefully noticed in her mirror her face had taken on a new radiance. She was, indeed, prettier. She had been attending to her toilette with more care and the results were showing.

Clint had a new awareness, too. By candlelight one night he gazed upon the gardenia white of her shoulders and throat in the low-cut pink gown that revealed the tempting cleavage of her full breasts. He suddenly felt ill at ease and embarrassed that he was so stirred. Damnit, he wanted to make love to Susan!

She had looked up to see this desire in Clint's blue eyes and it encouraged her. While it did not materialize that evening, she just knew she was going to win back Clint's love.

When Elise paid her a visit she brought her up to date on everything that had been happening since she'd last seen her. "God, Elise, I guess I've always loved Clint! I guess that's why I started envying you so when Clint first introduced us and you were going to be his guest . . . remember?"

"I remember, Susan. I also remember how much we liked one another from that first minute."

"Yes, that's right. But when he returned from Cuba with you I was shattered. I saw you standing there and Clint's eyes adoring you so. I guess that's when it all started. I truly liked you but oh, lordy, I hated you too, for being so darn beautiful. It really churned me up when Clint was going to marry you."

"Susan, I must confess something to you." She laughed softly. "This seems to be confession day, but then perhaps it will help. When I returned to Lance, leaving Clint after all those months of his generosity, I had a qualm of conscience. Then it dawned on me; Clint never loved me or he'd never have let me go. Lance didn't. Instead he searched for me for months. Had Clint not brought me to him that night he would have fought Clint for me. Don't you see, Susan? That was the difference in Lance's love for me."

How simple and uncomplicated Elise made it sound! A slow smile came to Susan's face for she saw the truth of Elise's words. "Oh, Elise, thank you!" The two collapsed into one anothers' arms. Tears and laughter came forth. When Clint Barron strolled into his study from his inspection of the fields he heard the laughter in the morning room, never guessing he was the topic of their conversation.

The change in Susan was nothing short of miraculous; no one could have been happier than Zack Hart. He was so overcome with emotion after her visit with him that he shed a few tears in the privacy of his study. There was hope for his pretty, spoiled daughter and her marriage to Clint Barron. He felt as if a giant boulder had been lifted from his chest.

Susan, realizing how happy she'd made her father, felt a surge of happiness within her as she traveled back down the road to Shady Oaks. Her day had been so good she decided she should try to install herself back in the good graces of Madame Le Clere. After all, Bellefair was on her way home.

Never did she fail to be impressed with the magnificent grounds of the fine old estate. Its original owners, before the Le Cleres had acquired it, had been a French Creole family, but Susan could not remember anyone living there but the Le Cleres. The grounds and gardens were laid out by the first residents, but inside the palacial mansion the handiwork was all Annette Le Clere's.

Susan took a deep breath of air as her driver helped her down from the carriage. As she started up the steps a small child caught her eyes as she ran across the carpeted grass. Susan hesitated. Perhaps she'd picked a bad time to visit Madame Le Clere; it seemed she had guests. Tempted to turn around and return to the carriage, she saw the child take a tumble, rolling down the slight incline. Lifting her skirt, she rushed to the whimpering child. Poor baby, she'd surely hurt herself, Susan concluded.

Giving no thought to the grass stains she'd get on her gown, Susan fell to the ground and cradled the child in her arms, asking, "Are you hurt, precious?"

The tiny miss nodded her head covered with dark brown curly hair. Her topaz eyes shone up at Susan. She returned the smile Susan was giving down to her. In that moment, Susan fell in love with the beautiful girl and hugged her close to her bosom.

"You pitty, and . . . and you nice to Dommi," the child mumbled, snuggling close as if it was natural and easy.

"Well, thank you. Dommi? Is that your name, precious?" Again, the child nodded. Susan was swept with a strange, wonderous feeling, but she felt it must surely be similar to the fulfillment a young mother felt when holding her baby. The glorious warmth made her almost giddy.

Annette stood on the veranda, frozen to the spot. The tenderness in Susan Barron's face as she held the child shocked and delighted her at the same time, and she did not intrude for a minute.

Finally she did join the two, inviting Susan to tea. Dear little Dominique lingered close, that sweet smile coming to her face each time Susan's attention went to her.

Annette prayed the whole afternoon was for real and not crazy madness. Could it possibly be that the day would come when Clint could claim Dominique as his daughter and Susan would accept it? What a miracle that would be!

A sly smiled creased her face as she thought out a wild idea. Just maybe she would help a miracle happen. Tomorrow, she promised herself, she'd seek out Elise's opinion about the idea.

*   *   *

Clint Barron choked on the bite of roast he was eating when Susan talked about meeting the darling little Dominique at the Le Cleres. Her words were tender and filled with love as she spoke of the little girl. His heart overflowed with admiration and love for Susan that moment.

Later that night he knocked on the bedroom door. As she bid him to enter and he walked through the door Susan knew: it was there in his eyes. She stood, heart beating rapidly and her head dizzy just looking upon the huge, virile maleness of him. His blue eyes played for a moment on the intoxicating beauty she truly was.

Susan stood, waiting. Her copper-colored hair flowed over her shoulders, looking even brighter against the white of her skin, sensuously exposed to Clint's eyes. The gown was sheer and clinging in a most flattering color of blue green. It gave a turquoise color to her blue eyes. She found herself awkward, knowing not what to do with her trembling hands. Did he know how she was quaking inside? she wondered.

All doubts were swept away in a swift, simple gesture by Clint. Holding out his strong arms to her, he painfully remarked, "How foolish we've both been, Susan. Such precious time wasted! Come to me and love me as I ache to love you."

"Oh, yes, my darling Clint." She rushed into his waiting arms, tears caressing her cheeks.

He took her completely, and she gave all her love to him willingly. No image of Elise remained before Clint's eyes after Susan's overwhelming response.

"Little darlin', I love you so much," Clint huskily whispered in her ear as they lie delightfully exhausted. He was not even aware of his term of endearment. It had been his special love-word for Elise until now. That night so long ago in Cuba when he found the poor little thing he'd picked her up and soothed her, calling her "little darlin'" and it had remained his name for her until now.

He continued to hold Susan close to him, afraid to let go now that they found this wonderful bliss with one another. "Always love me like this, Susan," he sighed, pulling her closer to him. "I want you. Love me."

And she did.

The days and nights to follow were filled with such happiness that Susan kept pinching herself to assure she wasn't dreaming. A week later when she brought little golden-skinned Dominique to Shady Oaks to stay for a few days, Clint Barron's cup of happiness overflowed.

Never suspecting that the inventive Annette Le Clere had tricked her by faking illness when Susan paid a visit, Susan offered to take the small child so that Annette could have rest.

To Clint that night at dinner she reasoned, "You know, Clint, she's not a young woman anymore, and while Dommi is a good child, she's still a very active one."

Clint heartily agreed, but still he wondered. No one dared sell Madame Le Clere short, for he considered her a very clever woman. But the impossible had happened, and he did not care how it had all come about. Never would he have hoped to have Dominique under his roof.

The two-story house emitted an infectious happiness affecting all the occupants of Shady Oaks. Old Callie was the happiest of all as she went about her kitchen humming constantly. "Dis hous is livin' agin!" The broad smile on her face appeared to be frozen there.

Little Dominique's few days at Shady Oaks stretched into a week. Susan could not have been more delighted and Annette could not have been more pleased, as was Elise when she heard about it.

However, Elise was shocked by her husband's reaction. But Elise had not noticed his preoccupation as she'd chattered away, which could have prepared her for his rather aloof manner.

"Elise, I have only one thing to say about this little game Madame Le Clere is playing. God forbid that it backfires on her. The results would crush Susan. What do you think she will do if and when she finds out about the real mother of this child? How would you feel, Elise?"

His stern, harsh tone tore at her. Her chin went high in defiance, but she still answered him honestly. "I . . . I would be—"

"Mad as bloody hell, *ma petite!* In fact, knowing you, I'd be lucky not to be murdered in my sleep." Oh, he knew her so well. She could not help a slight smile breaking out. He did not stop there though, and his manner remained the same. "I've said it before and I'll say it again; Clint should have been man enough to have cleared this mess up long ago."

"You're a hard man, Lance. So . . . so unforgiving." She regretted the words the minute she'd said them, for she, of all people, should have known better than that. It was more the defense of Annette than Clint Barron that prompted her statement. Yet, in principle, he was right.

It was not the time for something like this to take place as far as Lance was concerned. Her outburst wounded him more than she could possibly have known. Hard and unforgiving was he? A sudden rage exploded within him remembering that he could not sweep out the tormenting memories of Joaquin Ruiz, and yes, Clint Barron. Last, but not least, there was Jean Laffite sniffing around every chance he got. Perhaps he had spoiled her too much. Perhaps he should show her what an unforgiving man he could be, he mused.

He turned, staring at her. Elise did not like what she saw in his eyes. Seeking to make amends, she spoke up. "I meant, Lance, that you have no sympathy for anyone weak. Most people aren't as strong as you."

"Well, love, it's some consolation to know

317

you realize that much about your friend Barron!" He turned his back to her, rummaging for something in the desk drawer.

"*Our friend!* He is a friend to both of us, Lance. What in heaven's name is the matter with you today?"

Picking up the papers, he paused in front of her. He wanted to kiss her, but the anger in her eyes was flashing a message not to touch her. Should she have turned from him in that moment he might have forced her as he had once before. It was the only time he'd ever felt such a rage toward Elise, and never would he erase the night that he took her against her will in the cabin of his ship. Roaring drunk, trying to blot out the scene he'd witnessed at Shady Oaks when he looked upon her for the first time after months of searching for her, he'd forced her to his bed and it was forever etched in his mind. Hearing her say she was going to marry Clint Barron had seared his heart like a branding iron, and when she'd followed him to his ship docked in harbor, he wanted to hurt her as he hurt. He did by raping her.

Something about her standing there now reminded him of that night. She was pleading with him that night to listen to her, hear her out. Her eyes were pleading with him now, but he could not give in for some reason even he didn't understand. Too much was on his mind today. Things he couldn't tell Elise.

Francois Le Clere's revelation had been a tremendous shock. He felt the highest esteem and respect for the fine gentleman and he admired the man's courage to keep the truth from his wife. It was urgent, Francois had confessed to him, that he meet with Lance. When Francois told him he hoped Annette could seek Lance's wise counsel if she'd need it after he was gone, Lance felt a swelling pride engulfing him. He was honored that Francois thought of him so favorably. As the two had departed Lance sank into a depressed state that remained throughout the rest of the day.

He'd rode home that gray November day, a shroud of gloom seeming to hang over the countryside. The bright sunshine was hidden by ominous clouds threatening approaching storms.

Chapter 21

General Andrew Jackson had returned to Mobile and prepared for the move to New Orleans now that the British had abandoned Fort Barrancas. However, a British fleet with many troops plowed through the waters toward the Louisiana coastline under the command of Major General Sir Edward M. Pakenham. In his quarters the documents and charts pinpointing strategic spots along the coastline represented many months of work by British spies.

Pakenham's destination was Chandeleur Island at Lake Borgne. According to all the reports he'd received the port of New Orleans would be easy pickings. He'd been assured that they even had the loyalty of the fierce Jean Laffite and his band of pirates, numbering into the hundreds. From the west the Baratarians would attack; the British would assault the eastern coastline.

Pakenham held a very important session in

the confines of his cabin. Two of his most able men sat with him, sipping from his private stock of whiskey and listening to the major general as he spoke in a serious tone.

"In ten days, gentlemen, we'll meet again. And I pray meet in victory. You understand all your instructions? This contact in New Orleans will direct you once you're in the city. My blessings go with you. The destruction of the warehouses of ammunition and arms will put the city at our mercy."

For months the two men sitting at his desk had prepared for this mission. They allowed their beards to grow heavy on their faces, and their garb depicted them as any ordinary river boatman traveling the Mississippi. Both were seasoned, able seamen and had been picked for their ruggedness and ability to take care of themselves in any situation.

Bill Conner and Henry Townsend had volunteered for the mission knowing the danger involved. They were two of a kind, always the first to join in any fight aboard ship or on shore. Now that the time had arrived, they were eager to get started on their mission. They were wound up like two springs ready to snap.

An hour later the two descended into the longboat awaiting them and faded into the foggy shroud gathered over the waters. A few hours later, just before sunrise, the dark figures made shore, pulling the longboat up. Hacking away at the long branches of the underbrush they concealed the boat, and after a period of rest and several slugs of liquor they made for their first destination.

The River's End Tavern reminded Lance Edwards of the Seafarer's Inn in Le Harve, France, with its dining area separated from the tavern and bright table cloths. He sat in the smoke-filled tavern reminising of times long ago, and waiting for Zack Hart to join him. The small tavern area was hazy with smoke and smelled of tobacco when he'd sauntered in, taking a corner table near the entrance so he could see Zack come in. At first he'd paid no attention to the occupants of the booth next to his.

As his eyes adjusted and he slowly sipped on his drink, he surveyed the room, seeing four seamen sitting to the rear of the room. Then, out of the booth a rugged-looking gent emerged, ambling toward the rear of the building and returning shortly. He did not notice Lance sitting back in the dark corner and joining his companions he spoke a name that made Lance's ears perk.

Laffite's name was repeated a couple of times. Lance's long fingers played around the edge of the glass and he strained to hear more. Feeling certain he recognized a very distinct tenor voice he was curious as to why Laffite would be associating with these men. A strange association, indeed!

Had his curiosity not been whetted, he would

have given up on Zack's joining him, returned to his office to gather up some papers and gone on home. Instead, he remained.

With his glass dry, Lance decided to be on his way. As it would happen, the three left their table at the same instant. Lance's eyes saw it was indeed who he'd suspected.

"Hello there, Burke." Lance noted Charles did not seem too pleased and gave out a grunt for a greeting. He seemed to be more than eager to get out and away. But Lance gave no serious thought to his reaction as he started to the warehouse. It was fast becoming dark and the thoughts of his own warm hearth were anticipated.

He gathered up the papers and spoke briefly with one of his men, Captain Keane. For one fleeting second he dwelt on the two ruffians with Charles. He had never been very impressed with the man; a real queer duck. He'd heard the rumors of his gambling and womanizing. Yes, old J. William the banker had himself a no-good son, Lance concluded. For the life of him, he could not see the women's attraction to him. Lance was reminded of a fop.

He paused just outside the door, lit up a cheroot and waved at Captain Keane down on the quay. Otherwise, it seemed to be deserted down on the wharf. With the sinking of the sun, darkness closed in on the waterfront, with only a hint of light over in the western skies. He was going to be arriving at Montclair after dark now. He hastened his pace knowing Elise would have an apprehensive look on her lovely face when he arrived.

As he turned the corner of the building a sharp, smashing blow to his head gave him no opportunity to defend himself. The slight incline from the levee gave the two men all the cover they needed to wait for their victim and provided the same concealment from the road above to load the limp body into the bed of a waiting wagon.

"Throw that old tarp over him," Henry Townsend ordered the other man. "Hurry up!" He was already perched on the seat, reins in his hands as his comrade leaped up beside him.

Unfamiliar with the streets of the city and interested only in getting to the outskirts, Henry reined the wagon down the first side road. He wanted to get this business over as soon as possible, for this was something they had not planned on. The stupid Burke had raised a horrible howl when Townsend had insisted the man had to be taken care of; they could not chance that he might have heard their conversation.

The sidestreet came out on a rather secluded area, Henry noticed. Had it not been for the old sea captain down by the wharf he'd have just shot him and been done with it. He pulled up on the reins, his ears picking up the loud laughter and music coming from a big two-story house, brightly lit with people milling around.

"Bill, what do you think? Perfect, eh?" The explosion of one well-aimed shot would never be heard over all that commotion. Bill leaped down and pulled the dead weight from the back of the wagon, dragging it over into the cluster of trees.

Henry pulled out his pistol and followed behind. The shrill calling of a night bird made him jerk nervously.

A wall of trees surrounded them but the loud music still resounded, along with shrieks of female laughter and raucous male voices. Henry aimed directly at the helpless form lying there, his finger about to pull at the trigger.

A very distinct cracking of underbrush caused a slight quiver of Henry's trigger finger. Acrid smoke wafted to his nose but the sound of hurried footsteps urged him to make a hasty retreat, and he and Bill leaped to the wagon to make their getaway. He couldn't be sure he hadn't bungled the job.

It was not unusual for Titus to take an evening's jaunt through the woods next to La Maison. It was relaxing, and he enjoyed the night sounds after his chores around the house for Fifi. It was the quieter time for his services. He was always needed in the late night hours and so he was free to do his roaming, as Fifi called it.

But his quiet woods was strange this night. Even before the shot had disrupted his solitude, he'd heard something—some un- natural sound he couldn't place. Then the blast of gunfire and the smell came in the same instant! Titus rushed toward the cluster of trees from the footpath where he'd been. It was no animal laying there, Titus knew that before he knelt down. Blood covered the man's face and head, but he breathed shallowly.

"Oh, Lord God Almighty!" Titus's echoing footsteps along the path had saved the man whether he realized it or not. The shot meant to end Lance Edwards's life had only slightly glazed the side of his head and the tremendous flow of blood was due to the harsh blow he'd received back at the warehouse.

The huge black man hoisted the equally tall man's limp body up. "Big man here!" Titus mumbled as he struggled with the burden. By the time he reached the back entrance of La Maison, he was heaving deep and labored breaths.

"Git Madame Fifi, Prissy! Right now!"

Fifi wasted no time in answering Titus's summons, and when she saw who the injured man was she wasted no time sending word downstairs to the gaming table where old Doctor Barlow was. Luck was with her on that score.

While the doctor administered to Lance Edwards Fifi called Tawny and instructed her to take over for the evening. She'd have to get word to Bellefair as soon as she could, for she was certain there was no way Chickie's son was going to make it home this night.

With a heavy dose of laudanum in him Lance would rest for several hours, Barlow told Fifi. The injuries were minor, and by tomorrow he would be feeling much better. "A very healthy specimen," the doctor remarked. "Now, Fifi honey, I'll get back to my game with your permission."

"You just do that, Doc!" She let him out the door and turned to summon Titus to sit with Lance while she made the trip to Bellefair. "I'll get Toby to drive me."

An hour later Fifi was being ushered into Annette's cozy sitting room and she saw that her friend was alone. Trying to act casual, she inquired about Francois's absence. Annette informed her that he was not feeling well and had retired early.

While the hour was not late, Annette was curious about Fifi's nocturnal visit. Serving Fifi a glass of her favorite brandy, she sat down beside her on the settee.

"Chickie, your son's at my place. He's had a slight injury but it's not serious. He was shot at, Chickie."

Annette's face paled so that Fifi hastened to reassure her that he was all right. "He's sleeping like a baby. Now, you just calm yourself, honey. He's strong as a bull."

"Oh, Fifi, I appreciate your taking care of him. I care so much for him, even though he doesn't know it."

"Someday, he'll know! As for what I did, that was nothing. I was glad to do it."

"*Mon Dieu*, who would have tried something like that?" Annette seemed to sink with relief into the overstuffed chair. First Elise and now

Lance! Was the whole countryside going crazy?

"Don't have the slightest idea. Titus found him. Saw two men running away—took out in a wagon. That's all I can tell you. Got Barlow with him and he's sleeping like a pussy cat now. Thing is, Chickie, what do I do? Do I go tell his wife—this Elise you talk about so much—or what? You tell me!"

"Oh, yes! She's probably frantic now with worry. He's over three hours late. Oh, Fifi, you must get to Montclair right away. I would go with you but Francois isn't feeling well tonight."

"No, dear, you've no need. You . . . you think my being—well, you know what I mean. Do you think she'll—"

Annette interrupted her, "Elise is not that way, Fifi. Dear God, yes. If I know Elise Edwards at all she'll jump in that buggy with you and return to the city."

"Then I'd best be on my way and save her any more worry, eh?"

Hearing the carriage roll up the drive, Elise rushed to the window, sinking into even deeper despair when she saw the figure emerging was not her husband. Who was this though?

Before she could get downstairs the woman had been admitted. Midway down the stairs, Elise announced, "I'm Elise Edwards."

"Then it's you I wish to see," Fifi told her. Elise joined the woman and ushered her into the parlor. The young woman's beauty took Fifi's breath away even in the dimly lit parlor.

"Forgive me, Madame Edwards, for not introducing myself right off, but I had my reasons. It was for your sake."

"My sake? I fear I don't understand," Elise replied, guiding her to a seat. Elise tucked her deep green robe tighter around her as a sudden chill swept over her. There was a severe look about the lady dressed all in black, until as they took their seats and she removed her veil concealing her face. Elise saw her heavily painted face and flashy earrings dangling low. Elise first noticed the lady's warm, kind eyes.

"Yes, dear," Fifi answered, removing the black kid gloves. "I'm Fifi La Tour—the La Maison. Perhaps, you've been one of the ladies yet to hear of me. Not that it matters, but I'm not, shall we say, accepted in respected circles."

"Yes, I've heard of La Maison, Madame La Tour," Elise mumbled. All kinds of thoughts did battle within her. Thoughts she found more than disturbing.

"Well, a nice lady like you might not have. Anyway dear, to the reason I'm here. There's no simple way to say it, Madame Edwards, but to come right out with it. Your husband's at my place, hurt."

"*Mon Dieu*, is it serious?" Her face drained of color and Fifi saw her hand tremble as it flew up to her mouth.

329

"No, but he was sure not up to a ride home in a carriage or horseback so I bedded him down and got a doctor."

Fifi was not prepared for Elise's response but it confirmed everything Annette had said about the young lady. Elise moved out of her chair, flung her arms around the voluptuous Fifi and exclaimed, "Oh, bless you Madame La Tour! Could I please return to the city with you?"

"Well, sure honey." Fifi broke into a smile, satisfied she had done the right thing coming out to Montclair. That Elise Edwards had no qualms over entering a brothel to get to her injured husband would forever favorably impress Fifi.

She sat, watching the tiny miss rush away, black hair flowing down her shoulders. Like most people she saw the breathtaking beauty of Lance Edwards's wife, coupled with a bold spirit Fifi instantly admired. Quite a woman, she mused, waiting for her to reappear. She did not have a long wait, for Elise had been impatient to be on the way to La Maison and Lance's side. Yet, just to know that he was alive was enough to heave a deep, relieved sigh.

Returning to the parlor, where Fifi sat waiting for her, she anxiously declared, "I'm ready, Madame La Tour." Fifi nodded, thinking they could have been going for an afternoon jaunt around the countryside like a pair of old friends.

Fifi joined her at the archway. "Call me Fifi,

honey. I'd feel much better and probably answer faster." She laughed.

Giving out a light laugh, Elise took her arm. "If you will call me Elise."

"A deal!" She had to bite her tongue, for she'd come close to calling her "Chickie." Then she realized part of the reason she instantly warmed to this young lady she'd met for the first time a mere half hour ago: She was the image of Chickie at a younger age. Same raven black hair and emerald green eyes. The one exception was Elise's dark complexion compared to the gardenia white skin of Annette Le Clere.

The midnight ride through the sleeping countryside passed swiftly as the two women chatted constantly. Before either of them were aware of it the two-story establishment was there before them, ablaze with light.

Fifi led the way through the back entrance. Not once did her young companion hesitate or appear shocked at the goings on within her establishment, and as Fifi spoke to this one or that one, Elise followed along. To say the least, Fifi La Tour found her an astonishing woman. A rare jewel, to be sure!

The blasé Fifi La Tour knew by instinct this young lady had seen a part of life somewhere along the way that had not been too nice. No, she'd not always lived the existence of a pampered mistress of a fine plantation like Montclair. Fifi smiled, and her natural Irish curiosity wanted to know more about Elise Edwards. She was a rare young lady, for she held in the palm of her dainty hand the hearts of two of the most dashing rogues Fifi had ever known. That in itself set Elise apart from most women.

Chapter 22

Her husband's firm body looked out of place among the satin, lace-trimmed pillows and the other feminine decor in the room. His tanned bare chest heaved with even breaths and he slept soundly, knowing nothing of her arrival inside the room. "I'll take over now, Titus. You can get some rest."

Titus hesitated to move out of the chair and Elise smiled, explaining that she was the man's wife. "Oh . . . oh, yes ma'am. He restin' jus' fine."

"Yes, it would appear that way," she whispered softly. "And thank you, Titus."

"Yes, ma'am." He shuffled slowly out of the room, looking back just once at the petite woman gazing down at the man lying there.

Drugged heavily, Lance knew nothing of the warm body lying beside him. She'd stripped down to her chemise and crawled into the bed for some much needed sleep, for it had been an unusually long, exhausting night. Only then, and for a brief moment before her eyes became heavy with sleep, did she ponder why this had been done to Lance.

Once, in the early morning hours, Lance roused slightly to smell the sweet fragrance of jasmine. One of Fifi's girls had good taste, he vaguely thought to himself before turning on his side to go back into a deep sleep.

Elise woke up feeling amazingly refreshed. Lance still slept, so she dressed and went downstairs, seeking a cup of coffee she needed badly.

Slipping out the door, she was about to descend the stairs when an accented voice inquired, "You a new girl?" Elise turned to see a charming, dark-haired lovely with the blackest eyes, skimpily clad, coming down the hall.

The sheer wrapper left no mystery about her small but curvy body, and the beautiful Rita swayed up to Elise with no shame or embarrassment about her nudity, as though it was natural and normal.

Mischief took over in Elise as she answered the girl. "I might be. Tell me, where would I find Fifi?"

A dark brow raised. "Fifi! *Dios*, you don't dare call her that!" Who did she think she was?

"Oh?" Elise displayed a naive innocence. "But could you tell me where I might find her?"

"In our dining room." With a wave of her long, slender fingers she pointed out the

334

direction as they reached the base of the stairs. She turned in the opposite direction, calling back to Elise, "Oh, I'm Rita, honey, and I'll see you later. What's your name, by the way?"

"Elise." She found it all very amusing that one of Fifi's girls would take her for one of them. She had no idea that Rita could not wait to tell the other girls about the new arrival, and that in Rita's calculating mind, she reasoned that the new arrival would be the reigning queen before too long. What she couldn't know was that all this concern would be for naught.

As Rita's mouth went nonstop with three of the other girls, Elise spoke with Fifi and enjoyed a croissant and a steaming cup of coffee. By the time she excused herself to see if Lance had finally wakened Fifi decided she liked that young lady even more.

When Tawny entered the dining room to report to the madam about the evening before and how things went during her absence, Fifi was quick to point out to the sultry mulatto, "Tawny, my dear, you just passed a lady of quality. Lots are labeled so, but there went one." She proceeded to relate to Tawny the events of the night before and why she'd had to take her leave of La Maison. Tawny was her oldest girl now at the ripe age of twenty-four, and also her most reliable one. Fifi remembered that when Clint Barron had brought the beautiful Delphine to her she was struck by the resemblance of the two. They could have been sisters.

*　　　*　　　*

Now that the long hours of sleep had passed and no effects of the drug remained in his body, Lance rose on his elbows. It was a struggle, and he found himself engulfed by weakness. The sweet odor of jasmine came to his nose again and he remembered vaguely the same fragrance permeating the room earlier. Elise watched, saying nothing.

His muscled body began to tremble as he propped himself up, and he gave way, sinking back down on the bed. Without saying a word, Elise bent down and kissed him fully on the lips. "*Mon cheri*, I love you so."

"Elise?" Surely he'd heard wrong. Elise— here?

"Yes, it is Elise, my love." She smiled down on him and his arms reached up encircling her neck.

"Kiss me again, sweet," he urged her. She did gently and then rose. Her hands cradled his face tenderly.

"I dare not get too carried away for fear of your poor aching head. Does it still hurt?"

"A little, love. How . . . how did you get here?"

"Fifi came and got me," she told him in that forth-right, matter-of-fact manner of hers.

A devilish gleam came to his eyes, and he managed a hint of laughter. "Leave it to you, little vixen. What other woman in the city of New Orleans can say she's been at Fifi's!"

Elise giggled gaily. "Oh, Monsieur, what wife

336

can boast of sleeping with her husband in a brothel, eh? I did last night. The only thing is you knew nothing about it."

Fifi heard the soft laughter inside the room and thought to herself that Elise was all the tonic needed to cure what ailed the man inside the room. Hesitating to disturb them, she lingered a moment before knocking. Feeling sure the carafe of coffee would be welcomed by him, she rapped softly.

Elise bid her enter, and Fifi called out, "Can't honey. Got a tray."

Elise rushed to oblige her, apologizing. Fifi shrugged her off, looking at her improved patient and teasing him by intimating she knew what it took to get him well.

"You're right, Fifi! Can you blame me?" He reached out to squeeze Elise's hand, and his lazy black eyes told the story to Fifi better than all the words he could have uttered.

"No, the only way I'd ever blame you, Lance, would be if you were ever fool enough to let her slip through your fingers," the jovial madam declared, giving Elise a wink. The old gal liked his wife, Lance realized, watching the two exchange amused glances.

"Fifi, my darling, we'll promise you that never will it be told in the city of New Orleans that there was an occasion when a wife shared her husband's bed at La Maison. We'd never want to destroy the image of your establishment." Fifi roared with laughter at the thought of it.

After a mammoth breakfast and shaving with Elise's help, Lance dressed in preparation to go home. Titus would drive them, Fifi offered, and this pleased Lance for he was eager to get to Montclair. Impatience gnawed at him to regain his strength; he had a gentleman to seek out and deal with—three gents to be more exact. He planned to start with Charles Burke; he'd recognized the two ruffians who'd hit him even in the darkness.

Reckless he was, but a fool he was not, so Charles Burke made a quick exit from New Orleans, realizing that he'd allowed his hot temper get the best of him. Beating up Susan Barron had been one thing, but tangling with Lance Edwards was another. The two seamen had not done a thorough job, he was informed. Damned old Titus for coming along when he did! New Orleans was a dangerous place for him.

As dawn broke the next morning he rode west atop his fine red roan. His saddlebags bulged with all the funds he could muster in a few hours' time, along with some of the smaller family heirlooms, such as the exquisite jewelry of his mother's. The present Mrs. Burke, Andrea, would be dealt a devastating blow when she later learned she would never see it again.

His decision had been a wise one, for the next few days Lance Edwards thought of nothing else but revenge. Elise understood when he told her who, but it still perplexed both of them as to why. Lance made no mention of Jean's name to her.

The only clue Lance could cipher out of the whole insane mess was the name Jean Laffite.

A courier arrived at the Governor's mansion the last day of November bearing the glad tidings that General Jackson and his troops would be arriving in the city of New Orleans within a few days. There was a flurry of excitement and preparations were set in motion. There was also a sombering effect on the citizens of the city, for it brought forth the stark reality that the war that had yet to penetrate their homes and countryside was an actuality.

As the influencial men met with the Governor and officers of the militia, their ladies busily prepared for a ball to fete the esteemed General Jackson.

Elise's gown for the ball was the color of jonquil, which Madame Vivienne informed her led the list of the most fashionable hues.

"And you, my pet, can wear it to perfection!" she exclaimed, delighted with the effect of her creation. "Your friend has my other masterpiece; a magnificent pearl-gray gown."

"Oh?" She must be referring to Annette.

"Yes, Madame Le Clere. She was as surprised as I when she tried the shade. Something about her hair and the material. Oh, la, la—it was divine!"

"She is always attractive. Like you, I find the

color hard to picture though."

"Wait, *ma petite,* until you see her. You will see," Madame Vivienne assured her, helping her unbutton the miniature buttons on the long sleeves of the gown that gave it a unique effect. That was the perfection of its simple, soft lines, and the light softness and sheerness of the silk. Elise's beautiful shoulders were partially bared by the deep neckline, and the smooth, molded bodice exhibited her bustline. The slight fullness around the hips merely emphasized the wasplike waist.

Against the chill of the December night Madame had made a matching cape, lined in satin of the same color as the pale yellow gown. There was no doubt in Madame Vivienne's mind that the appearance of Elise Edwards would bring forth sighs over the gown, as well as the beauty wearing it. She could ask nothing more than to display her skills to the aristo-cratic elites of the city. More than once she'd had some lady come in and request a gown be made for her, and from the description Madame Vivienne knew they'd observed Elise in a similar one at one of the galas. While the generous Lance Edwards was one of her most prized patrons, she'd often pondered that it was she who should pay his wife for showing off her gowns so marvelously.

Vivienne fell exhaustedly in the chair. Her stockroom overflowed with a bevy of many colored gowns, each labeled now with the name of the customer. A vivid blue tagged for

Madame Barron, the pearl-gray for Madame Le Clere and Andrea Burke's magenta one.

While Vivienne's expertise touched all of them, some were her favorites, like the women wearing them were her favorite ladies. Such a match was the brilliant emerald green gown due to be picked up in the next hour or two.

Vivienne felt somewhat like Cinderella, for she found herself yearning to attend the grand balls just once. She had only visions of what it might be like to dance the night away in some Prince Charming's arms in one of her lovely creations. Who would she wish was her prince? she mused in her whimsy.

Two men came hastily to mind; the dashing, handsome Lance Edwards and the charming rogue Jean Laffite. Vivienne, being a perfectionist by nature, had resigned herself to the fact that her work would replace a husband. The men she would have found attractive and desirable did not move in her social circle. The men who did had never interested her.

So she had settled for making her beautiful creations and daydreaming from time to time about the fabulous nights she shared through her exquisite gowns.

Part III

Love's Glorious Reward

Chapter 23

The streets of New Orleans were alive with a mixture of milling crowds and aromas from the foods and flowers of the vendors on every street corner. It was a day churning with excitement and anticipation, beginning with the noon-day event of the governor welcoming General Jackson to the city. Lance and Elise were among the honored couples to sit on the stage during the ceremonies.

After that they were to go to a luncheon at the Governor's mansion. After the luncheon, the gentlemen were to hold a session and Elise, like the other ladies, would retire for a rest in the afternoon before the Grand Ball that evening.

As with most social events the schedule was running late, and by the time Lance escorted her to their carriage to be returned to their suite of rooms at the hotel it was past two. Elise was more than ready to get to their rooms and take off her new slippers and flop across the bed for an hour or so.

"Sweetheart, be sure you lock the door, eh? I'll be there . . . oh, I'd say in a couple of hours," he said, giving her a hurried kiss on the cheek before closing the door.

He found himself wishing that she had been accompanied by Annette Le Clere, but they had decided to forego the activities during the day and attend only the evening gala. Francois could not shake the lasting effect of a recent cold, so Annette was limiting their social events.

Lance waved to Elise as the carriage took her away, but he was not satisfied at all about her being alone while he was in the meeting. The city was teeming with people, and he'd taken notice of the crowded lobby of the hotel where they were staying. All kinds of dandies were roaming around ogling the ladies. It was a carnival atmosphere in the city.

Too much had happened lately for him not to be leary of his or his wife's safety. For the time being he had to shelve the revenge he'd plotted for Charles Burke. He satisfied himself that the man had skipped out of New Orleans for parts unknown. Still, he'd continued to search for the two husky ruffians who had attempted to do him in. His eyes wandered over the wharves and streets of the city in hopes of finding them. So that left one clue yet to investigate; Jean Laffite.

As Lance returned to his meeting with

twelve other gentlemen of influence, Elise was making her way through the lobby of the hotel, unaware that she was the subject of much animated conversation.

The minute she breezed through the entrance the two young gents stood spellbound by the sight of her. Both were having their own thoughts, saying nothing to the other. The taller of the two French Creoles nudged the other with a lusty look on his good-looking face. "That, *mon ami,* is choice!"

"*Oui,* I would say so. Beautiful! Beautiful! She puts Deirdre to shame, eh?"

"Deirdre and Agatha. Most of them."

Both shifted their positions, moving around the column blocking the view. Elise had now turned the corner to go toward the steps. The two young men continued to let their eyes follow her. She had no idea that the back view of her gave a signal like a beckon to the gents. Her feisty walk was just a part of her. All her movements were fast and animated.

"Who is she? Did you ever see such a cute behind?" One of the finely attired young Creoles asked his friend as they stood waiting for a particular lady to join them.

"You don't know?" The other Creole with fine aquiline features gave out a broad smile. "I've heard through a friend some very saucy tidbits about the beautiful lady."

"Tell me, Jacques." So his friend bent over and whispered in his ears the rumors related to her. Michael Morot's hot blood surged, and he trembled.

"Shall we test her out?" The devil-may-care Morot prodded his friend for he had forgotten any anticipated pleasures he'd harbored about the afternoon tryst with the wealthy matron who was a good ten years older than him.

"Shall we?" Jacques suggested and they both hurriedly rushed to catch up with their prey.

Elise noticed the two following her and when they attempted to approach her with a flippant remark, she shrugged them off with a sharp retort of her own.

"Ah, the beautiful lady is without mercy," Morot mimicked, and he winked at his friend with no intention of giving up his quest. By this time Elise was too angry to be frightened. She swung her parasol jauntily with a devious smile on her lips; the tip had a sharp point equal to any dagger, and she'd not hesitate a moment to apply it if she had to.

As it would happen the trio had been observed at the end of the hallway. But the two dandies had not noticed the formidable figure just waiting to see what they'd attempt on the lady. He recognized the beautiful woman in the rich gold-colored gown immediately, and he adored the sight of her sashaying down the thick-carpeted hall. He noted the brightness of her eyes, not one ounce of fear reflected there. No, it was more the look of mischief. It was his reason for not rushing immediately to her side and sending the two fops on their way. His ever-alert eyes caught the sharp tip of her parasol

348

and he knew exactly what she had in mind for the two. He could read the little minx's mind!

Only when she came to a halt at the door and the two began to form a barrier around her did he move and move swiftly. With anything but gentleness, he took hold of the collars of the finely tailored coats and the two were hurled fiercely across the space of the hallway. Their thudding bodies vibrated against the paneled walls with a resounding thump.

It took a moment for Elise to react, and then she exploded with laughter as Jean's arms enclosed her. "Oh, Jean, how wonderful to see you, and how glad I am you happened to come along," she said, still laughing lightly.

"Not half as glad as I, *ma petite*." While he didn't add the words he was thinking, he thought them to himself. It was no day for a lady like Elise to be anywhere in this city.

The docks and wharves were still astir as he'd come from there earlier. Drunken seamen were sprawled on the crates doing their brand of celebrating, some were laying with wenches from the waterfront taverns. Fights were spasmodically erupting on the levee, with the rivermen in disagreement. He laid the blame of it all on General Jackson's arrival and the reality of war actually upon the city of New Orleans. Chaotic conditions were bound to prevail. Its effect on people usually brought out astonishing traits of bravery or weakness. So far the battles to the north and east had not left any impact on New Orleans. Now they were to feel it, too.

Jean and Elise seemed to share the same feeling of awkwardness just standing there in the hall. Was she reluctant to invite him into their suite? he wondered. If that was so, he decided to remedy that right away. "Could you join me in some refreshments downstairs, *ma petite?*" he suggested.

"I have a much better idea, and besides, there's someone inside who would like to see you." She took his arm and guided him through the door.

"If you insist, my lady." Jean smiled at her.

"There is no reason why two friends can't have a drink, eh?" She called out for Jessamine and the young girl came through the door, smiling. She recognized Mister Jean's voice before Elise had called out to her.

"Why, Mister Jean! Nice to see ya'!"

"And it's nice to see you, Jessamine. My, if you aren't getting prettier all the time," Jean remarked with that charm of his. Jessamine's face lit up with pleasure. She left the room giggling to get the wine and glasses Elise had requested.

"And how is your husband, Elise?" He heard about the recent accident and questioned the attacks on both of them in the last two months.

"Appeared to be fine about an hour ago," she declared. "Jean—why? Who could have wanted to do him in?" She knew who had taken a shot at her, but Lance's attackers had been men— two ruffians. Lance had even mentioned rivermen, perhaps.

"I have no idea, Elise, but we're living in crazy times and New Orleans does have a lot of riff-raff coming and going. To some a life means nothing. Lance is a wealthy man, so perhaps it was for the funds in his pocket or the jewelry on him."

"No, it could not have been that, Jean. Nothing was taken. No, whoever it was wanted him dead!"

"Has he any clues at all?"

"Not that I know about."

It had to be nice for someone to care so much, he mused with envy flooding him. Desire overwhelmed him sitting by her side, but he fought it.

Changing the subject he inquired about the renowned Andrew Jackson. "What do you think of him, *ma petite?*"

"I liked him very much. He is warm and friendly. A sincere, honest man, Jean."

"Perhaps I will get the opportunity to meet him tonight."

"So, you are going to attend?" It pleased him to see her face brighten up.

"If I'm not held up. That reminds me Elise, I've been distracted already too long by your charms."

"Jean! Your silver tongue has no effect on me," she teased him back and laughed softly.

"But it's true, Elise." He ached to say more. Instead, he pulled a paper from his pocket and handed it to her. "Would you see that General

Jackson gets this, my sweet. There is the remote possibility something could detain me. I make you Jean Laffite's courier." He smiled broadly flashing his fine set of white teeth. Turning more serious, he pointed out how important it was that Jackson receive it.

"Of course I will Jean, but hope that he will get to meet you in person. I have no doubt that the two of you will like each other."

She joined him, standing up from the settee. Together they strolled toward the door. He fought the urge to encircle her tiny waist with his arms and press his lips against those honey-sweet lips as he had done once so long ago.

She thanked him again for coming to her rescue earlier. Jean looked deep into her bright eyes. His voice was low, smothered with passion as he spoke. "You should know Elise, I will always come to your rescue if I can."

What she saw burning in his eyes made her nervous and uneasy. When she replied she tried to control the tremble in her voice. "Thank you, Jean. I . . . I hope you get to see the general." She felt like a fumbling, bumbling idiot.

"We'll see, sweet. But now I must be on my way," he said, bending to give her a light peck on the cheek. Even this he should not have done for it left him wanting her all the more. Such punishment was foolish!

As his carriage pulled around the corner through the boisterous crowd, another carriage arrived at the hotel. Edwards thought it was the

Frenchman he'd just passed. Damn the Baratarian! He pulled angrily on his cheroot, questioning where Laffite had come from, and wild suspicions sparked at once with the hotel so close and his wife there alone. Was it just coincidence? he wondered.

Lance hated this thing within him that gnawed and chewed away at times like this. He should have realized from the first that Elise would be a woman sought after and fawned over by admiring gentlemen. He hated his rages of jealousy; considered it a weakness in a man such as himself. He resented any denting of that self-assured man he'd known himself always to be. Weakness he could not abide.

Damned if he'd even inquire of Elise if Laffite paid a call on her. He was just a little past the lovesick stage of some romantic fool not thirty-five. He hardly fit that role. Could loving make a man a jellyfish?

But even as he shrugged aside the plaguing thought of Laffite, something told him there would come a day when something would determine who was the better man. He knew it from the first time their eyes had met, challenging and daring each other. When it would happen he didn't know, but it would.

Jessamine had been out on the balcony surveying the exciting, lively streets below. She observed Laffite leave and Captain Edwards arrive. Which of the two virile handsome devils would win her heart, she quizzed herself. Lordy, it would be hard!

Now that Baptiste boy was one she could go for. She'd set out and managed to catch the youthful stable boy, and he certainly seemed to enjoy ogling her as she walked by. Giggling, she thought about how she'd added that extra swish to her hips. Baptiste's eyes fairly looked like they'd pop out of his curly black head.

She interrupted her whimsical daydreams hearing the captain's heavy footsteps padding through the sitting room. She made no effort to leave her balcony seat, for Missy's soft voice was not calling her yet.

Something told Elise not to mention Jean's visit. She had finally become aware of her husband's deep-seated resentment of Jean, and Annette Le Clere had made her see that he probably suffered more from his outburst of jealousy than she did. The matronly Madame Le Clere pointed out that when a man such as her husband loved so completely, with such hot-blooded passion, his fury when provoked was explosive.

Tonight Elise wanted no explosions. After all, there was nothing to feel guilty about, her conscience answered.

One look at her in the delicate yellow gown made him forget any moodiness he'd indulged in earlier. As he draped the cape around her shoulders, he vowed to not leave her side. While she gave him her sweetest smile, she secretly prayed that he would grant her some freedom to carry out the mission for Jean. She must do this favor for him.

"No, my pet, I wouldn't trust a saint standing next to you tonight. God Elise, it seems you get prettier each day," he declared candidly.

"Why thank you, my darling." She gave his arms a tight squeeze. "You are a remarkable man, Lance Edwards. I am a lucky woman!"

"Never forget it, love!" He took her hand and led her out of the room to go to the gala affair of the evening.

From the mammoth crowd milling around the ballroom it seemed everyone in the city had turned out to pay tribute to General Jackson. With all the gay decorations, finely attired guests, and lively music filling the room, one could hardly associate to the threat of war lurking in the background.

Yet gentlemen in uniform were very much in evidence among the dancing couples and crowd. Elise suddenly realized how many strange faces there were. She searched the room for some sight of Susan and Clint, or Annette and Francois. She saw Flo Maynard and her husband. No one could miss Andrea Burke hanging on the arm of Major Hopper. Elise gently led Lance in the opposite direction. He smiled smugly to himself.

Making their way to one of the several refreshment tables, Lance allowed her only a sip of champagne before taking her out on the floor to dance. "Got to show you off, my pet."

She could not help feeling pleased by his attention and admiration. An hour later she was beginning to believe that his earlier comment was not in jest; he continued to stay close to her side. They'd danced and spoke with the Le Cleres. Then he danced with her again. She searched the crowd for some sight of the general, who they'd not yet spotted among the guests.

The music stopped and Lance was leading her off the floor when a deep male voice called to him. She turned to see the tall, lanky general standing behind them. "I've been watching you, sir, and it's time you allowed us other gents a dance with your pretty lady."

Lance smiled. "I plead guilty, general." He placed Elise's hand in Jackson's outstretched hand. All of them broke into light laughter.

As they danced, Elise noticed the weary look on the rugged-looking general's face, and he had a nagging cough. The poor man probably needed to be in bed resting instead of dancing. What better way to present Jean's message to him as they sat in some secluded corner, she thought to herself.

"I don't know about you, General Jackson, but I'm about to fall in my tracks. It's been a very busy day." She sighed dramatically.

"Young lady, do you read minds? I swear you're as perceptive as my Rachael," he said, admiring her forthright manner and natural-ness. Had he not liked her before he certainly was impressed now.

Elise followed, as he led. She was equally impressed by the forty-seven-year-old man.

356

While his face was not handsome, there was great strength there. One could not help being aware of this masterful, powerful personality.

Stopping to help themselves to champagne, they found a secluded corner perfectly screened by a giant palm plant. As they seated themselves, the general remarked, "I must make a point of letting Captain Edwards know what a jewel he has in you, Madame Edwards."

"You are most kind, General Jackson." She dared not waste one minute, already fumbling in her reticule. The general was the honored guest, and she had no doubt the minute they were spied sitting there someone would intrude on their privacy.

"Sir, while we are alone I must give you this. This is a message from Jean Laffite. Perhaps you've heard of him?"

"Who, indeed, hasn't? Hmmm, Jean Laffite." Taking the message from her dainty hand, he found himself curiously interested as to just why this pretty lady would be the deliverer. He'd heard the rumors of Laffite being a rogue and a rascal. It was natural for him to question, why her?

After reading the message he folded it and placed it in his pocket. "Tell me, madame, what is your opinion of this Laffite?"

"Well, General Jackson, you will find me to be prejudiced. You see, Jean saved my life." Elise told him of her capture by Sebastian, and Jackson listened spellbound by the adventure and this young woman's obvious bravery. He'd always admired boldness and courage, in a man or a woman.

"My God, little lady, you've certainly done more than sat on your cushion doing needlepoint, haven't you?" He laughed with a twinkle coming into his tired eyes. "Yes sir, we've got to get you and my Rachael together. Still call her my little sweetheart."

Elise giggled, "Why General, you're a romantic!"

He winked and whispered, "Don't say a word. It would ruin my image."

"I wouldn't dare," she assured him, returning his wink with one of her own. "Tell me about your Rachael."

He spoke freely of their marriage and the ridicule his pretty lady had been subjected to due to the crazy legislation. The divorce they thought was valid when they first married was not, so they'd lived together for three years not legally married. In 1794 a second marriage was finally recognized.

"You can imagine how the vicious tongues tore poor Rachael apart." He reached over to pat her hand, adding, "And I, my little lady, can imagine how those same kinds of tongues tore you apart, living many weeks at Barataria."

"Yes, it's true. Perhaps that is why I can't see Jean Laffite as the river-rat, as some call him. Why, the people on Barataria love him as they would a king."

That kind of man could be a great asset in the days to come, Jackson calculated. "And I venture to say his men would follow him to their deaths in battle?"

"Yes, I think they would, General Jackson."

"Well, young lady, that's all this general needs to know. I'll send my courier to Laffite the first thing in the morning. But I must tell you, Madame Elise Edwards, I've enjoyed this moment with you tonight, and you saved a forty-seven-year-old general from collapse on that dance floor." He stood up so tall he looked like a giant. Looking down on Elise he offered his hand.

Walking back toward the crowd, he told her, "It's been a pleasure little one. Now, let's see if we can find that lucky husband of yours."

Elise smiled radiantly, unaware that her husband stood watching them from behind. His brow furrowed with a frown, his mouth tightened with clinched teeth, and his black eyes blazed with angry fire. Her superfluous praise of Jean Laffite galled him. She made him sound like some hero.

Having no knowledge of the earlier part of the conversation, Lance could only ponder why or how the subject of Laffite had come up between Elise and General Jackson.

Once again he was to be plagued by the damnable Baratarian and Elise's admiration of him. He wanted the pirate out of his life, once and for all.

Chapter 24

At the end of his second day in New Orleans, General Jackson knew he faced a dire situation. He was unprepared to defend the important gateway and the long coastline of Louisiana. He wasted no time in preparing batteries and enlisting the aid of men like Lance Edwards. He agreed with Edwards that gunboats should be situated at St. Louis Bay, out of the city some sixty miles to the northeast.

A group of men was sent out to secure the services of able-bodied men for the fight that was soon to be. The British fleet had been sighted out of the harbor. The days were short before they would be nearing their destination.

Six American gunboats stationed themselves on Lake Borgne. The Hart-Edwards Fleetline warehouses, along with Clint Barron's warehouses were beehives of activity day and night as weapons and ammunition were stored.

Elise found it a depressing time with Lance's long absences from home. She and Susan passed the time in the afternoons, for a new bond of friendship existed between them. Susan had become the full-fledged surrogate mother to little Dominique now that Francois Le Clere's health had taken a turn for the worse.

When Elise had last visited the Le Clere's she could hardly disguise the shock she felt viewing the frailty of Francois. A shroud of gloom remained with her when she had returned to Montclair, and she could not shake the gnawing feeling of foreboding that lingered. So absorbed with concern about her dear friends, Elise shrugged aside her own personal concerns about Lance's recent strange behavior. Oh, she understood his long absences away from home, but since the night of the ball he had not attempted to make love to her.

That night when they'd returned from the gala he'd fallen on the bed, drunk, and was asleep by the time his head hit the pillow. She had not thought too much about it that night. A man had the right to drink too much on occasion. Yet Lance was a man who could hold his liquor. Had she been unaware that he was drinking so much that night? She did not think so.

It was the next day that she remembered seeing her husband drunk only once before—so drunk he didn't know what he was doing. That was the night she'd gone to his ship moored in the harbor to explain that she'd thought he was dead.

All the misery and grief of the time when she was captive of Joaquin Ruiz came back like a rushing current. Their reunion here in New Orleans had been horrible. Lance, as a guest of the Harts, had attended that party at Shady Oaks. It was the night Cling Barron was to announce their marriage. Dear Clint, so proud and excited about Elise finally accepting his proposal! Elise had finally decided that Lance was dead as Joaquin had told her back when they were in Havana. Oh, that horrible moment was branded on her memory as if it had happened yesterday.

She stood laughing and talking with Zack Hart when Lance ambled over in their direction. He'd heard her tell Zack she and Clint were to be married. Their eyes met and she could not take the hate and anguish in his dark eyes. She had fainted. Later she knew she must go to him. Never could she marry Clint. Lance lived! She found him in the cabin of his ship, roaring drunk, hellbent on hurting her as he hurt. Even with all the torment and anger, a wild savage desire burned in him and he took her forcefully. But as it always was with them their love won out and the hurts and pains were swept away.

What was his torment this time? Elise pondered. She could think of nothing she might have done that had displeased him so. Even Jean Laffite could not be faulted, as far as she could surmise. Not lately, at least.

Elise had no inkling that it was Jean again that was the infuriating culprit. Having no knowledge that Lance had heard her praise of Laffite to Jackson, she was innocent about his wounded pride. That, and the fact that she had omitted mentioning Jean's apparent visit to her during the afternoon.

Elise did not get to confront him that evening as she had planned for she was asleep when he arrived home. The next morning he was already gone when she woke. He had decided the night before that he, too, planned to face her with his fact. Finding her already asleep that night, he vowed that after dinner that night he would speak to her.

With he and Elise there had never been games, and he would be damned if they'd start now. This had gone on long enough. Lately she had been far too polite and quiet, not his flippant, lively Elise, with her quick retorts. This Elise he neither understood nor liked. She made him feel like a stranger, and he hesitated to draw her into his arms or make love to her. He didn't need this added tension right now.

That evening during dinner he found her with the same disturbing, casual manner. Both found the other impossible to relate to, and neither touched their meals.

South of Montclair, lighting up the dark night skies an ominous orange-yellow glow reached up into the sky. Elise or Lance had taken no notice of it. Now that the meal was over and Lance had dismissed the serving girl,

363

he informed Elise they must talk.

His serious mood made her prepare for the news that the time had come for him to join the forces of Jackson on one of his packet ships, which had been armed to aid the blockades to be set up to protect the long coastline of Louisiana. She had expected this announcement each day and had dwelled in her own torment. The thought of him being in danger sent her into a panic.

However, their conversation never took place for their majordomo interrupted the quiet of the dining room by ushering the panic-stricken servant Henri through the door.

Lance insisted that he have a brandy and catch his breath before trying to speak. His words were jumbled and Lance could not grasp the sense of anything he was trying to say.

Still stammering, but somewhat slower, Henri told him, "I tried to get her to come with me, but she would not leave monsieur."

"What . . . is Francois worse tonight, Henri?" Elise prodded.

The old servant broke down again, covering his face with his hands. "Monsieur died tonight, Madame Edwards. Madame was with him when the three broke in the house. They tie me and Cecile up—we have no way to warn madame upstairs. They go through the house like vultures—monsieur's gun collection, the silver—everything they can put in their sacks. That little woman—she was so brave standing up to them. Poor madame! They slam her on the head.''

Elise could hardly catch her breath until he added that Annette was only injured.

But Henri was not through with his tale of horror. He told how they'd fired the mansion and urged Lance and Elise to look out the window where they could see the inferno still blazing in the distance.

He stammered out the story of how the intruders had burst into the bedroom of his mistress as she sat in the shock of finding Francois dead. He had passed away in his sleep. In their frenzy of destruction their shot had gone into a man already past feeling; he had expired a few minutes earlier.

Lance and Elise stood frozen, unable to speak for a moment. They stared in shock at the golden glow lighting up the sky to the south. ''Dear God!'' Lance shrieked!

Elise muzzled her mouth to hold back the scream trying to erupt. The countryside had gone mad, it seemed to her. From that moment until the next day, Elise moved through the hours in a maze. It was as though she was having a horrible nightmare she could not come out of.

Within the next hour she and Lance accompanied Henri back to Bellefair. Once they arrived Lance took charge of everything that had to be done. Annette Le Clere lingered in dazed disbelief, still not aware of everything that happened to her world.

Elise had no inkling of the time spent at

Bellefair before they prepared to return to Montclair with Annette.

Two days later when Francois was laid to rest Annette showed no concern over the devastation of her palacial home in the background from the small knoll where Francois was buried.

It was decided that Annette must return with them to Montclair for the next few weeks. During those weeks Lance spent time from sunup to sundown seeing to the removal of the charred ruins and the clearing and salvaging of any articles worth storing in the sheds.

Elise allowed Annette all the solitude she desired in the guest room she stayed in. But when Madame Le Clere sought to chat and visit Elise gladly joined her. She admired the older woman's courage, doubting that she would be as strong and brave in the same situation.

It came as an unexpected shock the morning Annette came down the steps to join Elise in the morning room and inquired if she might have the use of the Edwards's carriage and a driver. She joined Elise to have some coffee and heated croissants, along with delicious red plum jelly.

"Henri, Cecile and I must go into New Orleans, *chérie*," she announced, calm and casual.

"Are you sure you're up to it, Annette?" Elise thought she looked so tiny and helpless. "Shall I accompany you?"

"No, dear, you and Lance have done quite

enough." Annette pushed back her chair. "I can be ready to leave in an hour. I shall be gone most of the day."

Elise nodded her head and went to summon one of the servants to send word to Baptiste to ready the carriage.

Elise pondered throughout the day what Annette's purpose for the trip into the city was all about. When the petite Madame Le Clere returned late in the day she resolutely announced that the next day she was taking up residence at her house in New Orleans.

"I could never live at Bellefair without Francois. Bellefair was Francois, Elise. Someday I wish it rebuilt, but for now that will have to wait. Ah yes, someday I want to see some loving couple live there, and live and love within those walls as we did. But for now—"

Elise hugged her warmly and tears emerged in her eyes. She understood so well what Annette meant. She felt the same way about Montclair. Without Lance, it would all mean nothing.

"I see you understand, *chérie*," Annette murmured, patting Elise's hand. So dearly did she love the young woman who was married to her son. She knew she must do as Francois had requested of her shortly before his death. But she could not bring herself to do it while she was a guest under his roof.

Chapter 25

Restlessness flooded her and Elise could not have pinpointed its cause if she had tried to. All she knew was nothing held her interest or entertained her. She was like a butterfly flying from one thing to another. The soft pelting drops of rain falling against the windows had lulled the children off to their afternoon naps and Lance had gone into the city for a meeting at Townhall. She seemed to be the only living soul moving aimlessly around the huge house.

The damned dreary weather prevented her the pleasure of a ride, she muttered under her breath after she'd tossed the knitting aside. She laid the book aside after a couple of pages of reading. What was the matter with her?

A cozy, rainy day was usually welcomed by her, and she found herself relaxed and serene. Like a kitten, she liked to curl up by the hearth to watch the flames of the logs burning in the fireplace, but this day it did not soothe her. Instead, she strolled to the windows to look out at the countryside. How gray and ominous the skies looked! So dismal and gloomy!

Suddenly she thought of Francois Le Clere, and she found herself realizing just how much his loss had affected her. Dear God, it was hard to imagine never seeing that tall, dignified man again! She could envision that head of snow white hair and his classic features—such a handsome man! Thinking of Annette and how she must miss him she concluded that life was so unfair. She pondered her own life without Lance and how unbearable it would be. What was the cause of his serious preoccupation lately? It seemed forever he'd left her out of his thoughts and his time, she sadly mused.

The next morning the sun broke through the gray skies and the sight delighted Elise. She made immediate plans to go into the city to shop for the approaching holidays. Eagerly dressing in a dark green outfit and a perky hat with brown and green feathers, she added her emerald earrings. Her spirits were already lifted as she dashed down the stairs, unaware that Lance was in the study.

The door of his study was open and he sat at his desk watching her dash down the hallway. What was she about? he wondered. He called out to her and she stopped short, turning on her heels to return to the study.

"Yes, Lance? You called me?"

"I did. Where are you off to in such a rush, *ma petite?*" He rose from his chair, striding around the corner of his desk. His black hair fell carelessly over his forehead and as he brushed it back Elise noticed the weary look in his eyes. He'd been putting in too many hours lately. In turn, he was thinking how utterly beautiful she looked. She would remain young long after he was an old man.

"I'm going shopping and by Annette's, *mon cheri.*"

"The city is full of rabble, Elise. You should not go alone. Take Jessamine." His tone was far harsher and sharper than he intended and he saw the flashing resentment in her green eyes at once.

"Lord, Lance! I'm not a child. This . . . this darn threat of war can't stop our lives! It's all so . . . so, depressing with nothing going on—no parties, nothing! I'm going to buy some gifts for the children."

"Then make sure you leave long before late afternoon so you won't be after dark on the road coming home. Get Jess to drive you." He did not enjoy the thought of her being the target of the soldiers' ogling eyes, and the streets were full of them. His bossiness brought out hostility in Elise.

"I hear you, Lance," she snapped, bouncing out of the room.

He knew that look and he could have

mellowed that authoritative tone. Never had that worked with Elise and he of all people should know that.

Elise found Lance's manner vexing, and she thought about it during the ride into the city. However, as they arrived at the outskirts of New Orleans she began to understand what he'd cautioned her about. Drays filled with goods moved along the streets and strange, accented voices, and men as rough looking as the seamen ambled around carrying weapons and dressed in buckskins. They seemed to take no notice that their vulgar, earthy words were loud and easily heard by the few ladies like herself going in and out of the shops.

One store merchant told her, "We got some good men in those Tennessee men and Kentuckians. Tough as leather, and brave as bulls. Followed Jackson down here to fight for us."

This eased Elise's concern as she went about her shopping. With some gifts for Christmas for young Andy and a special cuddly doll for Lanissa, she made one more stop, adding a waistcoat of buff kerseymere and another of white marseilles. She was more than pleased with her gifts so she prepared to go spend an hour with Annette before starting back to Montclair.

An hour later Elise emerged from the house amazed that Annette seemed to have accepted her life without Francois. The hour's visit had passed all too swiftly. They'd chattered away about Lance, the children and Elise's gifts for the family. Annette, in turn, had told her of Jean's visits with her. "He's been most thoughtful. But then I am such a blessed woman to have so many good friends." She omitted mentioning the constant visits of Fifi La Tour during the nocturnal hours.

Elise stepped outside the iron gate in preparation to board the carriage, totally shocked by the figure rushing out of the concealing bushes. He was a thin man, heavily bearded and dark complected, and as he spoke she noticed the heavy accent of his voice. "*Señora*—a minute please!"

A million horrible memories rushed back to her from the past, and she turned abruptly to face the man. A deep, heavy sigh of relief escaped her lips. How foolish she was not remembering that Joaquin Ruiz was dead by her husband's own hands years ago—but Ruiz had called her "*señora.*"

Looking him straight in the eyes, she shrugged away the ghost haunting her momentarily. This man's eyes were black as night, not the pale, silver blue of Joaquin's that gave him a sinister look. However, he was a Latin. But in the city of New Orleans there were many people of Spanish descent.

"You speak to me, monsieur?"

"Yes, *Señora* Edwards."

"But, how—" He knew her name, but she did not know this man who now took hold of

372

her arm. Young Jessamine's head was now stuck out of the carriage inquiring about her. Elise assured her it was all right. "I have no time for games, monsieur. I demand an explanation for this!"

"You do not recognize me, do you *señora?* I must have aged in that *cárcel.* But there in my cell—it proved to be such a small world—we have mutual friends, *señora.*"

"*Mon Dieu,* will you quit going all around the world and get to the point. I am running late, whatever your name is?" She jerked away from his hold on her arms.

The man laughed showing off a set of white teeth and Elise began to tremble. "Ah, I think maybe you now remember Juan and that night in the bunk on the *El Diablo,* eh?"

"I could hardly forget it, you bastard!" She felt humiliated even now remembering the night Joaquin Ruiz's first mate had his way with her after she'd been abducted by the Spanish buccaneer from the inn at Bogner Regis where she and Lance had gone on a pleasure jaunt. Dear God, it had turned out to be anything but a pleasure trip.

It initiated many months of separation from her husband, and she'd remained the captive of Joaquin Ruiz. Later, after that night when she'd been forced into the role of Joaquin's mistress, he'd anguished that he'd let the first mate take her for his pleasure. Elise never forgot that night and it changed her thinking drastically, she was to remember. Lying in that filthy bunk that night, so alone, without protection, she vowed to use her beauty and her body if she must to survive. Use it she did and she had survived! A new Elise was born that night.

She had not thought of the possibility that the first mate lived. And now he stood here smirking, that devious smile taunting her. Dear God, she'd forgotten him!

"This time, *señora I have no time to enjoy your beautiful body, although I must say it is as tempting as it was, perhaps more so. No, what I have need of, most desperately, is a small portion of your vast wealth. You see, I have no desire to be caught up in a war. I wish only to leave New Orleans behind and go west, but I find myself without funds now that I'm out of jail."*

Dear Lord, she would be glad to give him all she had in her reticule to be rid of him! Fumbling inside the reticule, she handed him everything left.

"Don't play me for a fool, señora or I might just have to seek out that husband of yours. Tell me, have you ever told him about our wonderful night together? Do you still have that cute little mole under the—let's see was it the right or left luscious breast?" He smiled wickedly down at her. Lust burned brightly in his dark eyes.

"Oh, you are disgusting! I have nothing

374

more with me." It dawned on her that, in truth, she had never mentioned Juan. Could Lance accept that? She didn't know anymore.

"Oh, but you have, on your ears. That would take me many miles away. Nice sized emeralds, and several diamonds."

While it broke her heart to part with them, she gladly took them from her earlobes and handed them to him. Thank God she wore gloves, and he had not seen the magnificent matching ring of emerald and diamonds.

"Begone. Don't press your luck any further, Juan! My husband would not hesitate to kill you as he did Joaquin. Bear that in mind!" She turned from him and took the hand Jessamine offered her gratefully.

"Ma'am, are you all right?" Jessamine wanted to know. That man sure didn't look like any man who should be talking to her mistress, and it was obvious he had disturbed her.

"I'm fine, Jessamine. I am just fine. Don't worry."

"Yes, ma'am." Jessamine knew she need not ask any more of her mistress for her rosebud lips were clamped tight and her eyes flashing. Jessamine knew there was a volcano boiling inside the tiny miss.

A thousand excuses she could use to cover up her loss of the prized gift came to mind. Her husband was most observant, and sooner or later he would inquire about it. She accepted the fact that she would never see the beautiful earrings again, but perhaps the price was small. Their loss pained her tremendously.

When she considered the possibility of Lance finding out about that debasing time, and that she'd not told him all these years, the earrings were not that precious!

Chapter 26

The air of the room could have been cut with a knife. That the governor had to sit at the same long table as Jean Laffite galled him. General Jackson had insisted that he be included, for it was now crucial, and Jackson accepted the fact that he was going to be outnumbered by the British force.

From this moment they had to be prepared for attack by British troops and ships. The night before the alert eyes of guards placed around the Hart-Edwards warehouses had saved the firing of the buildings. It was obvious that spies had infiltrated the city of New Orleans to spawn havoc and destroy their precious ammunition.

The governor turned the meeting over to Jackson and took his seat. Jackson had no patience to pamper the disgruntled governor. He'd never been the most diplomatic man anyway. He certainly had no time for it now.

He welcomed Jean to their midst. "I, for one, welcome you and your men to join this fight to protect New Orleans and its citizens. It will be noted in history—a part of this young country's history. We shall win, gentlemen. The British will not take New Orleans, for we cannot allow it."

Cheers went up all over the room. In his rugged, assured manner the general had fired his audience into believing it to be possible. Incentive and will won many a battle.

Jackson raised his arms up to quiet the group. His face took on a somber demeanor, but there was still a masterful strength in his voice for all the men to hear. "It will not be easy, for we know that we're far outnumbered in men and forces. But we fight for our land and our homes and that makes us a formidable foe. I thank you gentlemen for your time and attention." With that said, the general moved around the long conference table to shake the hands of all the men in attendance.

The group disbanded. Lance heard his name called and turned to see Clint hurrying to catch up with him. "How's it going at Montclair, Lance?" Lance waited for him to join him.

"Pretty good. And you?" Lance inquired.

"I'm weighing the wisdom of bringing Susan and Dominique into the city to stay with Nelda Chambers. Not too content to be away for God knows how long once this thing erupts with them stuck out there alone. How about you?"

A frown etched in Lance's brow. It was a

thing plaguing Lance for the last few weeks, but his stubborn wife might just fight him, defy his wishes to leave her home. "I'm not sure yet, Clint."

There was always the competent Dake Coulter to keep an eye on things. But the time was growing short now and it was something he and Elise had to talk about without delay. The city would offer more protection with him away.

Another voice broke into their conversation and the imposing figure of Andrew Jackson stood behind Clint Barron and Lance. "Gentlemen, could I invite you back to my quarters for a drink? I have a spare hour to indulge myself before reviewing some volunteers who've just had a fast course in training. Forty good men from up the river."

Clint Barron excused himself. "I've got a lot waiting for me at Shady Oaks, sir." He tarried no longer with the two.

"How about you, Edwards?" Jackson prodded. It was really counsel with Lance that he sought.

"Fine, general." The two departed, saying their good-byes to Barron. However, they never made it to Jackson's quarters. Instead, they entered the door of the Cock and Bull down by the levee at Jackson's impulsive suggestion.

The Cock and Bull was operated by a middle-aged couple named Ramon. Ramon's hefty wife Yvonne helped him in the tavern. Lance frequently went there as it was close to the warehouse by the levee. At one time Yvonne Ramon had been a very pretty lady. Rumor had it she'd been disowned when she married the riff-raff José Ramon, far below her station.

She served him as usual, and she was overcome to know that the famous General Jackson was gracing their humble establishment. They drank one drink and ordered another when the woman bent down to wipe the table before serving the next drink. A gleam caught his eye instantly.

Lance's eyes were drawn like magnets to the earrings on the woman's ears. There could not be two pairs like the ones he'd had made in England. He found himself unable to concentrate on Jackson's comments. He had to know where Yvonne had obtained those earrings. It stabbed him in the gut like a dagger. If Elise had lost them perhaps, and had been afraid to mention it to him, that he could understand. It had to be something like that.

Jackson was puzzled by the captain's sudden strange behavior and swift exit from their table, muttering some lame excuse. He watched him approach the woman at the bar.

Lance's heart pounded as he patted her lightly on the shoulder. "Madame? May I inquire about the magnificent earrings. They are exquisite!"

"Why, thank you, Captain Edwards." Yvonne Ramon blushed. For a man such as the captain to admire her husband's taste was a compliment. As a woman she'd always admired the handsome partner of Zack Hart. Never did he yell out at her like some of the men. No, he always showed her respect. Always called her "Madame Ramon" when he wished to be served. He was always polite and gracious.

"I could not resist asking you, Madame Ramon. You see, my wife appreciates jewelry so much." Lance played it as casual as he could, although he found it a strain. The more his eyes beheld them the more certain he was that they were his wife's. He'd designed them out with special care.

"Well, my José surprised me with them. A bargain, captain! A real bargain, my José told me. A man . . . he needed money in a hurry to leave the city and José gave him what he was asking," she informed him.

"Well, that was indeed a lucky turn, wasn't it?" Lance did not know where to go from here. She would suspect something if he asked for a description of the man. Damn!

She fingered the earrings almost lovingly. "José says I'm crazy to wear them while I'm working, but I cannot resist for they are so beautiful."

"That they are, Madame Ramon. The man must have needed to leave New Orleans very badly to part with them. I could almost envy you and the fact that I didn't encounter the man first," Lance forced a laugh, which took effort.

"Well, captain the odds against that would

be slight. José mentioned that he'd never seen him before that he could recall. However, as he was leaving he spoke to a man we both know very well—Pierre Laffite. And Pierre told José that they'd shared a cell at the cárcel a few weeks ago."

There was that damnable name again, plaguing him. He returned to the table to join the general almost as perplexed as before he'd questioned Madame Ramon. He learned little. A sudden urgency gnawed at him to get home as soon as possible and speak to Elise.

He found it hard to believe that she could have lost the jewelry and not have been upset. Knowing her, she would have been grief-stricken, damnit! Everything within him cried out that fact. Logic deemed it so.

As he rode home in the chilling December weather he was convinced Elise knew the emeralds were no longer in her possession. He knew some insidious trickery was afoot.

As he galloped around the last turn of the road and Montclair came in sight, a number of troublesome thoughts were making his gut turn inside out.

The day had been miserable for Elise. All day she had been torn in two directions. She did not like any type of fakery between her and Lance. He had so much on his shoulders lately. His services rendered toward the cause and the extra time in helping Annette. It seemed like ages since they'd lain in one another's arms to make their wonderful loving, and she felt the knots in her stomach from the aching to have him quench the thirst.

His preoccupation had been so complete of late that he'd arrived home and left in the mornings without kissing her. She'd tried to overlook or excuse it. But other times she'd let herself imagine all kinds of wild things.

Was it too inconceivable that Lance had taken a mistress? Few gentlemen in New Orleans married this length of time did not have a quadroon mistress housed in the city. Perhaps one of the luscious lovelies at Fifi's had caught his eye?

Capable of as wild and vivid an imagination as she had been when she was that wide-eyed sixteen-year-old back in Le Harve, Elise envisioned her husband's muscled, virile body entwined with some female. She'd kill him, she told herself, if she ever found out he'd taken some woman to bed.

She ran the gamut from that whimsy to the other extreme. In defiance, she vowed she'd show him—she'd take to herself a lover. Finally shrugging her small shoulders, she came back to reality and swore it was the madness around the countryside that caused her to waste time in such idiot thoughts.

She chided herself about this crazy lethargy she'd sank into and decided to turn her energies to more meaningful endeavors. Tomorrow she planned to work along with Annette Le Clere at the hospital making bandages. Time would work out the problems.

She ordered a special dinner prepared for the evening and scurried upstairs for a romp with the baby before having a warm bath and dressing for dinner.

Delight swept over her that little Lanissa was in her image, since Andy was his daddy's boy in actions as well as looks. Lanissa was a constant miracle of changes now, almost daily, it seemed. While Andy seemed a fast doer as a baby, Lanissa seemed to be starting everything sooner. Elise felt she was mimicking her older brother. She pondered Lanissa's strong, stubborn will and spitfire temper. Lance pointed his accusing finger at her, always laughing. If in a fit of temper she flung her doll down he never failed to say, "Just like her mother!"

Elise would always retort, "Well, good! I don't want her to allow people to run over her!"

After almost an hour with the baby the hands of her locket watch told her she must be about her toilette. When she returned to her room Jessamine had it prepared and the aroma coming from the heated water and bath oils was pleasing and inviting.

"You need anything else, ma'am?" Jessamine anxiously asked. Elise detected her impatience to be about her way.

"Not a thing, Jessamine. You may be on your way. Baptiste waiting?" She turned to look back over her shoulder and smile at the flushed girl. That missy didn't miss a thing, she realized.

"He's going to take me to see the new colt.

Oooh, he say it's so cute, missy."

"I bet it is, Jessamine," Elise replied, trying her best to not show amusement. The colt was not the attraction, as far as Jessamine was concerned, and Elise knew it! She liked both the young people.

"Be off with you, Jessamine," Elise urged her, stepping out of her gown and sinking down on the bed to remove her slippers. Sweeping the thick hair from the back of her neck, she slipped a comb in it to hold it in place.

She could not resist glancing at her naked body in the full-length mirror for a fast appraisal before stepping into the tub. The birth of her children had certainly enhanced the fullness of her breasts, but she would never have ones like Susan Barron's. Her bottom was firm and rounded and her waist was as tiny as ever. She turned to one side and then the other and surmised she had nothing to be ashamed of as far as her body was concerned.

The warm bath felt good and she lingered in its liquid warmth, with the fragrance of jasmine intoxicating her. This was the sight Lance came upon as Jessamine, in her haste to meet Baptiste, had left the door slightly ajar. Elise had no inkling that he stood watching her.

Momentarily, he forgot what was uppermost on his mind. The sight of her set him afire with desire and the tremendous ache in his groin made him weak. He turned away so she would not see the swelling bulge of his pants.

Sensing his presence in the room, she raised

up slightly to turn in his direction. *"Mon cheri,* you're home already! I did not expect you for at least another hour."

With his back still turned to her, he removed his coat. "Yes . . . yes, I'm a little earlier than usual." He hesitated, feeling no relief from his fever. The fragrance of her satiny body wafted up to him.

"I'm glad, Lance. It's seemed so depressing lately and I've ordered your favorite dinner tonight. Only I *was* going to be all beautiful for your arrival and you—well, as you can see I'm not quite dressed." She giggled.

Unguarded, he turned forgetting his resolve and she stood there in the tub like a naked goddess for him to behold. He stood mesmerized by her spellbinding nudity. His own body pulsed with yearning. Like someone walking in his sleep, his black eyes devoured her. He strode across the room to the tub. His hands reached out to take hold of her waist. "You need no gown, love."

The intense look in his eyes had a hypnotic effect on Elise as he lifted her into his arms, her body still wet. He pressed her firmly against him, his clothes absorbing the dampness. As if in anguish, he groaned, "God, what you do to me!" His mouth took hers in demanding kisses. His tongue prodded her parted lips and Elise responded as his touch ignited the fires of smoldering passion in her.

She yanked at his shirt to feel the bareness of his chest and the soft cluster of hair resting there. Her breasts tingled with the wild sensations, the soft featherlike touch. Thrusting herself against him with a weakness engulfing her legs, she clung to his neck.

Lance pressed her back on the bed and hovered over her. In impatient yanks, he removed his shirt and raised himself enough to remove his pants.

Elise arched up to meet him with her warmth enfolding him. Fused together, they swayed to the beat of the music their bodies demanded. A sweet andante to a maddening allegro.

As the music subsided, Lance continued to hold her to him. They lay there quietly, saying no words but trying to catch their breaths. It was Elise who finally moved and remarked, "I warn you, *mon cheri*, dinner will probably be a little late."

She rose reluctantly from the bed, smiling down on her husband's lazy face. "Are you, *mon cheri*, just going to forget about supper, eh?"

"No, Elise." Had she not turned from him to start dressing she would have seen the sudden frown on his face. She could not know his motive when he called out to her to wear her green velvet gown so casually. It was no rare thing for him to suggest certain gowns for her to wear and Elise had always appreciated his fabulous taste in fashion.

By now he had got off the bed and stood stretching his magnificent, naked body before preparing to dress, too. Elise stepped into the rich, warm velvet and backed up to him for assistance in fastening the back.

"You are always more beautiful in green than any other color, *ma petite*. Can't imagine why," he remarked, giving her a laugh. With her gown fastened, he strolled over to the other side of the room. "Ah, yes, with that you must have the emeralds, yes?"

Elise turned sharply to see him lifting her jewelry case. *Mon Dieu*, she prodded her mind to think of something and fast! "No, I think the topaz tonight, *mon cheri!*" Her words were too sharp and panicky.

She could hardly catch her breath and her hands were trembling for he was picking through the various pieces. He would not find them.

"Elise, I don't see your emeralds. Have you lost them?" He felt a pang of disgust playing this game of cat and mouse with her. He had only to look at her to see she was pale as a ghost, but there was something else reflected there. He feared what he saw in her face.

He waited for her to reply. Finally, she stammered, "I must have." Her blunder was obvious to her the minute the words were out. God, if she was going to lie why didn't she just say "yes" definitely.

"Must have? Dear God, Elise! You'd surely realize the loss of your earrings." Rage exploded in him now for he knew she was lying or covering up something. Why?

Anger made him struggle to close his shirt. "I was under the impression you cherished those earrings."

"I did . . . I do! Damnit, Lance . . . why are you acting this way?" Panic grabbed her.

He turned sharply to face her. Damn that mask of such sweet innocence displayed there! This time there was guilt! He knew it, felt it deep inside.

"Because, madame, I've seen your earrings." He watched the shock of his words and the gasp she gave as a reaction. "How—"

Elise sank down on the bed. He waited, but she remained silent and that infuriated him more.

That she sought not to confide in him hurt him and in a blind rage he started out the door. No, he would not be put off! He marched back inside. Towering over her he demanded to know. "How?"

"Could we first have dinner Lance, and then calmly and quietly, I'll tell you."

"Dinner? Christ, woman—I couldn't swallow a bite."

"All right—a glass of sherry in your study?"

He gave in to her wishes and she rose from the bed, walking and thinking desperately how she might possibly relate to him what he was demanding to know. She knew this black rage he was in, and what she must now tell him was going to be more difficult. How could the heavenly bliss they'd just indulged in turn so suddenly into a tormenting hell.

She cursed silently that Juan had entered her life again. She cursed herself for not facing Lance with the truth. At least he would have respected her courage to tell the truth. Now she could not go back and undo the damage.

Chapter 27

Elise had hoped a few sips of the sherry would help calm her, but it didn't. Searching her thoughts on how to begin her revelation was in vain. There was no simple way. So she told him about Joaquin Ruiz's first mate on the *El Diablo*.

Lance's masculine rage and ego exploded. "Christ, all this time and you never told me. Dear God, Elise!"

The last hour had played on Elise's nerves as well as her husband's, and her own firebrand temper exploded. "And you, Lance—have you confessed to me every whore you took when we were apart?"

"Don't change the subject, *ma petite!* What I want to know—and you damn well know it— is when this . . . this Juan came back in your life and what he has to do with Madame Ramon now wearing your earrings that cost me a fortune?"

"A few days ago, as I was leaving Annette's, he approached me wanting money to leave New Orleans with. He'd . . . he'd just gotten out of prison. I had very little—as you know I'd gone shopping—so he took the earrings." She had no knowledge of how Madame Ramon had ended up with them.

"Why did you give them to him, Elise? I'm assuming you must have offered them to him. You weren't alone. Jessamine and the driver were with you."

"Because I wanted to be rid of him."

"Did he threaten to come to me if you didn't?" He wanted an answer to this. It was the most important question.

"Yes."

"And you did not want me to know? You have little faith and trust in me after all this time." Had he been such a fool all these years to think their love was so solid and sure? There was something disillusioning and disappointing about it.

Elise did not like for one minute the portrait he was painting of her. She held her chin in defiance and snapped at him, "As you're acting now, eh? Perhaps, Lance, it was exactly for this reason I wished you not to know of Juan." Elise was now past the point of guarding her words.

In the heat and confusion of argument his pride exhibited itself. "I am a man, Elise. I—"

Fury blazed in her as she interrupted what he was about to say. "Are you? You remind me more of a spoiled boy about Andy's age tonight!" She vented her frustration by flinging the glass against the hearth and marching out of the study.

The minute she shut their bedroom door she allowed the tears to flow. Before flinging herself across the bed she marched back to the door and turned the lock.

No dinner was eaten that night at Montclair. Instead of following Elise up the stairs, as he was tempted to do, he remained in his study and proceeded to get roaring drunk.

It was past midnight when he stumbled upstairs to find himself barred from their room. Like a rampaging bull he rammed the door, crashing into the room.

A startled Elise jerked up to see the irate figure approaching her side of the bed. The liquor on his breath made her gag as he placed his strong hands on either side of her face. Black eyes blazing like onyx glared at her.

Cruelly, he held her face like a vise and smirked. "Never do that again, love. No damn locked door would keep me away from you! If I wanted you, nothing would keep me from you." He released his hold on her face and staggered to his closet. Then he was gone, and Elise was stunned by the stranger she'd seen.

The next morning she welcomed his absence from the house when she went downstairs. The night before had its effect on her; sleep was impossible the rest of the night. She lie looking up at the ceiling and the shadows of dawn's first light. She knew not how to deal with the hate she's seen on Lance's face, nor did she intend to remain at Montclair and endure it. She had grave˜ doubts the damage could be undone.

It was in this state that Jean found her, and the mere sight of him lifted her spirits. When he pulled from his pocket and placed in her hand the emerald earrings, she could not hold back the flow of tears. Only later, after he'd comforted her, would he enlighten her that he'd—by chance—gone to the Cock and Bull, seen the earrings on Yvonne Ramon, and paid the price required to secure them for her. "The Ramons and I go way back, *chérie*."

Jean confessed that he'd admired them, and that no one else should ever wear them. "They were on your ears that day I rescued you from Sebastian, remember?" She nodded, still mopping the tears from her cheeks. Once again, dear Jean had come to her aid.

"Oh, Jean, what would I do without you. You are my friend . . . my very good friend!" She wrapped her arms around his neck and kissed him on the cheek.

He felt her body tremble as she clung to him. She broke away from him then and asked if he'd mind if she and the children went back into New Orleans with him.

"You have no need to ask that, Elise. You know I'll be most happy to take you." He thought nothing about her request until she summoned Jessamine and informed her to pack an overnight bag with clothing for her and the children. Then his black brow did rise in puzzlement.

"Elise . . . what . . . what's wrong?"

"I'll tell you later, Jean. Now, if you'd excuse me for a minute I'll go upstairs and change and we can be gone from here." Her voice rang with urgency.

Whatever it was driving her from her home, he could not imagine. Only yesterday he'd seen Lance at the meeting, and as chance would have it he'd stopped in at the same tavern as he and Jackson left.

She returned shortly, reticule in one hand and her toilet case in the other. Jessamine followed shortly with the babe in her arms and young Andy in tow. Elise seemed anxious to leave as she yanked up the hood of the velvet cloak trimmed in sable.

The group consisted of Elise, Jessamine, the two chidren, and Jean Laffite. As they drove out of Montclair Lance sat astride his horse, back in the lane, observing their departure.

She'd turned to Laffite, and to make matters worse she was taking their children. The bitch! Stop them he could but he would not upset the children, especially Andy. He would get them back when he chose. She or Laffite would not stop him, he vowed. Andy and Lanissa were his. They would be residing at Laffite's house in the city, he decided dejectedly. How dare she!

As they traveled to the city, Elise told Jean about the horrible night before, and Jean was tempted to try to persuade her to go to his home for as long as she wished. Forever, would have been his dearest wish. In his heart he loved her still. Looking upon the two black-haired tots, he could have imagined them his own—his and Elise's.

It was to Annette's home that Jean took Elise and the children. Overjoyed to see them, Annette greeted all of the unexpected guests. Jean excused himself quickly, assuring Annette he would come by another time.

"Business awaits me, Annette darling." He bent over to kiss her. "See me to the door, Elise."

As Elise took his arm and walked with him, Annette herded Jessamine and the children back to the cozy sitting room. Perplexed and disturbed, she ordered some hot chocolate to be brought to them.

Jessamine left, following Annette's servant to the room she was to share with the children. The baby was ready for a nap and beginning to fret. Young Andy remained in the sitting room with Annette and anticipated with delight the chocolate he liked.

Jean looked deep and long at Elise. "Once before I said these same words to you. I repeat the offer to you now. All you have to do is let me know if you need me. I'll be here, Elise."

"I know, Jean, and I treasure your friendship. I feel almost guilty. I've always asked more of you than I've given." Elise sighed dejectedly.

He squeezed her hands and soothed her.

"No, that's not true. You are in no position to measure what you've given me."

"Jean! Jean! You are such a wonderful man."

"I've tried to tell you that so many times." He smiled, flashing his pearly white teeth. He would have liked to express so much more to her there. A new hope sprang alive that he might stand a chance to win her. He'd fight for her, if he must.

They parted and Elise went to face an inquiring Annette Le Clere. Andy was sent upstairs for his nap and Elise and Annette talked.

Without stress or constraint Elise told Annette everything about the episode with Juan and Lance's shocking reaction the night before. It broke Annette's heart to see the anguish on her face as she spoke.

"I know you are miserable Elise, and I'd venture to say that Lance is, too."

"If only I'd not have lied to him at first. It's . . . it's always been utter honesty between us, Annette."

Annette smiled knowingly and then corrected her. "Ah *chérie,* there is no such thing as complete honesty. A little lie once in a while we are all guilty of. You are far too harsh on yourself. But right now your mind is a muddle and your world is turning topsy-turvy. It is a time to just catch up on a little rest, eh?"

Annette suggested a warm bath and a nap before the dinner hour and Elise agreed. She would not have been very good company anyway, and she was feeling a bit embarrassed, inviting herself and her children to be guests. What an imposition she placed on Madame Le Clere.

When she'd expressed these thoughts Annette quieted her immediately. "Elise, I adore you! I always have! You're my idea of a daughter dear, and I'm old enough to be your mother, you know." She kissed her on the cheek. "Now, you say nothing more on this subject."

The rest of the afternoon seemed forever for Annette as she sat alone with her thoughts. She prayed that her foolish son would come to his senses and burst through her door. Whatever it took to convince Elise to go home with him he should do. The temptation, and her mother's instinct, was to go to Montclair to talk to him, but she restrained herself.

The dinner hour was pleasant and quiet, considering that both she and Elise were not themselves. Preoccupied about Elise, she'd given no thought about the possibility of Fifi's impromptu night visits.

Sometime after ten Fifi appeared, and Annette was ever so grateful that Elise had retired. It was not the time for her to explain her friendship with Fifi La Tour. Neither was it the night for Fifi to tell her what she did.

"Holy Christ, Chickie, it's been a night!" She shed the veil and pulled off each of her kid gloves.

Annette was not prepared for Fifi's explanation of why it had been such a night. She'd merely considered it meant that it was very busy at La Maison.

"Oh, God, if only that was it I'd be delighted. Can you imagine how I almost swallowed my teeth when your son came in asking for a woman?"

"Oh, no Fifi!" Annette was shocked and horrified. She got up hastily and shut the door. "Is he still there?"

"No, but he may be coming after me with murder in his eyes tomorrow. I stalled him for a while with the excuse that he had to wait for Tawny. Well, he wanted no part of Tawny or Rita. He was a real pain in the ass."

Fifi went on to say he'd insisted the girl had to be blond and blue-eyed. The madam admitted her genuine liking for Elise. "I didn't want the fool doing something he might live to regret. Damnit, men can be such fools. That little girl surely broke his heart when she went off with Jean today. I just couldn't believe all his ramblings though. I had him well into his cup before I turned him over to Marta."

"Elise is not with Jean. She's here with me, Fifi. She and the children are upstairs right now," Annette told her. So her son thought Elise had gone with Laffite and that was why he never darkened her door during the afternoon or evening.

"Someone sure better set him straight fast then. He's gonna' kill Jean or darn sure try."

"You said he wasn't at La Maison now. Is that where he went, Fifi, to find Jean?"

Fifi had a sheepish look on her face. "Don't be mad at me Chickie, but it's like I said earlier, I was with Elise Edwards long enough to take a real liking to her. I . . . I gave Marta a little potion to knock him out and had Titus take him home. That's why I said he'll probably come gunning for me tomorrow."

Annette erupted into laughter and so did Fifi. "Oh, God love you, Fifi," Annette exclaimed, hugging her friend.

Laughing so hard that tears flowed down her chubby cheeks, Fifi declared, "Hey, what are friends for, eh? I felt I had to protect him from himself. The man was not himself tonight. I saw those two together—remember? If ever two people are crazy in love it's that son of yours and his little wife. A love like that don't wash out that easily. I don't know what happened, but it must have been something pretty drastic."

Annette told Fifi the story from beginning to end. Fifi remembered Elise's visit to her brothel and how the goings-on there didn't seem to shock her. It cleared up the mystery for the madam. "Figured that pretty little miss had some guts and backbone. Knew, by gosh, she'd not lived all her life in the cloistered surroundings of a fancy plantation house."

It was long past midnight when Fifi's carriage pulled away from the Le Clere's house. Elise stared out the window, seeing the familiar bulk of Fifi La Tour being helped into the carriage.

Why, of all people, would she be calling on Annette Le Clere? Everything seemed to be whirling with madness and insanity. Nothing seemed right or real this night. It should not be that she and her children were bedded here instead of Montclair.

She'd left no note for Lance, but it was obvious he knew they were not there. Had he even cared enough to try to find them? One thing was for certain, he had not sought Annette Le Clere, her closest friend. She had to accept the bitter, cold fact that he did not care enough to try to find her or the children.

How could she sleep without the man she loved by her side? Could one small lie destroy a lifetime of the love the two of them had so gloriously shared?

Chapter 28

The room was dark with the drapes still drawn. It was like second nature to him to fling his arm out to draw the soft, supple body to the curve of his own, but his arm encircled only a void. The reality made him open his eyes to face the cold, hard fact that Elise was not lying there.

He rose slowly, questioning how he'd arrived home. It had to be one hell of a state for he could not remember. He sat for a moment trying to remember how the evening had gone. There was Fifi and him drinking. Damn, Edwards, he thought to himself, were you with a woman or not! Any fool should know that.

It took concentrated effort to conjure up the image of the woman. Christ, there had to be a woman. You didn't go to Fifi La Tour's and not bed a beautiful woman.

He ran his long, slender fingers through his tousled hair. A throbbing at his temples distracted his attention. Blond and willowy, he vaguely envisioned her, but for the life of him he could not remember the feel of soft lips caressing him. Any magical pleasures she gave him were a total blank.

Cautiously, he moved off the side of the bed. Looking at his discarded clothes neatly folded and placed on the chair it struck him as funny that a man coming in so drunk would be so neat. Recalling the times when he and his first mate Jud Morgan made the rounds, drinking and whoring as they sailed the coasts of England and France, clothes were hardly this neatly arranged. Thinking on those times with Jud he mused how he could sure use the Irishman's humor. Yes, Jud Morgan's presence would be welcomed.

It took effort to pull on his pants, for every time he bent his head down even slightly pains assaulted him. Weakness engulfed him and he sunk back down on the bed. Old Jud would have ripped his sides if he had been there. But then that damn Morgan would probably have been in league with Elise. Like everyone, it seemed, he adored the green-eyed vixen. Damn her! Damn Jean Laffite!

Gathering another surge of strength, he reached for his shirt. It didn't take as much effort to sit and slip the shirt on. But drawing on the boots was more effort than the pants. Lord, he was weak!

Finally dressed, he checked the contents of his pockets. He found it strange that he had no money missing from his wild night of pleasure.

Crazy! Fifi La Tour liked him, but not that bloody well.

Then his eyes went to an object that he'd not noticed before and the sight of it sobered him swiftly. There on the chest lay Elsie's emerald earrings. How had she managed to get them back? However that had been accomplished it was obvious she'd left them behind, wanting no part of them when she left with her Laffite. It was like a slap in the face.

He bolted out the door yelling, "Jess!"

"Yes, sir!" The black man came rushing down the hallway.

"Tell Baptiste to saddle my mare and tell Susie to brew a strong pot of coffee. And Jess . . . tell me something. Did you let me in last night?"

Jess hesitated for a moment before saying anything. "Well, sir . . . I didn't exactly let you in."

"Quit talking in riddles, Jess! What the hell are you saying?"

Old Jess tried to mask his amusement, remembering Titus struggling with the limp, heavy body of his master. "If the captain will pardon me for saying so, you weren't walking yourself. The man Titus brought you and helped me get you up to bed, sir." Jess turned his eyes to the floor, uncertain what the captain's next reaction would be. He'd never witnessed such rage in the master.

"Thank you, Jess." Lance felt rather foolish and realized the embarrassment he was causing old Jess. "See to my coffee, Jess. That will be all for now."

The crisp winter air helped to clear his head as he galloped atop his mare toward the city. The day was already half gone but he planned to waste no more time. It had been in the air for months and he'd known it long ago. He had a score to settle with Jean Laffite, and the sooner the better.

He traveled down the street where Annette was now in residence. Jean's townhouse was only a few streets away. His pulse beat hard and fast as he marched up to the door. He searched himself to see just how much control he'd have if he came face to face with Elise or the children there under the bastard's roof. His heart pounded waiting for the door to open.

Dorrie answered his knock. "Mister Jean isn't here. I don't know when he'll return, sir."

"Then perhaps you could announce me to Madame Edwards?"

The mulatto woman's face frowned. "Sir?"

"Madame Elise Edwards!"

Puzzlement was written on Dorrie's face. "Madame Elise is not here, sir."

Oh, how clever the two were, Lance told himself. He smirked. "Oh, she isn't here now either, eh? She hasn't been here I suppose— say yesterday or last night?"

"No, sir, she sure hasn't been." Something about the woman's manner impressed him as being honest. He walked back to his mount in a perplexed state leaving Dorrie standing there in the doorway.

Well, he certainly wasn't through. He'd hit the known hangouts of Laffite and his band of riff-raff. He rode back down the street where Annette lived. Only moments before, Elise had turned from the window looking out on the street. Had she lingered there a second longer she would have caught sight of her husband riding by.

The deep, angry voice resounded to the back room where Jean sat talking and drinking with Dominique You, Beluche, and young Julio. Whoever it was certainly was in a foul mood and giving old Jason a hard time.

"Just a minute, sir." He looked through the peephole to see who the ruffian was in the smithy's shop. There was no mistaking the tall, towering figure of Edwards standing there, his face looking like a thunderhead. The situation demanded he stay cool.

Jean smiled and went through the wooden door. "Edwards, you wish to see me?" He moved up to him with that usual jaunty air; self-assured and unruffled. It accelerated Lance's ire.

"That's right, Laffite! It's you I want to see. In private though." He was like a spring ready to snap and Jean had a cautious respect for that.

"That can be arranged, Captain," Jean said, gesturing with his hand for Lance to follow him into the back room. Upon entering Jean dismissed the three sitting there. Lance's piercing eyes measured the three getting up to leave. The tall youth with a mop of black hair looked out of place with the other two.

Jean pointed to one of the wooden chairs and invited Lance to share a drink. But Lance refused. "No, I don't plan to be here that long. I want only one thing from you, Laffite. That, plus a warning."

"And what is that, Edwards?"

"My wife—where is she, and no lies?"

"I don't think I have the right to tell you that if she wishes you not to know, monsieur."

"Men have been killed with justification for harboring another man's wife, Laffite."

"There would be no justification in this case for I will tell you I'm not harboring your wife. She is not with me, although she could be if she'd wished to be, Edwards. I won't deny that."

"I saw you drive away with my wife and children. Elise has that right for herself but not my son and daughter. You could save her a lot of grief, Laffite."

Jean drank deeply of the brandy and his fingers played for a moment around the rim of the glass. "I don't blame you, Edwards. You may find that rather hard to believe. You have a very stubborn wife. I happen to know having had her as my guest on Barataria for weeks."

His words were rubbed salt in the wound, and Lance looked like he was about to lunge at Jean. Jean raised his hand in protest. "Please let me finish. I must add that you are a fool if you don't know that the beautiful lady's heart belongs to you. *Mon Dieu*, it galls me to say it. I tried to win her love even when she thought you and her son had gone down with your ship. Cherish it, Edwards, for I don't take you for a fool. In fact, you're one of the few men in New Orleans I respect. In truth, except for the fact that Elise stands between us, we might be friends."

He was either the most honest man Lance had ever met or the biggest liar.

"Have another drink, monsieur. I have more to tell you—promise you. I'll not deny to you that I'd take her in a minute if I thought I could. But alas, I'm no dreamer."

Lance finished the remaining liquid in the glass and as much as he resented the dark Frenchman across from him, he respected his straightforward manner.

"I'll remember what you've said, Monsieur Laffite. In fact, if Elise wants you, she can have you. But my children will not go with her."

Jean's brow raised, his dark eyes sparkled. What a proud man this Edwards was! He could not help goading him once more. "You would not fight to keep her, Captain Edwards?"

It was Lance's turn to smile. When he spoke it was through clinched teeth and with hellfire blazing in his black eyes. "Monsieur, when she was taken from me once a long time ago, I searched for months until I found her and killed the bastard who had wronged me. Yes, I'll fight or kill. But I'll never share my wife!"

He turned to take his leave, unaware that Jean was following him. As the two emerged out of the back entrance of the smithy shop darkness was slowly descending. It had been a short day for Lance, and the thought of food came to mind. However, everything was swept away in the wake of two fast explosions and the sharp impact of Jean's hand on his back.

"*Mon Dieu!*" Jean's mumbled voice came beside him as they both sprawled on the dirt. From the fence at the back of the smithy shop Jean heard the familiar voice of Dominique You calling to him that all was well. Footsteps rushed around the building.

A moment later the chubby pirate came through the gate, inserting his pistol back in the waistline of his baggy pants. "Beluche and me got 'em, boss. Those sonsofbitches won't bother anyone again."

Laffite, followed by Lance, peered through the broken planks of the wood fence. One man was dead and the other gasping his last breath. His final spray of venom was directed toward Jean. He hissed laboriously, "You bloody traitor!" Then his head flopped to the side.

"Christ! That's the two!" Lance muttered, causing Jean to turn toward him. Lance looked upon the two he'd sought.

"You know them, Edwards?"

"I do. They tried to do me in. More to the point, what was that bucko talking about, Laffite?"

"A long story, Edwards. But I think,

perhaps, these two may explain the warehouse fire the other night. They are British spies. You see Edwards, I was approached by the vermin to help the British. I only played them to suit my purpose. Hell would freeze over before I'd help the British take over New Orleans. Now, Claiborne might not believe that, but Jackson does. My men and I were discussing this very thing when you happened along."

Now Lance knew what had brought up Jean's name that day in the tavern when the two were in the company of Charles Burke. And the reason for the attack on him was to make certain he could not inform the authorities. They obviously thought he'd overheard them plotting with their cohort Charles Burke. That mystery was now solved.

He found himself telling Jean about his name being tossed into the conversation. Jean was ready with a simple answer to Charles's implication. "He's a wastrel and a scoundrel of the worst sort. Money, monsieur, was the inspiration for Charles. He'd sell his mother or his soul. His leaving New Orleans was good riddance."

"I only regret that I didn't get my hands on his rotten hide before he left," Lance grumbled.

"Charles is not an idiot. When the word reached him that you lived he knew what you'd do. He didn't wish to stay around to find out. He, among other things, is a yellow-bellied coward. Always did have his dirty work done for him."

410

It was hard for Lance to have to admit in his mind that in the space of the last hour or so he'd changed his opinion of the Frenchman. He had pushed him out of the way of the gunfire. He could be no less a man than to thank him, even though it did sear his gut to do so.

"I owe you one, Laffite. . . . The push awhile ago. For that, I am grateful," Lance said somewhat reticently.

Jean appreciated the effort it took for this man who gave no quarter to anyone. He gave him only a nod of his head, watching as he walked toward his mount. Lance flung his leg across the roan and reined the horse around. Jean's voice called out to him. "Monsieur—go to Annette Le Clere's if you want to see your wife and children. That is where I took her."

A deep laugh broke out in the evening quiet. "*Merci, mon ami.* . . . I owe you twice!" He rode like the wind down the road in the direction his heart demanded he go. Even the brisk winds at his back seemed to urge him on faster.

Chapter 29

As he dismounted and flipped the reins around the hitching post a spasm cut through his stomach. Food could come later he told himself, shrugging off the weakness washing over him at the same time.

He hurried up the flagstone walk to the house ablaze with light. It was perhaps the dinner hour now but he'd taken no particular notice of the time this crazy day.

Mimi, Annette's housekeeper, ushered him into the parlor and young Andy beat Annette into the room. Giving a loud shriek of joy at seeing his father, he leaped into Lance's waiting arms.

Underneath her breath, Annette thanked God. She was pulled two directions. Gratified that he'd finally come to see Elise, and yet, irritated that he sought out the brothel last night to drown his sorrows. But she put forth her usual grace and charm, inviting him to have a seat.

Apologetic about his bad timing, he said, "I . . . I just found out that Elise and the children were here. Could I see Elise, you suppose?"

No one had to tell Annette that her son had endured his own share of anguish. Deep lines and dark hollows were there for her to see around his tired-looking eyes. "You could if she was here, Lance. I expect her any minute though, and you're welcome to wait. May I ask, my son, when you last ate?"

He gave her a weak smile and confessed, "I really don't know, Madame Le Clere."

Compassion melted her irritation with him. This was her son, and for all his bulk and strength, he took on the image of the helpless young boy she remembered from so long ago. Her heart ached, wanting to put her arms around him and comfort him.

He continued to hold Andy in his arms, planting a kiss now and then on the tot's cheek. The happy little boy loved his father very much, that was obvious, and Annette knew she would employ any trick to see that Elise and Lance were united again with these two darling children.

"You must eat with us. Elise should be returning soon." Annette did not wish to show her concern over Elise's delay. In fact, she'd expected Elise back from Montclair two hours ago. Had Lance not appeared when he had Annette would have been certain that the two were there at Montclair patching up their quarrel.

"Come, we shall eat and I'll inform Mimi to keep something warm for Elise, eh?" She rose and Lance gave her no argument. He was determined to face Elise before the night was over.

He had not realized how famished he was until he took a seat at Annette Le Clere's table. He ate a hefty meal. Later, after Andy was sent upstairs and he and Annette had enjoyed a brandy, he fell asleep in the overstuffed chair by the fireplace.

Annette sat, enjoying the sight of her sleeping son, and she thought of Francois. His presence was so strong with her that December evening. Under her breath she promised her husband that she would tell her son the long overdue truth.

After Lance Edwards had left Jean Laffite, the disposing of the two dead men had been taken care of. But Jean was to find some startling evidence in the men's coats. It was disturbing to say the least. The two had been very busy making maps and charting the terrain of the countryside. Names appeared on the papers that disturbed Jean. It listed places known to him as the plantations situated near the river or waterways. It was obvious they'd pinpointed certain places to set up for bivouac. Seeing Montclair on that list made him deeply anxious. Shady Oaks or Bellefair was not included.

Without hesitation he made his way to Jackson's headquarters. The young aide informed him the general was with the governor and so Jean decided to wait.

Elise had left Annette's that morning after she and Annette had enjoyed a late breakfast of coffee and croissants. She'd paced the floor of the guest bedroom most of her first night away from Montclair, and the fact that Lance had not sought to come to her convinced her that he wanted no part of her. So be it!

When she'd left with Jean her departure had been so hasty that she had Jessamine gather up little for her and the children. After breakfast she requested the use of Annette's carriage and driver so she might return home to get more things. Midday she was less likely to encounter Lance, she knew.

Old Jess and Baptiste had been thrilled to see her arrive. Just as suddenly their smiles had faded when she told them she'd be leaving later, as soon as she packed some of her belongings.

She went immediately upstairs and she saw the earrings lying where she'd placed them the day before. Suddenly she hated them and what they reminded her of. Taking them in her hand, she flung them across the room. As much as she'd adored them at one time she hated the sight of them now.

Old Jess rapped softly on the door and Elise bid him enter. "Thought Missy might like a nice cup of coffee."

"Oh, Jess, thank you." She smiled. Old Jess saw the mist in her eyes and her smile, always so beautifully radiant, was a sad one. Jess excused himself hastily. It hurt the old black man to witness such unhappiness invading this house and the people he'd grown to love so much.

Elise finished in her room and went down the hall to the nursery to tackle the same chore. Packing some things for the children only made her sadder.

It wasn't right, any of this! She slumped down in the rocker and cried. Lance and she had loved one another far too much to allow anything or anyone to destroy them like this. She found the whole situation utterly insane. How could he forget so easily?

She sat in the rocker and rocked back and forth, deep in thought. Susie's voice broke the quiet, announcing that Clint Barron was downstairs wishing to speak to her.

Dabbing her eyes and straightening the falling wisps of hair where she'd cradled her head, she rushed down the steps. Tears were solving nothing!

Clint stood in the hall and she noticed the anxious look on his face. "Elise, where's Lance?"

"I . . . I don't know right this minute, Clint. Why?" She could not bring herself to tell the truth to Clint.

"I just came from the city to take Susan and Dommi to Nelda's and the city's buzzing with the news. The British are heading toward Lake Borgne. Lieutenant Jones is stationed out there with six gunboats and he's sent a dispatch to Jackson. They'll probably be landing on Chandeleur Island by nightfall. Jackson sent out orders less than an hour ago. That's why I stopped by to tell Lance."

"Well, I'll . . . I'll tell him, Clint."

"All right, honey," he said, turning to go. "Hey, are you going to stay here?" He paused in his hurry to leave and Elise thought she saw a note of concern on his face. "I think you and the children would be safer in the city, Elise. Your land is awfully close to the river. Jackson cautioned that marauders will possibly infiltrate the countryside. I really think you should go to the city, Elise."

"Thank you, Clint. I appreciate your concern, really. I probably will. And Clint, take care of yourself," Elise urged him.

"I will, Elise. I've got too much to live for. While I'm about it I just want to say thanks to you for what you did—you and Annette Le Clere."

She took his extended hand and patted it warmly. She saw happiness in Clint Barron's face. "No one could be happier for you and Susan than I am, Clint. You know that."

"I do know that, Elise. Someday, when Susan's love for Dominique is so strong that the truth won't matter to her I'll tell her. I just can't chance spoiling anything yet."

"You'll know when the time is right Clint."

Elise stood on tiptoe and planted a kiss on his cheek.

Clint's blue eyes went soft and mellow and he smiled down at Elise. "I'm about to tell you something that is no betrayal of Susan or Lance, but something I want you to know. I . . . I will always cherish that time we shared in our lives. It was a wonderful interlude, something precious and dear."

"I know what you're saying, Clint. I feel it, too. No, neither of us are taking anything away from Lance or Susan." She gave him a sly wink. "It will be our little secret."

"Agreed!" Kissing her, he left.

Elise stood, smiling and watching the tall, blond Clint Barron go on his way. Clint had found happiness finally!

Baptiste rushed up to her and she talked to the young Creole for a while. She realized he was curious about what was going on at Montclair with his master and mistress.

As if he was clutching for straws, he quizzed her, "What about Midnight? He hasn't been out for days now."

"Then why don't you take him out, Baptiste?"

His dark eyes flashed and he exclaimed, "Oh, may I?"

"Of course, Baptiste. You and Midnight will both enjoy yourselves. Oh, Baptiste, I may not be here when you return. I just wanted you to know."

Her words had a dulling effect on his

enthusiasm and he mumbled good-bye as he strolled away. She watched him kick at the earth as he made his way to the stable. She suspected that part of Baptiste's disappointment was that he wouldn't be around Jessamine. She certainly recognized the pout on Jessamine's mouth when she instructed her to remain with the children at Annette's.

Her stay at Montclair was much longer than she originally planned. Baptiste had left and she'd gone to find Jess with instructions to have one of the house servants bring her packed articles down and load them into the carriage when Dake Coulter came to the house seeking Lance. Once again she had to cover for her absent husband. It was obvious Lance had not been with the overseer out in the fields or barn. She pondered where he might be, for the afternoon was fading fast and soon twilight would be descending.

Suddenly she remembered the presents she'd purchased for the children and Lance and she rushed back up the steps. She was hardly filled with the happy holiday spirit, but nevertheless, it was less than two weeks away.

She went back into the room shared with her husband and got the articles from their hiding place. "Oh, I've got to get out of here," she mumbled to herself. The sun was already down below the cluster of trees to the west and with the winter months the darkness would be upon her before she got back into New Orleans.

Susie's shrill scream and old Jess's indignant

voice made her rush to the top of the stairs, but she saw nothing to enlighten her as to the cause. Moving slowly down each step, she trembled with a foreboding that something was not right. At the base of the stairs she slipped to the front door to see a wagon laden with goods and six saddled horses. What should she do? Go to the barn or stables or slip to Lance's study where she knew his pistols were? She couldn't forsake Jess and Susie.

She wondered if the intruders were the marauders Clint had warned her about. She moved with care to make no noise to the study. No one was in the parlor or dining room as she passed through. The door of Lance's study was open. Thank God for that! The heavy carved oak door never failed to squeak.

She made it and a sigh of relief escaped. The thought of the overwhelming odds of six armed men against one small woman with a pistol never entered her mind.

All she could think of was getting a pistol to protect herself and going to the rescue of her servants. She moved toward Lance's desk, so engrossed in her purpose she did not notice the burly character sitting in the corner watching her with a salacious gleam in his blue eyes. His comrade stood ready to grab her. As he clasped his two arms around her, the two exploded in laughter.

"Look what I caught, Roger!" He whirled her around roughly to face him. Elise felt herself spinning. Coming to an abrupt stop her eyes locked into his.

"How dare you break into my house! What have you done to my servants? I heard screams." Elise fought to release herself from his strong hands.

Both broke into another round of laughter. "Ooooh, this fine lady don't like us, bucko."

The burly-looking red-haired man imitated a bow, sweeping his hands in an animated gesture. "Pardon us, madame."

Elise didn't like the look in his eyes. Without speaking, his eyes spoke his lusty thoughts. As it had been with her Uncle Edwin and his beady eyes, Juan, and Joaquin Ruiz, she sensed it and diverted her eyes.

"Do we stick her in the pantry with the other two?" the man still holding her in his arms asked of the one he called Roger.

"No, take her upstairs and tie her up," he ordered his cohort. This made Elise shudder, knowing full well his intentions. If only she was with Jess and Susie she would have not been half as frightened.

As he pushed at her back to move out of the study, she noticed the loot lying on the floor ready to be put in bags. Lance's study had already been plundered by these two and she supposed that the other men were going through the other rooms of the house and perhaps the larder and pantry.

That the man left her after tying her to the bedpost left Elise grateful. That one she did not fear anyway. It was the other one who made chills run down her spine. Before she'd been the victim of a beast like him.

The minute he went out the door, she tugged to see just how secure the bonds were. She sunk back dejectedly knowing it was hopeless. They were too tight.

Minutes passed and she happened, by some miracle, to look at the reflection in the mirror to see the post of the bed. The wood higher on the post came to a point, and if she could move up she might just free herself.

The strain on her body was painful and the least movement was tedious. She forced herself on even though her whole being trembled from the exertion. It was the only chance she had.

Out the window it was totally dark, and she knew she could manage to climb down the trellis if only she freed the bonds holding her to the post.

An interminable time went by as she struggled, and her being cried out for Lance to come to her rescue. Reverberations of laughter and breaking glass told Elise the marauders were no doubt drinking their fill and helping themselves to the foods in the larder before they took their leave.

With each resounding crack of glass, Elise envisioned the fine pieces of cut crystal being destroyed and it pained her. Such heartless destruction! Surely, war could be nothing but waste if this was what it bred. What Elise did not know and what would have repulsed her with a sickening contempt was that some of the marauders were not British. They were locals who had joined the British for the handsome reward of gold. Their loyalty was bought by the British.

They'd filled their wagons with foodstuff, liquors, and blankets, among other goods confiscated over the countryside and they would be leaving to load their bounty aboard a waiting flatboat down on the river. Their mission had been a success, for they'd receive high praise and reward for the goods and firearms along with the vital information about possible encampment sites along the river banks.

She had just about given up hope on wearing thin the bonds when she felt the breaking of her shackles. Moving swiftly to the window, she urged herself to make no noise. She tackled the task with light pressure on the window. One sound could ruin everything. Much to her delight it opened without too much exertion and Elise wasted no time flinging out her leg. She only prayed that the slats would carry her weight to the bottom.

Two or three moves on the trellis were made before she felt herself halted and saw her skirts caught on one of the rough edges. "Damn!" She yanked and pulled at the material. Hearing the tearing of the gown, she gave out a sweet sigh of relief and moved farther down on the trellis. She was halfway down now. All the time she gathered more confidence that she would make good her escape.

Her soft, dainty hands were cold and scratched by the dried, sharp branches that had blossomed only a few months ago. Less than twelve feet from the ground now, she froze, clutching at the slats. A noise sounded directly underneath her. Dear God, no! She shuddered!

A voice whispered, "Missy? *Mon Dieu*, is that you, Missy?" Baptiste stared up at her in the darkness, his eyes disbelieving what they beheld.

"Dear God, Baptiste . . . you almost made my heart stop! She was now low enough to take the youth's hand he offered to her. "We must hurry, Baptiste! Dear Lord, I'm so glad to see you." Overcome with exhaustion and fear she collapsed in the young boy's comforting arms. Baptiste never felt so much like a man in his life.

"Come, Missy. I have Midnight back in the woods. They didn't get him." He supported her with his arms around her shoulders and again he felt so strong. How tiny she was! He'd never noticed it before but he towered over her.

Elise could not stop the chattering of her teeth, and like a gallant Baptiste took off his woolen jacket and slipped it around her as they made their way in the back of the house and beyond. "Just a moment, Missy." He led her toward the stable door and urged her to stay there while he grabbed some blankets and another jacket for himself.

He returned hastily and flung one of the blankets around Elise. "Come on, Missy." The two figures ran across the clearing toward the grove of trees. Only after Baptiste had lifted her up on the huge black beast and leaped up behind her did he begin to breath normally.

"We'll make it now, Missy! We'll make it!" He urged the huge horse on and they rode with the wind at their backs toward the city of New Orleans.

Chapter 30

Two other night riders rode through the countryside as Elise and Baptiste did. Jean Laffite, accompanied by young Julio, left Jackson's headquarters after he'd informed Jackson about what he'd found out from his search of the two British spies' bodies.

He had to warn Edwards about his plantation being named a bivouac point. Having just missed Lance by a matter of minutes and Annette's informing him that Elise had not returned from Montclair, he felt a desperate urge to get there as soon as possible.

"Where did Edwards go?" Laffite prodded the frantic woman, who by now was deeply concerned over her young friend.

"He was going to the warehouse. He carried no weapon with him. Like you, he was concerned about Elise not arriving."

Jean asked no more questions. Elise, alone, could only provoke a dangerous situation.

From those papers it didn't take any brains to figure out that the British were coming in via Lake Bourne and would set up their headquarters at Montclair.

He didn't want to contemplate what would happen should Elise be out there when they arrived.

He cautioned young Julio to keep an eye out for any unusual sights along the countryside as they galloped along the strip of dirt road running adjacent to the river.

It was a clear night, which added to the chill in the air. No clouds shrouded the moonlight shining down on them as they rode along.

Baptiste and Elise had not taken the main road. The cascading Spanish moss draping down from the live oaks had slapped Elise in the face and tangled in her flying mass of hair a couple of times. She'd cried out in pain and surprise, feeling she was being yanked from Midnight's back. Gently, Baptiste had untangled her long hair.

They traveled on through the edge of the wooded area until Baptiste reined Midnight in the direction he was sure would bring them out on the river road. He didn't see the two mounted figures up ahead of them. Jean and Julio had both spotted the riders coming and halted their mounts back of the road to see who was riding so fast.

There was no mistaking her as they galloped by, and Jean yelled out for them to stop. But Baptiste paid no heed, spurring the horse to go faster. The outskirts of the city were in view before Jean and Julio overtook them.

Pulling his horse up by their mount he saw blood on Elise's pale face and suspected the worst. She told him that she was only exhausted and tired. Until then she'd taken no notice of the scratches on her hands or face.

Poor darling. He dared not tell her that her husband might be riding into the nest of British housed at Montclair. He had to think fast of what would be best for Elise. She looked ready to fall off the huge stallion. So he urged them to take the back streets to his house in the city and Elise gave him no fuss.

In that masterful manner of his, Jean lifted her down from Midnight. He took no notice of the resenting look in young Baptiste's eyes as he remained upon the horse.

Dorrie opened the door, not recognizing the waif wrapped in the old, ragged blanket as Elise Edwards. She questioned who the other young lad was, but she recognized young Julio, for he'd been at the house before with Mister Jean.

He barked out orders impatiently to Dorrie. "Send Cassie to make some hot chocolate, Dorrie. A lot! Then you come upstairs to help me with madame. She's chilling!"

"Yes, Mister Jean." She turned her attention to the two young men standing awkwardly, uncertain as to what or where they should go. "Come with me to the kitchen and Cassie will give you some chocolate and you can warm yourselves. You both look like you are frozen stiff!"

Both gave the woman a grateful smile and followed her willingly. As willingly, Elise allowed Jean to help her out of the blanket and jacket. "Sit down, *ma petite*," he ordered her, pressing her back toward the bed. Kneeling down, he removed her ruined slippers. "Christ, look at your legs! You look like you've been in the thickets." A trail of scratches ran down from her knees.

"They tied me to the bedposts in my bedroom and after I managed to free myself I climbed down the trellis. I . . . I guess the branches did that," Elise said. Her voice still trembled. She wondered what it would take to warm her chilled body.

Jean gathered her in his arms, kissing her cheek. "My brave baby—you've had a hell of a night." His hands rubbed first her hands and then took her feet, massaging each in turn. Wisely, Dorrie entered with a bottle of brandy and two glasses. What that little miss and Mister Jean needed was the instant, warming liquid.

"Here, missy. You and Mister Jean will both feel better after you drink this," Dorrie told them, handing each a glass.

Jean gulped down the brandy and left Elise in Dorrie's capable hands to join the two young men waiting for him in the kitchen. There he questioned Baptiste if his master had ever arrived at Montclair. He thought better of asking Elise about Lance.

"No, monsieur. I have not seen him since yesterday. Miss Elise arrived back home today and packed some things to return to the city. She suggested I take Midnight out for a jaunt this afternoon, and that was why I wasn't there when the men arrived. Miss Elise told me we had to get help. They'd taken old Jess and Susie prisoners before she'd gone downstairs. She thought they were somewhere to the back of the house. Two of the men had taken her as she went into the study to get a gun."

"So Captain Edwards wasn't there as far as you know?"

"No, monsieur. The only thing that warned me of their presence and made me leave the horse back in the trees were the wagon and horses in the drive. I . . . I just had a funny feeling so I slipped up to the house and found Miss Elise coming down the trellis. Guess one thing that made me wonder what was going on was the house looked so dark. Susie always has a lot of candles burning come dusk."

"You're a smart lad, Baptiste." Jean told the young Creole.

Baptiste considered that a great compliment coming from the fierce Baratarian pirate. "Finish your hot drinks before we start out again into the cold night," Jean directed them, not looking forward to the mission they must go on.

When Lance had left the Le Clere house after the delicious meal and the much-needed nap, he realized his fuzzy state when he left Montclair to find Laffite. To face the pirate with his accusations was sheer insanity, he rationalized now.

Elise's mad folly of traipsing around the countryside without even Jessamine was the last straw. The only thing bothering him was the unlikelihood that Elise would stay overnight at Montclair with the children in the city with Annette. No, he could not buy that.

While he would be the first to admit that Elise was impetuous and stubborn, she was smart enough to start back toward the city before darkness descended over the country roads. He'd give her more credit than that. Logically, that left only one thing; something had happened to prevent her arrival at Annette Le Clere's home.

By the time he armed himself and left the warehouse he was a man driven by madness. Montclair *had* to hold the answer to where Elise was, and all he could think to do as he rode through the night was pray that nothing had happened to her.

Had Elise and Baptiste not cut through the fields to stay off the main road they would have met him only a few minutes before Jean encountered them. By that time Lance was riding into the long drive of his home. The outside of the house was completely deserted by this time and the marauders had left only minutes before. Much to the disappointment of the marauder called Roger he found no traces of the little beauty whose sensuous body he'd planned to make use of.

Her escape and knowledge of their being there prompted the decision to move farther down the river road to quarter the men. The wench's escape made that necessary.

Consternation flooded Lance as he leaped down from the roan. Without any doubt something was amiss here. He moved cautiously around the corner of the house instead of going in the front entrance. The windows displayed nothing to him as he slipped down the side, nor did he see Baptiste, who'd have normally rushed out to greet him. Lance had always teased him that his ears could hear a hoofbeat a half mile away.

There was an eerie quiet choking him, and finding the back door ajar confirmed his worst fears. He knew there had been trouble when he almost slipped on broken glass. The overwhelming odors of tobacco, liquor and, sweat wafted to his nose.

Slowly, he moved through the whole downstairs, satisfying himself no one remained. Lighting a candle he surveyed the havoc in his study and saw his prized collection of pistols was gone.

Elise! Dear God, could she be upstairs? He

flew up the steps and bolted through the different doors to find no sign of her. He was filled with mixed emotions: glad she wasn't across the bed, molested or worse, and plagued as to where she was.

He saw the evidence of her packing and then he gasped, seeing the ropes remaining around the bedpost. In the same instant he noted the opened window. The weather was far too chilly for windows to be opened.

The ungodly quiet seemed awesome as he made his way back down the steps toward the back of the house. He stopped short. A moan! A moan and a thumping sound came from nearby. He rushed to investigate the noise with fearful thoughts invading him. Opening the pantry door he saw Susie huddling back in the corner with fright in her dark eyes and old Jess lying on the floor. His blood splotched the floor from a blow to his white head.

"Dear God!" Lance rushed to tend to both of his servants, in a quandry over what had taken place in his absence.

Susie's deep relief broke loose a flood of tears with the repeated declaration that it was the master and not those horrible men coming back. Lance's concern was mainly for the aging Jess. Susie's injuries were slight.

"Help me, Susie!" They moved Jess out of the narrow room and Susie applied a cool compress to the wound before attempting to move him to his small cubicle of a room at the rear of the house.

Once the matter of Jess's comfort was settled, Lance questioned Susie about what had taken place that afternoon at Montclair, and where her mistress was.

"See, we were in dat pantry. But I did hear Miss Elise's voice. I heard noises up the stairs," Susie told him. "I . . . I don't know where Missy is tho'."

Lance's frustration made him slam the table with a mighty blow. He didn't blame Susie but damnit, it told him no more than he already knew. The rest of the story was pretty easy to figure. Montclair had been ravaged by advance soldiers of the British. They carried away his liquor and food, along with anything else of value that suited their fancy. The throbbing, tormenting question was whether they carried away his wife. Damn them all to hell!

Hoofbeats resounded as riders approached the house. Lance tensed, drawing his pistol as he went to the window. Three figures leaped off their mounts. A familiar voice called out. "Captain Edwards?"

Lance relaxed and placed the pistol back in its resting place. "Baptiste . . . that you?"

"Yes, sir." By this time Lance recognized Baptiste's companions as Jean Laffite and the young lad Julio.

"Laffite, we meet again," he remarked before turning his attention to Baptiste. "Your mistress, Baptiste . . . do you know where she is? Were you here when they hit Montclair?"

434

Jean spoke before the young Baptiste could inform Lance. "She is safe—a little worn and weary but Dorrie is seeing to her."

"Dorrie?" Lance frowned.

"My housekeeper. Julio and I came upon her and the boy here after they'd made good their escape from the bastards."

Ignoring Jean, Lance quizzed Baptiste. "Did they harm her, Baptiste?"

"Just a little, sir," Baptiste mumbled.

Lance's fury turned on the boy and he grabbed his shoulder roughly. Jean pulled Lance by the arms and led him to the side of the boy. Lance yanked away from Jean's hold. "Damn it, what's a little?"

"Simmer down, Edwards. They didn't rape her, if that's what you're wondering about: a bruised cheek and rope burns from being tied to the bedpost. She got other cuts and scratches from climbing down the trellis."

Lance exhaled a deep sigh of relief and walked to the young boy's side. Patting his shoulder, he confessed his remorse for being rough. "And I thank you Baptiste for being here to help her."

A tremendous explosion broke through the night and the four stopped short any conversation. All exchanged glances knowing this was it. This was what had been anticipated for many weeks. It had started, and the first exploding blasts of cannon-fire had been sounded.

Any thought of going to Elise had to be put aside, Lance realized. He turned to the other

435

three who were occupied with thoughts much like his own. "Men, I think we've been summoned. Shall we make for New Orleans." Making a brief retreat back in the house with instructions for Susie and a flurry of orders for her to pass on to Dake Coulter, he joined the others. They rode toward the city.

The British entered Lake Borgne to encounter six American gunboats under the command of Lt. Thomas Jones. Compared to the massive British forces, Jones's small flotilla seemed to be no obstacle to the British.

However, the British were soon to realize the task would not be so simple. Their losses were seventeen killed and seventy-seven wounded. The Americans lost six brave men and thirty-five were wounded.

Elise and Annette labored many hours every day at the hospital set up in the church not too far from Annette's home. The first day left Elise exhausted and sick to her stomach as she witnessed the blood-spattered men being brought in. Some appeared no older than Baptiste.

During the daylight hours she was too busy to think, but at night she found herself wondering about Lance. She had no way of knowing what had gone on that night after Jean had deposited her at his home. It was not until the next evening that she returned to Annette's house.

Annette told her of his stop at the house, but

she did not know of Jean and Lance's encounter later that same night. So it was that the men's whereabouts the last four days remained a mystery.

The city streets were madness as Elise and Annette walked the short distance home. The news came that only two vessels, the *Carolina* and the *Louisiana,* were holding off the British. Jackson and his troops were preparing to move about four or five miles below the city. The Chalmette plantation was to be their headquarters.

Was that where Lance was? Elise wondered. Why had he not sent her some word? Even Jean had not dropped by to see her since the night he'd left her with Dorrie. The world was all topsy-turvy!

A rattling munitions wagon rolled past the two women as they made their way to the house after their long nine hour shift. Mud sprayed generously on their skirts and Elise shook hers in irritation and grumbled.

Annette patted her shoulder, remarking, "You are overtired, *chérie*. We'll go home and have a glass of wine and a good warm bath, eh?" It was taking all of the will Annette could muster to put forth a brave front. A general at the hospital had related some very pessimistic views of the battles.

"Seven thousand British troops landed on Lake Borgne this morning. Jackson may be a great general but who the hell can outfight three times what's facing him," the wounded soldier and officer dejectedly grieved to Annette as she dressed his wounds.

All day Annette had thought about what he'd said. Somewhere her son was out there fighting. Maybe he'd die never knowing that his mother was alive and loved him so much.

Chapter 31

The cloaked figure hurried down the street
through the chilling mist. Jack Maynard reined
his gig up to the edge of the street calling out to
the petite figure to hold up. Even with the full
flowing cloak he recognized that walk as
belonging to Elise Edwards. He pondered what
was she doing out on such a day, walking alone
with all the riff-raff milling in the streets.
While he realized Lance, like most of the able-
bodied men, were doing their bit for the war, it
was certainly unwise for that pretty little thing
to be going down the streets alone.

Elise heard the male voice calling to her and
turned to see Jack smiling at her. "Can I take
you somewhere Elise?" The sight of her
brightened the dreary, gray day.

Elise gave an eager nod of her head and took
the hand he offered her. "You certainly can,
Jack. I've got a sick boy and Annette is very sick
with a chest cold. I was going to see if I can get

Doctor Barlow to come by the house."

"Hear Doc's been going day and night. I . . . I feel sorta' bad about this leg laying me low while all the others are giving their all," Jack said. He was given to a moment of whimsy thinking about what his wife Flo would say if she knew about this. Lord, it was a sin how she hated this little woman.

"I know. Annette and I've been putting some time in at the hospital. I'm not so concerned about Andy. He'll probably be up romping by tomorrow. But Annette's running a high fever and I can't bring it down, nor can I get her to eat."

"Flo went to the hospital one day but she couldn't take it. Here we are, Elise. I . . . I'll be glad to wait and see you back home."

"No, Jack. I appreciate what you've done, but I don't have any idea how long it will take me to find him if he's making his rounds. Thanks anyway." She gave him a wave and bounced up the steps.

Jack sat watching the sway of her back, stirred by the nearness of her during the brief ride. Thinking to himself that he might just hang around as he had nothing better to do. There was an absolute standstill of business with all this chaos, and the thought of going home to Flo's hysterics certainly depressed him.

Besides, Elise could be a little lonely with her man not around. A hot-blooded lady like her took a regular ration of loving. He'd bet a

440

handsome sum any day of the week on that score. He lit up a cheroot, leaned back on the leather cushion, and propped up his booted foot to linger awhile.

After several minutes, Elise came out the door followed not by the doctor, but Nelda Chambers. It was impossible for the doctor to break away, but Nelda's knowledge was the next best to any doctor's, Doctor Barlow had assured Elise.

It was a disgruntled and disappointed Jack Maynard who carted the two women back to the Le Clere house. But gallantry deemed he could do no less.

Reading Jack's thoughts, Elise bid him good-bye and her thanks as the two disembarked from the gig.

Striding up the walk the two began to laugh, finding a tidbit of amusement in the otherwise bleak winter day. Nelda Chambers voiced her matronly observations to Elise. "That man's sure to get murdered in his sleep by Flo, sure as God made little green apples."

"Especially me, of all people. Flo never did like me anyway," Elise chimed in, unlocking the front door and urging Nelda into the house.

Mrs. Chambers laughed. "Anyone would know the reason for that, dear."

In a professional manner Nelda checked Annette and then young Andy. Afterward, she joined Elise for a cup of tea in the small sitting room. "Your son's doing fine, Elise, no fever to speak of. Madame Le Clere's age makes her a more serious case, and actually you and Mimi have been doing all the right things. You have to make her eat broth to fight the extreme weakness."

Elise felt much better hearing Nelda's opinion. It was nice to have a brief chat with Nelda over the cups of tea and hear about Susan and Dominique. Clint had joined Jackson's troops the first night, she told Elise. She'd had no word from him since he left.

As Nelda rose to leave Elise expressed her regrets that she must walk back to Doctor Barlow's. Nelda jested, "Who knows . . . you suppose Jack might be out front waiting!"

It was nice to have that brief reprieve to laugh at nonsense. The atmosphere was dominated by gloom lately.

Even though she felt horrible doing it, Elise gave no quarter that evening when Annette shrugged away the broth Mimi had prepared. "Damnit, Annette. Quit acting like a spoiled child. I'm bone tired, and I don't intend to trot up these steps for nothing. Eat it or I'll spoon it down you!" Elise's harsh tone shocked Annette and she turned to stare at her young friend suddenly realizing it was out of concern for her well being. She'd been so thoughtless and selfish.

"I'll try, Elise. I really will." She gave Elise a wan smile. Later, she was pleased to see every drop of the broth was consumed and she took the tray downstairs to sit in the kitchen with Mimi to eat her own dinner. It was too lonely at the long dining room table.

She enticed Mimi to sit and join her in a glass of wine. Sadly, Elise lamented to Mimi, "It's going to be a bleak Christmas this year, I fear."

"Yes, ma'am, it looks that way."

Both women became alert at the sharp rapping on the front door for the hour was late for callers. Mimi rose to go to the door. Elise was gladdened by the sight of the tall dark man strolling into the room. His handsome face looked tired and weary. But he flashed a smile at Elise.

Elise went to meet him, her arms outstretched, and they stood enfolded in a warm embrace. "Oh, God Jean, I've wondered . . . it's been terrible not knowing. I've not had one word from Lance."

"I figured as much, *ma petite* and I've only got a minute. I brought Midnight to you. Baptiste is going with me and my men. There's ground fighting going on not too far from Montclair, Elise."

"Is Lance out there, Jean?"

"No, honey. He's at Chalmette. They're throwing up a parapet at the Rodriguez Channel to hold the British at bay. I don't think the man's stopped to sleep for the last three days. I'd be there too but I'm taking my men in the opposite direction. My Baratarians know these bayous and swamps better than anyone."

"Jean, take care," Elise urged him.

"I shall, *ma petite*. Just for a lucky charm I wish one kiss before I leave. One touch of you to go with me, Elise." His eyes devoured her as if the moment would have to last him a lifetime. Like a magnet his heat pulled her to him and he took her in his arms, looking deep into her green eyes before his lips caught hers in a long, lingering kiss which left her weak when he finally broke away from her.

Whether she said it or not, he knew his touch had aroused her. Her eyes told him so as well as the tremble of her soft body. He was afraid to hope foolishly.

He flashed that familiar smile of his, his black brow raised as if to dare her to deny it. "Good-bye, *ma petite*—until we meet again."

He was gone and Elise stood weak and perplexed at the sensations stirring in her. She wondered, standing alone in the quiet house, how far she'd have allowed Jean's lovemaking to go if he'd sought to remain.

But any further thought of the matter was aborted by the rapping on the door. She opened the door to see a young, awkward man standing before her.

"Ma'am, I was instructed to give a message to Jean Laffite. Is he here?"

"I'm sorry, but he and his men have been gone just a few minutes."

"Begging your pardon ma'am, but do you know if they were going to the south to join the forces there."

Elise had to think for a moment. It was the Rodriguez Channel he'd said Lance was at. "All I remember is he spoke of him and his men being best adapted for the bayous and swamps. Does that give you some idea where they might be heading?"

The young man gave her a hint of a smile. "No, ma'am. Not really. There's a lot of swamps and bayous and it could be one of a dozen." Bewildered, he pondered which direction.

Elise saw the frustration on the young man's face and it suddenly dawned on her who this youth in baggy trousers was. "You're Julio, aren't you?" The night had been a haze for the most part, but he'd ridden with Jean the night she and Baptiste met them there on the country road.

"Yes, I'm Julio." He could not help feeling a certain awkwardness looking upon the face of the most beautiful woman he'd ever seen. Lola could not hold a candle to her. He'd not changed his opinion on that since he'd first laid eyes on her there in Sebastian's cabin. After she'd left Barataria, he'd not seen her again until the night he and Laffite had ridden toward Montclair.

The boy looked tired and cold and Elise considered the least she could do was offer him something warm to drink. But Julio refused politely. "I must see if I can warn Mister Jean before it's too late, ma'am. Word just came in at headquarters, and that's why I hurried over here, to stop him."

Julio did not tarry, but his words left her in a quandary. Jean's men were to join the forces at the Rodriguez Channel to keep the British in

445

check, that was Julio's urgent message. Heavy concentration of British troops were gathering at two points on land. The gunboat *Carolina* was firing into their ranks.

There was no sleep for Elise that night; the exploding artillery of the British could be heard. In retaliation, the rumbling fire from Jackson's camp answered swiftly. All Elise could think about was that somewhere out there was Lance.

Elise could not stand to lie in the bed. She slipped into her wrapper and looked in on Annette and the children before slipping down the steps. Helping herself to some brandy, she sat in the chair. Only sheer exhaustion brought on sleep. It was young Andy who woke her up the next morning with a kiss on the cheek. Mimi stood smiling at her.

"He is well madame, and I'm happy to report that Madame Le Clere is much improved. Even Henri is up and about."

Elise stretched lazily and slowly came alive. Hugging Andy to her and delighted to see him lively again, she declared, "Well, this is a good way to start off the day." The night had been long and miserable.

It was only after breakfast was over that it dawned on Elise what this day was—December 25. She determined to make it a festive day for young Andy's sake if nothing more.

With greenery they gathered outside she and Mimi decorated the room. Henri was able to concoct some of his magnificent custard dessert. Annette was able to come downstairs at midday, delighted to smell bayberry and spices wafting from the kitchen area.

Like Elise, Annette's spirits were lifted, and the threatening sounds in the distance could be forgotten inside the Le Clere house. To make the evening complete Elise decided she must make an attempt to find some little gift for Henri, Mimi, and Annette. Many of the shops were closed down, but she just wanted something to say it was a holiday, she reasoned.

Rushing upstairs she grabbed her shawl and reticule and hurried back downstairs. She'd walk, she decided. The day was mild, unusually so for the end of December.

Annette cautioned her to be careful out on the streets. She watched her go, envying Elise's surge of vitality. She was glad to see a hint of lightheartedness in Elise's face, for she knew the torment of the last several days she'd endured. The uncertainty of Lance's whereabouts, the ravaging of Montclair, and tending to her while she was ill had been a tremendous burden.

Elise walked jauntily up the street, the reticule swinging from her hand and her other hand holding the shawl snuggly around her. The sun felt good on her face, dulling the slight chill. She took no notice at first to the wagon loaded with soldiers until she recognized the driver as the chubby Dominique You. He threw up his hand to wave. She smiled and returned his wave.

447

Following a little behind the wagon came Jean atop a dappled gray gelding. "Elise!" He reined up the gelding. "*Ma petite*, did you see our catch?"

"You mean they are British soldiers!"

"*Oui*—twelve prisoners. Waylaid them in the swamps. Killed twenty and took these prisoners. A long night's work but well worth it." He leaped down from the gelding and called to Dominique You to herd them on to the jail and he would follow shortly. In an easy, casual motion, he led his mount and snaked his other arm around Elise's waist. "I want at least one Christmas toast with you before going about anymore dreary business, eh?"

Laughing up at him, she nodded her head and matched her steps to his. They strolled down the street with Jean's dark eyes devouring her warmly and Elise's smiling face welcoming his attention. Each seemed to be trying to recapture a time when there was a lighthearted gaiety in the fabulous city of New Orleans. But to some soldier who had traveled through the early morning hours from his encampment to the city with a twenty-four-hour leave the sight would leave a bitter taste. It would appear to everyone observing them that the two strolling in such an intimate embrace were lovers delighted to be reunited. Arms entwined and faces warmed by the sight of each other was the sight Lance's eyes beheld gazing at them.

Weary in spirit and body, he was too

disheartened to intrude. The private, wonderful reunion he'd envisioned with Elise was not to be, so he shrugged his shoulders, turned sharply on his heels, and walked away. Dismal and crushed he recalled the night before— Xmas Eve.

Chapter 32

Lance had never spent such a lonely, depressing Christmas Eve as he had last night joining Jackson in that miserable tent. His body ached with tiredness from the long fourteen hours he'd put in. There had been periods but for raw guts and courage the Americans could have been subdued. No one was more aware of that than Andrew Jackson.

Like Lance, with his thoughts about Elise and the children at the holiday season, Jackson was reminded of his Rachael. The two sat drinking generously of the whiskey that helped to heat their insides. Jackson rubbed his bearded face, which had gone without a shave for days now, and his voice cracked with hoarseness as he spoke. "You know, Edwards, I envy women. At least they can shed their tears and not be considered fools."

Lance appreciated fully what he was trying to say. He had only to think of his home and how perfect Elise had made everything last year at this time. She was so on his thoughts tonight that he couldn't concentrate on anything else, and Jackson knew it.

Once again, he let Lance know they shared sentiments. "My Rachael is probably just as sad as I am. Bless her sweet heart! You know, Edwards, there's nothing like a good woman's love. You got yourself a prize. Knew it the minute I met her. Pretty as hell, too."

"Yes, she is," Lance lamented. Dear God, an ache in his groin hit like thunder just thinking about the sweet fragrance of her body and clinging arms around his neck. Jackson's ramblings sure as bloody hell weren't helping him any. He wouldn't be worth a grain of salt so consumed with these wild thoughts, he mused. Like Jackson, the whiskey soothed and eased the tensions of the last few days. The two of them needed that.

Jackson's gray head cocked to one side, and through the raised bushy brows, the general's eyes locked into his. "I can't go see my sweet wife, but by God and all that's holy, you can, Edwards. That is, if you want to ride the five miles into the city. I order you to get the hell out of here and take a retreat for the next twenty-four hours."

"You serious, General?"

"Serious as the devil. There's no man we can't do without for one day. Besides, that damn fog's so thick they can't see us anymore than we can see them."

451

Lance wasted no more time in argument, but bid the general good-bye and saddled up his roan mare. While he knew he would forfeit almost two hours of the precious time, he had to detour by Montclair.

He arrived at Montclair and took Elise's Christmas gift from its hiding place. His vanity urged him to have Jess draw a bath before presenting himself to her and the children. Deep inside his being he wanted no hints of battle and strife remaining on him. He was ever so glad that he'd selected a perfect hiding place so that the marauders had not found the gift. Months ago he'd selected the emerald and diamond bracelet from Caron's and it was perhaps the reason the incident about the earrings had infuriated him so.

When he rose out of the tub of water his head felt like it was whirling, and he realized he'd had no sleep in . . . hell, he couldn't remember. It would be no good to Elise or himself if he tumbled from his horse en route. With orders to Jess to wake him in three hours, he collapsed across the bed.

In three hours, Jess sought to carry out his orders. But three more hours were to pass before the elderly Jess could budge the strong master from his deep sleep. Lance's anger was directed toward himself and not Jess as he hurriedly dressed. In his haste, he almost forgot the bracelet.

He made record time riding into the city. He felt like a young boy, anticipating seeing his family. He had no doubts about finding Elise back at Annette Le Clere's now. After all, that was where their children were, and Elise would be with them. Perhaps, some time in the future, he mused, he would be able to conquer these black rages sweeping with such fury over him when he saw the heated desire in every man's eyes who gazed upon her ravishing beauty. Would she ever age? Sometimes he doubted it!

He gave a deep, throaty laugh, thinking how he had his work cut out for him.

Upon his arrival at Annette Le Clere's he had only to step into the hall with bayberry wafting to his nose to feel the holiday spirit consuming him. The touch of Elise was there warming him thoroughly, and Annette's announcement that she was out slapped him with instant disappointment. Annette soothed him that she was certain Elise would not be long. Lance satisfied himself for over an hour with the children. While he enjoyed holding his baby daughter and romping with his son, it was Elise's presence his soul cried out for.

Annette watched his impatience grow and she wondered what was delaying Elise.

Annette knew as dear as the children were to Lance that they were beginning to vex him since his patience was wearing thin. She suggested Mimi put them down for their afternoon nap before the evening's festivities.

As soon as they were dismissed, Lance asked Annette to excuse him. "Think I'll take a look for my prodigal little wife." His casual, offhanded manner did not fool Annette at all, and she felt compassion for her son. After he'd gone she realized that she'd been offered a private time with him to reveal her long-kept secret. Yet, it did not seem the right time.

Nothing was as he'd anticipated it! His visions of taking Elise into his arms and kissing her honey-sweet lips were hardly in order there on the streets, with Laffite hanging possessively on her arm. It shattered the peak of that wild anticipation growing within him from the moment he'd left Jackson's tent.

It was he that beautiful face should be looking up at so warmly and inviting, not Jean Laffite. He froze in his tracks, unable to move, nor did he know whether he wanted to as he watched them walk down the street, arm in arm. He watched them go into the little tea room and take seats at the small table for two, and he turned away feeling like he'd be an intruder to disturb the gay mood both seemed to be in. He turned away, disillusioned and angry.

Annette was dismayed when he returned. His hand was as cold as his heart and the black fire in his eyes was as chilling as death. "Tell Elise I wish her a happy holiday. She appeared to be enjoying herself immensely." As an afterthought, he bent and kissed Annette's cheek. "Happy holiday!"

"You saw her? But Lance, why . . . where. . . ."

"It doesn't matter, Annette." He hugged the tiny woman and quipped, "I'll just give you the hug I intended for her." His brave attempt to mask his anguish pained Annette.

She could not resist pleading, "Please, my son . . . stay." It was futile, she knew.

"No . . . no, I must get back to camp. Goodbye!"

Apprehensions engulfed her, and she could not help wondering what had happened. How could Elise possibly do something to hurt him so at a time like this?

Breezily, Elise came through the door, going directly to the small sitting room where she was sure Annette would be enjoying the sun and possibly doing some needlepoint.

"You're back," Annette remarked. There was a tone in her voice Elise did not understand, and the woman's green eyes held the reflection of hostility, or something resembling it.

"Yes, Annette . . . I am back. Are you feeling all right?" Elise saw displeasure on Annette's face, but why?

"I am fine, Elise and it's obvious you are, too."

"Yes, I am. I . . . I will put these things away and get us something to drink. Would you like that, Annette?" She pondered what she'd done or not done that had displeased her hostess so much. Everything had changed in the brief hour, or was it two hours, since she'd left the house. She had felt it so overwhelmingly, standing there before Annette. For the first time since she'd known Annette, she felt uneasy, almost unwelcome in her home.

"Sit down, Elise. We must talk. I hope you will take what I'm going to say to you in the spirit it's given. That I love you as a daughter is no news to you, so I feel it gives me the right."

"And I love you, too, Annette. Tell me what I've done wrong."

"I don't know, *ma petite*. But I do know that your husband came like a lovesick calf to see you. So happy he was, Elise, but he was so tired. His eyes showed it. He left angry and hurt from seeing you somewhere. You know where, or perhaps I should say who."

"*Mon Dieu!* He—"

"Why, Elise . . . why would he be so angry?"

"Because, Annette . . . he saw me with Jean, and we were laughing. For one short moment, it was nice to see an old friend and be gay," Elise said, hoping Annette could understand.

Sadly, she did. But it did not ease her concern for her son's state of mind. She wondered if Elise would think of the danger of such preoccupation.

Elise sank dejectedly on the settee beside Annette. How wrong everything had turned out! If only she'd not rushed out to pick up the meager little gifts for the members of the household she would have been here to greet her husband. But damn his stubborn soul, he

456

could have come to her even if she was with Jean! So Elise fluctuated between qualms of conscience and flurries of anger.

"He looked tired, you say?" She looked at Annette, who still seemed withdrawn. Elise felt hurt by this aloofness toward her.

"Yes, Elise. I could tell it when he tried to play with Andy, and of course, you can imagine how the boy was beside himself seeing his father. He cuddled little Lanissa for a while. But it was you, *chérie*, he needed so desperately."

Elise stood up abruptly. No need to carry this any further, she decided. "I did nothing this afternoon to apologize to Lance for. If he misunderstood what he saw, I can't help that," Elise declared defensively, and started to stalk out of the room. Never would she want to say something to Annette Le Clere that she'd later regret. Nor would she allow Annette to reprimand her for her actions. This overprotective attitude for Lance puzzled Elise.

"Baptiste came this afternoon, Elise. I thought you might be glad to know. He's sharing the quarters above the carriage house." Annette tried her softest voice, realizing the harshness of her words earlier.

"Yes, I'm glad to know he is safe. I . . . I think I'll go see to the children, Annette. See you at dinner," Elise remarked, not turning back to face her friend.

"All right, dear." Madame Le Clere sat thoughtfully after Elise left. She wished most desperately for her old friend Fifi. How cruel the times were, and what havoc they were playing with the lives of the people she loved so dearly. She had not helped the situation. She had no right to criticize Elise. Her stubborn, headstrong son was not blameless in all that had gone wrong lately.

Elise peeped in the room at the sleeping tots and continued down the hall to her own room. It was dusk, she noticed. Somewhere in the twilight, Lance was riding back to the encampment near the channel. Tonight there could be a battle—men being killed or wounded. One of those could be Lance. Dear God, he could not die thinking she did not love him! She knew what she must do!

She rushed down the steps and out the back of the house, passing Mimi and Henri in the kitchen. They stood with mouths gaping as Elise streaked past them without even speaking.

The carriage house steps squeaked as she mounted them hastily. It took some fierce knocking to rouse the weary Baptiste from his deep sleep. "Miss Elise!" he mumbled, bleary-eyed and brushing his rumpled hair out of his face.

"May I come in, Baptiste?"

Stammering, he admitted her, trying to come out of his daze. "Forgive me, ma'am. I'm just not awake. Guess I was tired, I've been without sleep so long."

"I understand Baptiste, and it is you who

must forgive me. I need your help or I wouldn't have bothered you. Then I promise to leave and let you go back to sleep."

"Of course, Miss Elise. How can I help you?" He sat down on the cot.

"I don't have time to explain everything to you. But what I want is your clothes. I'm sure you can borrow something later from Madame Le Clere's boy. He's about your size. I have no time to tarry. Do you have a cap?"

Miss Elise looked rational enough, but what kind of folly was she up to? He stood saying nothing.

"Well Baptiste?" Every minute was merely an unnecessary delay.

"Of course, Miss Elise. You know I'd do anything you ask me."

"Then start undressing and I will, too." She wasted no time removing her shawl, looking up to see the boy's blushing face. "Oh, Baptiste . . . I'm sorry! Look, we'll turn our backs on each other, and you take off your clothes and get under the blanket. Call to me when you've finished. All right?" She had no time for modesty.

The whole idea made him tremble but he did her bidding. First, he removed his pants and then the shirt. With only his underthings remaining, he slid under the blanket and lay down on the cot. "All right, Miss Elise."

Elise was already down to her chemise, and she walked over to the pile of clothes on the plank floor. The shirt fit rather well since

Baptiste was lean and small-framed, but the pants were inches too long. But that was no problem; she rolled up the excess material. She was ready except for her hair.

"A cap, Baptiste—do you have one?"

"The brown wool one there on the peg where my coat hangs." Elise went to where his finger pointed. The hassle of getting all the mass of hair underneath the cap was more than she could manage and she begged his help, sitting down on the edge of the cot as Baptiste awkwardly helped his mistress tuck the long strands of black hair inside the cap.

She would never know the aching pain he experienced in his groin when she finally took leave of his quarters. Nor that his young manhood was pulsing from the stolen look at her as she stood in her chemise. For all his honor and respect for the fine lady, Baptiste was only human, and male. He could not resist one peek.

Sleep was delayed for Baptiste. Elise made her way to the stable knowing only that he was curious as to her crazy masquerade. As soon as she ordered Midnight saddled, she went back to the house to tell Annette of her plans. While she knew Madame Le Clere would think she was insane she did not care. She was going to her husband. She had to let him know she loved him beyond any and all things.

Annette's reaction was one of shock. "Elise, you are crazy, and foolhardy as well!"

"Annette, I can see you going to Francois

just as I'm going to Lance. Deny it, if you can." Elise's green eyes locked into another pair of green eyes, daring her to say otherwise.

A slow smile came on Annette's gardenia white face. A twinkle gleamed in the eyes. A sudden surge of warmth filled her being. "That, I can not do and you know it! So, *ma petite*, God go with you, eh?" She held her arms out to the young woman and Elise went to her.

"Oh, Annette, I love him so. If anything happened to him and he thought I didn't care I'd never forgive myself."

"I hope you a safe journey. Take care, and Elise, let me give you something." She went to the drawer of the liquor chest and pulled out Francois's pistol. "Take this, *chérie*."

The thought of encountering danger had not entered her mind until now. She took the pistol, kissed Annette, and left the house.

Chapter 33

On December 25, while Lance was in New Orleans, the British troops had been slowly massing and building until they numbered 8,000 under the leadership of Major General Sir Edward Pakenham. Jackson's total infantry numbered 5,000.

The American ship the *Louisiana* was stationed some two miles below Jackson's encampment, and the *Carolina* was farther down the river about a mile. The armed ships were the bastions they must destroy, Pakenham decided, and then, he felt, victory would be theirs.

As he left the Le Clere home Lance's thoughts were not on the British or Jackson's troops. He pondered the mad insanity his own life had been swirling in, and for one fleeting moment it seemed to him that to leave New Orleans and its turmoil behind and head for the high seas in one of his slick-lined schooners would be heaven.

That whimsy left as soon as it had swept across his thoughts. Once before he'd tried to run away and not face the truth, and how well he remembered not finding the peace he'd sought.

La Maison came in sight and he decided to pay Fifi a call. A drink was what he could use before the five-mile ride back to camp. A woman he'd have time for, too, if he desired one. But he wanted no other woman except Elise. A substitute might work for some. It didn't work for him. God knew he'd tried it a couple of times since taking Elise as his wife. After the feast of Elise he never wanted crumbs. He'd been left wanting and still hungry. The little vixen had spoiled him and he cussed that fact. She held him with as much masterfulness as he her. Yet he knew it made her all the dearer to him. From the minute he assumed the role of Elise's protector he knew it would be a constant challenge.

So his hour's stay at Fifi's was merely a little lighthearted conversation with the madam and a couple of drinks before mounting the roan to ride toward the outskirts of the city. He still had not spent the twenty-four hours alotted him. The sun was down, but he set the roan in an easy gait.

Another rider atop a jet black horse set her pace at a springing gait, as though there was no time to lose. She would have been incredulous with delight had she known that she was swiftly

463

closing the gap between her and the rider ahead of her.

Lance had gone about a mile when he sensed the rider behind him, but the darkness now over the countryside made it impossible for him to make out anything about the rider. Elise's horse blended in with the night. Lance questioned if it was friend or foe coming up on him so fast. Caution demanded he find out.

He reined the roan to go faster. Jackson's camp was less than a couple of miles away. Soon the outbuildings of the plantation would be in sight.

For one fleeting second Elise had thought she spotted a rider up ahead of her, but Lance had had a start on her and he would be farther ahead of her than that. According to calculations, he should have made the five miles and been back in camp easily by now.

The night was dark, except for an occasional break of the clouds that allowed the bright moon to light up the countryside. Elise was hopeful she was drawing near the plantation where she would find her husband.

Sugarcane fields lay on either side of the rutted road, and she was certain she was on Chalmette land. Suddenly she reined up on Midnight and leaped down. Would it be wise to ride into the camp in her boy's garb? Could she be taken for the enemy? With that in mind, she guided Midnight, clasping the reins in her hand, and started walking down the road.

Lance sat atop the roan observing the

464

mystery rider. He'd reined his horse behind the giant bougainvillea by the side of the road. Was the culprit trying to slip up to their headquarters to observe the movement around the camp? It seemed strange to him that the rider would suddenly dismount, as if he did not want his presence known.

The man was so short that Lance pondered if it was a young lad sent to do the dirty work: small, and not easily spotted. The horse was black as the ace of spades, too. Ah, the British were smart, thinking of every angle. If it was any of Jackson's young couriers they would not have hesitated to ride on into camp.

He found it interesting that he approached with no weapon drawn, only leading the horse cautiously behind him. Lance slowly dismounted and tied the reins of his horse around a branch. The youth was almost even with him now. He continued to watch, making no move for the moment.

Unconsciously, his booted foot moved just slightly causing the snapping of the underbrush. The noise was enough to alert the intruder and he broke to the right, dashing into the field at the side of the road.

That reaction denoted guilt, and Lance rushed in hot pursuit of the swift, agile figure running ahead of him. Damn little bastard was going to give him a hell of a chase, Lance decided, exerting all his effort to catch him. Like a gazelle the figure darted through the fields.

Elise knew she must make for the buildings up ahead. It was her only chance. She thanked God she had on Baptiste's pants instead of the riding ensemble she normally wore. He was gaining on her and she did not have to take the time to look back to know that. She could almost feel his heavy, hot breath on her neck as she bobbed and weaved down the rows of sugarcane. She pulled from all the reserve strength remaining, noticing a building of sorts now less than a hundred yards away. Someone just had to be there who would aid her. Gasping for breath, she ran on.

Then it happened. She stumbled over a stump of one of the sugarcane stalks. Her face burrowed into the cold earth and she felt the taste of her own blood from her lips. She had no time to worry about that as she scrambled to raise her tired, panting body from the ground.

The effort was for naught as a heavy, muscled body slammed across her, smashing her back into the ground. She muttered a long string of curse words, fighting like a wildcat. Kicking her legs and flailing her arms, she twisted back and forth on the ground with determination to free herself. The brute was wearing her down fast now.

The running had taxed Lance and the struggle to subdue the youth was more than he'd bargained for. Finally managing to flop one of his strong thighs over the legs, quieting their movement, he concentrated on those two battling arms that had hit him repeatedly on the face.

Flipping the small body over, he managed to straddle the youth. Now that he sat astride the youth the kicking legs were doing no damage, and now he held the two hands in a viselike grip. But then he felt the body arch trying to prod him off, and he slammed his body down hard against the heaving chest of the youth. Chest pressed against chest.

There were two mounds of firm, flesh jutting into his chest. Two rounded mounds that no male would possess. He gasped, "Holy Christ!" Rising slightly, he looked down to see Elise! The moment he spoke, Elise had known who sat astride her. She gasped with equal disbelief.

Flinging his heavy weight off of her, he could only sit a moment to catch his breath and gather his wits about him. This wasn't happening! It was a nightmare . . . madness! This was some kind of apparition conjured up because she'd been on his mind so intensely. Yet, looking over to see the black hair fanned out on the earth and the round little hills of her breasts heaving up and down, he knew it was reality. His wife!

As if to completely satisfy himself, his hand reached out to touch her face. "Elise, tell me what all this is about. You dressed like a boy riding through the night with all hell breaking out over the whole countryside." His voice wasn't raised or harsh. Instead, he was more like a man dumbfounded and totally beaten. No fight was left in him.

His perplexed face did look tired and weary just as Annette had said. He looked down on her like a father would a child he'd given up hope for. It made it hard to answer him. She'd never seen this Lance Edwards before.

His eyes searched her face. Dear God she was beautiful, lying there so still as if she was waiting for him to make love to her. Drawing in deep breaths as if he was heated in passion, he felt himself being aroused. He was seized with the wildest desire to make love to her there on the ground.

"Lance! Oh Lance!" She slowly, almost sensuously raised her arms with her fingertips touching his cheek lightly. "I had to come, *mon cheri*. I had to." A single tear dampened her cheek. "I had to see you."

"Why, Elise? Why would you feel compelled to chance the danger of riding through the night to find me?" He did not know whether he wanted to hear the answer, knowing how brutally honest she was. He knew what he'd seen with his own eyes.

She rose to a sitting position. Her legs brushed against his and her honeyed lips were so near he could almost taste their sweetness. "You, Lance Edwards! You! I love you too much to allow you to go back to fighting with any doubts." He must believe her! He must!

He gave a deep, throaty laugh, clasping her to him, and his hungry mouth took hers, savagely kissing the lips he starved for so. He knew he had to have her, for denying himself now would drive him to the brink of insanity. In an abrupt release, she felt herself lifted up to stand on her own two feet. With an impatient tug on her arm, she felt herself being hauled back through the sugarcane field. Lance said not a word but she felt the tenseness of his firm, muscled body as he strode beside her. Led by Lance they marched back through the field.

Elise allowed him to lead her, having no idea where he was taking her or his plans for her. But Lance knew exactly where he was taking her. There on the ground he had decided that. He had to have her once more.

He tied the horses to a sapling at the side of the outbuilding and led her through the door standing ajar. Elise concluded the building was deserted as they moved through the darkness.

"Lance, not so fast! I can't see a blasted thing. Can't we use that old lantern there on the post?"

"No, *ma petite!* I want no intruders. My twenty-four hours is almost up." He led her to the corner where hay was piled halfway to the roof. He stood, whirling her around to face him. His black eyes were brooding with a strange, haunting look that puzzled Elise. His voice shook with a depth of emotion Elise did not understand. "I need you Elise, so goddamn much. I want you to wash away the hurt."

"Oh, *mon cheri* . . . foolish, foolish *mon cheri,*" she mumbled, her mouth taking his with her tongue wickedly taunting and teasing him. She knew now what he yearned for and what she would give. As it was for her, it was with him.

With her petite body pressing feverously against the front of him, his hands cupped her hips to fit snugly to him. More than ever, Elise knew she'd done the right thing by seeking him out this night.

Unaware that they'd sunk into the hay, they clung to one another with lips and hands caressing and heating wherever they touched. The winter chill had no meaning as they burrowed into the hay.

Lance's hands yanked the shirt she wore out of the pants and slipped it up to cup each of her pulsing, firm breasts, playing the tips with his thumbs in a slow, sensual motion. Her body swayed against him in the stirring pleasure he was igniting there and he felt the tense hardening.

She sought to pleasure him, letting her small hands trail over the hairy cluster on his chest down to his waist and below until she heard his deep intake of breath as she caressed the pulsing essence of his manhood. "Dear God, Elise!" He trembled with the rapture she was creating by her touch.

But this wild ecstasy demanded more and Lance tore away from her long enough to remove his clothing for he wanted nothing between his body and hers. With his own clothes tossed aside, he pulled Baptiste's pants down letting his mouth touch the bareness as he undercovered her. Elise moaned with anxiety and eagerness to be filled with his being.

"*Je t'aime,*" she moaned, blazing with the flames of passion leaping and licking her body. Sensation followed sensation.

"Ah, always, love. *Je t'aime!* You and I, my darling!"

She could have sworn he was punishing her instead of loving her for her body surged up for his taking of her. He laughed with the savage delight he was causing. This was his Elise, his woman. This was why no other woman could compare to her. The sweet giving as well as the eager taking was what made this heaven's rapture so wonderful.

In the next few moments he knew why she was surely passion's woman as he covered her and she arched to him to receive him so eagerly.

They moved with the perfection of two dancers. The movement was one, in perfect time, up and down, side to side, round and round, slow and fast. Even abrupt stops.

"I want this to never end, love. Dear God, you feel so good!" Lance moaned, knowing he was soon to make that ultimate thrust that would carry them to the pinnacle of heaven belonging to lovers exclusively.

Elise felt herself being swept wildly upward to that peak, and Lance went with her all the way. There they soared the heights together in a whirling frenzy of passion.

Both fell into a deep, exhausted sleep encircled in one another's arms. Neither had any idea for how long. Lance had roused up first, thinking he'd heard gunfire. He listened for a moment before nudging Elise gently. "A belated merry Christmas to you, love." He gave her a broad, handsome smile that warmed her.

She grinned devilishly, saying, "Thank you, *mon cheri* for . . . for the most wonderful gift you could give me."

"Ah, Elise . . . it's all I ever want . . . all I ever need. That you love me as you just did. You are my life, *ma petite*. I admit it to you," he told her. As he held her in his arms, he remembered the bracelet in his pocket. He hoped it was still there after the struggle on the ground back in the sugarcane field.

He sighed with relief when his fingers touched the bracelet still resting there. Pulling it out, he pulled her over on his lap and took her arm. Placing it around her wrist he fastened it there securely. "With all my love, Elise."

"Oh, Lance." She pouted. "I don't have anything to give you. It's at home." Her eyes were misty with emotion.

He imitated her pout, letting his lips come to hers. "No, no, *petite amie*. You gave it to me last night. That's what I wanted most of all. Anything else would never equal that." He smiled at her lying there with his cloak covering her naked body pressed down in the hay. The night's chill began to affect him and he reached for his pants and shirt. With his clothes back on the delightful madness they'd just indulged in made him throw back his head and roar with laughter.

Elise jerked up wondering what had brought that on. "Lance?"

"Hmmm?"

"May I share in whatever it is you find so comical?"

"Tumbling with my wife in the hay on a winter's night with the almost certain possibility of a battle any minute." As he made the comment the reality, and serious danger to Elise, hit in the pit of his stomach. What was he going to do with her? She couldn't stay here!

In a deadly serious tone, he ordered her to get her clothes on. "I've got to see about getting you back to the city, Elise."

"I got myself out here so I'll get myself back, Lance," she retorted.

"Not alone, love," he declared firmly. She knew there was no point in pressing the point, for he would not be swayed. She certainly would not argue with him now.

"I'm ready," she announced. "Where are we going?"

"To headquarters." He guided her through the wooden door barely hanging by its hinges to where he had tied their horses.

Lance wore a look of consternation pondering how in the devil he was going to explain her presence to Jackson. As they rode the short distance to headquarters, the skies exploded with the sound of thunder. But thunder it was not! A fierce, heavy bombardment was in progress.

"Hurry, Elise!" He shouted at her. He cussed himself for allowing her to be caught up in this hell. He should have made her turn around on Midnight and ride right back into New Orleans. Instead his own selfish desires had put her in jeopardy. Nothing must happen to her. He couldn't live with that.

As they hastily dismounted, troops were rushing in all directions. One of the officers informed Lance that the ship *Carolina* had been bombarded with hot shot and was burning. All Lance could say was "Oh, Christ!" That left only the *Louisiana* to hold off the British.

Chapter 34

With Midnight tied to the back of one of the wagons taking wounded back to the city, Elise sat on the seat with the young soldier. Other wagons made the trip into the city a few hours later. The British push was hard and unrelenting for the next twenty hours, feeling they would encounter little opposition.

Jackson's troops fought with fierceness, sustaining a small loss of eleven men, while the British lost seventy-six. Pakenham decided to withdraw and wait for reinforcements to arrive. The lull in the fighting gave Jackson's men a chance to catch up on some much needed sleep, tend to their wounded, and bury their dead.

Elise quizzed each new load of soldiers with some faint hope of hearing the news about what was taking place. As she tended and dressed their wounds, she always asked about Lance in hopes that one of them knew something. Each day and part of the night found her working by the side of Doctor Lawrence at the hospital. She trudged home so exhausted that sometimes she fell into the bed to tired for the warm bath prepared for her.

Annette Le Clere's strength was not restored to the point to allow her to give her services at the hospital. She tried to play the mother role to Elise's two during her absences. Elise caught fleeting glances of Susan Barron from time to time, as she made the daily rounds. One day seemed to melt into another, with the same never ending routine. That a brand new year had been ushered in one week ago did not bear any significance. There was no time this year for celebrations or galas. The usual flamboyant lavishness flowing forth at this time of the year was missing in the city of New Orleans.

Elise had lost track of the dates for her thoughts were so disturbed about her husband's welfare. Seeing the daily parade of men being carried in on stretchers, their clothing soaked in blood and the once handsome faces marred with ugly gashes and cuts, she realized more and more how it was getting to her. When would this torment and hell all end? That other world she'd existed in seemed so long ago and faraway.

Suddenly she felt the need that morning to leave the confines of the makeshift hospital and just walk in the crisp, cool air. Otherwise, she felt she would start screaming, and it might not stop. Rushing down the corridor to grab her cloak, she bumped into a massive figure and looked up to see the weary, but beaming face of Clint Barron.

"Elise! Hey, how nice to see you," he said, holding her by the shoulders to settle her. "Sorry, honey . . . I happened to be standing in the wrong spot."

Elise slumped against his broad chest. It was so good to see him, a dear friend. She thanked God there were no wounds on him. She was sick to death of bandages and blood and gore.

"Elise, you're worn out!" Clint's concerned eyes scanned her face. "Come next door with me and have some coffee or tea, all right? Besides, I'd like to talk to you awhile. It's been a long time."

Elise readily agreed to accompany him, and it was only then that she noticed his limp. "You're injured, Clint!"

"Yeah. Nothing serious, but enough to send me out of any fighting. 'Fraid I'm on my way to Nelda's after we have some refreshments. Truth is, I'm thinking I'll gather up Susan and Dominique and get back to Shady Oaks. Just don't think this thing is going to last much longer, Elise. We had those damn British falling like flies last night. Christ, I don't know where all of them are coming from."

"Clint, can we just forget the fighting for a moment?"

"Oh, Elise, I'm sorry! You know me, the oaf! How are the kids? Missing their dad, I bet?"

"Oh, yes! So am I. It will be so nice to go

home and start living again."

By this time he'd guided her to a table and seated her in the chair opposite his. With the eagerness of a young boy, he told her of his plans for Dominique. "I have these friends in London and I think it would be best for her. I've not mentioned anything to Susan yet but she's just got to see it my way. I'll make her. We could always go over there to see her until the time when she could come back to Shady Oaks. What do you think, Elise?"

"You've got to tell Susan sometime, Clint," Elise told him.

"I intend to, honey. I've just got to be sure there's a deep enough feeling there to sustain the shock. I love them both so much, Elise. You can understand that, I know."

Elise reached across the table and patted his huge hand. "Of course I do, Clint. You are the judge of that. Somehow, I know it will all work out right."

"Thanks, Elise." His eyes warmed, thinking of so many, many memories. "We've traveled many miles since that night so long ago in Havana, haven't we, little darlin'?" He felt the times warranted him calling her that one more time.

She smiled brightly, remembering, too. "That was another lifetime, Clint. A lot of water's gone under the bridge."

They parted company and Elise turned to go back to the hospital for a few hours more. She had not noticed the motley group coming up the street.

A familiar voice called to her and she turned around to see the chubby, short pirate she'd come to adore waving and calling to her. A smile broke on her face as she rushed out to the street to join him and his band of men. "Dominique You, what a sight you are, and how glad I am to see you!"

"You're the prettiest sight I've laid eyes on for a long time, Miss Elise!" His swarthy face wore a broad smile. His barrel chest seemed to swell when he announced that he and his band of men had captured the shackled prisoners they were now marching to jail.

"Then I will not keep you from your duty, Dominique. It was good to see you, and good luck to you." She planted a friendly kiss on his cheek and watched him march down the street with his prisoners in tow. His three pirate comrades wore smiles on their faces because her light kiss had brought a rosy blush to Dominique's dark face.

The rest of the afternoon somehow seemed lighter, having seen Clint Barron and the chubby Dominique You. However, once past the entrance to the hospital, the antiseptic and fetid odors mingled. Elise felt like she could retch, but she willed herself to bear the next hour or two before going home.

Arriving at the Le Clere house at the same time the sun was setting, she went directly upstairs and ordered Jessamine to prepare her bath. This night she wanted to rid herself of the odors; any reminder of the fighting so close by.

She lingered in the sweet-smelling tub of water for a leisurely time, letting the perfumed oil absorb into her body. She washed her thick hair and sat wrapped in a large towel while Jessamine rubbed the excess dampness.

"Shall I tell Madame Le Clere you're here, Miss Elise, and that you will be joining her for dinner?" Jessamine inquired, as she prepared to leave the room. Except for the finishing touches to her hair and dabbing some jasmine at her throat and eyes, Elise was dressed and very refreshed by the toilet.

"No, I'll go down shortly, Jessamine." She fingered one stubborn wisp of hair determined to go the wrong way. A few minutes later as Elise jauntily reached the base of the stairs, she noticed the dining room was dark and the table was not set up for dinner. This seemed odd to Elise. She stood for a moment to question what had disrupted the normal routine of the household.

She heard the lilting laughter of Annette coming from her cozy sitting rom, and even though the door was closed light escaped under the threshold. Then came the deep resounding voice of another female. Elise tried to remember just where or when she'd heard that voice. As she stood there listening, Mimi's soft footsteps approached from behind her.

"Madame?"

Elise whirled around, sighing from the unexpected voice and appearance of Mimi.

Mimi was sharing the same feelings, and both of them gave out a nervous laugh realizing the reaction of one to the other.

"I'm truly sorry I startled you. We were certain you'd be running past the dinner hour so I was instructed to keep you some dinner warm. Madame and her friend were having theirs on trays."

"Oh, I see." Elise was preparing to have hers served up in her room when the door opened. Annette had heard the voices and recognized Elise's. There was no way to explain Fifi's dining with her except to tell Elise the truth that was long overdue. Annette did not have to tell Fifi of her intentions either, for she knew.

"Ah, *ma petite*, how pretty you look! Come, join us. Uh, Mimi, bring Madame Elise's tray in here and perhaps another bottle of the Madeira."

Elise tried her best to act perfectly natural, for she had nothing against the vivacious madam. It simply surprised her to know that the two were obviously friends.

She strolled into the room. "Madame, how are you?" Elise smiled, acknowledging her. The earthy, plump woman urged her to sit down next to her with such a casual air that it merely whetted Elise's curiosity. Even Annette Le Clere was unruffled and calm. Elise could almost be vexed and annoyed with the two who sat so smugly, letting her fret.

Her tray was brought by Mimi and Annette poured and served the Madeira before taking her seat. "Eat, my dear, and then Fifi and I will tell you a magnificent story—one you will understand and appreciate, I think."

The two women enjoyed their wine while Elise ate her dinner. She was ever so grateful that it was a light meal. Annette refilled her glass of wine and confessed, "You don't know how many times I've been tempted to tell you in the past Elise, and after I finish you will understand why you've been so very dear to me."

In that next hour, Elise experienced emotions ranging from shock and sympathy to amazement and delight. So many things were easy to understand now. Of all the ladies, Annette had shown her the most compassion about her past. And theirs was the strange warmth the two of them had felt from the first moment they'd met. The one insignificant trait Annette shared with her son—and Elise doubted that either was aware of it—was the similar way they raised an eyebrow when they questioned something. And there were the same animated gestures they used when they spoke.

It was a rare night for all three women. Annette was so greatly relieved by her daughter-in-law's reaction that she drank far more wine than usual. The three talked so late that Fifi La Tour did not make it back to La Maison. Elise slept the deepest sleep she had experienced for many weeks. She, like Fifi and Annette, had drunk far too generously and climbed the steps swaying from the effects of the wine.

Elise would need that rest most desperately the next day and night. The worst was yet to come.

Troops were stationed across the river from Chalmette, and a fierce battle took place throughout the day and into the evening. Jean Laffite and his men, along with the Tennesseans and Kentucky riflemen plowed down the waves of British soldiers only to find another coming across the fields. For many days British ships bombarded Fort Saint Phillip with everything they had. While the Americans suffered their losses, the British losses were tremendous.

The English asked a truce of two days in order to bury their dead. Along with the many British soldiers killed, Major General Sir Edward Pakenham was wounded and later died.

The Americans also buried their dead and carried their wounded to the makeshift hospitals in the city. Elise's hours at the hospital for three days were long and tiring. She wondered if this nightmare would never end.

After three days it was all she could do to make herself get out of the soft bed and trudge the short distance to the hospital to work another day by the side of Doctor Lawrence.

This morning was like the last three days, with more patients to be tended to. Elise would have sworn yesterday not a single new space could have been filled in the ward. However, walking down the rows of cots with the doctor she saw new faces peering up at her. At the end of the aisle, she stopped short. Jet black tousled hair lay on the pillow. It was a sight she'd imagined many times in the several weeks she'd worked at the hospital. She'd wondered how she would cope with finding her husband mangled and horribly scarred for life.

She rushed to the cot knowing full well before she looked upon the face of the man lying there that it had to be Lance. As if the patient sensed her approach, he turned as she stood by the side of the bed.

"Oh, dear God!" Elise gasped, her small hand going to her mouth. The handsome face was without any apparent injury to it.

"Bon jour, ma petite!" He gave her a slight smile, and reached his hand up to take hers. Elise realized the effort it took. Taking his hand, she put it back down to rest on the blanket covering his body.

"What happened, Jean?"

"I got it in the leg—nothing too serious. Thanks to your husband."

"Lance and you were together?"

"We were. I guess I must have blacked out for a few minutes. I don't remember leaving." He laughed. "Anyway, you must thank him for me. I didn't get a chance to."

"So . . . so he is all right?"

"Last thing I remember he was fighting like a fool, and doing a hell of a job. A good man, Elise!" He saw the tormenting concern she felt.

"It can't last too many more days. We were fighting stragglers down on that river bank. Over on another point of the river we couldn't bring out any return of fire from our artillery."

"Oh dear God, Jean . . . I pray you are right. I truly do."

He gave her that handsome smile of his and managed a devilish wink of his dark eye. "Believe me, Elise! Have I ever lied to you, eh?"

Elise managed to laugh and bent to kiss his cheek. "Jean Laffite, I adore you!"

His eyes warmed, knowing that this was as much of the beautiful Elise's love he'd ever possess. While the pressures of the times had taken their toll on her she was still the most beautiful woman he'd ever seen. There was a grain of truth to what Nadja had told him. It was never to be, and who could argue with destiny.

At least he'd shared some memories and he'd cherish them forever.

As it would happen Jean Laffite was right. A few days later the troops led by Andrew Jackson rode into the city of New Orleans. They had won their victory. Shop windows and houses were adorned with flags. People lined the streets shouting and screaming their praise for their brave, courageous men.

Elise churned with that same wild excitement as she rushed out of the house, lifting her muslin skirt so she could walk faster. She was so eager to get out of the house that she grabbed her light-weight shawl instead of going upstairs to get her cloak. Her hair was loose and flying in the breeze as she scurried up the street, and her eyes were as sparkling and green as the emeralds on her ears.

Impatient and anxious, she watched each man atop his horse pass by. Where the devil was Lance? Jackson had passed, looking down at her and smiling as he tipped his hat. A dozen or more paraded by, but not Lance.

She stretched her small, petite body to the fullest to look up the street. All around her couples were reunited, warmly embracing and kissing eagerly. Dear Lord, she wanted that, too. Eager to see his face, she stretched once again, only to feel her slipper fall from her foot. She had to turn slightly to reach for it. Bending down to slip it back on, she felt herself hoisted in midair. Lance's muscled arm held her tiny body up, suspended by the side of the red roan. As if she was light as a feather he shifted her with ease atop his horse, holding her close to his chest.

His lips sought hers in a long, hungry kiss as the horse trotted along. "Oh, love . . . it is so good to hold you close to me."

"Lance, I love you so! I thought you were never going to come by." She kept planting kisses here and there all over his tired, handsome face.

"Got here just as soon as I could, *ma petite amie.*"

"Lance . . . how did you know that was me

you were grabbing up like that? You couldn't see my face."

He laughed a deep throaty laugh, thinking how sweet and innocent she looked at that moment. He knew she'd retain it, he knew it! "Well, love . . . let's just say your bottom is as well known to me as your equally beautiful face."

She tapped him playfully on the chest. "You are a wicked man, Lance Edwards! But I adore you!"

He was suddenly caught up in devious whimsy but hesitated to voice his thoughts. The roan trotted down the street toward Annette Le Clere's house, and for the moment he wanted her alone.

Elise pressed against the front of him and felt the tremendous bulge in his buckskins molded tight around his thighs and legs. She could not help the smile playing on her face and he saw it. The wanton little vixen! Never could he fool her when his blood burned with desire.

Dare he suggest what was beating like drums in his head? To hell with it, he'd dare it!

His lips touched her ever so gently, moving sensuously to conquer any protest she might make. Then he let them travel to the side of her face, murmuring with his hot passioned breath, "Want to go to Fifi's with me, *chérie?* I need you, love, need you desperately."

"I thought you'd never ask! And Lance, hurry!" she fervently exclaimed.

Her mutual impatience to be alone with him

only fanned the flame of passion higher, so the ride to the back entrance of La Maison was made posthaste.

Fifi La Tour was more than pleased to give the young couple her finest room, along with a complementary bottle of champagne. As the two were about to close out the rest of the world and Lance was about to guide Elise through the door, Fifi saluted the two. "Enjoy yourselves." Giving a wicked wink, she strolled down the long hallway.

It was much later that the champagne was opened. Their thirst for one another was more overpowering and demanding. More than once during these last weeks, Lance found the beautiful face and ravishing body of his wife was the driving force that made him stay alive. Death had come so close a couple of times out on the field down by the river.

He flaunted fate, refusing to succumb—not when he had rapture's bounty waiting for him back in the city of New Orleans. Now he claimed that bounty as his reward.

Sated to the point of weariness, they slept. They both woke up at almost the same moment. Lance strode from the bed, suggesting now they would have a toast. Elise noticed for the first time that his magnificent body bore no marks from the fighting. What an exciting figure of masculinity he was! How grateful she was that the perfection was not marred in any way.

As always, he adored her appraisal of his nude body, so open and unashamed. As a man, he found her so easy to worship with his whole being. He was doing it right then as she sat up in the bed propped up on the satin pillows, her glossy black hair fanned out and those emerald eyes staring straight at him. Her honey lips lifted with a smile, warm still with the intimate moments they'd just shared.

As he poured the champagne in two glasses he watched her out of the corners of his eyes. Languorous, she stretched her body covered by the satin sheets. Watching the satiny rise and fall of the mounds of her breasts, he knew he must have her again before they left the room.

Handing her the glass, he sat down on the side of the bed. Elise sipped the champagne. She hardly anticipated his next words. "Tell me, Elise, how are the children and my mother?"

Sputtering and gagging so she sprayed a mist of champagne over the sheets, she finally managed to speak. "Lance . . . you know about Annette Le Clere? But how could you possibly know?"

He finished the champagne, set the glass on the nightstand and answered her. "Francois told me when he found out he was dying. He knew how petrified she was about telling me, and as always, Francois tried to make it easy on her. He adored my mother, he said, from the moment they met. As I have you, Elise." His eyes caressed and adored her.

"Oh, Lance." She sighed, snaking her arms up around his neck. "I couldn't live without you. I wouldn't want to."

"Oh, little vixen." He pressed his hands on her back and pulled her to his chest. A flame of ecstasy consuming him, he urged her, "Love me again, love! I can't get my fill of you, it would seem."

And she did!

Epilogue

There was an air of serene contentment washing over the couple sitting by the hearth that winter night in 1830. They sat in the overstuffed chairs watching the dancing, darting flames of the burning seasoned oak logs. Toying with their glasses of brandy, each was lost in private musings.

As always, their traditional ball had been a great success, and all the guests had departed over an hour ago. The two of them had sought a quiet relaxed minute before retiring, and Jessamine had served the brandy before retiring to her quarters where her husband waited.

It never ceased to amaze Jessamine, as she left the two alone, how they remained eternally young. Her mistress had her petite figure and moved as lively as ever. But for a sprinkling of gray in her thick black hair no one would guess her to be forty-one. The master remained, as he always had to Jessamine, the handsomest man she'd ever seen. He, too, had a mass of gray around the temples, which only gave him a more dignified look.

As Jessamine closed the door on them and ambled down the hall, she heard the soft laughter of her mistress. Elise had just made an interesting observation to her husband. All their guests were eager to hear about their recent visit with the president of the United States, Andrew Jackson, and his wife Rachael. Elise had never forgotten Jackson referring to her as "his sweet Rachael," and his prediction that the two women would be friends had come true.

This year's celebration at Montclair had been a joyous one. Their son Andy had returned from a tour of the Continent accompanied by his bride-to-be. Elise and Lance could not have been more pleased, for they both adored Dominique. Soon she would be the new mistress of Bellefair. Annette Le Clere had given Bellefair to Andy. Never did she wish to live again at Bellefair without her beloved Francois. So she had remained throughout the years at the townhouse in New Orleans.

"You know, *mon cheri*, somewhere up there I can almost hear Delphine laughing," Elise declared. "Think of it! Can you imagine how mortified some of them would be if they knew Dommi was the daughter of the octoroon Delphine?"

Lance pulled her over on his lap. "You and mother are a devious pair. Both of you are green-eyed vixens! Between the two of you, I've bloody well had my hands full!" His eyes sparkled as his finger tilted her chin.

"Ah, but we've been worth it."

"I suppose." He tousled her hair playfully.

Elise knew of Lance's displeasure about their daughter Lanissa running away with the Baratarian Julio Vega. The two of them now resided in Corpus Christi. For her, it had been easy to accept, for she had only to look upon their two radiant faces to know of their love.

"Next year this time you'll feel differently about Lanissa, I'm sure," she said, patting his leg.

She could not see the look of amusement playing on her husband's face, but she could feel the heat of his strong hand caressing her neck and shoulders. What he had not told her was that he'd already come to terms with Lanissa, and soon they'd travel to the Texas coast to pay a visit to them. But he'd surprise her later with that news.

He pulled her closer to him and continued to let his hand caress her. It was a touch she knew well after all these years, and still it affected her.

"Lance. . . ."

"Hmm?" He smiled, knowing that particular softness of her voice. The two of them moved from the chair to their newly acquired furry rug situated in front of the hearth. With Elise encircled in his arms and gazing into the blazing fire, he found himself carried back in time to that night in Horsham, England at the Blue Goose Inn when he'd made wild ecstatic love to her on a pelted rug. Who was to say he couldn't do it again?

His lips devoured her soft, yielding mouth, parted, eager, and willing. Her soft, supple body pressed against his broad, pulsing chest and he felt himself swell with overwhelming passion. He gave a deep, throaty laugh and dared Dame Destiny to deny him this extra bounty of rapture. He was not denied!

There on the furry rug they made love with the same intoxicating ecstasy and all-consuming rapture, defying time or age. Forever, it would be!